SCANDALOUS PASSION

When she reached the door, Gwendolyn whirled around so quickly that her body collided with the viscount's. His arms came around her, to prevent her from falling.

"Oh, do forgive my clumsiness, my lord. I fear—"

He never gave her the opportunity to finish the sentence. He slid his right hand around the back of her neck, angled her head upward and then his mouth came down boldly upon hers. Captivated, Gwendolyn felt utterly at his mercy, as he coaxed and teased, modulating the pressure and angle of his mouth, urging her to respond.

Catching her lower lip between his teeth, he nibbled brashly. Gwendolyn gasped, then shivered when the hot, wet tip of his tongue edged out, skimming across her lips. They throbbed at the contact and she opened her mouth. Misunderstanding, he seized the opportunity and slipped his tongue between her lips.

Something instantly changed. The undercurrent of attraction Gwendolyn had been fighting nearly burst into flame. Time held still as her breath mingled with his and she became lost in a haze of pleasure. The kiss deepened and lengthened. Fire licked between them and he pressed his body against hers, letting her feel the evidence of his growing desire for her . . .

D0051225

Books by Adrienne Basso

HIS WICKED EMBRACE

HIS NOBLE PROMISE

TO WED A VISCOUNT

TO PROTECT AN HEIRESS

TO TEMPT A ROGUE

THE WEDDING DECEPTION

THE CHRISTMAS HEIRESS

HIGHLAND VAMPIRE

HOW TO ENJOY A SCANDAL

Published by Zebra Books

HOW TO
ENJOY A
SCANDAL

ADRIENNE BASSO

ZEBRA BOOKS
Kensington Publishing Corp.
www.kensingtonbooks.com

ZEBRA BOOKS are published by

Kensington Publishing Corp.
850 Third Avenue
New York, NY 10022

All Kensington titles, imprints, and distributed lines are available at special quantity discounts for bulk purchases for sales
promotion, premiums, fund-raising, educational, or institu-
tional use.

Special book excerpts or customized printings can also be created to fit specific needs. For details, write or phone the office
of the Kensington Special Sales Manager: Attn. Special Sales
Department. Kensington Publishing Corp., 850 Third Avenue,
New York, NY 10022. Phone: 1-800-221-2647.

Zebra and the Z logo Reg. US. Pat. & TM Off.

ISBN:13: 978-0-8217-8041-1
ISBN:10: 0-8217-8041-7

First Printing: April 2008
10 9 8 7 6 5 4 3 2 1

Printed in the United States of America

To Millie's girls:

Elaine Colucci, Marilyn McBride, and Angela Casale

Sisters through marriage, friends by choice—
you've helped make the good times even better
and the tough times tolerable.

Hope you like your book!

Chapter One

Yorkshire Countryside, England
Early Summer, 1817

"We are nearly there, *my lord*. Do you wish to remain inside the coach or would you prefer to finish the journey on horseback? I can instruct the coachman to pull to the side of the road so your horse may be unhitched from the rear of the carriage."

Jason Barrington slowly raised his left eyelid and glared at his valet, Pierce, who was sitting on the red velvet squabs opposite him. Though he had been drifting awake from his dreams, Jason had missed neither the sarcasm in the servant's voice nor the condescending manner in which the words were nasally spoken. *My lord,* indeed.

If not for the fact that Pierce could tie the most intricate cravat imaginable, shine a pair of Hessians until you could see your reflection in them and shave a jaw so close it was lacking in even a hint of whiskers, Jason would have sacked him years ago.

"I shall stay inside the coach, Pierce." Jason tapped the

roof of the carriage with his fist, effectively slowing and then stopping the vehicle. "However, you shall ride atop the box with the rest of the servants. I am sure John Coachman will appreciate your congenial companionship for the remainder of the journey."

Now it was Jason's turn to be sarcastic. The coachman and valet were hardly companions. They tolerated each other, as upper and lower servants were required, but mostly tried to stay out of each other's way.

"I am certain the fresh air will invigorate my spirits, *my lord*," Pierce replied. The valet sniffed with a faint air of disapproval that belied his words and Jason felt a flash of guilt.

It was wrong of him to punish Pierce because the man was a stickler for propriety and possessed in abundance what Jason admitted he himself lacked—a conscience. Truth be told, Jason was not a lord. He was the son of an earl and the brother of a viscount, a man raised in wealth and privilege, but lacking a title, as was the case with most younger sons.

However, in this case, being a younger son was a consequence of mere minutes instead of years. His identical twin brother, Jasper Barrington, Viscount Fairhurst, was born seven minutes before Jason. Throughout the years, especially when they were youngsters, the twins had enjoyed switching places, playing pranks and fooling others with regards to their identity.

Yet this time, Jason had not set out with the intention of impersonating his brother. He was traveling north to Jasper's estate in Yorkshire, and at his brother's request was using the viscount's coach, with the Fairhurst coat of arms etched prominently on each carriage door.

It was therefore a perfectly honest mistake for the innkeeper at their first stop to assume he was in truth the viscount. Jason was unaware of the confusion at first, but the quality of service he received at that establishment left him inclined *not* to correct the mistake. Nor to deny it at the next inn or the next, and thus he had spent the past week and a half of his journey to the north country as a "viscount."

The rest of the servants that made up their small traveling party thought it a great lark. Except for Pierce.

"Do you know why I am going to my brother's estate, Pierce?" Jason asked his servant.

The valet, who had been in the process of donning his cloak in anticipation of leaving the comfort of the carriage, even though it was summer and fairly mild, halted.

"I am certain it is none of my concern," he replied, infusing a bit of backbone into his already-stiff spine.

"True, but that does not mean you cannot be curious about the matter."

Feeling magnanimous, Jason tapped on the roof of the coach a second time and signaled that they should continue. Pierce's face took on a more relaxed expression when he realized he would be spared from riding atop the vehicle.

"Since your brother rarely visits his estate, I assumed your trip somehow involves a task Lord Fairhurst has asked you to undertake. Is that incorrect?" Pierce finally asked.

"Yes. There have been problems at the estate that my brother has been unable to solve. Serious problems." Jason shook his head. "It appears that someone has been helping themselves to a large portion of the estate's profits."

"Thieving?" Pierce's thin, pointed chin lifted in indignant shock. "'Tis appalling. They should be sacked immediately. And then arrested."

"They will be," Jason said in a confident tone. "Once they are caught."

"By you?"

Jason glared at his servant and the valet had the grace to look slightly embarrassed.

"Do not underestimate my abilities," Jason said lightly. "When I was a mere lad of twenty-two I rescued my sister, Meredith, and two other young noblewomen from certain death."

"I have heard a thing or two of that tale," Pierce admitted. "Even though the incident took place the year before I came to work for you."

"Saints above, you have been with me for six years?" Jason grunted out a small snort of laughter. "It seems longer."

The valet sniffed. "For both of us, *my lord.*"

Jason grunted again, then turned his head and stared out the window into the depths of the green, rolling countryside and the heather-covered moorlands. But he saw none of the bounty and beauty spread before him. His mind was racing, his stomach churning with memories that his disturbing dreams had evoked.

Elizabeth! It had been a very long time since he thought of her so intensely, yet for some reason she had been on his mind constantly since this journey began. Years ago he had fallen in love with her the very moment he had set eyes upon her delicate, blond beauty. Newly arrived from the country, she was sweet and naive and refreshingly honest.

That memorable Season he had eagerly attended any London event where she appeared, always braving the wrath of her fiercely protective older sister, who acted as her chaperone. Each conversation, each dance, each stolen moment had put him further under her spell and she had unknowingly and unintentionally captured his heart.

Through skill and luck and sheer determination, he had been able to save Elizabeth, along with her sister, Harriet, and his sister, Meredith, from the clutches of a madman. Yet from that moment, the sweet, delicate Elizabeth had forever associated him with that horrible incident and was unable to bear the sight of him.

He had wanted her for his wife, yet she could not tolerate being in the same room with him for more than a few minutes. She had sobbed and begged his forgiveness, had asked with embarrassed honesty for him to try and understand. Given no other choice, he was forced to leave her alone. As the years passed, he eventually came to understand that she had not meant to wound him, that she was sincerely sorry she lacked the ability to alter her feelings.

Yes, he understood. He even managed to forgive. But he never forgot.

Elizabeth's rejection had bled his heart, had crushed Jason's spirit, had left him feeling every sting of hurt that an unfair and unjust world could produce. He could still remember the wave of nausea that had rolled through his stomach when he finally admitted to himself that Elizabeth would never change her mind about him. The pain had unleashed his volatile nature, had made his already outrageous behavior even more daring, more reckless, more scandalous.

Within a month, he had been embroiled in a notorious affair with a very married, and much older, duchess. The following month it had been a famous Italian opera singer, who was soon replaced by a recently widowed marchioness. As the years passed, the names and faces, hair and eye color, size and shapes of Jason's female companions began to change with the same regularity as the seasons.

And he never thought about marriage again.

"The driver has signaled that Moorehead Manor is within his sights."

Pierce's voice drew Jason away from his melancholy reflections. He blinked his eyes and focused as the estate came into view, realizing it had been years since he had last seen it.

The manor house sat at the bottom of a rolling valley, its red brick wings stretching across a wide expanse of open land. Windows glittered under deep dormers, and ivy clung to the walls like a green curtain. A formal rose garden lay to the south of the house, its beds a riot of yellow, red and pink.

The residence was surrounded by acres of rolling green fields and, beyond them, patches of dense green forest. From what Jason could see, the crops looked tall, lush and healthy. By all accounts, this was a well-maintained and profitable establishment. Yet the funds deposited each quarter from the property had steadily dwindled over the last year.

"Shall I continue to address you as Lord Fairhurst once we arrive at the manor house?" Pierce asked, as the carriage swung down the gravel drive and sedately approached the manor.

"Yes." Jason, who had been mulling over the idea the entire morning, made his decision quickly. It would make his investigation easier if the household believed he was the viscount. "Do I look the part?"

The valet cast a critical gaze over his employer, who was dressed in dove-gray breeches and a bottle-green coat that set off the flecks of emerald green in his eyes. A crisp white cravat, starched and intricately tied, a silver threaded embroidered waistcoat and a spotless white shirt completed the ensemble.

"A man's breeding cannot be bought with expensive fabrics nor elevated unduly by an expert tailor. In the end, blood will tell." The servant brushed a small piece of lint from Jason's coat sleeve. "You look splendid, my lord."

There was no sarcasm this time, merely an honest assessment, with a dash of flattery thrown in for good measure. After all, Pierce was a man who understand which side his bread was buttered on. Still, Jason felt more at ease knowing he had his valet's support.

He stepped out of the coach, but before he had two feet firmly planted on the gravel drive, a middle-aged man rushed forward. From the detailed description that Jasper had given him, Jason knew it was the estate's steward, Mr. Cyril Ardley.

"This is an honor, as well as a pleasant surprise, Lord Fairhurst." The steward bowed low. "Though if we had known of your impending arrival, the staff would have had the opportunity to prepare a special welcome."

"Ardley." Jason ignored the comment, angled his left eyebrow and narrowed his gaze, in what he knew was a perfect imitation of his twin brother. The lack of notice that he was visiting the estate had been deliberate. Far better to catch everyone unaware.

The steward was a man of average height, with gray hair and sharp, dark eyes that regarded everything with keen scrutiny. He did not back away from Jason's narrowed gaze, but instead met it head on. The steward was both Jasper and Jason's key suspect regarding the missing funds from the estate and in that moment Jason knew he would prove a worthy adversary.

Ardley strode forward and held open the manor's front door. With a nod of thanks, Jason stepped inside to a dim and cool hall that stretched to the back of the house. A gallery ringed it, the intricately carved woodwork dark and shining and smelling pleasantly of beeswax. On the stone floor of the hall stood at least twenty servants, divided equally in two neat lines, their eyes turned curiously in Jason's direction.

He acknowledged the butler, housekeeper and cook first, pleased he was able to correctly ascertain their positions from their clothing. Then, feeling ridiculously like the returning prodigal son, Jason made his way slowly down one line and up the other, smiling and nodding a greeting to each and every one of servants. Thankfully, it had been at least three years since his brother had visited the estate, so there was no expectation of him knowing any of the lower servants by name.

When he was finished, Jason announced he would retire to the drawing room to relax after his journey. He graciously accepted the housekeeper's suggestion of a light meal and instructed that it be served to him informally in the drawing room.

Fortunately, the manor house had a traditional configuration, with the drawing room on the second floor. Jason was able to find his way without escort, though a footman eagerly dogged his steps, awaiting his command. He shooed the eager young servant from the room and collapsed into a horsehair stuffed chair, which he soon discovered was stiff and uncomfortable.

Rising from the chair, Jason elected to pace the room instead, feeling a bit cramped from sitting so many hours in the coach. He located a decanter of whiskey and helped himself to a sizable glass while awaiting the arrival of the aforementioned light meal.

Through the window he could see the walled garden, with its many rosebushes, neat paths and swaths of rambling wisteria. A pretty sight, if one enjoyed flowers. And the country. Two things of which Jason had never been especially fond.

He turned away from the pastoral scene and took in the furnishings of the drawing room. Jason had no strong recollection of the estate, though he had visited it on more than one occasion when he was younger. Perhaps knowing it would one day belong to his brother played a part in his lack of memory, but as a rule Jason was uninterested in houses or decor.

The drawing room was a good size, fitted with fine French antiques, accented with several long windows allowing in the natural light. Those many windows were dressed in long silk yellow draperies and the upholstered furniture scattered throughout the room was adorned with floral patterns in dominant shades of yellow. Even the lush Aubusson carpet in the center of the room featured an intricate weave in complementary shades of yellow.

Clearly whoever had outfitted the room had an unusual preference for any shade of yellow. Or perhaps an unnatural affinity for butter? Whatever the reason, Jason promptly decided if he spent too much time in this room his complexion would take on a very sallow hue.

Laughing quietly to himself at his foolish joke, Jason finished his drink, then poured another. He sat on several of the chairs and couches, relieved to finally discover one that wasn't so damn uncomfortable. As he sipped his whiskey and mused over the unappealing color scheme of the room, the door opened. Expecting the servants with his food, he turned his head slightly.

"My lord!" A large-bosomed woman with glossy dark hair cut short and curling around her face entered the room and hurried toward him. He rose automatically to his feet, hoping against hope that this was not someone he was supposed to know.

Fooling the servants would not be too difficult, but impersonating his brother to the local gentry might turn out to be a bit more tricky than he had first imagined.

"Good afternoon." He bowed low at the waist and gifted the middle-aged female with a dazzling smile.

"Oh, my." She paused, momentarily seeming to forget her purpose, but she soon regained her composure and smiled. Very broadly.

Jason felt a trickle of alarm bolt up his spine.

"Do forgive this impromptu call, but we stand on far less ceremony here in the country than in Town," she said.

"How refreshing."

"Oh, gracious." The woman tittered, then held up her hand to her mouth as if trying to stop her giggles. "I fear you will think me terribly forward by presuming upon our previous acquaintance, my lord."

Damn! He was supposed to know her. "In my experience, a beautiful woman can never be too presumptuous," Jason replied in a charming, seductive tone.

Her eyes widened like two saucers and a hint of curiosity entered her expression. "Goodness, you have become quite the charmer these past three years, Lord Fairhurst."

Jason's smile froze on his face. Bloody hell! He had been here less than an hour and already he was giving himself away. His twin was far more restrained around everyone, especially women. If he had any hope of successfully keeping up this masquerade, he would do well to remember it.

"It must be the country air causing my frivolity," he said hastily. "So much more informal, as you said."

The woman nodded. A light knock sounded at the

door and Jason beckoned the footman into the drawing room. The young man was pushing a serving cart crowded with silver-covered dishes.

"Take the food back to the kitchen, with my apologies to Cook, and bring tea instead," Jason said.

The footman paused. "Will Mrs. Hollingsworth be staying for tea, my lord?"

Jason looked to Mrs. Hollingsworth as the servant waited, feeling such a sense of relief at learning her name that he did not mind inviting her to tea.

"Would you be so kind as to take tea with me this afternoon, Mrs. Hollingsworth?"

Color washed into the older woman's round cheeks. "I would be truly honored."

"Inform Cook I have a guest."

"Very good, my lord. Shall I serve the tea in here?"

It was the customary location, but Jason doubted he could stand to sit amongst all the yellow in the room without eventually becoming dizzy.

"I believe I would enjoy breathing some of this invigorating country air. I have been cooped up in my traveling coach for too many days. Will you brave the elements with me, Mrs. Hollingsworth, and take tea on the terrace?"

Jason looked to the older woman with a questioning arch of his brow.

"It sounds lovely, my lord."

"Excellent."

Jason struggled to seem interested as Mrs. Hollingsworth proceeded to engage him in bland, boring conversation focusing mainly on the weather and the society happenings of the local gentry. Time and again, Jason's mind kept wandering and he found it necessary to force himself to concentrate.

"Tea is served, my lord," the footman finally announced.

"Splendid."

He offered Mrs. Hollingsworth his arm and she began to guide him in the direction of the terrace. Feeling oddly like a guest, instead of a host, Jason allowed himself to be led away. Outside, the sun was shining with a crisp glow, and a pair of sparrows sat on the branch of a large tree that shaded the terrace.

Smiling, she moved him off toward a table covered with silver trays laden with a large assortment of individual cakes, cookies, pastries and tiny finger sandwiches. It was an impressive spread, even by London standards. Jason made a mental note to convey his thanks to Cook for a superb job on such short notice.

At his insistence, Mrs. Hollingsworth poured the tea. She handed him a cup that he accepted politely. Taking a small sip, he hid his grimace and thought longingly of his whiskey glass.

"Oh, my goodness, what a delightful surprise. 'Tis my daughter, Olivia."

Mrs. Hollingsworth's voice had taken on a false, cheery brightness that indicated she was lying. Relying on the skills that had aided him for years in avoiding matchmaking mamas for years, Jason decided this little surprise was anything but a coincidence.

Still, he could not be rude. He rose obligingly to his feet and greeted Miss Olivia Hollingsworth, who was a younger and slightly thinner version of her mother. She was dressed in a saffron muslin gown embroidered with roses. Jason nearly winced when he noted the shade, wondering if yellow had some mysterious meaning for country folk, rather like purple did for royalty.

After a token protest, Miss Olivia joined them for tea. She declined the food, but at her mother's insistence, finally selected a fruit tart from the silver tray. It was a gooey confection of pastry, custard and fresh strawberries, with the pretty green stems intact. She balanced her plate precariously with one hand and Jason kept glancing her way, waiting for the pastry to slide off the plate and fall in her lap.

Unfortunately, Miss Olivia completely misunderstood his interest. Glancing at Jason from beneath her lashes, she grasped the largest strawberry by the stem and lifted it near her mouth. Using the tip of her tongue, she licked the custard that coated the bottom of the fruit in an amazingly suggestive manner before slowly sliding it between her lips.

Jason set his teacup down on its saucer and cleared his throat.

"Your mother was mentioning how it has been an usually warm spring this year."

Without the slightest hint of embarrassment Miss Olivia pouted her lips, then opened them to reply, but she was interrupted by the arrival of two matronly females, with five younger women in tow.

Within ten minutes, another matron and her daughter arrived. Jason soon realized the females in the area must be unaware of his brother's recent marriage, since they were stalking him with all the tenacity of a hunter on the scent of fresh game. In his experience, only single men were afforded this kind of attention.

More cups and plates and a second pot of tea was brought. Jason tried to divide his time equally among the women, but it was difficult to concentrate and nearly impossible to keep their names straight. After twenty minutes he admitted defeat—there was no controlling this particular gaggle of determined females.

He thought briefly of making a reference to Lady Fairhurst, but that might bring up too many sticky questions, namely where she was and why she had not accompanied her husband to the estate.

No, better to let the word leak out in a more dignified fashion—through the servants. Jason would instruct Pierce to make a few pointed references in the servants' quarters about his lordship's marriage tomorrow morning. Within hours, the news would be the main topic of conversation at breakfast tables throughout the county.

Until then, he would have to endure this female onslaught with good humor, knowing his twin would never forgive him if he alienated the local society. With an inward groan of dismay, Jason smiled politely as he was introduced to yet another matchmaking mother and her giggling young daughter.

He bowed stiffly and hoped fervently that in addition to the informal manners found in the country, they also had much shorter visiting and afternoon tea hours.

"If you do not hurry, Aunt Mildred, we shall not arrive until well beyond tea time," Dorothea Ellingham cried in frustration. "For pity's sake, can you not walk any faster?"

"If I had known we would be sprinting about the countryside, I would have worn my walking boots," her aunt responded in a puff of shortened breath. The older woman's round, florid face was flushed and gleaming with a thin sheen of perspiration, but she gamely tried to keep pace with the much longer strides of her niece. "Besides, I hardly think it is appropriate that we descend upon the viscount so soon after his arrival. Gracious, the man only arrived at Moorehead Manor a few hours ago."

"Nonsense," Dorothea insisted. "We are not going to call on the viscount. Our visit shall be with Mr. Ardley. If perchance we happen upon the viscount, I would be pleased to make his acquaintance. Though he is a fine London gentleman, I am sure he would appreciate being made welcome by a local to our quaint community."

It was a pretty speech, well-spoken and well-meaning and so blatantly false that even the normally bold Dorothea had difficulty meeting her aunt's eye after she had uttered the words. They both were very aware that Dorothea had never cared a fig for Mr. Cyril Ardley, steward of the manor, and was using Mr. Ardley's close friendship with Uncle Fletcher, Aunt Mildred's husband, as an excuse to gain entry to the house.

Their knock was answered by a tall, wide-shouldered footman. He was brimming with excitement and did not bother to ask their names or why they had called. He made a slight bow and announced, "Please follow me, ladies."

Dorothea's eyebrows lifted at his odd behavior, but not wanting to challenge her luck, she quieted her aunt with a stern look and obligingly followed the servant. He led them through the main foyer, down a long wide hallway and through a set of French doors.

Dorothea's initial elation and excitement vanished the moment she stepped out on the sunny terrace. Her heart sank as she beheld the bizarre scene. It seemed as if every unmarried female in the area between the ages of sixteen and thirty had precisely the same idea as she had. The normally open and airy terrace was crowded with women of all ages, shapes and sizes. She assumed the viscount was somewhere among them, but it was difficult to see anything beyond the sea of muslin gowns and straw bonnets.

Dorothea nearly stamped her foot in frustration. If only it had not taken Aunt Mildred so long to get ready, *they* could have been the first to arrive. Now it was much too late to make a singular impression.

Drat! She knew she should have left Aunt Mildred behind and brought her sister Gwendolyn along as chaperone. Gwen never fussed with her appearance, walked at a quick and even pace and could be supportive in any situation.

As an added bonus, many of these stuffy females would most likely flee in horror at being in the presence of a "fallen" woman, thus thinning out the crowd considerably. It went against Dorothea's nature to expose her sister to any sort of ridicule or pain. Yet Gwen constantly claimed she was not in the least bit upset over her banishment from the local society, an unfortunate and unfair event that occurred four years ago.

Gwen's little mishap was part of the reason Dorothea had come to the manor today. The sisters all needed a fresh start, a way to escape this closed existence. And the only way to do that was through marriage. To a peer. A rich peer.

"My gracious, what a crush," Aunt Mildred said as she took a sip from the cup of tea she had snagged from a passing footman.

"If only we had arrived earlier," Dorothea muttered, then she clamped down on her jaw so hard an ache throbbed at the back of her teeth. It would do no good to insult or upset Aunt Mildred at this stage. Better to see if there was some way to salvage the situation. "Do you see Mr. Ardley in attendance, Aunt?"

The older woman raised herself up on her toes, no small feat for a female of her girth, and surveyed the crowd. "I fear I do not."

"Pity." Dorothea clicked her tongue against her two front teeth, a nervous habit that revealed the depth of her frustration. "I was depending upon Mr. Ardley to introduce us to Lord Fairhurst."

"That would be the proper course of action," Aunt Mildred agreed. "Shall we ask one of the servants to fetch him?"

"Lord Fairhurst?" Dorothea asked in horror, seizing her aunt's hand to prevent her from signaling one of the servants.

"No! I shall ask for Mr. Ardley. Goodness, where has your head gone today, Dorothea?"

"I am not sure," Dorothea replied, her mouth twitching.

This most unexpected glitch in her scheming was quite vexing and Dorothea found it difficult to get her bearings. She never was one who could think fast in a crisis, who could salvage a situation with a clever new approach at a moment's notice. That was her sister Gwendolyn's area of expertise.

Dorothea felt the frustration sweep through her. It had been a good plan, a solid plan, a brilliant plan. Trouble was, it had not been a *unique* plan. Every other unmarried female, and their scheming mamas, had apparently formulated the same approach to capturing the viscount's attention. *Double drat!*

"That must be the viscount," Aunt Mildred whispered, smiling at the blond man on the far end of the patio. "He is certainly a handsome man. A very handsome man."

Dorothea did not even attempt to be coy. She lifted her chin and stared boldly across the patio, hungry for her first glimpse of her intended target. Her eyes widened, surprised she had not seen him sooner.

The viscount stood far above average in height, a fact emphasized in a gathering of women, many who barely reached his shoulder, even in their heels. His hair was a deep golden blond, his eyes a glittering shade of green, his jaw square, his nose prominent, but not intrusive.

He was far more than she had ever hoped. Dorothea smiled with pure pleasure. No matter what the cost, no matter what methods of flirting or teasing or trickery she needed to employ, she would have him. As her husband.

All coherent thoughts fled the moment Jason set eyes upon the statuesque blond. Her looks and manner reminded him so much of Elizabeth that his breath caught in his throat. The shade of her hair, the curve of her nose, the arch of her neck. Even the way she stood, with her back straight and her head tilted at an attractive angle.

An alarm sounded in his brain. Without even speaking a word to her, Jason knew he would be susceptible to her charms, would be vulnerable to her beauty, would listen attentively to her conversation, no matter how inane.

Knowing it was his only means of survival, Jason found himself turning away from her, shutting himself off from any absurd possibilities. The large crowd that had previously annoyed him was now considered a blessing. At worst he would be forced to meet the angelic blond; at best he could avoid her completely.

And, he vowed, somehow, he would continue to avoid her for the remainder of his visit to the manor.

Chapter Two

"Gwendolyn, wake up!"

Gwendolyn Ellingham was pulled from the depths of a pleasant sleep by a hissing in her ear and a hard shake of her left shoulder. She snuggled deeper into her feather pillow and tried to shrug off the interruption, but the shaking and hissing continued. As she drifted toward wakefulness, thoughts formed and separated in her mind and she felt as if she were swimming against a strong tide.

Surrendering to the persistent disturbance, Gwendolyn opened her eyes gradually, cautiously, and beheld her youngest sister, Emma, crouched on the mattress of her bed, a single lit candle held high.

"Emma?" Gwendolyn croaked.

"Yes, 'tis me," Emma answered in a harsh whisper.

"What's wrong?" Gwendolyn lightly touched her sister's cheek. "Did you have another bad dream?"

"No!"

Emma blushed and lowered her head and Gwendolyn wished she had not been so tactless and blunt. Though only fifteen, Emma fancied herself a strong, mature, intellectual woman. She did not like to be reminded of her frequent nightmares.

"Then tell me what is wrong," Gwendolyn asked.

"I'm fine. It's Dorothea who is in trouble. You must come at once."

"Is she ill?" Gwendolyn asked in alarm. "I told her not to eat that second helping of trifle, but she seemed so out of sorts at dinner that I did not have the heart to insist."

"Dorothea isn't ill," Emma replied in an anxious tone. "She is gone!"

"Gone? From your bedchamber?" Gwendolyn patted Emma's hand comfortingly. "I'm sure there isn't anything to worry about, Emma. Dorothea often wanders about the house when she is feeling restless and cannot sleep."

"She is not in the house, Gwen. I've looked everywhere for her."

"Oh, Emma, I am sure you are mistaken. No doubt Dorothea is hiding from you. You know how she enjoys being secretive and mysterious at times."

"This is different. Please, Gwen, you must believe me."

Gwendolyn shook her head, but the protest she was about to utter caught in her throat. Startled, she saw a large tear roll down Emma's cheek. Though sensitive and occasionally dramatic, Emma rarely cried.

She lifted the corner of her bed sheet and wiped Emma's face. "Don't fret. Tell me why you are so distressed. What do you think has happened to Dorothea?"

Emma lifted her head and gave her a sorrowful gaze. "'Tis Lord Fairhurst. She met him this afternoon and was instantly smitten."

"Viscount Fairhurst? But he lives in London."

Emma's mouth tightened. "He is here now, at Moorehead Manor. He arrived early this afternoon."

Gwendolyn felt an uneasy prickle shiver up her spine.

"If he has only just arrived, how did Dorothea meet him?"

Emma licked her lips nervously. "She paid a call at the manor this afternoon."

"What? Are you certain?"

"Yes. I saw Dorothea and Aunt Mildred hurrying from the house and when I asked if I could join them on their walk, I was told to go home. They would not even say where they were going." Emma wrinkled her nose in displeasure. "It seemed most unfair, so I followed them to the estate. They went into the manor through the front door, but I could hear voices coming from the terrace, so I snuck around the side, through the rose garden, and peeked."

"What were they doing?" Gwendolyn asked, knowing she should not encourage such behavior in Emma, but feeling too curious to scold.

Emma shrugged. "I could not find them in the crowd, but I am sure that is where they went. It looked like the viscount was having a garden party, but it was very odd, because there were only women in attendance. I recognized Mrs. Hollingsworth and Olivia and Mrs. Tiltondown and her two daughters."

Gwendolyn felt a brief, momentary stab of pain, but it vanished as soon as it appeared. If the viscount had held a garden party or some other social event, Gwendolyn knew she would not have been included. Still, it hurt to think that her sister and aunt had not even mentioned the garden party to her, nor had they said anything about it at dinner this evening.

"A party given by Viscount Fairhurst is big news for our little social community," Gwendolyn replied. "It would hardly be kept a secret and yet I heard nothing about it."

Emma chewed on her lower lip for a moment. "Perhaps it was not a *formal* party, but there were enough people there to consider it one."

Gwendolyn rubbed her eyes and tried to force her mind to clear. The viscount was the highest ranking peer in the area, a man who was gossiped about and speculated over on a regular basis, even though he was rarely in residence. If he had come to Moorehead Manor, his arrival would not have been kept secret for long.

It was possible that her sister and aunt had made an afternoon call, though that seemed a far-fetched notion. The three sisters were the granddaughters of a baron, through their mother's side of the family. Their father had been of respectable birth, but was hardly of the same social standing of a man who was a viscount and heir to an earldom. Yet in the country, the lines of social standing were drawn a bit hazier than in Town.

"I am sorry, Emma, but I still do not understand what all of this has to do with Dorothea."

"She has fallen in love with him!" Emma declared. "And now she has gone to him. In the middle of the night. As we speak, they could be preparing to run off to Gretna Green together!"

Gwendolyn hung her head to hide her smile, wanting to spare Emma's feelings. At times such as this, it was important to remember that Emma was only fifteen and despite her intelligence and maturity was still given to bouts of girlish imagination and dramatics. A steady diet of romantic and suspenseful stories by Minerva Press only fed into that imagination. Running off to Gretna Green. What a truly ridiculous notion. Gwendolyn's smile widened.

"Why would you ever think Dorothea was eloping with the viscount?"

"She left a note."

The smile disappeared from Gwendolyn's face. It was then that she noticed Emma clutching a scrap of paper in her hand. She snatched it away from her sister.

"Hold the candle higher so I can read it."

My Dearest Sisters,

When you awake, you will find me gone. Do not worry, I have gone to Moorehead Manor to be with my one true love. Please, at all costs, you must wait until morning to follow me there and make certain that you bring Aunt Mildred and Uncle Fletcher when you come. Again I say, do not worry. I do this willingly and with a joyful heart.

Dorothea

"Now do you believe me?" Emma asked.

"Yes," Gwendolyn whispered. She stared down at the parchment she held in her hands and noticed they were trembling. Gracious Lord what a bloody mess!

Emma might naively believe this to be a hasty elopement, but Gwendolyn knew it for what it was—entrapment! If by some miracle the viscount and Dorothea had instantly fallen in love, there would be no need to hide it. More than likely, Dorothea was instead plotting to force the viscount into a situation that would demand he make her an offer of marriage.

It was no secret that Dorothea had long despaired over finding a husband wealthy enough to take her away from this country life she found too restrictive and boring. Dorothea was a beautiful girl, spirted and fun, and at age twenty should have had her pick of suitors.

But the number of men that called upon her sister was small, and Gwendolyn felt a deep sense of guilt, knowing she was the reason. The scandal that had made, and kept, her an outcast from this closed society four years ago had also tainted her sisters. Loyal and protective, they had defended her actions and her character and had suffered for their support.

Yet that scandal would pale in significance beside this latest escapade of Dorothea's. If Gwendolyn could not successfully rescue her before morning, Dorothea's reputation would be torn to shreds and life would become unbearable for them all.

"Help me dress," Gwendolyn instructed as she leapt out of bed. "I need my grey muslin gown, walking boots and dark blue cloak."

"I want to come too."

"No!" Gwendolyn whirled around. She grasped her sister's hand and gave it a quick squeeze. "I need you to stay here, Emma, in case Aunt or Uncle wake up."

Emma's chin jutted out mutinously. Worried, Gwendolyn added, "Please, no arguments and no following me after I have gone. Promise?"

Emma seemed to think it over, but she clearly knew she had no choice. "I do not want to, but if you insist, then I will stay behind. But you must tell me everything."

Gwendolyn mumbled what she hoped Emma would believe to be a positive response. Then she wretched her night rail off and began to dress. With Emma's help, she was soon ready. After repeating her warning to her sister to stay behind, Gwendolyn quietly slipped out the side entrance of her aunt and uncle's house.

It would be faster on horseback, yet impossible to saddle a horse by herself and then hide it once she reached the viscount's estate. Gwendolyn thought briefly of asking for Emma's help, then discarded the idea. She would have to walk.

Moorehead Manor lay two miles to the east. Gwendolyn

set out on a route she was familiar with, through the open fields. There was little chance of encountering anyone at this time of night, but she stayed near the border of trees edging the fields, just in case.

The night smelled different from the day. It had rained briefly at sundown and the air was thick with the smell of mossy trees and damp earth. The low, mournful call of an owl sounded, repeating in a series of short bursts.

Her heart skipped and Gwendolyn was relieved to realize the night rustling was one she recognized. Moonlight guided her way as she walked swiftly, praying she would arrive in time to prevent a real tragedy.

She let out a soft cry of relief when the manor house at last came into view. Bathed in the glow of moonlight, it stood tall and proud, dominating the grounds around it. The windows were dark and shadowed and all was quiet. The household was sleeping.

She quickened her pace as she crossed a wide expanse of manicured lawn. Gwendolyn's boots made a loud crunching sound as they tread along the gravel path through the south gardens. She safely reached the back of the house, then paused, staring at the French doors, bemused. What now? How could she possibly reach Dorothea without awakening the entire household?

Perhaps Mr. Ardley could help? Gwendolyn gnawed her lower lip as she considered the possibility. She had visited Moorehead Manor on several occasions, thanks to her Uncle Fletcher's friendship with Mr. Ardley, the estate steward. She did not know him well, but felt kindly toward him, since Mr. Ardley was one of the few gentlemen in town who did not cast a frown of disapproval her way whenever they happened to meet.

She believed he could be trusted, but was fearful to

test the theory. If her assumptions were correct, this would prove to be a most indelicate matter. The less that others were involved, the better. It was safer to somehow solve this problem on her own.

It was at times such as this when she missed her parents most. Their gentle guidance, loving support, and optimistic belief that any wrong could be put right would have been a real asset at this difficult moment. Though truthfully, if they had been alive, this situation would not have even occurred. Their deaths a few months apart eight years ago had left all three sisters unsettled and fearful. Uncle Fletcher and Aunt Mildred had done their best, but it was not the same.

Gwendolyn shoved the memories of her beloved parents and happier times out of her mind. It did her no good to remember the long-gone past. Her problem existed very much in the present and if she did not find a satisfactory solution soon, it would escalate to unbearable levels.

Gwendolyn stood at the back terrace, her hands on her hips, pondering her next move. She had a vague knowledge of the layout of the manor house. If Dorothea was already in the viscount's bedchamber Gwendolyn felt confident she could locate it. But how would she possibly gain entry to the house and keep her presence a secret from the staff? Break a window?

Gwendolyn shut her eyes tight and tried to remember if the estate dogs slept in the house or in the stables. They were placid, friendly animals when one met them in the light of day, eager for a pat on the head or a scratch behind the ears. Yet she was fairly certain she would receive a far different greeting if the dogs heard her break a window and suspected she was an intruder.

Unfortunately, there was only one way to find out. She

searched among the flower beds for a large rock. Brushing off the dirt, Gwendolyn held the stone in her right hand and planted her feet, poised to hurl it at the window. She drew her arm forward, then back, practicing the motion several times, took a deep breath and . . . nothing.

Darn! Frustrated at her lack of nerve, Gwendolyn angrily dropped the stone, stalked up the terraced steps and reached for the handle of the French door. To her utter amazement it opened quietly and without any resistance.

With a pounding heart and a small smile of satisfaction, Gwendolyn silently entered the house. It was the middle of the night and Moorehead Manor was as quiet as a tomb. Hoping against hope, she made a hurried dash around the formal rooms on the first and second floors, disappointed, yet not surprised to find them empty.

Letting out a deep sigh, Gwendolyn crept up the main staircase to the next floor, then down the long corridor of the east wing, thankful the tall window at the end of the hall allowed in so much bright moonlight. She was thankful also that she had always been able to see well in the dark.

Gwendolyn paused as she reached the first chamber door. She had no idea which bedchamber belonged to the viscount, but since there were no other guests in residence, the other rooms should be unoccupied. Approaching the problem in her usual, thorough manner, Gwendolyn started at one end of the hall and began quietly opening each of the doors, knowing eventually she would locate what she sought.

As she finished one side, she turned and started on the opposite side, wondering how many wings of the manor held bedchambers. But her diligence was at last rewarded when she opened the next door. It was obvious the moment she stepped inside that there was something different about this chamber.

Inside there was an intangible feeling of life, a vibrant air of breath and bodies. Gwendolyn allowed a moment for her eyes to adjust to the darkness before taking another step farther into the room.

A shaft of moonlight slashed through the room, cutting across the bed. Gwendolyn could discern two distinct shapes among the bed linens and then, to her horror, noticed a bit of movement beneath the covers. Gwendolyn stared at the image and a rush of intense warmth came over her, but she had come too far to lose her courage before the final confrontation.

She had only a split second to consider the appalling consequences if this was *not* the viscount's room, or if one of the occupants in the bed was *not* her sister.

Gwendolyn cleared her throat.

"Psst, Dorothea. Dorothea." She heard the breathlessness in her own voice and tried to cover it by lowering the pitch of her tone. "Dorothea, I have come to bring you home. Get out of the bed. Hurry, before any of the household awakens."

As dreams went, it was a fairly erotic one. Someone was stroking his hair, with a light even touch that made Jason relax even as his body began to tighten with a stirring of desire. Next, the kisses began; sweet, tender, plump lips pressing quick kisses to his cheeks, his forehead, and then finally his lips. Still drifting in a dream-like state, Jason moved closer to his phantom lover, breathed in the scent of lemon soap and felt his lower body come alive.

He reached out instinctively, cradling the warm, feminine softness. He could feel the smoothness of this lovely apparition's skin under the thin gown she wore, but it wasn't enough. The contact, though part of a luscious dream, sparked something deep and primal within him. He wanted more, he needed more.

His last love affair had ended months ago and there had been no dalliances since that time. He knew now that he had been too long without the physical company of a woman, especially if his body's needs were torturing him as he slept. Tilting his head, Jason swept his tongue across his partner's lower lip. She gasped, and when she parted her lips, he plunged inside, stroking, exploring, needing.

The glorious fantasy continued. He deepened the kiss and tugged on the soft fabric of her night rail, pulling it higher and higher until it bunched in his fist. With his other hand, he stroked the bare skin of her upper thigh and hips, then slid his fingers up her back. She shivered and wrapped her arms around him.

Fearing he would wake up too soon, he anxiously ground himself against her, rubbing his arousal against her sweet belly. She gasped, flexed into him, then moaned softly.

A buzzing noise invaded his conscience, an annoyance that distracted him from his pleasure. Jason frowned in his sleep and tried to ignore it, but the noise persisted.

Dorothea. Dorothea. What? Someone was calling for Dorothea. Who the hell was she? The dream lost its edge of delight, turning quickly into a nuisance. An irate husband barging in just when things were starting to get interesting was hardly the stuff of an erotic dream. It was more like a nightmare.

"Dorothea! Dorothea!"

Mentally grinding his teeth, Jason tried one final time to recapture the fantasy, but it was lost. The disappointment of the moment faded sharply in the next few uncounted minutes as he realized two things simultaneously.

This was most definitely not a dream or a nightmare and he was not alone in his bedchamber. His eyes slowly opened.

"Merciful heavens, is that you, Gwendolyn?"

The lovely female who lay beside him in bed spoke, her voice a hissing whisper.

"Were you expecting someone else?" came the dry reply from the shadowy figure standing near the doorway.

"You know very well that I was. Didn't you read my note?"

"How else would I have known where to find you?" The shadow sighed. "You have made a colossal blunder, Dorothea, but there is no time to explain. You must come with me at once. Hurry, before the viscount awakens."

Though he tried, Jason could not let pass this golden opportunity to insert himself into this most bizarre drama. "Too late, ladies. The viscount is already awake."

His voice echoed through the room, a deep booming baritone. The woman in his bed shrieked.

"Quiet!" He and the shadow commanded at the same time.

Eyes narrowing, Jason stared sightlessly ahead into the darkness, wishing the shadow would move closer to the shaft of moonlight in the center of the room so he could see her, could distinguish her features.

The silence that followed was so strange it could not even be labeled awkward. Jason was a sophisticated man, with jaded tastes, who had experienced many surreal events in his lifetime, especially when women were involved. Hiding in wardrobes, leaping off balconies, even once dressing as a serving wench to avoid being caught by his lover's husband. But this moment entered an entirely new realm.

"I know there is some sort of explanation for all of this," he began in a calm tone of voice. "And I confess to being very interested in hearing it."

"I have been compromised, my lord." The woman in his bed started to tremble. "And I expect that as a gentleman, as an honorable gentleman, you will set things to right."

Bloody hell! Entrapment! Ever since he was a young man, many had tried, and failed, to wring a proposal from his lips. He was an old hand at avoiding the marriage trap, an expert many would say. It took a moment for Jason to realize he was not breathing. Were all the years of chasing women, having brief, torrid affairs and successfully avoiding anything that even hinted at a relationship going to end now?

The shadow shifted and he thought he saw her shake her head. "He is married. Do you understand, Dorothea? Lord Fairhurst already has a wife."

His bed partner made a strange choking sound and even in the dimness of the moonlight he could see her face drain of all color. "Is that true?"

He sensed the eyes of both women upon him. "There is indeed a Lady Fairhurst."

Though a rake and rogue and a mostly unscrupulous fellow, Jason had never been much of a liar. He avoided the entire truth when it suited his advantage, omitting details that were not specifically asked. But this was the truth. There was a Lady Fairhurst. His brother had married a few months ago and only recently undertook a second wedding ceremony so his bride's family could bear witness to the union.

Jason, who had supposedly compromised this innocent female, was unmarried, but that was not the query.
His breathing slowly took on a normal rhythm as he realized he was safe. There would be no outraged father
insisting he must save his daughter's reputation by marrying her, because these women believed he was Jasper.

"He is married!" The female at his side let out a withering cry and pressed the back of her hand to her forehead.

"Steady, Dorothea," the intruder commanded. "You
will make even more of a muck of things if you faint."

The lithe creature in his bed shifted away from him
and pushed herself into a sitting position. Her face
briefly fell into the shaft of moonlight and Jason sucked
in his breath. It was the blond beauty from this afternoon's tea, the woman who reminded him so much of
Elizabeth.

"I shall not faint, Gwendolyn," the blond said, tossing
her glorious hair over her shoulder. "I promise."

"Nor scream?"

"Nor scream."

A rustle of sheets told him she had successfully slid out
of the bed. Her footsteps made no noise on the carpet as
she ran to the woman. The shadow she called Gwendolyn.

Jason's eyes strained in the darkness, trying to see
what they were doing. He heard a clanking noise and
supposed the blond was putting on her shoes. And then
what? Would they quit the room, leave the manor house
and melt into the night?

"We are going, my lord."

He coughed in shock.

"Was there something you wished to say?" the shadow
demanded.

Jason blinked at her. There were few females who

managed to catch him by surprise, but this pair had done an admirable job.

"I have nothing to say, madame," he answered in a priggish tone. "Frankly, I am struck dumb by the bizarre events of this night."

The shadow huffed. "Then I suppose I must wait for your wits to return, my lord," she replied in a sharp tone. "Though I fear that will take more time than we have at present. Come along, Dorothea."

"Wait!" Jason reached over and fumbled for the flint he knew was on the bedside table. He struck it, then lit the candle that was perched in the brass candlestick on the same table.

Though only a single candle, it provided the necessary light for him to examine the pair closely. The blond was disheveled and shivering in a thin cotton night rail that left little to the imagination. A beautiful woman, to be sure, and Jason was stunned by his complete lack of interest in her. Her resemblance to Elizabeth was uncanny, but his earlier reaction of excitement and dread was gone.

It was the shadow who captured his attention completely. She was as dark as the other was fair, with raven hair and deep, chocolate brown eyes that were fringed with long, lush lashes. Her nose was pert, with a slight upturn on the end and her unfashionable full lips looked perfect for giving and receiving kisses.

Yet it was not her physical beauty that so intrigued Jason; it was the force of her presence, her spirit that seemed to fill the room. Standing tall and proud, with an expression of righteous indignity, she was the very essence of female power. Anyone who took her as a pretty, uncomplicated woman would be committing a grave error.

She had removed her cloak and was wrapping it around the blond, who was now shivering. "We are leaving," she announced. "I trust you are at least enough of a gentleman to hold your tongue over this most unfortunate matter."

Jason was accustomed to making quick decisions. He was not about to let them walk away without some sort of explanation. Yet he did realize this was hardly the most opportune moment for a lengthy conversation.

"This is far from over, ladies. I expect you both to call on me tomorrow. At noon."

There was a pause of silence. This time the blond broke it. "You need not drag Gwendolyn into this mess. I will come alone."

Jason raised his brow. "I would be a fool indeed, if I received you without a witness. I insist that you both attend me."

"You will not receive me," the shadow stated bluntly.

"Excuse me?"

"I am not received in polite society," she repeated in a bland tone. "Ask anyone. Mrs. Hollingsworth, Mrs. Tiltondown, or even one of your staff. I do not relish coming all this way only to have the door slammed in my face."

Jason blinked, then refocused on her face. She did not appear to be lying, yet her matter-of-fact pronouncement was unsettling. Not received in polite society? Why? What could she have possibly done to warrant such treatment?

"I do not care about the opinions of others nor do I follow the dictates set down by the rigid rules of society," he replied.

"That's not what I have heard."

Damn! She was right. His brother Jasper was a most upstanding, proper fellow, with a moral outlook and attitude that bordered on priggish. Thank heavens he now had a wife who would temper his rigid tendencies.

"I am unconcerned with what you have heard," Jason stated, as he tried to bluff his way to credibility. "I give you my word that you shall be admitted to my drawing room tomorrow at noon and I expect you to comply with my request. If not, I shall be forced to come to you and that would put me in a foul temper."

That got her attention. She stared at him for a long moment. "We shall be here at noon," she finally replied, nodding her head.

"Excellent." His lips quirked. Jason liked getting his own way.

The women disappeared from his room in silence. Jason left his bed and hastily dressed. He glanced at the clock and allowed five full minutes to pass before he stepped out of his bedchamber. Hurrying, he descended the main staircase, slipped out a side door, then halted.

His eyes scanned the area, quickly finding what he sought. Jason let out a loud curse when he realized his recent, uninvited house guests were traveling on foot. Grinding his teeth together in annoyance, and sincerely hoping they were not going too far, he set off after them.

After following them at a safe, undetectable distance for nearly an hour he realized there was no need to be so cautious. The pair were too absorbed in their harshly whispered conversation to take much notice of their surroundings.

The open pasture they crossed eventually gave way to a dirt path, that lead past a cottage and barn, then the path turned to cobblestone as they entered a short drive. The house that stood at the end was not overly large, yet was stately in design.

Not a soul was in sight.

He stored the information away in his head, knowing it might prove useful in the future. That was partly the reason he had trailed the women to their home, to discover all he could about them. The equally important other reason was to ensure that no harm came to them as they traipsed about the countryside, alone, in the very early morning hours.

Jason Barrington was many things, but above all, he was a gentleman.

Chapter Three

Soft streaks of pale sunlight crept in through the thin draperies while an open window allowed a gentle breeze to flutter into the chamber. Gwendolyn felt the coolness on her cheek and slowly opened her eyes. As she gradually came awake, she hoped the bizarre images in her mind would turn out to be a bad dream, but her cloak was thrown hastily over a chair instead of being hung in her wardrobe, evidence of her recent nighttime excursion.

Gwendolyn let out a long, slow breath. It was all true. Her wildly impetuous sister had tried to entrap the viscount into marriage and the plan had backfired dreadfully. Even more alarming was the acknowledgement that they were not out of the woods yet.

The viscount could make life very difficult for them if he so chose and Gwendolyn knew it would be her responsibility to somehow prevent that from happening. Unfortunately she was hardly at her best this morning. It had been very late when they had returned home and Gwendolyn had retired to her bed with a hard knot of tension in her stomach. She spent those few hours before dawn grappling with the situation that faced them, trying to decide how to dissuade the viscount from retaliating against them.

There was a discreet knock at the door and the maid, Lucy, entered the bedchamber. "Are you ready to get dressed, Miss Gwendolyn? Or would you prefer that I come back after I've attended to Miss Dorothea and Miss Emma?"

"See to my sisters first, please," Gwendolyn replied.

Since their Uncle Fletcher had an eye toward economy, all three sisters shared the maid's services. In an effort to be fair, each morning Lucy alternated which of the girls she went to first, but more often than not, Gwendolyn sent the maid to her sisters, preferring to be on her own.

Gwendolyn tried to rest after Lucy departed, but it was impossible. Giving up, she went to her wardrobe and scrutinized the contents, deciding to wear one of her newer gowns, knowing she would need a boost of confidence today. After a few minutes, she selected a white muslin day dress trimmed with blue satin ribbon. When Lucy returned, the maid finished fastening the buttons on Gwendolyn's lower back, then arranged her dark hair in a loose upsweep.

Gwendolyn was the last to join the rest of the family at breakfast, and she tried hard to appear as if nothing was amiss. She had not slept well, nor from the look of her, had Dorothea. Though dressed in one of her prettiest gowns, a simple muslin dress of pale pink, trimmed with darker pink satin, Dorothea's face carried the same hints of fatigue as her own.

Emma buttered her toast, then reached for the jam and Gwendolyn tried to pretend she was unaware of her youngest sister's intense gaze. It was obvious to anyone who cared to notice that Emma was near to bursting with curiosity and questions. Fortunately, she was wise enough not to say anything while their aunt and uncle sat at the table with them.

Aunt Mildred accepted a plate piled high with ham and several slices of toast from their serving girl, then asked for a second cup of coffee. Gwendolyn tried to engage their aunt in small talk, since Emma seemed cautious about speaking and Dorothea was depressingly silent. Thankfully, Aunt Mildred had always been a woman who relished the sound of her own voice, so it was not difficult to keep her talking.

Uncle Fletcher never spoke at the breakfast table, though Gwendolyn was certain he listened, even if only with mild interest. Gwendolyn found she had little appetite, but she managed to force down a few bites of toast.

Finally, Uncle Fletcher set down his coffee cup and pushed back his chair. "I've business matters to attend to this morning and an appointment with Mr. Ardley this afternoon. I shall see you all at dinner. Have a pleasant day."

Gwendolyn sucked in her breath, certain the mention of Mr. Ardley would elicit a comment from her aunt about the viscount, since Ardley was steward at the manor. But Aunt Mildred was too caught up in the telling of some ridiculous tale about Mrs. Hollingsworth to take note of her husband's remarks.

With their uncle gone from the room, Emma seemed to find her tongue. She asked Aunt Mildred a question that launched the older woman on a new topic. Gwendolyn used the distracting opportunity to lean over and whisper to Dorothea.

"Uncle Fletcher mentioned an appointment with Mr. Ardley this afternoon. We must make certain we arrive at Moorehead Manor precisely at noon, so we can take our leave before Uncle gets to the estate. If we are lucky enough to remain unseen, we might be able to keep our meeting a secret."

"Is it really necessary for us to go to manor today?" Dorothea asked.

Gwendolyn reached over and took her sister's hand. "Lord Fairhurst was rather insistent. He said he would come to us if we did not honor our promise to meet him and I for one take him at his word."

Dorothea's blue eyes darkened with distress. "But how would he know where to find us? We did not reveal our full names to him last night."

"He knows that you are Dorothea and I am Gwendolyn. The infamous Gwendolyn, who is not received by our local society." Gwendolyn exhaled sharply, wondering if it had been wise to tell him that fact. "The viscount strikes me as an intelligent man. With only a few choice questions, he will easily learn all about us, including where we live."

"I suppose you are right." Dorothea glanced away, tears welling in her eyes. "I am so sorry that I made such a muck of it all."

"It could have been far worse. What if one of the servants had found you in the viscount's bed? The disgrace would be complete, your ruin assured." Gwendolyn squeezed her sister's hand. "I have thought about it long and hard and concluded it is most doubtful Lord Fairhurst will want any of the details of the incident revealed. He will keep this secret safe, if only to guard his own reputation."

"Perhaps." Dorothea looked away, her expression worried. "Lord Fairhurst is only half of our problem. How are we both going to slip away without telling Aunt Mildred of our destination? We need something to keep her occupied."

"Or someone," Gwendolyn added, casting her gaze at Emma. She would have preferred to keep her youngest sister removed from all of this drama, but she had no choice. "Emma is due for a fitting at the dressmaker's later this morning. Would you mind taking her, Aunt Mildred?"

"Not at all. It will give me a chance to check on the progress of my own new gown." Aunt Mildred liked nothing more than feeling needed.

Emma's mulish expression let Gwendolyn know she was not at all pleased with the arrangement. Far more clever, and knowing, than their aunt, Emma was quick to see that she was being used as a diversion.

Please, Gwendolyn mouthed silently to Emma as their aunt concentrated on finishing the food on her plate. *We need your help.*

Emma lifted both brows, paused, then nodded in agreement.

Knowing she would somehow have to pay back the favor later, Gwendolyn was still relieved to have her sister's cooperation. She took a fortifying sip of her now lukewarm coffee and tried to calculate how soon she and Dorothea could slip away from the house.

The morning had been warm, but a brisk wind swept across the open fields, keeping Gwendolyn and Dorothea cool. They walked at a steady pace, speaking occasionally.

"I wish we could have taken the carriage," Dorothea grumbled. "It is so much more elegant. If we aren't careful, we shall arrive at the manor looking sweaty and disheveled, despite this breeze."

"Aunt Mildred and Emma have the carriage,"

Gwendolyn replied. "It was either ride or walk and we both agreed it would take too long to change into our riding habits."

Secretly she agreed it was rather lowering having to walk, but not only because of the need to preserve their appearance. Gwendolyn knew the importance of looking the part of a well-bred lady when paying a social call, especially to someone with a superior social standing. Arriving in their uncle's old-fashioned yet finely appointed carriage would have made a far more elegant, respectable statement than arriving on foot.

Initially anxious about not being late, Gwendolyn now experienced a moment of regret as they reached the front drive of the manor. She glanced up at the sky and tried to calculate the time by the sun's position, worried about arriving too early.

Their steps slowed noticeably as they drew closer to the house until finally there was no way to delay their arrival any further. Dorothea lifted the shiny brass knocker on the front door. The sound seemed to echo through the large foyer beyond it. Standing beside her, Gwendolyn suddenly felt cold in the sultry summer air, wondering how she would keep her pride and dignity, if she were denied entrance.

Four years was a long time to be ignored by society, but knowing she had little choice, Gwendolyn had adapted. She quickly learned how to avoid situations that afford others an opportunity to openly snub or ridicule her. It had meant cutting herself off from nearly everyone of consequence in their small community, but after the initial feelings of loneliness and isolation had worn off, Gwendolyn realized she was surviving.

She was not a complete pariah. The merchants all spoke to her, as did the vicar and his wife, as did Mr.

Ardley. But they were the minority. It was an unspoken rule that she did not attend parties or balls or afternoon teas. She did not make social calls and when visitors came to their home, she did not stay in the parlor. On the rare occasion when there was an unavoidable, intolerable encounter, she had learned how to cope with the moment and then later, push it from her mind, to distance herself from the unpleasantness.

But there would be no avoidance, no distancing today. She would walk boldly into what might prove to be her most scathing rebuke to date.

The butler answered Dorothea's knock and it took every ounce of Gwendolyn's inner strength to appear confident. "Lord Fairhurst is expecting us," Gwendolyn said in what to her ears was an overly loud tone.

The butler made no response. He regarded them both for a tense moment, then opened the door wide. "This way, please."

They stepped inside, out of the gusting breeze. Gwendolyn's emotions were rioting. At least the viscount had kept his word, yet she could not help but wonder what wild tales he had been told about her past.

"Are you frightened?" Gwendolyn whispered, feeling her sister trembling beside her.

Dorothea let out a nervous giggle. "I am too numb to be frightened," she replied. They followed the butler at a considerable distance, so as not to be overheard.

"Numb this morning, yet last night you found the courage to sneak into this house and the viscount's bed," Gwendolyn whispered.

"That was different. Last night I had a goal to achieve. Today I wish only to forget it ever happened." Dorothea had the grace to look slightly chagrined. "I too have given a great deal of thought to how we should act and I think it would be best if when we meet the viscount, we pretend last night never happened."

Gwendolyn sighed, wishing it were that simple. "Ignoring a social gaffe to be polite is common practice, yet this is hardly equitable to forgetting to wear the proper gloves or using the wrong fork when eating the fish course at a formal dinner. We must tackle this head on and convince Lord Fairhurst that he is the one who will benefit most by keeping the incident confidential."

For a quick moment Dorothea looked as if she intended to argue the point, but then her chin lowered and she meekly stepped closer to Gwendolyn.

Lord Fairhurst was standing by the window, looking out on the lovely gardens when they entered. He turned, dismissing the butler, then motioned them to the settee near the unlit fireplace.

Gwendolyn fought to obey. She wanted to remain on her feet, believing that standing gave her more control, yet thought it prudent not to antagonize him so soon upon their arrival. She sank gracefully on the edge of the sofa and Dorothea copied her movements.

Lord Fairhurst took the chair opposite them. His face was stern, his stare intense. Though Gwendolyn found his scrutiny unsettling, she was determined not to give him the satisfaction of letting him know it. The idea that he was deliberately trying to intimidate her and Dorothea had the opposite effect. She stiffened her spine.

He was not what she had expected. Last night, it had been too dark to observe him. She had heard he was stiff, proper, a stickler for proprieties. However, in the light of day he seemed older, more sophisticated, and Gwendolyn feared that under that polite facade lurked a hard-headed male.

"First, I wish to know the nature of your relationship to each other," Lord Fairhurst said.

He was all business. A part of Gwendolyn was relieved there would be no polite, meaningless little conversation that was so awkward to sustain during social calls. Still, she was put slightly off balance by this direct approach, knowing it might be to her advantage to ease into the substance of the conversation gradually, after establishing a congenial rapport.

"Dorothea and I are sisters," Gwendolyn said calmly, wondering if he already knew the truth and was testing her honesty or if he had refrained from inquiring about their background.

"Sisters?" He looked from one to the other as though he were struggling to make the connection. "You do not resemble each other in the least."

"That is often the case with siblings," Gwendolyn responded defensively, imagining for the first time how striking they must appear with Dorothea's pale blond curls an almost opposite contrast to her own dark straight locks.

"Not always." The viscount laughed, and for an instant, the aura of sobriety was lifted.

His innate charm was almost overpowering. Gwendolyn found herself starting to answer his smile, then pulled herself back to reality. She forced her gaze down to her shoes, knowing it was utterly ridiculous to find him attractive or appealing.

"Do you resemble your siblings, my lord?" Dorothea asked.

"Not my sister, but it has been noted that my brother and I bare a passing resemblance."

Gwendolyn frowned in consideration, a pertinent fact niggling at the back of her brain. A passing resemblance? That was not right. Her head jerked up. Now she remembered. The viscount's brother was his twin and by all accounts the resemblance was nothing less than extraordinary.

Something shifted in his eyes and Gwendolyn realized that he was aware that she knew about his twin brother. For some odd reason, it appeared to unsettle him. Curious. Gwendolyn schooled her features into a neutral expression, in an attempt to conceal her own feelings.

"We are here, as you demanded, though I do not understand why," Gwendolyn said.

"I want an explanation for your sister's most unusual behavior last night," Lord Fairhurst demanded. "I own I am a man of varied experiences, yet you managed to give me quite a shock."

"I hardly know what to say," Dorothea hedged.

"Start at the beginning."

Dorothea cleared her throat; an obvious ploy to gain her more time. Gwendolyn glanced over at the viscount. He was looking straight ahead. Even in profile he was an extraordinarily good-looking man, with high cheekbones and a strong jaw.

"Honestly, my lord, there is no need for a lengthy explanation," Gwendolyn proclaimed, after it became clear that Dorothea was not going to say anything. "The events of last night were as they appeared and the sooner they are forgotten, the better for all of us."

The viscount looked at her thoughtfully, as if he were turning her words over in his mind. Gwendolyn returned his gaze directly.

"How did you know about Lady Fairhurst?" he asked. "Within an hour of my arrival at Moorehead Manor I was besieged by every unmarried female within a twenty-mile radius, all with one thing very much on their minds. Matrimony. I quickly surmised they were unaware of Lady Fairhurst's existence, yet somehow you knew, Miss Ellingham."

"I did." Gwendolyn stiffened. Clearly he knew more about them then he had led on, since he just used her surname. This fact merely enforced her first impression of the great need to remain cautious. Above all, she must be careful not to underestimate him. "I read a detailed description in the newspaper of a party held by the Duke of Warwick that mentioned you and Lady Fairhurst as honored guests. Since I know that your mother is the Countess of Stafford, the only individual who could hold the title of Lady Fairhurst would be your wife."

"Which paper?"

"*The Times.* Many of us in the area read it, but the delivery is hardly reliable. Our paper was over a month old, but it must have arrived before everyone else's."

He expelled a long breath. "Hmm. Obviously you neglected to share the information with your sister?"

Gwendolyn shrugged. "Quite frankly, I forgot. There hardly seemed a pressing need." She did not add that she had been reading the paper before going to sleep last night and thus had not had the opportunity to tell Dorothea. If she had, this entire mess could have been avoided.

Lord Fairhurst's eyes narrowed momentarily, as if he was trying to decide if he believed her. What an arrogant man! Was he suddenly puzzled as to why he was not the center of everyone's conversation? Did he really believe that he was the sun and the rest of them the planets which revolved around him?

"You just said you were besieged by unmarried females soon after your arrival, so my ambitions for an advantageous marriage were hardly unique," Dorothea interjected. "When I was at the manor yesterday afternoon, I realized that there was going to be a myriad of female competition, so I sought a way to gain your attention."

The viscount turned to stare at Dorothea. "I concede that you were not the only female with a pre-occupation toward matrimony, but certainly the most desperate." His eyebrows rose fractionally. "Are you breeding? Is that why you felt it necessary to resort to wedlock by ambush?"

Dorothea let out a gasp of pure indignity, but Gwendolyn managed to hold back her emotions. She was not overly surprised by the accusation. In all honesty, she could not even claim it was completely unwarranted. Anyone who was so bold as to slip into a stranger's bed in the middle of the night must be prepared to accept the harsh comments that would follow.

But she knew she could not afford to give Lord Fairhurst an inkling of her sympathy. She must never let him see anything but her outrage over his implications. Any chance of saving Dorothea's reputation rested on somehow forcing the viscount to acknowledge her sister as a lady, an individual who ordinarily would never dream of doing anything so improper.

"Dorothea's actions were an uncharacteristic aberration, an incident of momentary madness," Gwendolyn declared.

"Ahh, so the prospect of marrying me drives women to acts of insanity?" Lord Fairhurst looked at her, his expression mild and unperturbed. "I am uncertain if I should be flattered or appalled by that remark, Miss Ellingham."

Gwendolyn barely held back an exasperated hiss. The viscount was deliberately trying to be difficult and she quickly admitted there was very little she could do to change that attitude. Still, they had come here for a specific purpose and she at least had to try to get some assurance from him that he would say nothing about the incident.

"We seek not to make excuses, my lord, but rather to assure ourselves of your discretion. I am sure you do not wish to be the object of gossip and speculation."

"I suspect that my reputation will weather the storm intact." He stretched out his legs and crossed them at the ankles. "However, this is the sort of gossip that could ruin a young girl's prospects."

"Precisely," Gwendolyn agreed. "Which is why we ask that you show some empathy and remain silent about the matter. There must have been at least one time in your life when you acted on impulse, without giving due consideration to all the consequences of your actions."

Lord Fairhurst remained perfectly still, but for just a second his eyes blinked. She had made her point, and apparently also struck a nerve. Perhaps the viscount was not as stuffy and straight-laced as he appeared. Gwendolyn remembered hearing rumors that he had been a rather impulsive young man.

He lifted his head and looked into her eyes. For a moment their gazes locked and Gwendolyn wondered what he saw, what he was searching for when he regarded her. Wondered what in heaven's name he wanted from them.

"You speak from experience, Miss Ellingham. What, or rather who, precisely, ruined you?"

Dear Lord. In the four years since the incident, Gwendolyn had never been spoken to about it so bluntly, so directly. Was it his lofty position or his innate personality that bred such superiority?

Her fall from grace was something whispered about

behind closed doors, something invisible, yet tangible, that hung in the air whenever she chanced to encounter people who refused to acknowledge her existence with even the slightest nod of the head.

"Gwendolyn did nothing wrong. Nothing!" Dorothea said vehemently. "She has been treated abominably by these small-minded, petty women who are jealous of her wit and intelligence and beauty."

"You appear to be paying a high price for doing nothing wrong," he replied dryly.

"You don't understand," Dorothea cried.

"Then pray, enlighten me."

Gwendolyn's breath caught in her throat. They were not here to discuss her, but rather to avert a scandal with Dorothea. Yet somehow it seemed that no matter what the circumstances it always came back to Gwendolyn and her scandalous behavior. How had her life become so topsy-turvy?

Gwendolyn closed her eyes, searching for a brief moment of peace. She lifted her lashes and only then became aware of her tightly clasped fingers resting in her lap. She slowly loosened her grip. Pain shot through her hands and fingers as the blood began flowing normally again. She sighed, annoyed at her cowardice.

"Four years ago I was traveling to Town with my great-aunt," Gwendolyn began. "She had kindly offered to sponsor a modest debut into society, despite my advanced age."

"Our mother was her favorite niece and she wanted to do something in her memory," Dorothea added.

Lord Fairhurst looked startled. "I was unaware you lacked the guidance of a mother."

Dorothea shot him a mighty frown. "Our father is also dead."

"A recent loss?" the viscount inquired as he tapped his fingers thoughtfully against the scrolled, padded chair arm.

"No. They have both been gone for many years," Gwendolyn responded.

"We are all alone in the world, my lord," Dorothea said in a pitiful tone. "In addition to Gwendolyn and myself, there is our youngest sister, Emma, who depends on us completely. She is barely fifteen."

Gwendolyn turned toward Dorothea, inwardly groaning when she caught the calculating gleam in her sister's eye. Dorothea had always excelled at playing the downtrodden, helpless maiden, yet Gwendolyn greatly feared that the viscount would not be among the many men who found this appealing. Especially under these circumstances.

"You are orphans?" A soft, but unmistakable snort erupted from Lord Fairhurst. "My God this gets more melodramatic by the moment. Is there a wicked guardian threatening to force you into marriage with a lecherous old man three times your age? Will you claim that is the reason you took such desperate and drastic measures last night and crawled into my bed?"

Dorothea gasped and her brows knit together in shock and indignation. Gwendolyn shared her sister's annoyance and her control stretched thinner.

"It pleases me to no end, discovering that you find our misfortunes so amusing, my lord." Gwendolyn could not restrain the urge to glower. "I am therefore most sorry to inform you that our aunt and uncle are both kind and loving and, while we are hardly wealthy, we are comfortably situated."

A ghost of a smile flitted across his face. "My apologizes for any insult you might have taken from my comments. I assure you, none was given."

Gwendolyn searched his handsome face for a hint of self-reproach, for an ounce of sincerity and found none. She realized in that moment the futile nature of their mission. He had already formed his opinion of them, had set his mind to the course of action he would take regarding Dorothea's behavior.

"Come along, Dorothea, we are leaving." Gwendolyn rose gracefully from the settee and straightened to her full height, which gave her bruised confidence a boost. Dorothea imitated her movements.

The viscount's eyes flashed annoyance. "We are not finished," he stated.

"Further discussion is pointless," Gwendolyn replied. "My past is immaterial in this instance and I believe that you have already made up your mind as to whether or not you will expose my sister to scandal."

His gaze locked with hers. "Now you are a mind reader?"

"No, my lord. I honestly do not know what you will do. I only know you have already decided and I doubt anything we say will sway your opinion. I can only hope that you will act as the gentleman you were raised to be and behave honorably. You were wronged by my sister, yet in the end no harmful consequence befell you. Any man with an ounce of compassion in his heart would take that into consideration before taking actions that would destroy a young girl's future."

He regarded her smugly and the frustration of last night, and this morning, bubbled up inside her. Without meaning to, Gwendolyn found herself issuing a parting shot. "Unfortunately, your behavior today has cast grave doubts as to the true nature of your character, but we can always pray for a miracle."

Chapter Four

It was an impressive exit line, worthy of a great actress and yet it would have sounded melodramatic if any other woman had spoken it. Though he did not want to, Jason could not help but recognize the honesty in her voice, the sincerity of her actions. Her cold stare enforced her words, while the rigid set of her shoulders emphasized her animosity, letting him know exactly what she thought of his opinions and character.

Jason felt a twinge of regret. He had not intended to be so harsh, but honestly, how could he possibly trust a word these two women said to him?

He almost wished he could explain to Gwendolyn that she had misunderstood him, but the most annoying part of the entire exchange was that she was right. He had mulled over the incident while shaving this morning, rethought his position at breakfast and had firmly concluded that no good would come out of exposing the silly Dorothea to any sort of scandal. This meeting was indeed unnecessary.

Initially, he had planned to tell the sisters of his decision within minutes of their arrival. There was no need for a lengthy conversation, no reason to listen to their half-baked explanations and apologies. But seeing Gwendolyn fully for the first time in the bright daytime light had distracted his thoughts.

Though a connoisseur of all women, Jason had always preferred blondes. He found their delicate pale beauty, ethereal coloring and white skin an almost irresistible temptation. However, Gwendolyn Ellingham's looks had him instantly re-thinking his taste in females. Her brilliant raven hair reminded him of the finest heavy silk, the intense color a striking contrast to her creamy white skin.

The perfection of her figure was enhanced by the delicate beauty of her face. Wide dark eyes, thick black lashes, a pretty mouth with lush lips. It had been a long time since he had felt this degree of physical hunger for a woman and he was intrigued by his response.

Even now, Jason wondered how he could find a woman in such a high pique so damn attractive. Instead of listening attentively to her words, he had found himself watching her luscious mouth and flashing eyes and feeling his own breath grow shallow.

Experience had taught him it was never wise to let an angry woman storm away, yet Jason was relieved the sisters were leaving. He stood automatically once they had risen and turned to ring for a servant to escort them out.

Not expecting Gwendolyn to cross in front of him, Jason rounded the corner of the sofa at a fast pace and nearly collided with her. She let out a faint, startled cry and took a stumbling step backward. Instinctively, he caught her, steadying her by grasping her shoulders with firm hands.

She regained her balance, but his hands lingered. When he realized how much he was enjoying the sensation of touching her, Jason let go. Being a man possessed of both his common sense and sanity, he took several steps away, distancing himself as if she carried some fatal, contagious disease.

"Forgive my clumsiness." Her voice sounded breathless.

"It was my fault." Jason puffed out his cheeks in exasperation, then exhaled slowly. "It seems as though I can do nothing right today."

"It has been an unsettling day for all of us, my lord."

"Indeed." His gaze drifted down to her breasts. "You were correct, Miss Ellingham. I have given this matter due consideration and I can assure you that the events of last evening shall remain a private matter, an incident known only to the three of us."

A tense silence followed. Gwendolyn's eyes held a mistrustful expression, but when she finally spoke, her voice was soft and filled with relief. "Thank you, my lord. I give you my word that you will not regret your decision."

He grinned a little lopsidedly and for the first time in his life, wished his experience with the female body was matched with an equal amount of experience with the female mind. What was she thinking?

Were her thoughts as devilish and improper and dangerous as his own? Or had she unknowingly, without trying, set off sparks in him, igniting his sensuality?

He stepped closer and color flooded her face. Jason smiled slightly. Good. He had not been imagining the attraction. That interested him far more than it should.

"We bid you good day, my lord." Gwendolyn's voice turned to a high-pitched squeak.

He bowed politely and reached for her hand. Due to the heat of the day, she wore no gloves. Her fingers were elegantly tapered, the nails short and smoothly filed, the skin velvety. He lifted her hand to his lips, then glanced at her, silently challenging her to protest.

An odd gasping, choking noise came from her throat. He worried that he had pushed her too far, too fast, had perhaps even frightened her and then realized that she was hardly in distress.

She was laughing! And not a nervous, maidenly giggle either, but rather a full blown burst of amusement.

"Miss Ellingham?" he questioned, with a quirk of his eyebrow.

"Lord Fairhurst," she remarked, pulling her hand back. "You are amazingly charming. And unfailingly predictable."

She sank into a graceful curtsy, then turned and left the room. Her sister made a hasty bob and followed Gwendolyn out.

Jason stared at the door for a full minute before reacting. Frankly, he was speechless. He could not recall *ever* having a woman rebuke him in such a fashion. Females of all ages clamored for his attention, were honored if he cast a look their way. Masquerading as his twin, a peer with an aristocratic title, should have made him even more appealing.

Of course his brother was married. That would certainly lessen his appeal with an unmarried woman, though Gwendolyn Ellingham did not precisely fit into the untouched, unmarried, must-act-with-honor category. She was, by her own admission, an outcast from polite society. The rules no longer applied in her situation.

Even stranger, Gwendolyn's lack of encouragement served mostly to whet his appetite further. Visions darted through his brain as he imagined bedding her. Jason wondered if he could convince her to engage in a brief affair during his visit. His body tightened. A man could get lost in those eyes, those luscious lips and curvaceous body and never care about finding his way back.

Jason sighed. Clearly Gwendolyn's tack was to ignore

this attraction. And unless he remained in close proximity to her, he would have no opportunity to change her mind.

Reluctantly, Jason admitted that was probably for the best. His brother would turn purple with mortification if Jason sullied the family honor and disgraced his lawful wife by carrying on an affair. If he was to continue masquerading as his twin, he was going to be forced to temper his actions and his lust.

The lovely Gwendolyn would have to remain off limits. For now.

"You laughed at him! Oh, Gwen, how could you?" Dorothea's voice carried on the wind, but the sisters were alone as they walked through the open field on their way home and did not need to censor their conversation.

"I simply could not help myself." Gwendolyn paused, her brows wrinkling together. "The meeting had gone so poorly for us from the beginning at that stage I knew I had nothing to lose. Lord Fairhurst's final display of possessiveness towards me was ridiculous under the circumstance. He is very much like so many men, I'm afraid. When in doubt, play the seducer."

Dorothea's eyes went round with shock. "Seduce? I thought he was merely flirting with you. Partially as a retaliation against me, a form of punishment for my disgraceful actions last night."

"That might have been a contributing factor," Gwendolyn conceded. "There is no other explanation I can fathom. 'Tis very obvious that the viscount is a clever man. There is hidden meaning in his behavior, a deliberate reason for all of his actions."

And there was something else, but Gwendolyn did not voice this observation out loud. The discovery that she could not in any way manage or reason with him had undermined her usual confidence. That had been the main reason she laughed. For it was either laugh or risk being charmed.

"Well, I for one found his behavior shocking," Dorothea huffed.

"Did you?" Gwendolyn flicked an eyebrow upward. "I find that an unusual reaction from a woman who less than twenty-four hours ago slipped into his bed."

Dorothea's eyes sparkled quite suddenly. "My behavior was entirely different. 'Twas born of desperation and affected no one but myself."

Gwendolyn knew she should argue the point, but decided to let it drop. "I suppose one would expect such a recently married man to act with more restraint and decorum," she conceded.

"Perhaps it was an arranged marriage," Dorothea suggested. "Perhaps Lord Fairhurst does not like his wife, nor she him."

Gwendolyn's frown deepened. *How could any woman not consider herself fortunate to have a man with the viscount's looks and virility as her husband? My goodness, if she was married to him . . .*

Gwendolyn swallowed, unable to finish the thought. "You might be right, Dorothea. It is possible that the viscount and his wife are not enamored of each other. It is a common practice among the aristocracy. At a party several years ago, I overheard a baroness say that she was pleased indeed that her late husband had never loved her because she knew she could never return that love."

Dorothea shuddered. "What an extraordinarily sad way to live your life."

"Yes, it is very sad," Gwendolyn agreed. "And I do hope that you realize now that you might have found yourself tied to exactly that sort of depressing, loveless marital situation with the viscount, had the charade you pulled last night been successful."

The remark snared Dorothea's undivided attention. "Though you clearly believe otherwise, I am not so much of a peagoose that I did not understand all the implications of my actions before I climbed into the viscount's bed. Including the possibility that he would reject me." Dorothea's lovely blue eyes took on a keen focus. "Furthermore, under the right circumstances, I will gladly marry a man I do not love."

Gwendolyn turned her head and stared directly at her sister. "It saddens me to know you would settle for so little."

Dorothea shrugged. "'Tis a matter of survival, Gwendolyn. If I am fond of the gentleman, if he is suited to my tastes, is pleasing to me in looks and temperament, and if he possesses an adequate fortune, then I would try to win an offer from him."

"What about love?"

Dorothea chortled. "Love is important, but there is no guarantee it will last. I would never marry a man unless the *possibility* of us falling in love existed. However, I would also prepare myself to be graciously accepting if no deep, passionate love between us ever grew. In that eventuality, I would find myself set in a perfectly acceptable marriage to a man that I liked and admired and I would be happy with it."

Gwendolyn was unsure how to respond. She could find no fault in the logic of Dorothea's thinking. Her ideas about a successful match were in fact a far more realistic and practical approach than Dorothea took on most matters. Which was precisely what made it the wrong approach for her headstrong, impulsive, passionate younger sister.

"'Tis a most practical and well-thought-out plan," she said slowly.

"Yes." Dorothea nodded, obviously pleased with herself. "I understand that marriage is a matter of convenience and fortune. To want more from it would be sheer lunacy if you select the wrong partner."

Gwendolyn stopped walking and stepped in front of her sister. "Is that why you pursued the viscount with such single purpose? Because you thought he was the right partner for you?"

"He was convenient, titled, handsome and rich. And, I believed, available." Dorothea gulped. "Yet the moment I saw him, I also believed he had the right elements to be a good partner for me. Circumstances forced me to be far too hasty in my judgement. Upon further reflection and interaction with Lord Fairhurst I have come to realize that it would have been a mistake to become his wife. A dreadful mistake."

A broad smile broke over Gwendolyn's lips, though she had no idea why this made her feel so pleased. She hooked her arm through Dorothea's and they continued walking, soon arriving on the grounds on the edge of their uncle's property.

"I just hope Lord Fairhurst will easily disregard your mirthful exit." Dorothea skidded to a halt, gasped, then grabbed her sister's arm tightly. "Do you think there is any chance that he will go back on his word and reveal last night's incident?"

"He had better not." Gwendolyn fought to ignore the thread of doubt and unwelcome surge of panic. They would be powerless to stop the viscount if he changed his mind.

"'Tis over, Dorothea. The best thing we can do now is to push it from our minds," Gwendolyn said, as she tried to reassure her sister, and herself.

As she had intended, the bold statement calmed Dorothea. Yet uncertainty gnawed at Gwendolyn's insides and with each step she took, her worry continued to build.

"What did you discover about the Ellingham sisters, Pierce?" Jason asked his valet an hour later as he changed into his riding clothes. The restless, edgy feeling that invaded his body would not dissipate, especially since he kept replaying the exchanges of the afternoon in his head. He was hoping a punishing ride would clear his mind and settle his body.

Pierce pivoted on the heel of his finely polished shoes, and strode across the room, his hands carefully cradling Jason's freshly pressed riding jacket. "I had heard a rumor below stairs that the women paid a call on you earlier in the day, though there seemed to be a great debate as to whether or not you would allow the older sister to stay. I assumed you had and were then able to uncover all you needed to know during that meeting."

"The women started to tell me about the scandal involving the older girl, but the conversation veered off course." Jason let out a low sigh of frustrated puzzlement. "What could possibly have happened to make Miss Ellingham such a *persona non grata*? The servants must be aware of the details. You must have learned something."

Pierce cast his employer a haughty glare, the one he

reserved for ill-mannered lower house servants. "It is necessary for me to remain discreet when making inquiries into these matters. As a Town servant I am already regarded with a healthy dose of suspicion by the staff. I can hardly start questioning them all as if I were a Bow Street Runner hot on the trail of some criminal."

Not in the mood to gainsay the valet's attitude, Jason met his servant's haughty glare with an even harder stare. "Are you telling me that you have learned nothing?"

"You neglected to mention why you needed this information," Pierce said.

"Nor shall I." The incident in his bedchamber would remain a closely guarded secret, something Jason suspected he would take to his grave.

Pierce sighed dramatically. "Though I have never been one to take notice of gossip before, at your behest, I have endeavored to discover what I can. And I shall thus admit in the past twelve hours I have heard enough scandal to write one of those dreadful Minerva Press novels. Maybe even two."

"Concerning the sisters?" Jason asked eagerly.

"Most definitely. Cook is a woman eager to gossip. I need only mention the name of Ellingham and she overwhelmed me with far more information than I should ever care to know."

Jason took a step forward. "Well, out with it, Pierce. What is the great scandal?"

The valet glanced at Jason, the expression on his face making it clear he had grown exceedingly tired of this topic of conversation. He held up the bottle-green riding coat and Jason turned and shrugged into it, gritting his teeth with impatience as Pierce smoothed the line and brushed the imaginary specks of dirt from the shoulders.

Jason appreciated looking well, but Pierce took the state of his clothing far too seriously.

"The scandal?" Jason prompted.

Pierce cupped his hand to his brow as though he were trying to remember, a gesture done purely for effect. "According to Cook, the incident is over four years old, yet does not seem to have lost any interest among the locals."

Jason nodded, pleased to finally be getting some answers. "I know that she was traveling to London with her great-aunt when the incident occurred."

"Yes. That is how it all began. But they never arrived in Town. The poor aunt took ill and died unexpectedly in Berkshire."

"And somehow Gwendolyn was blamed for it?" Jason asked in a befuddled voice. "How could she possibly be responsible? Was foul play suspected?"

"Murder?" Pierce's eyes lit with speculative interest. "Now that would make this a fascinating tale. One actually worthy of a novel."

Jason's mouth fell open in disbelief. He was stunned. "They accused Miss Ellingham of killing her relative?"

The valet bowed his head in apparent disappointment. "Alas, no. There is nothing of that nature to report, though I insist that would make a far more juicy tale."

"Bloody hell, Pierce, stick to the facts," Jason snapped.

The valet drew in a long breath through his nose, but after a stern glare from Jason, resumed the story. "After the older woman died, of natural causes, her niece stayed in Berkshire."

Jason frowned. "After the funeral?"

The valet shook his head vigorously. "No, after the death, Miss Ellingham stayed in Berkshire. At the local inn. Alone. For seven days and six nights, she resided at the inn without the benefit of a proper chaperone, without another female companion, not even a maid."

"Why?"

"The aunt's servants were sent posthaste to inform Miss Ellingham's family of the death. Apparently at that point there was some confusion about making the arrangements for the body and it took the girl's Uncle Fletcher seven days to arrive in Berkshire. Hence, Miss Ellingham was alone."

Jason tapped his fingers impatiently on the window sill. "Surely someone in the community offered assistance to a lone female traveler in such dire circumstance? What about the local vicar?"

Pierce crossed his arms over his chest. "She refused all offers of help and according to Cook there were many. Not only did Miss Ellingham take up residence alone at the inn, she proceeded to conduct herself in a wildly inappropriate manner. Shopping for expensive clothes that were highly unsuitable for mourning, taking her meals in the inn's public parlor, drinking spirits, engaging in conversations with men. It was most scandalous."

Jason reached up, unlatched the window and pushed it open. The breeze was warm, yet soothing. "Were there any witnesses to report on this behavior?"

"Not precisely. Apparently Mrs. Hollingsworth has distant relations in Berkshire and they informed her of what occurred, though there seems to be some debate as to whether or not this relative was a reliable source."

"But these tales were believed?"

"Oh, yes. Miss Ellingham was condemned before she even returned home. In my opinion, what Miss Ellingham truly needed, and unfortunately lacked, was a witness who could defend her behavior, who could claim that she conducted herself with great propriety at all times under the most difficult of circumstances."

Jason let out a short grunt. "So she has, in essence, been condemned for what she might have done?"

"In a manner of speaking." Pierce retrieved Jason's riding boots from the armoire and held them toward the light, inspecting the shine. "There was no disputing that Miss Ellingham stayed alone, unchaperoned, in a public inn for several long days and nights and when questioned by the members of this community, she freely admitted it. Thus sealing her fate."

Jason moved away from the window, sat upon the chair Pierce indicated and obligingly raised his right foot. "Lord, I would hate to be a woman," Jason muttered as the valet grunted and groaned and struggled to get the tightly fitted boot properly positioned. "'Tis a monstrously restrictive existence."

All things being equal, it hardly seemed such a heinous crime. Miss Ellingham had not sought to be on her own initially. Circumstances had landed her in a trying and emotional situation and while ultimately she had not made the most prudent decisions, the punishment she received seemed excessively harsh.

Jason's thoughts shifted to his sister Meredith, who was an intelligent, free-thinking female. She too had experienced great difficulty being accepted into society. If not for her marriage to a marquess and the staunch support of her father-in-law, the Duke of Warwick, Meredith might have easily suffered a similar fate as Gwendolyn and been shunned.

His mind remained on Gwendolyn's plight as he rode over the grounds of the estate. His initial plan had been to make a careful study of the condition of the grounds, the fields, the orchards, the livestock and the surrounding tenant farms, but he had difficulty concentrating on the task.

Instead, Jason rode as he normally did when in the country—full-bore and a bit reckless. He jumped over streams and fences, pushing his very able mount harder and faster. When the animal was spent, he returned to the manor, his head feeling a bit clearer.

Once inside the house, Jason headed toward the study, intending to once again review the account books. As he turned toward the closed study door, his peripheral vision caught sight of Cyril Ardley. The estate steward was walking down the hallway, a distinguished looking middle-aged gentleman by his side. The pair were talking and laughing and at one point Ardley lifted his arm and thumped his companion on the back.

Feeling unexpectedly peeved at the sight, Jason turned away from the door and waited for the men to spy him.

"Good day, Lord Fairhurst."

"Ardley." Jason nodded, then inquisitively looked toward the other gentleman.

"You do remember Mr. Fletcher Ellingham?" the steward asked.

"Of course. Good day, Ellingham." Damn. His brother had at least a nodding acquaintance with Gwendolyn and Dorothea's uncle. This was an unsettling discovery.

"Fairhurst."

Jason held back his surprise at the familiarity of the address and concluded that Fletcher Ellingham must be a man of considerable social standing that put him on such close footing with a peer. Or else he shared more than just a passing acquaintance with his brother. It was frustrating having no way to clarify the matter.

Yet if Ellingham was a viscount's social equal, why

would he befriend an estate steward? He had obviously come to the estate with the specific purpose of seeing Ardley. Why?

"I hope your visit to the area will allow you time to come to my home one afternoon for tea," Ellingham said. "My wife would be delighted to make your acquaintance, as would my niece, Dorothea."

Jason gave him a straight look. "If I recall correctly, you have more than one. Niece of course, not wife."

Ardley laughed, but Fletcher Ellingham did not even crack a smile. Instead, Ellingham cleared his throat gruffly, then stared up at Jason with a look of mild unease. "Quite right, my lord. I have several nieces. Lovely girls, fine ladies. It was a great responsibility to assume their guardianship, but they were my younger brother's daughters and my wife and I agreed it was our Christian duty to take them in and care for them when their parents died suddenly."

Yet you failed mightily in your duty. The truth of the words echoed in Jason's mind. Jason felt a spurt of anger, knowing that Ellingham had not adequately protected Gwendolyn. Perhaps he was being a bit hard on the man, but ultimately the responsibility had to lie with someone.

There was a long silence that felt curiously like a stand-off. Ellingham broke the quiet by saying his farewells. Jason noticed the two men exchange a covert look and then Ardley also turned to depart. Jason decided to stop him.

"I require a word with you, Ardley. Now would be a convenient time."

Normally he would never conduct any sort of meeting, business or social, when he was so sweaty and muddy from his recent ride. But seizing the opportunity and gaining the element of surprise overrode Jason's personal need for fresh clothes and a bath.

"I am due at the stables in a few minutes to inspect a plow horse recently purchased from Mr. Kittering," Ardley replied. "The sale will not be final until I pronounce the animal fit."

"He can wait." Jason's eyes narrowed unpleasantly.

The steward's lids lowered. "As you wish."

Jason stepped back from the doorway, allowing Ardley into the study. He deliberately led him over to the desk and indicated that the steward should take a seat in one of the chairs in front. Jason then settled himself comfortably in the dark brown leather chair behind the desk, the position he knew that Ardley was accustomed to taking.

The gesture was deliberate. Jason wanted very much to emphasize his rightful place as the man who was in charge. Something Jason suspected the steward had conveniently forgotten, but the momentary flash of anger in the steward's eyes let Jason know he understood what was happening.

"I spent a few hours last night reviewing the account books before I went to bed and noted several mistakes in the addition of the columns," Jason said. He opened the leather-bound ledger and slid the book across the desk.

Ardley pulled it close and carefully examined the pages, frowning at the sections where Jason had circled the errors. At first, Jason had been surprised at how easy it had been to find these mistakes. It was almost laughable for someone to think it would be that simple to steal from the estate by adding the columns incorrectly and pocketing the difference.

But as Jason had worked through the numbers, he realized that not all the mistakes went against the estate. In some instances the total indicated more money had been collected, in others less. It would therefore be very difficult to prove it had been deliberate, even though in the final outcome the estate had been shorted funds.

Ardley's expression was carefully indifferent as he pushed the ledger back across the desk. "I apologize, my lord. I can tell by the dates of the entries that this is young Thomas Lee's work."

"Who is he?"

"My apprentice. Or rather my former apprentice." Ardley rubbed the fingers of his left hand across his forehead. "Early last year as a favor to one of the local families, I took on their son as an apprentice."

Jason settled back in his chair. "An inexperienced fellow should have been closely supervised."

"Quite right." Ardley nodded his head. "He was an eager pupil and a hard worker. In nearly all instances his work was exemplary. Unfortunately, I did not discover that he lacked the necessary mathematical skills to be proficient in the job until after he had been doing the accounts for most of the year."

"Rather neglectful of you," Jason said as he lifted his gaze to the steward's face and fixed him with a look guaranteed to freeze an opponent's blood.

But Ardley barely blinked. "I thought I had caught and fixed all of the errors. My apologies for missing those few."

"Is it a common practice to take on apprentices for a property of this size? "

"'Tis not uncommon. You may recall that I sought your permission to hire the lad and then later wrote to inform you of my decision to terminate the arrangement."

"I gave it only a passing notice," Jason said, certain

that if the agent had indeed sent his brother a letter, Jasper would have considered it carefully.

"As always, I appreciate your confidence in my abilities, my lord," Ardley replied. "Is there anything else you wish to discuss?"

"Not at the moment," Jason said.

He half-expected Ardley to storm off in a huff, but he soon realized the steward was far too clever to so easily give himself away. Still, as he turned to leave, Jason caught the hint of a frown line between Ardley's eyes. A rather small, but important sign that let him know he had managed to ruffle the steward's composure. Jason decided he would take it as a victory, the first on his way toward quickly unraveling the financial quagmire at the estate.

Unfortunately, it proved to be a premature impulse, for it was the one and only triumph Jason experienced for several long days.

Chapter Five

The days marched steadily forward and a week later, Jason was forced to admit that he had run himself to a standstill. He was no closer to uncovering the true state of affairs at the estate than when he arrived and his lack of substantial progress frustrated him.

Throughout the week he had made the rounds to all the tenant farms, speaking privately whenever he was able to the men who ran those farms. The results of their labors were clearly visible and Jason was convinced they put in an honest day's work. All the properties were kept in good repair. There was no overt waste of money and all the rents were paid to the current quarter.

To a man, everyone praised the efforts of Cyril Ardley, proclaiming him a fair boss and a reasonable individual. Jason reluctantly agreed. The prosperity of the estate was a testament to Ardley's deft management and hard work, yet there was no denying that money was disappearing from the estate.

Small inconsistencies abounded in nearly every aspect of estate affairs. Sums in the account book that did not add up, a double deduction when a single order was delivered, a rent payment recorded in one account book, yet not added into the total profits. Small amounts in all cases, easily explained as honest mistakes, yet when it was added together, it amounted to a substantial amount of money.

The simple solution would be to fire Ardley. As the estate steward, it was his responsibility to oversee all matters on the estate and clearly he had been neglectful in his duty. Jason suspected that Ardley was indeed the one profiting, but he hesitated to act without solid proof. His brother had hired Ardley years ago, when he had inherited the estate, and he held him in high regard.

Besides, it was wrong to ruin a man's reputation without evidence to back up the accusations, especially one of this magnitude. If proven true, Ardley would never work again.

Sitting alone in the study late in the morning, Jason held a writing quill in his hand, trying to compose a letter to his brother. It was a frustrating task, since Jason was not normally much of a letter writer, but the chore was made even more difficult because he had so very little of substance to report.

It was lowering to have to admit such miserly results, mainly because that was precisely what his family, and his brother, had expected of him. All he could confirm at this point was that money was indeed missing from the estate, a fact that had been established before he arrived.

The question of who was taking the money and what they were doing with it haunted Jason's days and nights. He knew very well that his brother would not be satisfied with only discovering the identity of the thief. Jasper would want to know why the funds had been taken and, more important, what had been done with the money.

The chief suspect remained the estate steward, Cyril Ardley. But Ardley had worked for the estate for ten years. Why was the money disappearing now? What had changed in Ardley's life or circumstances that could explain this occurrence? Jason was convinced that the key to solving this mystery was to learn more about Ardley's character, to observe him as often as possible.

"More invitations, my lord," the butler, Snowden, announced as he entered the study. "Where shall I leave them?"

"Place them on my desk with the others," Jason said wearily.

The servant did as he was bid, hesitated, then turned. "Since you did not bring a secretary with you, I would like to offer my services, if you need assistance."

"Thank you. It is most kind of you to offer to take on additional duties; however, I will manage to sort through the correspondence on my own."

"Very good." Snowden tipped his head toward him. "If I may be so bold my lord, you must not hesitate to ask me any questions concerning the locals. I would be honored to share my knowledge."

It was a tempting offer that Jason dare not accept. Though his suspicions remained squarely focused on Ardley, he could not yet rule out any of the upper house servants. It would be foolish indeed to place any sort of trust in the staff at this point in the investigation.

"I will remember to ask, if I find the need," Jason replied.

The butler bowed, then left. Jason swore under his breath. The servant's remarks darkened his humor, heightened his frustration. He would need help to accomplish his task and there were few he could ask. Since Ardley was an active participant in local affairs, Jason knew he needed to go out in the local society to learn more about him, to observe him closely in this element, but that strategy could easily backfire.

Though he had not been in residence for almost three years, it was obvious that Jasper knew many of the individuals in the social community. Through sheer luck, Jason had managed to bluff his way through meeting Mrs. Hollingsworth and Fletcher Ellingham, but it would be foolish indeed to enter into a social situation without assistance.

What he needed was someone who could help him navigate the local society. His mind suddenly filled with the image of Gwendolyn Ellingham. With a soft sigh, Jason discarded the notion, but the idea persisted to dog him.

In so many ways Gwendolyn was the ideal choice. She knew everyone. She was a clear-headed female with a sharp mind, and that could prove to be a great asset. And most important of all, she was beholden to him and desperate to keep her sister's behavior a secret. That would give him a decided advantage in negotiating some sort of arrangement with the older Miss Ellingham.

With a grim smile, Jason tried to imagine Gwendolyn's reaction to his request. She would be appalled, protesting that she did not frequent society functions because she was not invited. But who would dare to refuse her entrance if she arrived on Lord Fairhurst's arm?

In fact, the scandal of Gwendolyn's past would help distract people from noticing he was asking a great many questions. Ardley was clever; Jason knew he must avoid arousing any sort of suspicion.

And so, directly after luncheon, Jason put on his best tailcoat and finest linen shirt in preparation of paying a call on the Ellingham family. He rode the short distance on horseback, refusing to be driven in the carriage like a limp-wristed dandy. The ride, and fresh air, helped clear his head and settle his determination to be successful in his mission.

The Ellingham home was a modest-sized, rambling house constructed of local stone. It did not follow any particular or pronounced style of architecture that Jason could identify, but it was still a pretty structure, set in well-maintained grounds.

He steered his horse through the gates, pulling to a halt in front of the ivy-covered entry that led into a small garden courtyard. A rather overbearing, unattractive fountain was placed in the center. Its disproportionate size detracted from the beauty of the house, but the sound of the trickling water emitted a soothing noise that immediately caught the interest of his thirsty horse.

Jason dismounted and waited for a servant to appear to take care of the animal. After several long minutes of solitude, he decided he might have to be so gauche as to let his mount drink from the ornamental fountain if no one came soon.

Fortunately, a stable lad arrived just as Jason's horse was nudging his way toward the fountain. Touching the brim of his cap, the boy nervously asked if he could be of assistance.

"I've come to pay a call on the family. Walk my horse slowly to cool him down, then let him drink his fill," Jason commanded, tossing a coin in the lad's general direction.

The boy caught the coin as it arched high in the air, pocketing it with a smile. "I'll take good care of 'im, sir."

Trusting the boy to keep his word, Jason strolled up to the front door. His knock was answered by an older woman, who smiled with welcome and bid him to enter. The keys jangling at her waist proclaimed her the housekeeper and he was not overly surprised the household neglected to employ a butler. It seemed too formal an arrangement for such a casual home.

The housekeeper held out a small silver tray, causing him an awkward moment of hesitation. Jason had no calling cards with his brother's name and title. Yet another reminder of the consequences of his impulsive decision to impersonate his twin without fully considering all that would be involved in successfully carrying off the charade.

"Lord Fairhurst calling," he announced, sweeping his hat from his head. "Is the family at home?"

The question seemed to confuse the servant. She lifted the tray higher, placing it almost directly beneath his nose. "Your card, my lord?"

"I am afraid I am fresh out of them." He smiled charmingly. "Would you mind very much delivering my message verbally and inquiring if I am to be received?"

"Oh, they'll receive you, all right," the woman muttered. "I'll be back in a tick."

As predicted the woman returned in short order. He followed her up a winding staircase, down a corridor to a pair of closed polished doors. The decor he glimpsed in the rooms he passed was tasteful, if spartan, and the overall effect was attractive and comfortable. The Ellingham sisters might not live in the lap of extravagant luxury, but they were far from destitute.

The housekeeper gave a quick knock before throwing open the doors. At her nod, Jason preceded the servant into the room. His eyes quickly sought and found Gwendolyn. Quill in hand, she was bent over a writing table.

"Lord Fairhurst," the housekeeper announced in an awed tone.

Gwendolyn's head shot up and she squinted, as if not

believing she had heard the servant correctly. She snatched the parchment she was writing on, folded it, then stuffed it in a small drawer.

She gazed to her left and a look passed over her face that was far from pleasant. "Gracious, Aunt Mildred, you should have told us someone was waiting to pay a call."

The older woman to whom she had addressed her comment smiled vaguely and shrugged. Gwendolyn's jaw tightened in annoyance. She shifted her head and shot daggers of confusion at Jason, but she maintained her control. It was obvious she was both alarmed and wary at seeing him again.

He enjoyed seeing the penetrating glint in her eyes. Women with spirit were always far preferable than those who were spineless. He favored her with a guiltless smile. She leveled a piercing stare at him that penetrated to the bone, giving him a deliciously hot feeling of pleasure.

In that moment Jason thought he had never encountered a woman so lovely or appealing in his life. He had to fight against the temptation to draw himself closer to her, especially since they were not alone in the room.

His attention shifted to the other occupants. Dorothea's mouth was gaping open in slight horror. She studied him from beneath thick blond lashes, her gaze worried. He surmised that the third girl, sitting beside Dorothea, was the aforementioned youngest sister, Emma. She had a sketchbook in her hand and wore a solemn expression. He bowed in her direction and she perked up considerably, allowing a smile filled with curiosity to cross her face.

"This is a most fortuitous surprise, my lord." The final occupant, a stout gray-haired lady whom Gwendolyn had called Aunt Mildred, appeared beside him. "I am so pleased to finally make your acquaintance." She extended her hand and he took it, bowing gracefully.

"Mrs. Ellingham. Forgive my intrusion. Mr. Ellingham extended an invitation for me to visit when he was at Moorehead Manor last week and I decided to take him up on his most gracious offer. I do hope I am not intruding."

"Oh my, no." She tittered and rolled her eyes, as if the notion of him being any sort of a bother was totally absurd. "This is the perfect opportunity for you to meet my nieces. Girls."

It was clear that Gwendolyn was having a difficult time making herself obey the instructions, but eventually she moved in front of him, standing between her sisters, with slumping shoulders and a barely concealed frown. Mrs. Ellingham, her bosom swelling with self-importance, was too caught up in the excitement of the moment to notice. She made the elaborate introductions with a silly grin of triumph on her face that never once faltered.

Jason could not have been more amused. He was used to being fussed over by women, but as the younger, untitled twin, he was not usually treated with such deference. "I am delighted to meet you all at last," he said with a wicked smile. "Especially since I have heard so much about you."

Mrs. Ellingham blinked, looked directly at Gwendolyn, then pulled a face as if something truly pained her. Gwendolyn noticeably stiffened. Jason's amusement instantly disappeared. Curse his glib tongue! He had certainly not meant to make any implications with that remark.

Mrs. Ellingham compressed her lips. Jason was trying to decide if an apology would make the situation better or worse, when the older woman spoke. "Please, my lord, you must join us for tea."

He nearly sighed with relief. "I would be honored. Thank you." With a flip of his coat, he settled into the matching settee opposite Mrs. Ellingham and tried to ignore the frantic looks he was receiving from the two older girls.

Mrs. Ellingham rang for the tea cart. The girls sat down and he was surprised to find Gwendolyn beside him. Jason thought it was a good sign until she caught his eye and cast him another quelling glance.

Under Mrs. Ellingham's lead, they settled into the dullness of polite conversation. Jason could see it was an effort for Gwendolyn and Dorothea to be pleasant and civil, but they gave it a good try. The situation reminded him all too much of the London drawing rooms he so diligently avoided.

The tea cart arrived. Mrs. Ellingham bustled around it, instructing the servant as to how and where to place the items. With her aunt occupied, Jason seized the opportunity and leaned over to whisper in Gwendolyn's ear.

"You wish for me to do what?" Her voice rang out in astonishment, the pitch high, the volume loud.

The outburst earned them several curious stares from her sisters and aunt. He leaned forward, planted his arm on his knee and spoke softly, trying again to keep the conversation from being heard by the others.

Gwendolyn glanced over at her female relations. They were clustered around the tea tray, all making a concerted effort to appear engrossed in organizing the refreshments, but Gwendolyn felt certain they were straining to hear any and every word the viscount uttered.

Lord Fairhurst likewise stole a glimpse at the other women, then groaned beneath his breath. "Is there somewhere that we can speak privately?"

"Alone?" Gwendolyn stammered momentarily on the word.

"It would be best."

"Impossible! 'Tis rare enough that I was allowed to stay for tea. I am never present when the household receives callers."

"I must see you alone."

Gwendolyn straightened her back. "I can show you the rose garden. 'Tis not nearly as lovely as the one at Moorehead Manor, but it will afford us some privacy. We will bring Emma along for propriety's sake." At his dubious frown, she added, "Emma is the best choice of my three relations to act as chaperone. She can be remarkably quiet and inconspicuous when told."

"If you insist."

Fighting a powerful fear, Gwendolyn modulated her voice to a nonchalant tone. "Lord Fairhurst has expressed an interest in your roses, Aunt Mildred. I would like to show him the garden. Emma can join us."

Her aunt held up a plate of cream cakes, looking confused. "But the tea has just arrived."

"We will return before it grows cold." Gwendolyn gazed pointedly at her sister. "Emma?"

The young girl's eyes lit up. "I shall be delighted to accompany you," she replied eagerly.

Emma led the way. After a slight hesitation, Gwendolyn placed her fingertips lightly on the arm Lord Fairhurst extended toward her. Avoiding her aunt and Dorothea's curious stares, she left the room.

The narrowness of the hall caused her hips to brush against the viscount's upper thigh. He made no indication that he was aware of the contact, yet the heat of his body and the firmness of his muscles invaded Gwendolyn's senses. Her uneasiness increased.

Why had Lord Fairhurst come to call and why was it so vital that he speak with her alone? Though she longed to do otherwise, Gwendolyn knew it was prudent to acquiesce with his demands rather than openly quarrel.

They wandered out to the garden, following the main path. Emma chatted amiably, pointing out the finest specimens to the viscount, who answered in a polite, distant tone. When they reached the fountain of a fat cherub pouring water from an urn, Gwendolyn pulled away from the viscount, then reached forward and clamped a hand on her sister's wrist to gain her attention.

"I need a few moments alone with Lord Fairhurst. Would you please wait in the rose arbor for us."

"Gwen!" Emma rolled her eyes and looked up at the sky. "Why do I always get excluded from all the fun?"

Gwendolyn took her sister's hand in hers and squeezed it very hard. "Trust me, Emma, this is not one bit *fun*."

"That's what you always say," the younger girl grumbled, her lips forming into a pout. She shifted to stare at the viscount, her gaze one of calculated interest. "I will walk the perimeter of the small pond rather slowly, but only once."

"Thank you." Gwendolyn waited impatiently until Emma had reluctantly dragged herself away, then turned to the viscount. "State your request quickly, Lord Fairhurst. Emma's curiosity is infinitesimal compared to my aunt's. She will not allow us to stay out here long."

Lord Fairhurst arched one eyebrow. "You are exceedingly direct, Miss Ellingham."

"'Tis one of my finer qualities, my lord." She smiled with a sweet falseness. "Please, explain yourself. I was under the distinct impression we concluded our business last week in your drawing room. Why have you come here?"

"I wish to attend a few of the local society functions

during my stay at Moorehead Manor and I find they are far too tedious without a female companion."

"Then send for your wife."

"Lady Fairhurst does not enjoy the country."

"Pity." She cast him a highly skeptical look. "If you insist, I can speak with Dorothea, but I am uncertain if she will agree."

"'Tis not Dorothea that I want. 'Tis you."

Gwendolyn felt a spasm of warmth clutch the pit of her stomach. She was quiet for a long moment, her gaze growing distant and unfocused as she stared out at the blooming beauty of the garden. "Surely I misheard you, my lord."

"You did not." He took a step closer. "I want someone with a steady head and composed demeanor to be my companion. Therefore, it must be you."

His confidence that she would so easily comply irritated her. It emphasized all too well that he was a man accustomed to getting his way. Well, not this time. "There is one rather fatal flaw in your plan, my lord. I am not an accepted member of society, therefore I cannot be your society companion."

"My dear Miss Ellingham, that is all about to change."

The notion made her stomach clench. Gwendolyn struggled to exhale. It was not just his words, but the force with which they were uttered that stole her breath. Re-enter society. He was mad!

She gave a nervous little laugh. "Though your joke was in questionable taste, I will concede you the irony of the situation."

She turned, preparing to walk away. He seized her hand and pulled her close, locking her wrist securely within the strength of his hand. "I am deadly serious."

"You are seriously insane!" she retorted, twisting her

arm in a vain attempt to dislodge his hold, but his grip remained fixed in place. "Why do you need me?"

"A fair question." He gazed over her shoulder to ensure Emma remained out of earshot. "I would first ask for your word to keep what I tell you in the strictest of confidence. You must promise to tell no one, not even Dorothea."

Despite her anxiety, the viscount's mysterious attitude caught her attention. Ignoring her better judgement, Gwendolyn replied, "If that is what you wish, I will tell no one."

He nodded. "I do indeed prefer to have a female companion with me at a social event for various reasons, but it becomes a necessity in certain instances. You see, I have great difficulty remembering people's names, even after I have met them several times. I therefore find at times that it can be awkward and embarrassing to go about in public. Everyone knows me and yet I recall almost no one's name."

Gwendolyn shook her head and smiled thinly. "That might be awkward at a London affair, but here in Willoughby, it does not matter if you remember an individual's name. You are a viscount and they . . . well, they are not."

The corners of his mouth drew down in a frown. "'Tis appallingly bad manners not to address someone by their name, especially if you have been previously introduced."

Gwendolyn's smile widened. "That type of behavior is almost expected of you. Everyone knows that aristocrats are eccentric. It's a common excuse to dismiss their odd behavior."

Lord Fairhurst's eyes flashed a look of pure annoyance. "I am neither eccentric, nor odd, and I abhor bad manners."

The request still made no sense, especially considering her notorious reputation. Had Lord Fairhurst somehow forgotten about it? "You would exhibit the poorest taste imaginable if you brought me to any society affair," she replied lightly, hoping she had found a legitimate reason to dissuade him from pursuing this ridiculous idea. "I am not received in the home of anyone of consequence."

He sniffed. "The Barringtons *never* do anything in bad taste," he declared haughtily. "If you accompanied me to an event it would be perfectly acceptable."

Gwendolyn squinted at the viscount. "You have no problem recalling my name or my sister's. Perhaps you are getting better."

"Obviously, you are the exception. There must be something about the two of you that makes you extremely unforgettable." His lips twitched. "Unfortunately, that is not the case with nearly everyone else in Willoughby."

He was serious! Gwendolyn began rubbing her arms, hoping to stop the goose bumps of anxiety that were forming. "My wardrobe is hopelessly out of fashion. I shall be hard-pressed indeed to find something appropriate to wear to any of our local society affairs," she muttered.

The viscount's brow frowned in consideration. "It will take far too long to have clothing commissioned in London, but there must be a local dressmaker who could make you some fashionable gowns. Naturally, I shall cover all the expenses."

"You cannot possibly pay for my clothing! Everyone will believe I have become your mistress!" A fist of nerves knotted inside her stomach, but Gwendolyn forced them to unravel.

"My apologizes. That is a valid concern. I had not realized it might appear that way." His mouth tightened. "You shall order whatever clothes are necessary and I will reimburse you the costs. No one need ever know. Trust me, Miss Ellingham, I shall be the soul of discretion."

"I hardly find that reassuring." Gwendolyn snapped. "How will I explain a new wardrobe to my aunt and uncle?"

He released a huff of breath, obviously irked by her protests. "You have raised several legitimate points, but none that cannot be overcome with proper planning. I will call on you tomorrow morning and take you riding, so we may discuss this further."

"We'll need a chaperone," she said quickly, pleased to have another obstacle to throw in his path.

"Does Emma ride?"

"Not any longer. She was bucked from her horse several years ago but remembers the incident too vividly to feel comfortable riding."

"I'll bring one of my grooms."

Gwendolyn wanted to refuse. An inner warning told her nothing good could possibly come of any further acquaintance with the viscount. His idea of having her accompany him to any sort of social function was totally preposterous. Yet it was clear he was not a man who often heard the word "no."

Frustrated, Gwendolyn started walking slowly toward the house. She wanted to speak her mind fully, tell him that she refused to subject herself to any possible humiliation, yet she knew it was unwise to anger him so soon after the incident with Dorothea. He still might change his mind and create a scandal. It would be safer in the long run to cooperate. For now.

"Be here at eight o'clock tomorrow morning," she replied. It took all her composure to answer in a steady voice. "We should take our ride before it gets too warm and before too many others are out and about."

"As you wish." He bowed elegantly, the courtly picture of an indulgent male.

Gwendolyn's spine stiffened. She opened her mouth. Then closed it. Her wishes! What rubbish. They both knew that was hardly the case. For one mad moment Gwendolyn thought of arguing with him, forcing him to admit the truth of the matter. Whatever that could be. But she held her tongue. She had bought herself some time. Now all she had to do was make him see the utter foolishness of his ridiculous plan.

Chapter Six

The next morning, Gwendolyn hooked her knee over the side-saddle's pommel, secured her free leg in the stirrup the viscount's groom caught and held for her, and sat ramrod stiff as the viscount watched her every move. She could feel his heated gaze burning into her, but she refused to so much as glance in his direction. Except for a crisp greeting in answer to his own when he arrived at the stables promptly at eight, Gwendolyn had said nothing.

She steered her horse out of the courtyard. Lord Fairhurst's large black mount sidled close and walked at an easy stride beside Gwendolyn's mare. The groom followed behind at a discreet distance. By unspoken agreement they set the horses trotting the moment they left the drive.

A crisp breeze blew across Gwendolyn's cheeks and she turned her face up to a ray of sunshine. The morning was clear and fine, perfect for riding.

"'Tis a lovely day," she muttered.

"Beautiful," Lord Fairhurst agreed.

They turned a corner and Gwendolyn noted her

mare's ears perk up as they reached an open field. She knew the animal was longing to stretch her legs with a vigorous run. Reasoning she could avoid talking with the viscount if they were riding hard, Gwendolyn gave a light flick of her reins and the animal took off.

Not surprisingly, the viscount's mount chased after her, catching her with ease. They kept the horses at a brisk, safe pace, cantering through the open fields. The fresh air invigorated Gwendolyn's spirits and helped clear the dullness from her mind. She had gotten precious little sleep last night, tossing and turning and worrying over how to convince the viscount he was making a colossal blunder with his ridiculous plan of having her accompany him to society events.

They had gone for several miles when another set of riders appeared on the horizon. The viscount shouted to be heard above the pounding of the horses's hooves. "Do you know them?"

Gwendolyn looked up, drew in a breath and held it. Though the distance was considerable, she recognized the bright green color of the woman's riding habit. "I believe it is Mr. and Mrs. Merrick. Their property lies to the north of here. If we turn off ahead, we can avoid meeting them."

The viscount waved aside the comment. "No. 'Tis as good a time as any to test the waters."

"I do not think . . ." Gwendolyn began, but her protests were lost in the wind. Lord Fairhurst had spurred his horse forward and her traitorous mare eagerly followed.

The horses frisked and frolicked together until the viscount pulled his mount to a halt in front of the other pair of riders, who had likewise stopped. Though she would have dearly loved to ride past them, Gwendolyn too pulled up.

"Good morning, Mr. Merrick, Mrs. Merrick. Splendid day, is it not?" Lord Fairhurst tipped his hat and smiled broadly. "Miss Ellingham and I were taking the morning air. Won't you join us for a mile or two?"

"Not today," Mrs. Merrick replied grimly, acting every bit as horrid as Gwendolyn feared. Though she spoke to the viscount, she barely looked at him, glaring instead at Gwendolyn. "Perhaps we can arrange to meet for a ride another time, my lord. When you are alone."

Mrs. Merrick peered down her nose. Gwendolyn felt herself twitch with an involuntary tremble, her body raw with nerves.

"But today is the perfect opportunity," Lord Fairhurst insisted, a note of steel in his voice. "It would be foolish to waste it."

Mrs. Merrick made a bird-chirping noise of distress, then turned her harsh beetle-black eyes on her husband. Mr. Merrick's pallor heightened. He shook his head ever-so-slightly, but his wife continued to stare him down until the poor man looked at the viscount almost apologetically. "We are for home, my lord."

Lord Fairhurst's visage darkened. Gwendolyn feared there might be an explosion of temper, which would make matters far worse. He took a long breath as if trying to calm himself. "Your home is located to the north, is it not? How convenient that Miss Ellingham and I are going in the same direction. We shall join you."

"Our home lies in the opposite direction from where you were headed," Mrs. Merrick said indignantly.

A faint line of color touched Mr. Merrick's face. He turned away, facing his wife, mouthing something at her. Whatever he said somehow convinced her not to make a scene.

Not giving them further time to argue, Lord Fairhurst

spurred his horse forward. Everyone fell into step behind
him. The viscount allowed a few minutes of silence, then
began making small talk. Mr. Merrick obliged, awkwardly
doing his best to keep up his end of the conversation.
The women said nothing.

Finally, they came to the clearing that bordered the
edge of the Merricks' property. Suspicion sharpened
Mrs. Merrick's gaze as she turned to the viscount. "You
two are out here riding alone?"

Gwendolyn cringed inwardly, but refused to say anything, knowing it was pointless to defend herself.

"My groom is with us," Lord Fairhurst replied. He
turned and pointed to the mounted servant who kept
pace at a respectful distance. "Though I suspect the rules
of etiquette are somewhat more loosely observed here in
the country, I would never risk the reputation of a true
lady by anything less than the most proper behavior."

Gwendolyn saw the flash of anger in the older
woman's eyes. Clearly disputing the remarks, Mrs. Merrick opened her mouth to argue that Miss Ellingham was
most certainly not a lady, but the glare from the viscount
must have made her think twice.

"No one will ever dispute that you act the gentleman,
my lord," Mr. Merrick said, nervously tapping the tip of
his tongue to his upper lip. "Especially my wife, who
shares your deep commitment to all that is correct and
proper."

"I am truly delighted to hear that, sir," Lord Fairhurst
said. "It is important to maintain standards. I applaud
Mrs. Merrick's efforts."

At his compliment, the tenseness in Mrs. Merrick's face
broke and the wrinkled lines of anger at the corners of
her eyes began to fade. But Gwendolyn feared it would
only be a temporary lull. This was too perfect an oppor-

tunity for Mrs. Merrick to pass up. She would soon start regaling the viscount with stories of Gwendolyn's past.

Out of habit, Gwendolyn hung her head and wished she could close her eyes and disappear. What an amazingly powerful weapon that would be, to fade away from the unpleasantness and cruelty, to slip away from the pain effortlessly.

But there was no easy escape. All she could do was conceal the lines of vulnerability on her face and pretend everything was perfectly fine. They were fast gaining on the house. Gwendolyn bit her lower lip with worry, trying to decide what to do when the viscount was invited inside for refreshments and she was not.

But then at the last moment, the viscount positioned his horse in the opposite direction. Gwendolyn breathed a sigh of relief. Apparently he was not about to test the Merricks' hospitality by riding into their courtyard.

The couple bid him farewell while sending a crisp nod in Gwendolyn's general direction. She conceded to herself that if glares of disapproval held any heat, she would surely have melted into a puddle on the hard ground.

Lord Fairhurst's gaze studied the pair for several long minutes as they rode toward their stables and disappeared from view. "I think that went rather well, don't you?"

Gwendolyn could feel her face redden. "Went well? Compared to what? The defeat of Napoleon at the Battle of Waterloo?" She strove to make her tone match his, but it was difficult. "Now can you not see that your idea is completely ridiculous? Mrs. Merrick nearly swallowed her tongue when you forced her to acknowledge my presence. And we both know if you had not been here she would have ridden past me without so much as a glance in my direction."

"She would not dare snub you with me by your side," Lord Fairhurst smirked.

"I do not like Mrs. Merrick and it galls me to court her approval."

"You have your pride and I respect that, but you must also realize you will have eat a bit of humble pie if you wish to be accepted. It is my understanding that Mrs. Merrick holds a great deal of social power within this little closed society. If you win her over, then others will no doubt follow." A delighted smile burst upon his handsome face. "The first time is always the most difficult. I'm sure it will be easier the next time you face her."

Gwendolyn's fingers folded into a fist of frustration. He made it sound so simple and she was angry at herself for wanting to believe it. "You are delusional. I cannot imagine an exchange of conversation with that woman that would not be drowned out by the sound of Mrs. Merrick's teeth grinding."

"I am not delusional." He slowed his horse to match her pace, pulling closer. "I just like a challenge."

"At my expense." An odd rawness scraped at the back of Gwendolyn's throat, but she managed to force the hardness into her voice. "You have no idea what you are getting yourself into, my lord. I urge you to reconsider before things go too far array."

They had reached a small wooden bridge. The horses clattered over it, making further conversation impossible. Yet somehow Gwendolyn doubted this would be the end of the discussion.

When they reached the other side, Lord Fairhurst slowed his mount, then signaled Gwendolyn to do the same. She followed him as he veered into a clearing, halted and dismounted. Stopping her mare, Gwendolyn kicked free of the stirrups, swung her leg over the pommel and slid to the ground.

The viscount's groom appeared within moments to take her mare's reins. He led the animal to a tree where she noted Lord Fairhurst's horse was already secured.

"This will never succeed if you keep fighting me, Miss Ellingham," the viscount declared.

A light, warm breeze fluttered through the trees around them. Lord Fairhurst had removed his hat; the wind rustled the golden waves of his hair onto his brow. Gwendolyn resisted the most ridiculous urge to reach up and brush it back into place.

"I am not fighting you, my lord, I am merely trying to prevent myself, and you, a crushing embarrassment."

He gazed at her in a subtle, serious manner. "I have given this a considerable amount of thought and urge you to do the same. After hearing about the incident, I believe that you are not really ruined."

"Not ruined?" Gwendolyn let out an exasperated sigh. The sun had moved higher in the sky and was beating down on her straw bonnet, heating her head and face. "Then I have been shunned these four years for no particular reason?"

"I know all about Berkshire. Your aunt, the inn, the shopping. Everything." He leaned a shoulder against a tree trunk. "Your reputation is tarnished, yet salvageable."

"The shopping?" She knitted her brows together in confusion. Shopping? The memory returned in a flood and she threw back her head, filling her lungs with the warm, tangy air. "I had almost forgotten. My behavior was scrutinized and conjectured upon and the catalog of sins were so numerous 'tis hard to remember everything. I now recall there was a particular group of women who seemed most offended that I had the effrontery to visit the local shops after my aunt's death and insisted it was the most grave sin of all. I think that Mrs. Merrick was among them."

He crossed his arms, his coat stretching over his broad shoulders. "I agree that scandal can take on a life of its own, how the facts are exaggerated until they resemble very little of the truth."

His tone was calm and thoughtful and she got the distinct expression that he was speaking from experience.

"But there was truth in the stories," Gwendolyn replied. "I did stay at the inn, on my own, after my aunt unexpectedly died. So the scandal was born from truth. Not precisely as it was reported, of course, but then where would the fun be? What would everyone have to whisper and speculate about and be superiorly disapproving of me if only the truth were revealed? How could they, in good conscience, declare me a pariah unless I were a wretched person?"

Lord Fairhurst sighed and rubbed his neck. "I am not unsympathetic to your plight, Miss Ellingham. Unfortunately, when an individual reaches her lowest point that becomes the most opportune time for others to prove how beastly they can act."

"I did go shopping, that much was true." Setting her lips in a firm line, Gwendolyn kept her eyes forward. "I bought a bonnet."

He shot her a look of total surprise. "A bonnet?"

"Yes. I paid four guineas for it, a ridiculous sum considering how small and dainty a hat it was, but the moment I saw it, I knew Dorothea would adore it. I remember it had a peacock feather on the band and was designed to be worn at a rakish angle."

"The hat was for your sister?"

"She was very upset that she had not been allowed to

accompany me on the trip to London and I promised her a special treat." Gwendolyn turned her head, forcing her eyes toward him. "With my aunt gone, I knew I'd never get to London and I was loathed to return home empty handed. I also bought a fine set of sable paint brushes for Emma with the rest of my pocket money. She fancies herself an artist and I will vouch for her talent."

The viscount's green eyes lit up with speculation. "The shopping would be considered a lapse in judgement by those lacking the complete story, but I think staying on at the inn alone was the most damning. Was there no one in the village to offer you assistance in your time of need?"

Gwendolyn shrugged. "The vicar made a lukewarm attempt to bring me into his home. But his house was very small and he had a large family. His wife had recently given birth to her sixth child. I felt it was wrong to impose upon them and strain their already overextended household.

"I expected my uncle to arrive the next day. When he did not, I thought he would be there the next. And so forth. All too soon, seven days had passed and I had been alone all that time."

He fastened his intense eyes upon her. "We all make mistakes."

"Ah, but the results are not always so painful and punishing."

A flicker of emotion crossed over the viscount's face. "You must trust that I know what I am doing. I will not allow you to be hurt by anyone. I give you my word. But if you have any hope of overcoming this scandal, you must stand up to these people or else you will forever concede them the upper hand."

Halting beside her, he reached for her gloved hand, turned it palm up, then lifted it to his lips. Eyes locked on hers, he kissed the exposed flesh of her wrist. A strange tingling warmed her skin, the sensation bold and exotic. She felt herself softening, weakening.

Gracious—he was an expert at persuasion and seduction!

In a flash of panic, Gwendolyn broke away and stalked toward the horses. She walked as haughtily as she could manage, wanting her body language to portray her rejection of his argument, her mistrust of his motives.

"Please, Miss Ellingham, do not make this any more difficult for yourself. We both know that in this instance I will get what I want."

The words hung in the air as they remounted. She turned her mare toward home. There was an oddly tense silence between them as they rode and Gwendolyn was barely conscious of the terrain they passed. Her mind was replaying the events of the morning, focusing on the viscount's determination to bring her back into society.

And the realization that she was going to have to let him try.

She was worried. She did not trust Lord Fairhurst. She did not trust his motives or his methods and most worrisome of all, she could not determine if he was set on a course of seduction or retaliation. Either one would not bode well for her or her family.

A shiver shot through her. Though she was firmly seated upon her horse, Gwendolyn felt a touch off-balance. She shifted slightly. It was impossible to understand the feelings that enveloped her. Terror and trepidation coupled with restless excitement.

Yes, excitement. She was poised to allow the man who she thought so handsome and appealing, who was well beyond her reach socially, not to mention married to another, to launch her back into society.

It was sheer madness.

***

Jason lifted the oars from the water, turned them at an angle and dipped them into the lake, pulling hard. The sleek rowboat glided effortlessly through the calm water, cutting a smooth path. He felt a tug in the muscles of his arms and shoulders, but pulled again, pleased to have the opportunity to exercise.

He often turned to physical activity when he needed to clear his head, shift his focus. The only thing that would make the afternoon more enjoyable was a companion, sitting across from him in the boat, smiling and flirting.

A young, pretty, female companion.

A picture of Gwendolyn Ellingham entered his mind. The loveliness of her features, her remarkable dark eyes, the beautiful shimmer of her rich, dark hair. Yet it was not only her beauty. There was something about Gwendolyn Ellingham that appealed to him on a far deeper level.

Who knows what would happen if she were here with him now? Jason smiled with self-deprecation as he imagined her looking over the side of the boat, gauging the depth of the water. If he annoyed her, as he always seemed to do, she would most likely dive overboard and swim for shore.

He then imagined her dripping wet, her simple muslin gown clinging to every sensual curve. His body reacted instantly to the image, hardening, tightening, his breathing growing heavier. Her manner was never brazen or suggestive; she never flirted or teased him, which had the strange effect of making him want to touch her even more.

He had not been able to get her out of his mind since

their morning ride two days ago. Unknowingly his interest in her had somehow progressed to something far more than gaining her assistance with navigating the local society. He wanted to set to rights the wrong that had been done to her by the locals; he wanted to force them to accept that she was a lady who was as worthy as any of them.

He knew she doubted his ability to achieve this goal, which goaded him harder to succeed. He was waiting for the perfect invitation to orchestrate his plan and fortuitously it had arrived earlier in the day. An invitation to a ball given by none other than Mr. and Mrs. Hollingsworth. He could only imagine the shouts of protests when Miss Ellingham learned she was to accompany him to this very grand affair.

"My lord!"

Jason lifted his head and glanced toward the distant shore. His valet, Pierce, stood awkwardly at the edge of the water, waving something aloof.

"Go away," Jason shouted. "I am enjoying my solitude."

"I have brought the post from London," the valet replied.

Jason quickly realized the item in Pierce's hand was a letter. With a forlorn sigh, he rowed to shore. As he neared the shallow end of the lake, Jason hoisted the oars into the boat, paying no attention to the water dripping on his breeches.

"What was so important it could not wait?" Jason asked, then answered his own question when he recognized the bold strokes and distinct handwriting on the envelope Pierce held. It was from his twin brother.

"It was most fortunate that I arrived in the main foyer just as one of the stable lads brought in the post," the valet said. "I recognized Lord Fairhurst's seal immediately and decided it would be difficult to explain how you could be writing a letter to yourself from London while residing here."

The valet's comments were a none too subtle reminder that he had not informed Jasper of his plan to impersonate him while at the estate. It was even more galling to admit Pierce was right. It would have been a disaster if one of the servants had seen the letter, or even worse, if Ardley had inadvertently come across it.

Jason knew he would have to write to his brother at once and inform him of his actions, if for no other reason than to avoid any other mishaps. Still, Jason hesitated because he suspected his twin would not approve of the plan. Over the years, Jasper had become more and more stark in his manner and behavior, taking the duties he assumed toward the family and the family reputation to extremes.

Jasper had taken on the role of head of the household, even though their father, the Earl of Stafford, was very much alive. The earl made no objection to his son and heir assuming these responsibilities, since he wasn't all that interested in doing them himself.

Jason thought it was commendable that his twin was considered a man of integrity, that he was strong, capable, honest and forthright. A veritable saint. Yet he was also unyielding, priggish, stoic and impossibly restrictive. Everyone in the family—including their mother and sister—had agreed that overall Jasper had not changed for the better.

Thankfully, he was lucky to have recently acquired the love of an extraordinary woman to temper his somber, dull attitude. Gradually, Jasper was starting to return to a more balanced view of life, to realize it was possible to live his life happily without always getting his own way.

But most important for Jason, his brother was learning to accept others without always having to judge them and find them wanting when they did not meet his own lofty standards. The lessening of this impulse to pass judgment was the main reason Jason now stood a chance of repairing his strained relationship with his brother.

And more than ever, he wanted to prove his worth by fixing this problem at the estate.

"You were right to bring this to me immediately, Pierce. I shall write a reply now, but you will need to post it for me in Selby, which is ten miles from here." Jason stuffed the parchment into his coat pocket. "Once that is done, I will pen a letter to be delivered to the Ellingham household. For Miss Gwendolyn's eyes only."

Then with an invigorated sense of purpose, Jason strode toward the house, his mind intent on how he would phrase his various letters.

Gwendolyn paced her bedchamber, her pulse wildly clamoring. Lord Fairhurst should be arriving at any moment. Her aunt and uncle and Dorothea had left almost a half-hour ago. Though the viscount had disagreed, she had decided it would be best to keep her appearance at the ball a secret from her relatives. Except for her sisters. Both Dorothea and Emma knew of her plans and had embraced the idea with varying degrees of enthusiasm.

Their maid, Lucy, was also privy to the secret and she was overly excited at the notion of Gwendolyn sneaking off to the ball, with the handsome viscount as her escort. Though none voiced it, Gwendolyn repeatedly reminded herself he was the handsome *married* viscount.

Gwendolyn blew out her breath and resumed her

pacing, knowing this little adventure would end before it had even started if she could not calm her nerves. She stopped briefly in front of her mirror, checking her appearance, pleased that at least she was looking her best.

She had most adamantly drawn the line at allowing the viscount to pay for her clothing. Fortunately, Gwendolyn possessed an eye for style and a flair for design. Staying home from all the parties had given her more time to read *La Belle Assemble* over the years, making her something of a fashion expert. Dorothea, who was talented with a needle, had generously offered her help and Gwendolyn had appreciated her sister's support.

It had taken a good amount of creativity and some skillful stitching, but between the two of them, they had managed to transform an outdated satin ball gown into an exquisite, fashionable dress.

The blue satin fabric was embroidered with small gold flowers and tiny green leaves at the hem. The colors made Gwendolyn's skin look creamy, her eyes vibrant. The fit of the dress emphasized that she was every inch a shapely woman. It showcased her ample breasts and slender waist, and the plunging neckline highlighted the delicate turn of her shoulders.

Her hair was pinned up in a simple knot with a few strategically placed curls trailing down her neck. She wore a delicate gold chain that had belonged to her mother close to her throat and the matching earbobs dangled from her earlobes, glittering each time she moved. Gwendolyn marveled that her sister's inspired design gave her an almost fairylike delicacy even though she was a tall woman.

"The housekeeper just told me that he's here, Miss Gwendolyn." The maid's eyes were wide with excitement.

Gwendolyn's stomach clenched. *Why, oh why, had she ever agreed to this ridiculous scheme?*

"Wait." Emma rushed over. She lifted her arms and pinched Gwendolyn's pale cheeks, then fluffed her raven curls. "You look so beautiful, Gwen. I wish I were going too."

"Oh, Emma, I would dearly love to have your friendly face among the crowd tonight." Gwendolyn hugged her youngest sister tightly, then turned and hurried down the stairs.

She greeted Lord Fairhurst hastily, too nervous to say more than a brief hello, too agitated to react as he eyed her up and down, appreciation growing in his gaze.

They traveled to the ball in near silence. When the carriage pulled into the small courtyard of the Hollingsworth home and the footman opened the door, Gwendolyn's stomach clenched.

She knew she should feel pleased or triumphant or satisfied. She was about to re-enter society on the arm of most influential man in the area, assuring her success. All the slights, the snubs, the snide looks and comments would have to be stifled when she entered the party.

She kept telling herself she would be greeted with deference, acknowledged with envy, accepted back into the fold without any challenges because no one with half a brain would wish to anger or displease the viscount. To do so would be social suicide.

But there was no pleasure or triumph or satisfaction swirling inside her. In truth, Gwendolyn had never dreaded anything quite as badly in her life. It almost felt as if she were marching off to a funeral. Her own.

The waiting servant cleared his throat, startling her. Gwendolyn leaned forward out of the viscount's coach and glanced at the gloved hand the footman was holding toward her. "Are we the first ones to arrive?"

"Hardly. I believe you are among the last to arrive, Miss."

"Truly?" she asked, craning her neck to gaze about the courtyard. She noted two additional footmen standing attentively at the bottom of the steps, but no other coaches were in view.

Footmen! The Hollingsworths had spared no expense, or pretense, for this affair. It was a stark reminder of how important they felt it was and how furious they would be when she ruined it all by making an appearance.

Gwendolyn paused, sternly admonishing herself. She was being ridiculous. Even if things did not work out as Lord Fairhurst promised, even if she was not accepted, but snubbed as she so feared, it would not be the end of the world. People did not die of humiliation; it only felt that way.

Lord Fairhurst must have seen the unease in her eyes, for he leaned forward and whispered, "You have numerous outstanding qualities, Miss Ellingham, but the one I admire most is your courage. Surely, it will not desert you now."

Gwendolyn pressed her lips together, then put her hand on his arm. With his words of encouragement ringing in her ears, she marched up the steps and swept through the front door as if she were queen of the castle.

Chapter Seven

Gwendolyn's burst of courage lasted only until they reached the entrance foyer. A servant directed them to the second floor and her heart began to pound. Logic told her it was too late to turn tail and run and Gwendolyn climbed the stairs slowly, feeling absolutely ill with dread.

She lifted her gaze to the portraits that lined the walls, trying to distract her thoughts of panic. But even the sight of a couple dressed in the style of the previous century was distressing, since the stiff-faced woman garbed in a satin dress festooned with lace bore an uncanny resemblance to the current Mrs. Hollingsworth.

They reached the second floor, where a lavish array of candles lit the hallway. Positioned in front of a pair of open double doors, in a makeshift receiving line, were Mr. and Mrs. Hollingsworth and their daughter, Olivia.

Distant voices echoed through the open doors along with music, laughter and conversation. It appeared as though most of the guests had already arrived, but the host and hostess were waiting for their most distinguished guest to make an appearance. And wouldn't they be surprised when they saw who that guest had brought with him?

Gwendolyn could not contain a shiver of dread, knowing she was hopelessly out of place.

"Try to smile and appear aloof," Lord Fairhurst whispered as they drew close to the Hollingsworths. "You must make them feel honored that you have graced them with your presence tonight."

Gwendolyn let out a brittle laugh. Was he mad? That sort of superior attitude was bred within the bones of the aristocracy, not in someone like her. "I had not realized you were such a snob, my lord."

"Snobbery is among my finest qualities, an asset I have honed to perfection over the years." Beneath the twinkle of amusement, there was unmistakable confidence in his gaze. "I am also insufferably stuffy and formal and have been accused by more than one individual of being stiff to the point of near rigor mortis."

"Qualities that all most assuredly contribute to making you such a charming and sought-after companion."

He smiled. "'Tis good that you can jest at a time like this; however, it would be better if you could try to cease looking as though you wish to hurl yourself out the window."

"We are only two flights from the ground, my lord." Straightening her back, Gwendolyn stood up taller. "If I jumped at this height at most I would fracture a limb."

"True. Hardly worth the effort, is it?"

Gwendolyn knew it would be impossible to manage a smile, but with great effort she was able to force her features into a pleasantly stoic mask. And then they stood before their hosts.

Mr. Hollingsworth bowed in a decidedly fawning manner and blustered out a nervous greeting. Mrs. Hollingsworth dipped a wobbly curtsey to the viscount and turned graciously, but the instant her eyes fell upon Gwendolyn, her face contorted into an expression of ghastly shock.

Hellfire and damnation!

She knew it was not going to work. In that moment Gwendolyn wished that she had not been so foolish as to come here, wished that she had listened to her practical nature and refused the viscount's demands.

Clenching her teeth, Gwendolyn lowered her head. But she had underestimated the viscount's power and resolve. He refused to relinquish any outward signs of decorum and would not permit anyone else to either, especially his host and hostess.

"Miss Ellingham graciously agreed to be my companion this evening, though I'll admit I had a devil of a time convincing her to come. She had some strange notion that you would not bid her welcome. I assured her repeatedly that cannot possibly be true. Was I correct, Mrs. Hollingsworth?"

The older woman's lips puckered and the expression on her face pulled as though she were sucking on a lemon.

"With you as her escort, my lord, we could hardly refuse her entrance, even though she was not on the guest list, nor was she sent an invitation," Mrs. Hollingsworth replied, barely relaxing the haughty disdain from her face.

"I would expect nothing less than a gracious welcome." He pointedly reached down and moved Gwendolyn's hand into the crook of his arm. "My father, the earl, has always said those who doubt their own worth will cast aspersions on others. I am delighted to discover you are a woman of character." His voice lowered. "Though I suggest you try to display more of it whenever possible, madame."

Mrs. Hollingsworth actually blanched. Gwendolyn almost felt sorry for her, for it was clear she did not know whether to be insulted or flattered by Lord Fairhurst's comment. Her double chin wobbled with confusion and the pair of bright red ostrich feathers in her elaborately styled hair shook to and fro. Fortunately, her daughter came to the rescue.

"We are all pleased indeed that you were able to make it to our humble entertainment, Miss Ellingham," Olivia said. She smiled to demonstrate her sincerity, revealing a mouth filled with very white and very crooked teeth.

"Thank you," Gwendolyn murmured, glancing past her trio of hosts into the room beyond. It was filled with people. "'Tis lovely to be here."

Her obvious lie was not challenged by anyone. Lord Fairhurst executed a short bow, Gwendolyn sank to a graceful curtsy and they managed to escape their hosts without further incident.

Gwendolyn's breathing slowed as they walked through the doorway into the formal drawing room. Since the house did not have a ballroom, the drawing room had been cleared of furniture in preparation for dancing. Voices were raised in merriment and for an instant Gwendolyn thought she might be able to slip quietly into the mix without attracting too much attention.

That, of course, was totally impossible. Gwendolyn almost laughed out loud at her foolishness, for it was as if she had momentarily forgotten who her escort was, had forgotten he would be the center of everyone's attention.

Gradually the other guests began to take notice of the new arrivals. There were several clear gasps of astonishment and more than one cold glance. Gwendolyn could feel the loathing emanating from a few of the assembled company. She knew she must not panic, knew she must somehow keep her head held high. Still, her hand went to her throat as she tried to settle her nerves.

The extreme irony of the situation was that for four long years she had told herself that she did not care. She did not care that she was shunned, that she was an outcast. She did not care that she was thought to be a tarnished woman, an immoral female. Yet to her surprise, as she stood there facing the harsh stare of society, Gwendolyn realized that she was truly bothered by the treatment she had received.

"Do not let them sense any weakness or else you are doomed," Lord Fairhurst instructed as all emotions on his handsome face disappeared behind a bland smile.

The muscles of Gwendolyn's neck dragged her head and chin higher. The viscount was right, though she could not resist voicing an observation. "You sound as though you speak from experience, my lord."

"Far more than you would ever know," he muttered under his breath, his voice so low she was certain she must have misheard the remark.

They began to circle the outer edge of the room slowly, greeting the other guests.

"I can see your uncle casting daggers of surprise in our direction," the viscount said. "Obviously you ignored my advice and neglected to inform your relations that you would be attending the ball."

"Dorothea knew." Gwendolyn sighed. "It was pointless to mention the party to my aunt or uncle, since they could easily have forbade me to attend."

"Would you have obeyed them?"

"Contrary to popular opinion, I do not relish the role of being disobedient or notorious. It would have been difficult to defy them outright. Therefore I did not tell them of my plans."

She followed his gaze to where her relatives were clustered around the refreshment table. Aunt Mildred seemed mildly confused, but Uncle Fletcher carried a thunderous expression of disapproval on his face.

"We will avoid them until your uncle regains his composure," Lord Fairhurst decided.

"That might take all evening."

"Then we shall hope the party ends early," Lord Fairhurst drawled. He looked about the room, a slight frown on his face. "Your family is not the only ones exhibiting an extreme interest in us. Nearly all the women are peering at us over their fans and the men are hoping the milling throng will cover their open curiosity."

"Surely, you expected it," Gwendolyn replied, her voice sounding high and strangled, as if her throat were being squeezed.

Lord Fairhurst exhaled. "The key to our success lies in showing no hint of strain or stress. No matter what the situation, Miss Ellingham, you must learn to feign pleasure."

"A task you seemed to have very adeptly mastered, my lord."

"I have indeed. But there are certain instances when only real pleasure will suffice. I encourage you to learn the difference."

Warmth flooded her body at the brazen look he gave her and she struggled to ignore the heat rising up her neck to her cheeks. The very last thing she needed was to encourage an improper flirtation. "We should circulate among the guests," she suggested, needing a change of topic. "Together or separately?"

"Together to start. I will not abandon you like a lamb

to the slaughter," the viscount promised. "But as you obviously realize, we must eventually separate."

"I know," Gwendolyn said. "The gossip would be unbearable if we stayed glued to each other's side all evening."

Over the course of the next half-hour, Lord Fairhurst slowly made his way around the room, steering her from one group of guests to the next. Gwendolyn pretended to be unaware of the speculation in nearly everyone's eyes and though there were a few frosty comments now and again, no one overtly snubbed or ignored her.

As they approached another cluster he leaned close and asked, "Refresh my memory, please. Who is the gentleman in the ill-fitting dark blue coat standing next to Mr. Ardley?"

"Mr. Chelton. He owns the largest dairy farm in the county and fancies himself a country squire. It would delight him to no end if you addressed him as Squire Chelton."

The viscount did as she suggested and the conversation went smoothly. They had just started to move toward another group when a masculine voice interrupted them.

"Gwendolyn! We are astonished to see you here."

She knew it was her uncle without even looking. Fortunately he was not alone. Both her aunt and Dorothea were with him, blessed allies in Gwendolyn's opinion.

"The viscount was kind enough to offer his escort and I was pleased to accept his invitation," she said calmly, though her tone was more defensive than she had hoped to make it.

Uncle Fletcher pinched the bridge of his nose between his right thumb and forefinger. "I do wish you had consulted me first. It was just this sort of reckless, impulsive behavior that landed you in trouble four years ago."

Gwendolyn raised her chin, but before she could reply, the viscount spoke.

"The burden of that fiasco lies squarely with you, sir, and I expect you to offer Miss Gwendolyn the support she needs and deserves now that she is re-entering society."

Uncle Fletcher snorted, yet apparently he realized it was against everyone's best interest to make a scene, so he changed the subject. "The dancing will be starting soon. I shall partner you, if no one else asks."

It was a somewhat insulting remark, but Gwendolyn decided to be gracious. "Thank you, Uncle Fletcher. I doubt I will take to the floor, but I appreciate the offer."

Aunt Mildred laid a hand on her husband's arm, gazing at him with a long look of entreaty. "We only want you to be happy, Gwendolyn. Isn't that true, Fletcher?"

A tenseness cinched Uncle Fletcher's mouth, but he made no further remarks. The two departed, and Gwendolyn finally found a smile. She turned to her sister. Dorothea looked stunning. Her hourglass form was shown to perfection in a low-cut gown of white silk that made her hair seem an even lighter shade of gold. Gwendolyn was proud of her lovely sister. There was no question in her mind that Dorothea outshone most of the other simpering young women in attendance.

"I would like to join the gentlemen gathered at the sideboard for a round of brandy," the viscount said. "Will you be all right on your own?"

"I will stay with her," Dorothea volunteered.

He hesitated, his lips pursed in consideration. Gwendolyn could almost see the thoughts burning through his mind. Finally, he reached his decision. "I shall leave her in your capable hands, Miss Dorothea."

He turned, but Dorothea tapped him on the arm with her closed fan. "Do not stay away too long. I know bringing her here was all your idea, my lord. So I expect you to return to my sister soon."

"Pay no attention to Dorothea's fussing," Gwendolyn said. "I shall manage well enough on my own. In fact, if you wish to visit the card room, you need only follow the trail of men making their way across the hall."

"My goodness, Gwendolyn, everyone knows that Lord Fairhurst does not gamble," Dorothea admonished.

"Quite right," he chimed in. "Gave it up years ago."

His voice sounded oddly strained. Gwendolyn regarded him closely, noting how the momentary gleam of interest abruptly vanished from his eyes, causing her to wonder about his true feelings about gaming.

As Lord Fairhurst strolled away, Gwendolyn was able to fully appreciate how elegant he looked, especially among so many provincially dressed men. Dressed in black breeches that hugged his muscular thighs, a fitted black evening coat, and a starched white cravat tied to perfection, he was easily the most intriguing man in the room.

"It is rather unfair that he is so disturbingly handsome," Dorothea commented with a sigh. "But it is his title rather than his person that has been such an advantage for you tonight. I am so glad you came, Gwendolyn. I was worried that you would change your mind at the last minute and sit brooding in your bedchamber for the night."

"I did consider it," Gwendolyn admitted.

"Miss Ellingham, I believe this is our dance."

"Mr. Harper." Dorothea consulted the small card that dangled from her wrist on a white satin ribbon. "Yes, I see your name, written so neatly. You have excellent penmanship." She turned to Gwendolyn. "Are you acquainted with my sister, Mr. Harper?"

"Ahh, not formally. Good evening, Miss Ellingham."

Gwendolyn felt a flash of sympathy as the young man blushed and stammered, but to his credit he managed a polite bow and a civil greeting. Dorothea's lips quivered and a dimple appeared on her right cheek as Mr. Harper led her out for the opening dance.

The voices swirled around her, laughing, joking, gossiping. Gwendolyn found a comfortable chair, sipped a glass of champagne and sat back, feeling oddly relaxed. For the first time in four long years she was seated within the bosom of society.

Well, not precisely within the bosom. More like clinging to the outer edges, but no one had dared to cut her directly. On that point the viscount had been right. She glanced through the potted palm fronds across the crowded floor to the corner where the older women sat and gossiped, telling herself she was not their exclusive topic of conversation.

And then realized that even if she was, it did not matter overmuch.

The dance ended and the next one began. Gwendolyn could see her sister had a new partner and was glad. It was past time that Dorothea received some attention from the male population. But Dorothea dancing another set left Gwendolyn alone. She settled back and waited.

Suddenly, Lord Fairhurst swept by. He plucked the half-empty glass of champagne from her hands. It made a sharp click as he set it down on a mahogany sideboard near her chair. "How kind of you to save this dance for me."

Gwendolyn allowed herself to be pulled to her feet and led onto the dance floor, trying to suppress the feelings of panic when the viscount chose the center of the room. For the benefit of those looking discreetly, and the others who were openly staring at them, Gwendolyn faced him with a bright smile.

He took her hand in his, laid the other on her waist and in that moment she realized it was a waltz.

Oh dear.

"What's wrong?" he asked with concern.

The question jerked her out of her panic. "'Tis a waltz."

His brow furrowed as the strains of music began. "Do you know the steps?"

"I think so. My dancing master taught them to me many years ago, but I have never danced a waltz in public."

"It's easy. Just follow my lead."

And with that, he swept her into the dance. Gwendolyn closed her eyes for a moment, then opened them, as she fought to remember what she had been trained. Not surprisingly, the viscount was an excellent dancer. His movements were fluid, his hand on her back gently guiding her one way, then another.

Gwendolyn tightened her grip and felt his shoulder flex beneath her fingers. His hand, resting on the small of her back, moved lower and tightened. Her wits scattered as she tried to remember which way her feet must go.

He danced like an aristocrat, masterfully leading her every step, weaving her through the maze of dancing couples. Gwendolyn tried to relax in his arms, letting her feet follow his lead without too much thought. Heads turned as he whirled her around the room and she feared she would stumble and embarrass them both.

Though she did not voice her fear, he seemed to understand it. He pulled her closer and she soon realized that only mere inches separated them while the other couples were apart by almost a foot. Their bodies brushed, then touched, and she was surrounded by the feel of his chest close to her own.

She lifted her head and whispered, "I think you are holding me too close."

He met her gaze with a quizzical gleam in his eye. "I shall hold you however I wish, since I am leading the dance. Besides, I like it."

I like it too. Dragging in a breath, Gwendolyn tried to calm her emotions. Her senses quivered as she gradually surrendered to his dominance. She felt cocooned in his arms, his masculine strength and effortless grace hiding any of her flaws.

It was an amazing feeling. For the first time in her life, Gwendolyn understood what drove a woman to occasionally act rashly when in the company of a man.

As they were the last to arrive, Lord Fairhurst informed her they would be the first to leave. Gwendolyn was relieved. The strain of appearing as if everything were perfectly fine and normal was starting to wear on her nerves. She had somehow managed to get through the evening without making any major mistakes and she most definitely wished to quit while she could still claim a victory.

Mrs. Hollingsworth was not to be found, so after a brief farewell to Mr. Hollingsworth, they stepped out of the stuffy house into the cooler night air. A gust of wind skittered across the portico as they waited for the viscount's carriage to arrive. Gwendolyn felt the edges of her gown flutter in the breeze and she had to squash the most ridiculous desire to hold out her arms and twirl with delight in the wind.

It had worked! Not perfectly perhaps, but far beyond anything she could have accomplished on her own. The grin Gwendolyn had held inside burst forth. She had attended a society party and lived to tell the tale.

'Twas a glorious feeling!

Lord Fairhurst handed her into the carriage and followed, shutting the door firmly on the rest of the world.

"A triumph, Miss Ellingham. You should be pleased."

"I am."

The coach lurched forward and they started for home. Gwendolyn flushed faintly and sat back in the shadows, the glow of her success surrounding her. Within minutes, however, she noticed that her heartbeat had started racing, and her chest began to tighten with an unfamiliar emotion. Confused, she glanced over at the viscount.

He was staring intently at her. The shock of it sent a jolt through her entire system and Gwendolyn had to hold the edge of her seat to steady herself. She fought to ignore the way her senses seemed to have fixed on him, seemed to be pulling her toward a road that could only lead to disaster.

She snapped open her fan and fiddled with the edges, needing a moment to gather her thoughts. She was so absorbed in controlling her emotions that she barely felt the pressure on the padded seat as the viscount shifted his position.

Startled, Gwendolyn looked up at him and found herself so close to his handsome face that she was unable to utter a word. The tension between them that had begun while they were dancing grew with each passing turn of the carriage wheels. Gwendolyn's heart thumped inside her breast so forcefully she felt light-headed.

"There is only one way to properly seal such a victory

as we shared tonight." His expression was easy, yet seductive, as he met her gaze. "With a kiss."

Gwendolyn steeled herself against the effect his words had, fearing if just the mention of a kiss sent her heart racing, the actual kiss itself would leave her dizzy.

He lowered his head. With innate, and amazingly accurate timing, Gwendolyn turned her head just as Lord Fairhurst's lips reached her face and he kissed her cheek, instead of her lips. It was better this way, she sternly told herself, yet Gwendolyn felt embarrassed at the intense disappointment that swamped her.

She pulled away and glanced over at him, wondering at his reaction. In the bright moonlight, she saw his smile flash, but the gleam of predatory determination in his eyes did little to soothe her taut nerves.

"Did you sample the champagne?" she asked in a breathless rush. "I own I am hardly an expert, but I thought it a bit flat. What was your opinion of the quality?"

The viscount's gaze never wavered from her face. She had no earthly idea what he was thinking and wondered perhaps if that was for the best. Knowing what improper, seductive ideas were swirling through his head would surely send her into a witless panic.

After what seemed like an eternity, but was in truth only a few seconds, Lord Fairhurst replied, "The champagne was a decent vintage, but not properly chilled. A common problem encountered at this time of year."

"How interesting," Gwendolyn lied, in as casual a manner as she could evoke. "The Hollingsworths seemed to spare no expense on the affair, yet stinted on the amount of ice they purchased."

"A true pity." Lord Fairhurst's voice was amused.

With her pulse skittering as fast as a mouse racing from a cat, Gwendolyn racked her brain for another topic. "And the food? Did you eat any? I confess to being far too nervous to taste a morsel."

"I found the oysters especially delightful," the viscount replied. "I must find out where the Hollingsworths found such choice, fresh specimens this time of year."

She could tell by his expression that there was some sort of hidden meaning in his remark, but Gwendolyn was too rattled to try and sort it out. She persisted in pretending that all was normal and, with a strained effort, they gradually slipped into the natural rhythm of conversation.

Yet, Gwendolyn was very aware that Lord Fairhurst was regarding her with faintly amused interest. Still, he did his part to keep the conversation going, and for that she was grateful.

She nearly cried out with relief when the coach turned down the gravel drive. She was nearly home. Not surprisingly, there were no servants about when they pulled into the courtyard. The viscount's footman helped Gwendolyn from the carriage and she thanked him quietly.

She hurried toward the front of the house, following the light from the first story window that spilled onto the lawn. She could sense that Lord Fairhurst was close on her heels, but Gwendolyn chose not to acknowledge his presence.

When she reached the door, Gwendolyn whirled around so quickly that her body collided with the viscount's. His arms came around her, to prevent her from falling.

"Oh, do forgive my clumsiness, my lord. I fear—"

He never gave her the opportunity to finish the sentence. He slid his right hand around the back of her neck, angled her head upward and then his mouth came down boldly upon hers. Captivated, Gwendolyn felt utterly at his mercy, as he coaxed and teased, modulating the pressure and angle of his mouth, urging her to respond.

Catching her lower lip between his teeth, he nibbled brashly. Gwendolyn gasped, then shivered when the hot, wet tip of his tongue edged out, skimming across her lips. They throbbed at the contact and she opened her mouth. Misunderstanding, he seized the opportunity and slipped his tongue between her lips.

Something instantly changed. The undercurrent of attraction Gwendolyn had been fighting nearly burst into flame. Time held still as her breath mingled with his and she became lost in a haze of pleasure. The kiss deepened and lengthened. Fire licked between them and he pressed his body against hers, letting her feel the evidence of his growing desire for her.

Gwendolyn's body strained for air. Everything within her screamed to pull away, to act with decorum and decency, but Gwendolyn couldn't do it. She had fallen into the pleasure and desire with startling ease and could not seem to pull herself from it.

Gwendolyn had been kissed twice before, but never with such skill and passion. The viscount's kisses left her stunned and reeling and longing to fill the emptiness inside she had never before acknowledged existed. She was tingling, feeling as if her feet no longer touched the floor. Her body, as well as her mind, felt warm and languid, just as it had earlier tonight when she sipped the warm champagne too quickly.

He kissed her cheek, then nuzzled just below her earlobe. Without really thinking about it, she snuggled against him, savoring the moment.

Senses still reeling, Gwendolyn slowly opened her eyes. Lord Fairhurst was staring back at her, his pupils dark and wide. Her hand went to her throat as she tried to quell her rioting emotions.

"I will not apologize for kissing you," he whispered huskily. "For I wish to do so again. And again. I wish to get lost in the moment, fair Gwendolyn. I wish to get lost inside you."

She quivered at the notion, her belly clenching in a sharp ache. She was tempted. So tempted. More than he could ever know. But she could not afford to be foolish now that her life was finally turning around. She had been accepted tonight. Not willingly and not easily, but it had been a first step. She owed it to Dorothea and Emma, and yes, to herself, to try and bring herself away from the fringe of society.

"Oh, my lord," she said softly, her voice floating on the night air. "We must never kiss each other again."

The viscount's gaze roved over her features, his breath coming in shallow drafts. "That is far too depressing a way to end an evening."

Her heart wrenched, for in truth she agreed. But something in the back of her mind sounded a warning and she knew she must heed it. She was not the kind of woman who could partake in an empty dalliance and that was all he could ever offer her. She paused and looked straight into his eyes, to make certain he understood completely. "Never again."

Lord Fairhurst closed his eyes tightly for a moment, then reached down and took both her hands in his. "Sleep well, my dearest Gwendolyn. May your dreams be sweet and only of me."

He turned and walked away. Her feet remained planted to the ground, her eyes riveted to his back as he climbed into his vehicle. Then the carriage door closed and the coach pulled away. He was leaving.

A wave of regret welled up in her throat, threatening to choke her. Gwendolyn swallowed it back and gripped the brass knob of the front door so tightly her hand began to hurt. She struggled to fight off the most ridiculous impulse to go after him and ask him to take her on a moonlit walk in the garden.

Turning blindly, she yanked open the front door and stepped inside the house. Fortunately, there were no servants or family members about. Even though they had lingered in the carriage, she and the viscount had left early enough to beat her sister and aunt and uncle home from the ball.

Pushing the heavy door shut, Gwendolyn latched it, then leaned against it, listening to the sound of her loudly thumping heart. Thank goodness common sense had prevailed! She had pushed against the line of propriety, and yes, crossed over it, but returned before total disaster had struck.

The entire situation was highly improper, highly immoral. Lord Fairhurst was married. Despite how seemingly each of her senses was so intensely attuned to his, there was no possible future for them. It would be a brief affair or almost worse, a longer, illicit entanglement. Any relationship they formed would throw her into a quagmire from which she might never be able to extract herself.

The incident tonight must be considered a momentary bit of madness, a euphoric reaction to her success at the Hollingsworth ball. It must never, under any circumstances, happen again. She must never again allow her passion and emotions to sway her morals and principals, no matter how great the temptation, how intense the longing.

The viscount's kisses had left her breathless, almost

feverish. In that brief, single moment of passion Gwendolyn knew she had felt more alive than all the moments she had ever experienced added together. She was forever changed by it and the uneasy feeling that nothing would ever be the same lingered, the final disturbing thought echoing through her head before sleep claimed her.

Chapter Eight

Jason restlessly paced the floor of his bedchamber. He had removed his evening clothes and dismissed Pierce, knowing if the servant stayed any longer he would unfairly bear the brunt of Jason's foul mood.

Things had started out so well this evening. Gwendolyn's nerves and fear had been almost palpable, but she had conquered them and forged ahead. He was oddly proud of her success, pleased that he had been able to restore some level of dignity to her after four long years of being an outcast.

With her assistance, he had been able to move easily among the locals, with no one suspecting he was not who he claimed. Surprisingly, he had felt comfortable in the role of viscount, though there were times when having to do as his brother would have were a bit restrictive.

A few games in the card room would have been an excellent opportunity to engage the gentlemen in casual conversation, but that was not possible, since Jasper no longer gambled. And amazingly, the locals were aware of that fact; a none-too-subtle reminder to

Jason that he needed to be very cautious if he wished to pull off this charade.

Unfortunately, the strides he had made and the success of the evening were overshadowed by his appalling behavior once they had left the Hollingsworths. Once he found himself alone in the dark with Gwendolyn, cocooned inside the privacy of the carriage, he had acted on his impulses and desires in a way his brother *never* would have considered.

He had kissed her! What the bloody hell was wrong with him? Was he truly the sex-depraved libertine his twin accused him of being? Did he lack even the basics of moral fortitude? Did he possess no remnant of self-discipline?

Despite the scandal of her past, Gwendolyn was hardly the free and wanton type of woman who would come easily to a man's bed. She was the type of woman one married. Which was precisely the type of woman he always avoided. And given that he was impersonating his brother, a married man, there was no question that a relationship with Gwendolyn was an impossibility.

Jason's hand curled into a fist. Only a scoundrel of the worst kind made love to a woman who believed all he could offer her was a role as his mistress. It was an insult. She should have done far more than push him away. She should have slapped him silly!

With a sigh of disgust, Jason walked to the window and gazed out at the blackness of the night. He rubbed a hand along his jaw, feeling the roughness of the stubble that had already begun. Had his beard chaffed her delicate skin, leaving behind a telltale redness? It had been too dark to see.

Whenever he thought about those kisses, he felt very unsettled. He had kissed dozens of women in his lifetime, but taking Gwendolyn in his arms, pressing his lips to hers, teasing her sweetness with his tongue had been a truly moving experience.

There was fire inside her—fire and passion. All just waiting to be released. He could still taste her lavender-scented flesh, still hear her moans of pleasure. He cherished the way she melted in his arms, had clung to him as the heat flowed between them. It was far more than sensual pleasure, it was something that struck him on a more profound level.

With something akin to fear, Jason remembered the one and only time he had ever allowed such tender feelings to stew in his heart. His deep and unconditional love for Elizabeth had left him open and vulnerable to a pain that had nearly brought him to ruin when he discovered she did not return his feelings.

And now he felt himself again caught in the grip of something that he had long thought unnatural budding inside himself. Could it be possible, even though he had vowed it would never again happen to him?

Was he falling in love with Gwendolyn Ellingham?

Gwendolyn awoke the next morning feeling tired and out of sorts. Her sleep had been restless, her dreams unsettling and mildly erotic. Though she remembered no specific details, the sensation of warm masculine lips upon hers, the delightful shiver of pleasure as his tongue glided past her lips, and the heat blossoming throughout her entire body as his sensual touch had invaded her senses remained with her.

Her mood did not improve as she opened the curtains, allowing a strong shaft of morning light to stream into the bedchamber. Gwendolyn briefly considered returning to bed, but she knew she could not avoid her family forever. Her aunt and uncle would no doubt be filled with questions about last night and waiting for an explanation.

The rest of the family had returned from the party shortly after Gwendolyn had retired for bed. There had been a soft knock on her bedchamber door, but knowing she would be unable to discuss the evening without recalling the steamy kisses that had ended it, Gwendolyn had hidden beneath the covers, pretending to be asleep. Thankfully, Dorothea had left without trying to rouse her.

Gwendolyn scrunched her eyes tightly closed as she recalled her cowardly behavior. If she had difficulty facing Dorothea last night, how would she find the courage to deal with her aunt and uncle? She opened her eyes to small slits and considered her options. Unfortunately, there weren't many.

With a resigned sigh, she crossed the room and poured fresh water into the china bowl on the washstand. She washed her hands and face, her fingers lingering over her lips, remembering how they tingled with pleasure when the viscount kissed her.

"Do you need any help, Miss?"

Startled, Gwendolyn dropped the towel. "No, thank you, Lucy. I can manage on my own."

"Fine. I'll just put your laundry away." The servant bustled about the chamber, taking her time, obviously waiting for an opening to start a conversation. When her arms were empty, she turned, an eager smile touching her mouth. "Did you have a nice time at the party last night, Miss Gwendolyn?"

Gwendolyn calmly finished drying her hands. "Yes, I did, Lucy. I want to thank you again for all of your help."

The maid's smile broadened and she modestly lowered her eyes. "I was pleased to be a small part of your success."

"Your support meant a great deal to me," Gwendolyn said sincerely.

The maid blushed with pride, curtsied, then left. Gwendolyn slowly folded her damp towel, her head and heart rioting with emotions. She covered her face with both hands and shivered. Composure. She must focus on regaining her composure and dignity or else she would never be able to face her family.

Selecting a dainty gown of pale blue muslin, she pulled it over her head and tied it tightly. Concentrating on each individual task, Gwendolyn unbraided her hair, combed it through, then pinned it into a simple knot at the base of her neck.

As she finished preparing to join the rest of the family for breakfast, Gwendolyn hoped the furor over her appearance at the Hollingsworths' party had died down a bit. If she were very lucky, it might not even become the entire focus of the morning conversation.

Bolstered by the optimistic thought, she hurried downstairs, the last to arrive at the breakfast table. All eyes turned towards her as she entered the room and Gwendolyn felt a dull red flush creep over her face. Her optimism faded as she took her seat.

"Good morning, Gwendolyn," Aunt Mildred said cheerfully. "I hope you slept well."

"Yes, thank you." Gwendolyn avoided looking at her aunt and waved off the plate of coddled eggs, bacon, sliced beef and biscuits with marmalade the serving girl tried to place in front of her. "Just tea and a slice of plain toast for me this morning, Jane."

"Lost your appetite, have you?" Uncle Fletcher asked

as he poured a large portion of cream into his china cup. "Not surprising after your behavior last night."

She shot him a glare. He met her eyes steadily, then popped a whole hard boiled egg into his mouth. Gwendolyn glanced away and took a sip of tea to prevent the tightness from building in her throat.

"Gwendolyn's behavior last night was perfectly exemplary," Dorothea insisted hotly. "I for one think it was terribly brave of her to come to the ball in the first place. Her success is a triumph for us all."

"A triumph?" Uncle Fletcher's eyebrows rose and his throat moved visibly as he finished swallowing the remainder of his egg. "More like a shock. A most unpleasant shock." He held up a hand when Dorothea started to protest and turned his full attention on Gwendolyn. "Your aunt and I were flabbergasted to see you last night. Why did you not inform us of your plans?"

Gwendolyn lifted the small pot of tea that had been set beside her and poured more of the steaming brew into her cup. "I thought it unimportant and inconsequential."

"Balderdash!"

"Fletcher! Such language. And at the breakfast table, no less." Aunt Mildred fanned her face vigorously with her linen napkin. "I know you are distressed, and rightfully so, but there is no need for such vulgarity."

"I did not mean to upset your tender sensibilities, my dear. Forgive me."

Her uncle tried to appear contrite, but Gwendolyn was not fooled. He was angry, far more than Gwendolyn had ever anticipated. She glanced over at Dorothea. Her sister shrugged in confused agreement.

"I believe your uncle was rather puzzled by your choice of escort. Won't you explain to him exactly how you became acquainted with Lord Fairhurst?" Aunt Mildred prompted in a stage whisper as she leaned toward Gwendolyn.

"I met him when he came to call on us, Aunt Mildred," Gwendolyn said calmly. "In fact, the viscount told use came at Uncle Fletcher's invitation."

The reminder sent Aunt Mildred into a dither. "Yes, yes, of course. How foolish of me not to remember."

"And since it was you who invited him, *dear* uncle, there was no question in any of our minds that you thought him a suitable gentleman," Dorothea said in an overly sweet tone.

"He is a viscount! Of course he is suitable!" Uncle Fletcher yelled.

"Then there is no reason for you to be upset, Uncle," Emma chimed in. "Was it a lovely party, Gwen? You must tell me all about it."

Uncle Fletcher stiffened, his features turning stony. "Not now. I refuse to listen to a recount of that blasted affair. It will sour my stomach."

Aunt Mildred gasped, but this time there was no apology for the coarse language.

"It was a delightful party, enjoyed by everyone, except for Uncle Fletcher. I will happily relate all the details after breakfast, Emma." Gwendolyn felt her tongue swell with indignation. "Though I feel compelled to remark that Lord Fairhurst was a most charming and gallant companion and I greatly appreciated having someone to champion my cause after all these years."

"Yes, 'tis long overdue," Dorothea replied.

A muscle tightened in Uncle Fletcher's jaw as he leaned against the back of his chair. "You might believe Fairhurst is some sort of noble knight, but as your guardian it is my duty to question Lord Fairhurst's motives."

It was difficult to hold a glowering expression with a blush creeping up her cheeks, but somehow Gwendolyn managed. "He was my escort. Nothing more."

Aunt Mildred nodded her head enthusiastically. "Precisely! See, there was no harm in it, Fletcher. No harm at all."

Her aunt's deliberately solicitous tone grated on Gwendolyn's nerves. Why had it suddenly become necessary to placate Uncle Fletcher? He never before seemed overly interested in his niece's activities. Or was there something about Lord Fairhurst that he found particularly grating?

"I suppose there is no point in debating it after the fact," Uncle Fletcher eventually replied. "As long as it ends now."

Gwendolyn took a sip of her hot tea before answering. "If Lord Fairhurst invites me to attend another event, I shall accept his invitation."

"I think that most unwise, Gwendolyn."

Her uncle's tone was soft, but there was something in his voice that made all four women feel visibly uncomfortable.

"Is there something you wish to say to me, Uncle?" Gwendolyn challenged.

"I am sure your uncle only wishes to point out that you are under his protection, Gwendolyn. As are all of you girls," Aunt Mildred said, her voice laden with unease. "Isn't that right, dearest?"

Uncle Fletcher ignored his wife and kept his gaze firmly fixed on Gwendolyn. "Fairhurst is married. You are not. 'Tis highly inappropriate for you to be alone with him, even for a short carriage ride."

"At my age I am nearly a spinster. However, if you insist, I shall endeavor to have a chaperone along any time I am with the viscount," Gwendolyn replied. "And I will make certain to chose one who will exhibit unfailing attention to her duties."

"You were always headstrong, Gwendolyn, but I never thought you a fool." Uncle Fletcher grimaced. "Married lords such as Fairhurst do not have noble motives toward attractive young women."

A sudden chill seized her. He had voiced her worst fear with alarming accuracy. Blanching, she turned away from him.

"What a dreadful thing to say, Fletcher. My goodness, we hardly need to instill a sense of moral responsibility in the girls, especially Gwendolyn," Aunt Mildred said, her voice turning into a high-pitched squeak. "Nor should we question the motives of a proper lord."

It seemed a ridiculous statement, given the lax morality of the nobility and Gwendolyn's scandalous reputation of the past four years, but she appreciated her aunt's support. Uncle Fletcher seemed to finally realize that he was outnumbered and out-maneuvered. With a look of masculine distaste, he flicked open his newspaper and promptly disappeared behind it.

Aunt Mildred let out a sigh of relief and patted Gwendolyn's hand awkwardly. Gwendolyn answered with a slight smile. Shaking off the irritation of the conversation, she attempted to finish her breakfast. Yet each bite of toast seemed to lodge squarely in her throat.

Though Jason had half expected it, nevertheless, the next afternoon a sense of surprise stole over him when Snowden announced there were callers. Female callers.

"Where have you put them?" Jason asked.

The butler's eyebrow rose. "Nowhere yet, my lord."

The ladies are waiting in the foyer. I was uncertain if you were at home to visitors."

Jason blew out a breath. "That bad, heh, Snowden?"

It was difficult to tell what the butler thought, for not the slightest expression crossed the man's face. He smoothly extended a small silver tray, upon which rested three calling cards. Jason tilted his head and read the names.

Mrs. Hollingsworth, Mrs. Merrick, and Mrs. Tiltondown. The unholy trio of Willoughby society. Jason nearly groaned.

"Your orders, my lord?"

"I'd best see them. If not, they will only return tomorrow."

"Very good, my lord. Shall I show them to the drawing room?"

Jason thought of the bulbous yellow decor of the room and this time did let out a groan. "No. Put them in the front parlor."

"Shall I bring refreshments?"

Jason paused. "Don't bother. They won't be staying that long."

As he walked the short distance to the parlor, Jason's resolve hardened. He had a fairly good idea why the women were here and he was in no mood to deal with their criticism.

Jason entered the room, a stoic expression on his face. He bowed before his guests and they bobbed quick curtsies in response. At his invitation the women sat down, clustering together on three chairs. He sat opposite them, feeling far too much like an errant lad awaiting a scolding for his peace of mind.

Jason indulged the women with polite conversation for a few minutes as he sized them up. It quickly became clear that Mrs. Merrick was the leader of the group. She was dressed in a shade of green that did nothing to enhance her complexion and accented every flaw in her ample figure. His mind wandered fancifully as he idly realized she was shaped remarkable like a turnip.

"We felt it our duty to come here today and speak with you, my lord," Mrs. Merrick began, finally getting down to the real purpose of the visit. "After the events of last night's party, it is obvious that you are not aware of the situation regarding certain members of our community. We must therefore, in good conscience, caution you against forming any sort of connection with Gwendolyn Ellingham."

His temper flared, but Jason regarded them all with cool composure. "You must forgive me, ladies. I fear my hearing must somehow be affected by all this clean country air. For a moment I thought I heard you tell me how to conduct myself and, even more absurd, dictate with whom I may associate."

The women exchanged nervous glances.

"We would never presume to tell you what to do, my lord. However, by escorting Miss Ellingham to my party last night it became abundantly clear that you were unaware of her true nature," Mrs. Hollingsworth said.

"I have heard the rumors," he snapped. "And I have seen how you regard her: with suspicion and superiority and even contempt. It's disgraceful." He glanced from one to the other, to the third, waiting for their reaction.

Mrs. Hollingsworth puffed her chest out like an outraged bird. "'Tis Miss Ellingham who is disgraceful!"

Jason leaned forward, his voice low with purpose and command. "Are you aware of my reputation, Mrs. Hollingsworth?"

Mrs. Hollingsworth's mouth opened, then closed.

Wild-eyed, she turned toward Mrs. Tiltondown, who came to her rescue. "'Tis said that Viscount Fairhurst is a stickler for propriety, which is why we naturally assumed you did not know the truth about this girl."

Mrs. Merrick nodded her head vigorously. "We knew if you did know the truth, you would not be her champion. Not to mention that your wife would naturally never approve of the association."

"Ahh, so you are well-acquainted with Lady Fairhurst?" Jason raised his brow. "She has taken you into her confidence and expressed her disapproval of Miss Ellingham?"

Mrs. Merrick's face blazed red. "Why no, I have not had the honor of meeting Lady Fairhurst."

"Then you cannot possibly presume to know her mind." Jason's jaw clenched and a muscle ticked beneath his skin as he looked from one woman to the next. "I would therefore ask you to cease assuming that you do."

Clearly offended, Mrs. Merrick clasped her hand to her ample bosom. "I can certainly presume to know how a lady will react when her husband springs to the defense of a scandalous woman. It is disgraceful."

His features grew stoney. "Lady Fairhurst is a treasure among females, a woman with intelligence and wit who does not suffer fools. I know that upon acquaintance, she and Miss Ellingham will become fast friends."

They all three studied him for a moment, trying to decide if he was being honest.

"Lady Fairhurst's opinion will quickly change once she hears about Miss Ellingham's scandalous past." Mrs. Hollingsworth bristled.

Without being asked, she began to recount the events of the scandal, with a degree of detail that bespoke of great exaggeration and numerous re-tellings. After just a few minutes, Jason had heard his fill.

"Enough."

"But Lord Fairhurst, surely you must agree that—"

"Enough!"

"My lord—"

"Shh!" He brought a vertical finger to his lips. "I will not listen to another word."

Mrs. Hollingsworth's eyebrows rose so high they were almost lost under the rim of her bonnet. Mrs. Tilton-down looked near to bursting; holding her tongue was proving to be a Herculean task. She glanced frantically at Mrs. Merrick for guidance, but she shook her head slowly back and forth.

The silence was long and tense. Finally Mrs. Merrick spoke. "We did not intend to offend you, my lord."

"But you have." God, was this what his family had to go through on his behalf? Listening to an endless list of his transgressions and then being forced to defend him against snide remarks and sanctimonious innuendo?

And the worst part was that his actions were often indefensible. He was guilty of exhibiting churlish behavior and neglectful of observing even the most basic proprieties. He had done things that had shocked society, had behaved in a way that deserved comment. He had been, for many years, a scandalous fellow, while Gwendolyn's transgressions were minor and inconsequential, affecting no one but herself.

He speared Mrs. Merrick with a look of frosty disapproval. "It shocks and saddens me to witness such small-minded, petty behavior. I had hoped to spend more time in Willoughby, had even considered spending the winter holidays here, believing it to be not only a place of beauty but a place filled with noble individuals.

"I had even hoped to persuade a few of my unmarried male friends to visit and become acquainted with what I had thought to be a genteel society. They are always eager to meet new people, especially unspoiled young women. After all, the marriage mart does not only exit in London."

Jason noticed the look of horror on Mrs. Hollingsworth's face and surmised she understood his meaning. Good. All three women had unmarried daughters. Mrs. Tiltondown had two. The opportunity to have eligible aristocratic gentlemen so close within their grasp was irresistible.

Even if they wanted to go to the expense and bother of trying to launch their daughters for a season in Town, they most likely lacked the necessary connections to be invited to the best parties. They would be fools indeed to toss away this golden opportunity. He was gambling that their practical nature would override their stubborn pride and stiff-necked morality.

"We would not want you to think us backward in our thinking, my lord," Mrs. Merrick said. "But we must also uphold a standard of appropriate behavior to ensure our future."

Careful. Though he really wanted them to squirm, Jason decided it would be far wiser to make it easier for them to acquiesce.

"I am aware of things regarding this unfortunate incident that no one else knows, ladies. You must believe me when I tell you that the rumors are greatly exaggerated, the facts long lost in the re-telling of the story. Miss Ellingham is only guilty of using poor judgment, which given her age at the time of the incident can surely be understood. And forgiven." Jason cast them a grim smile. "I would consider it a personal favor if you could find it in your hearts and conscience to be the leaders of our community and embrace Miss Ellingham. For my sake."

All three gave him a startled glance. They all seemed shaken by his request, not expecting such a direct plea.

"We should like to agree," Mrs. Hollingsworth ventured, the first crack in the wall of intolerability. Her uncertain gaze drifted to Mrs. Merrick.

"Perhaps we have been hasty to judge, especially if all the facts were not revealed. Don't you agree, Mrs. Tiltondown?"

"That is a possibility." Mrs. Tiltondown's smile looked forced, but she did manage one. "Our opinion could be changed, if his lordship would be so kind as to enlighten us with what he knows."

All three turned to him expectantly.

Damn! Jason had hoped they would not call his bluff, but these old birds were tougher than he had anticipated. He searched his mind for an appropriate response, realizing any lies he concocted could make the situation far worse.

"I simply will not gossip, ladies." He lifted his nose in the air and assumed the superior expression that his brother had perfected over the years. The one that made Jason want to strangle him. "You need to look beyond rumor and innuendo and take my word on the matter. I firmly believe you are all courageous and enlightened enough to do so—pray, do not disappoint me."

He sniffed for good measure, wishing he wore a silly quizzing glass so he could peer through it at them and thus create a total look of intimation.

The women released a collective sigh. They stared silently at each other for several seconds before returning their gazes to him.

"If we do as you ask, will you then plan a house party with your friends and acquaintances from London?" Mrs. Merrick asked.

"Your unmarried male friends?" Mrs. Tiltondown added.

Jason cleared his throat. "I shall. The place will be knee-deep with eager young men of good character and breeding. And I promise to extend invitations to each of your families."

The concerned frowns slowly vanished. Though the women fought to conceal it, there was no hiding the triumphant grins that appeared on their lips.

"Then we are in accord, Lord Fairhurst," Mrs. Merrick said. "We shall do our best to ensure that Miss Ellingham is welcomed into every household when you are her escort."

He did not miss the limitations of their answer, but Jason realized that all things being equal, this was as good a bargain as he could strike at this stage.

"You are most gracious, ladies."

They all stood. Jason rang for Snowden, instructing him to show the ladies out. They paraded from the room like a gaggle of geese, with Mrs. Merrick firmly in the lead. It had been a rather delicate negotiation and Jason was pleased with himself. By tempering his emotions and considering how his brother would have reacted, he was able to successfully achieve his end.

And most surprisingly, Jason realized he was actually smiling when the women left the room.

Chapter Nine

The noise at the doorway of the library startled him. Cyril Ardley drew in a harsh breath to steel himself, but his panic disappeared when he saw who stood so near.

"You should not have come." He sighed and lowered his head. "Fairhurst is at home this afternoon. He already seems curious about our relationship. If he sees you have come again to visit me, he might start asking more pointed questions."

Fletcher Ellingham puffed out his breath. "I will not let that London dandy dictate my life." He strolled into the library, bold as brass, and stood in front of the steward. "We have been friends for years and I refuse to pretend otherwise. Let the viscount think what he likes."

As quickly as it came, the anger bled from Cyril's face. "We run a great risk, Fletcher. The viscount is no fool. He pores over the account books as if they are priceless antique tablets that hold the key to understanding the mysteries of civilization. He has already found several inconsistencies. If he continues to dig, I fear he will eventually uncover the truth. And then we shall both be ruined."

A heavy silence fell.

"'Tis merely a stroke of ill luck that has brought the viscount here at the worst possible time," Fletcher replied, helping himself to the bottle of port that sat open on Cyril's desk. "He will soon grow tired of our quiet country life and return to London, where he belongs."

Cyril dragged his fingers through his gray hair. Oh, how desperately he wanted to believe that would happen. "He seems in no hurry to leave, especially now that he has started showing an interest in the local society."

"He'll get bored soon enough. We are far from an interesting lot."

Cyril shook his head slowly. "I fear not, especially since he is showing a marked interest in your niece. A relationship that I would not encourage."

"I agree. If he were available, now, that would be an entirely different story." Fletcher gulped the remaining port in his glass and refilled it. "Too bad the man is married. With such deep pockets, he would make an excellent in-law. 'Tis just my luck he already has a wife."

"Is that not the only type of luck we have, my friend? Bad luck." The steward took a long swig of wine, barely tasting it. His brow lined with worry. He did not share Fletcher's confidence that the viscount would soon be gone. This trip was different somehow; the man himself seemed different. Cyril sighed. "You realize, of course, that I could lose everything."

Fletcher settled into a chair and leaned forward anxiously. "You have picked a most inconvenient and dangerous time to lose your nerve. You need to stiffen your spine and your resolve or else all surely will be lost."

Turning away, Cyril reached for the bottle and poured himself another generous serving. "There is actually very little I can do at this point. Except pray."

Fletcher's eyes narrowed slightly. "Fairhurst might have his suspicions, but he will not act without proof. And if he had that proof, you would not be standing here. You'd been in prison."

The notion horrified Cyril, far more than anyone could ever realize. To have risen so far and then fall so low was a terrifying notion. He had built this estate from near ruin. When he was hired as steward ten years ago the tenants were barely surviving. Their farms were in an abysmal state; their spirits even lower.

Cyril had several radical ideas for making improvements on the estate that the young Lord Fairhurst had listened to, and then, amazingly, had allowed him to try. The viscount had put his trust in him and, under Cyril's guidance, the tenants had been supplied with new equipment and encouraged to try new farming methods.

The gradual implementation of these new techniques and experimentation with different crops had saved the estate fields as well as the tenant farms. The results had been healthier produce and grains, higher yields, and increased incomes for everyone.

With the land producing a steady income, attention shifted to the manor house, which had also been in disrepair—overgrown flower gardens choked with weeds, the lake covered with a thick green carpet of scum, far too many of the nearly one hundred windows on the mansion broken and boarded up.

Lord Fairhurst had taken a more personal and active part in this project, but had still left Cyril to manage the majority of the work. The steward had enthusiastically supervised it all, from fixing the shaky banister on the main staircase to replacing the widows and repairing the leaky roof.

He had been charged with the task of turning the property into a thriving, profitable estate and restoring the house to its original beauty. As he looked around the library now, with its gleaming woodwork, silk draperies and priceless antique furniture, Cyril took enormous pride in knowing he had succeeded beyond his employer's expectations. And been handsomely rewarded for a job well-done.

Perhaps he should tell his lordship the truth? He was uncomfortable with the lies and evasions and worried about his chances of succeeding with this cover up. The viscount was a clever man; it was difficult to stay one step ahead of his thinking. A logical man must admit it would only be a matter of time before the truth was revealed.

Perhaps if he explained the situation fully, admitted his mistakes and promised to make restitution, the viscount would forgive his behavior?

Or he would have him thrown in jail.

"I know you have only paid back a small amount of the coin we *borrowed*, but how many items have you managed to buy back and return to the estate?" Fletcher asked.

Cyril squirmed uncomfortably. "Less than half of what we took."

Fletcher gasped. "We agreed the items would be put back first! I know I've given you money to buy more. How can it be that you have made so little progress?"

"The moneylenders are bleeding me dry!" Cyril exclaimed. "The interest compounds daily. Just when I feel I am getting close to being free, another payment is due. 'Twill be impossible to ever pay off the debt."

"Then you must give more to the moneylenders who hold our markers and less to the estate. Once we have settled up with them, we can buy back the reminder of the paintings, silver and other antiques we pawned."

"If only it were that easy," Cyril muttered beneath his breath. "I cannot get blood from a stone."

"Aye. Well, at least we no longer play at the tables. We have successfully beaten the gambling demon that had plagued us." Fletcher raised his glass to toast the sentiment.

Cyril lowered his gaze. Had they truly beaten it? He thought about the market day horse races they had each bet heavily upon two weeks ago, and lost, and wondered if they were merely fooling themselves. Just because they no longer played cards did not mean they no longer gambled.

Cyril could feel his teeth start to grind. "If I lose my position then all hope of making restitution is lost."

"I know."

The band of fear around Cyril's chest twisted tighter as he tried to squelch the burst of unfamiliar guilt. It had gotten out of hand so damn quickly. He had never meant to take so much money from the estate. It had started in small increments, just enough to cover his loses from a vigorous night of card play. He had fully intended to return the sum the moment his luck changed.

And he had. Within two weeks the money was back, along with a few extra shillings of interest to assuage his guilt for taking it in the first place. But the following month he had needed more funds and those were not so quickly returned. This time Cyril had pawned several antique vases, knowing that even if the servants noticed they were gone, they would never say anything.

He was forced to eventually replace them with cheap imitations, since he had never recovered the necessary blunt to buy them back, though he vowed to himself he would one day purchase the originals. Then, in a maudlin mood in the wee hours of the morning after drinking too much wine, Cyril had foolishly confessed his sins to his gambling companion, hoping Fletcher would be able to lend him some money.

Instead, Fletcher had asked for a "loan" of funds to cover some of his outstanding debts, forcing Cyril to steal twice the usual amount. Fletcher had promised to pay it back, yet over the course of the next year, the pair had taken far more than they had returned.

"We must keep our heads and pray that Fairhurst grows tired of the simplicity of country life and returns to the excitement of the city," Fletcher insisted. "Given enough time, we will be able to set everything to rights."

Cyril took another swallow of wine and clung to the precarious hope. "Though I have worked for him for years, I never knew him well. Yet somehow he seems a changed man. He not nearly as proper and stiff, nor as formal at times. It's a puzzling difference."

Fletcher shrugged. "Maybe marriage has changed him."

"Perhaps. But why does he live apart from his bride?"

"That might explain why he is so relaxed. Life is far easier without a female around to nag you every minute." Both men laughed. "Take heart, my friend. The viscount will leave, this muddle will be fixed and you and I will be freed from our financial burdens."

Cyril nodded glumly. "Yet never free from the guilt."

Fletcher snorted. "Do not speak to me of guilt. I have squandered the majority of my nieces' dowries in my quest to lift myself from this debt. Who would have ever believed that Gwendolyn's scandal would turn out to be such a blessing? No man of decent birth will have her to wife, which means there is one less dowry for me to replenish."

"Fairhurst seems to have taken a liking to her. That might spawn other men's interest."

Fletcher's face darkened with concern. "His lordship's

attention has not escaped my notice. With his help, Gwendolyn is trying to re-enter society, but given the strong feelings against her, I doubt even he will succeed in fully restoring her reputation."

"We might be able to use Fairhurst's interest in her to our advantage," Cyril ventured. Even in his semi-drunk state he knew he was crossing the line by implying an impropriety, but was feeling desperate enough to do it.

Fletcher shrugged. "Gwendolyn is too moral a girl to be of any use to us in that department."

Shocked by the response and angry with himself for even mentioning it, Cyril rose unsteadily to his feet and walked to the window. The sight of green fields reminded him of what he had worked so hard to achieve and could now possibly lose.

"You're fretting again," Fletcher observed. He put down his glass and joined his friend at the window. "You must not take it so to heart. You are hardly the first corrupt steward in England."

It was a truthful and wholly depressing statement. "I might not be the first, but if Lord Fairhurst uncovers my misdeeds before I have a chance to correct them, I could very well be the last."

Gwendolyn was quick to notice that the mood of the community exhibited a subtle change over the next few days. Though she never felt unconditionally welcomed at any of the events she attended, she nevertheless did not experience the same degree of censure from the local matrons. When she met them at these events, or even in the village, conversations between her and her neighbors was not as forced, not as strained.

At the viscount's behest, she continued in her role as

his social companion, though she arrived with her aunt and uncle and departed in the same manner. By unspoken agreement, she was never alone with Lord Fairhurst and Gwendolyn told herself she was not in any way disappointed.

She was, in truth, relieved. Relieved that the viscount was conducting himself in a wholly appropriate manner, was treating her in a polite, distant manner, as was proper and correct, given their circumstances.

It would be complete disaster to do otherwise. They were together for one reason only, so she could assist him in easily knowing the members of the local society. Once the task was finished, and it would be soon, she would rarely see him.

This evening's soiree had been hosted by the vicar and his wife and it had been a surprisingly pleasant affair, with good food, excellent wine and lively conversation. Gwendolyn was pleased to have been included and she once again acknowledged that her life had improved with Lord Fairhurst about. And while he might be a master at making her skin heat, her heart race, and her mind wander toward all sorts of improper thoughts, she steadfastly refused to cross the boundaries of propriety.

Gwendolyn looked out the carriage window at the night sky and sighed. She should be feeling a sense of satisfaction and pride that she was doing the right thing. Yet why did it leave her feeling so cold and empty inside?

"I imagine a picnic in the country can be different from those we have in London, Miss Ellingham. You must alert me to any specific customs so I commit no overt *faux pas*," Lord Fairhurst said with a charming smile.

"I would be honored, my lord."

Emma's voice held a breathless wisp of excitement and Gwendolyn did not have the heart to tell her younger sister that the viscount had not been addressing Emma with his question, but had instead directed the inquiry to her.

"Thank you, Miss Emma. I shall value your counsel greatly." The viscount bowed his head elegantly and Emma beamed a smile at him.

Gwendolyn smiled too, appreciating how the viscount did not correct the mistake, thus avoiding any embarrassment to her youngest sister. She settled back against the comfortable squabs of the open carriage and tried to relax and enjoy the remainder of the ride. They were off to a picnic at Bartwell's home, an event that Gwendolyn assumed would be over-the-top, since that was how Mr. Bartwell and his wife preferred doing things.

They were traveling in the viscount's carriage, a beautiful vehicle, no doubt the finest and most expensive made. To complete the picture, the viscount had brought along two grooms and three outriders, ensuring they would make an entrance worthy of the prince regent.

"I am sorry that Dorothea was unable to join us," Lord Fairhurst commented.

"I'm not," Emma said honestly. "She is going with Mr. Harper and his family, which makes it all the better for me. You only have two arms, my lord, and if Dorothea were along I would not get to hold on to one of them."

Gwendolyn opened her lips to scold her sister, but Lord Fairhurst's rumble of laughter drowned out her words.

"You are an original, Miss Emma," he said, the corners of his eyes crinkling with humor. "I vow, when you make your debut, you will have half of London's most eligible bucks dancing to your merry tune."

"Only half?" Gwendolyn questioned.

"Dorothea will have the other half," Emma announced. "In that instance, I shall not mind sharing."

"Most generous of you," Lord Fairhurst added.

Gwendolyn shook her head and glanced across the carriage at Lord Fairhurst. Though he spoke to Emma, he was looking at Gwendolyn. When she caught his eye, he smiled and winked. Gwendolyn shifted in her seat, confused anew about him.

The gesture was part of the mystery of his personality. He had not been wrong when he told her that he could be stiff and formal. He had displayed that trait more often than she liked over the past few days. Especially at the musical evening hosted by the Scarbrough family last night.

At the conclusion of the final piece, he had stared with his one eye through a monocle and pronounced the entertainment passably pleasant. His manner was mildly condescending, but it was the monocle, an affectation that Gwendolyn found exceedingly annoying, which was so objectionable. It seemed forced and unnatural and she longed to tell him that he looked ridiculous peering through it.

But she did not dare.

First, because she honestly did not want to annoy him and second because the formality served as a convenient way to distance herself from their previous inappropriate behavior.

They had been in each other's company several times since the incident and had never made any mention of the kiss they had shared. She knew it was for the best, knew that was truly the only way she could remain his "companion."

Yet she constantly wondered if he thought about it as often as she did.

They arrived at the picnic. Emma got her wish and held regally to Lord Fairhurst's left arm, while Gwendolyn held his right. As they greeted their hosts, Gwendolyn noted a vague irritation flashed in Mrs. Bartwell's eyes, but it vanished quickly and she was gracious and welcoming.

They said hello to several of the other guests and then, at Emma's suggestion, they hiked up a small slope, climbing three abreast, the viscount in the center. They debated where to rest once they reached the top until the viscount selected a spot with both sun and shade where they could easily observe the picnic.

Lord Fairhurst's groom, who shadowed them at a respectable distance, was sent to fetch a blanket. When he returned and set it out, they each took a comfortable spot.

Emma chatted amicably with the viscount and Gwendolyn was glad her exuberant sister was along to carry the conversation. As the two conversed, Gwendolyn was content to enjoy the lovely weather and surroundings, drinking in the wide views over the lush green fields to the glimmering water on the lake.

The sun shone brightly overhead and the air held a gentle breeze. The wind tugged a few wisps of hair from her tightly pinned chignon, but Gwendolyn did not fuss over her appearance. Instead, she turned her face upward to be warmed by the sun, moving her head slowly from side to side in the breeze.

"Best be careful or else you will ruin your complexion," the viscount warned.

Gwendolyn would have been pleased at the concern he was paying her, if he had not sounded so much like a fussy aunt. "A few freckles are hardly the end of the world," she intoned lightly, keeping her head steady. She waited for an additional scolding, but it did not happen.

"Are you ladies hungry?" the viscount asked. "I can signal for one of my grooms and have him fetch us a basket of food."

"What an inspired idea." Emma leaped to her feet. "I shall go along to ensure only the best morsels are selected. Do you have any particular requests, my lord?"

"Surprise me, my dear."

Emma blushed with delight and hurried away. Gwendolyn waited until she was out of earshot before speaking.

"She is quite taken with you."

Lord Fairhurst shrugged. "It has not escaped my notice."

Gwendolyn caught the waving wisps of her hair that had blown free and tucked them behind her ear. "I appreciate your kindness and patience toward her, but would ask that you tread softly. Emma is at a very impressionable age."

"She strikes me as a very sensible young woman," he commented.

Gwendolyn sighed. "She probably has the most common sense of all of us. But she is very young."

"And I, no doubt, seem very old to her and therefore a safe individual upon which to practice her flirting. I find her flattery charming."

"'Tis far more than flattery when it's true and spoken with sincerity."

"Bravo! Now that is an expert bit of flirting," he said in a deep, warm voice. "I commend you."

Gwendolyn waited until the blush on her face had receded before turning her head away from the sun and looking at him. He stared at her as if he knew what she thought.

"You misunderstood," she insisted.

"I think not." His gaze drilled into her. "I will not trifle with her feelings. Or yours."

"My lord—"

"I have a great favor to ask. When we are alone, would you please address me less formally?"

At his suggestion, a small thrill climbed up her spine. "I would consider it, but alas, I do not know your Christian name."

His eyes sparkled and she wondered why he would find that so amusing. "My family calls me Jason."

"Jason." She tested the name, letting it roll off her tongue slowly. "If I assume that liberty, you will no doubt wish to do the same?"

"How very absurd. Naturally, I too refer to myself as Jason."

There it was again! That mischievous streak to his personality, a sharp, clever wit that he appeared to be suppressing, yet at times seemed unable to help himself.

He bent his head and leaned close. She felt his breath waft over her left ear. Realizing how near he was, Gwendolyn caught her own breath and heard it distinctly, sharp and shallow. Lifting her head, she met his eyes directly. An intense, clear emerald green, they held more than a wicked hint of temptation along with a purpose she did not fully understand.

She felt an almost overwhelming urge to reach out and touch his cheek, but knew she had not the right. Planting her hands on his chest, she pushed. He immediately pulled away, but the intensity behind his eyes did not fade.

"Tell me more about our hosts," he finally said. "They seemed to have spared no expense for this event. Is that typical?"

Relieved at the change of subject, Gwendolyn's eyes spread over rolling green lawns of the property that were now dotted with scores of green and white striped tents. Ladies and gentlemen were clustered beneath these tents, feasting on a wide variety of culinary delights. Most were seated on chairs, but a few younger couples shared space on one of the many blankets also provided.

"Mr. Bartwell made his fortune in wool, and has been trying for the past ten years to remove the smell of trade," she explained. Gwendolyn noted that their hosts were seated on large armchairs, under a striped canopy that rippled in the breeze. From this vantage point they could admire the spectacle they had created, rather like a pair of Elizabethan royals. "Alas, I fear he has fallen far short of his goal."

A slow grin grew on the viscount's face. "He certainly knows how to throw a party. I challenge anyone to label this extravaganza a mere picnic."

At that moment Emma returned, with two servants in tow, each carrying a large wicker hamper. "I was unsure what you would like. So I brought a bit of everything."

"Clever girl."

While the ladies sat eating wafer-thin slices of bread and butter with cheese, the viscount indulged in a more hearty lunch—a sandwich of roast beef, half a roasted pheasant, a substantial wedge of cheese and a bowl of cut-up fresh fruit. They were finishing up the last of the raspberry tarts and lemon cakes when, without any sort of warning, the first fat raindrop hit.

"These summer storms can be drenching," Gwendolyn cried out as she scrambled to her feet. A gust of wind whipped at her skirts and she struggled to keep herself decently clad.

"I'll race you to the bottom," Emma shouted, and she took off running.

Gwendolyn accepted the challenge without thinking, slipping and sliding and shrieking her way down the hill, arriving a few moments after her sister. Breathless and laughing, the two took shelter beneath the portico. Gwendolyn turned to see what had become of the viscount.

He was marching down the hill at a clipping pace, shoulders straight, head forward, rain dripping off the brim of his hat onto the front of his blue superfine coat.

"Lord Fairhurst! Over here!" Emma waved enthusiastically.

The viscount turned his head and gazed back at them, unsmiling.

"My goodness, my lord, 'tis just a bit of rain. Surely you won't melt?" Gwendolyn said with a smile, as she noticed the drizzle beading on his cheek. "'Twould do you good to be less stiff-necked over these sorts of occurrences."

"You might find it amusing and freeing to be out in the rain, but I can assure you that my valet will nearly burst into sobs when he sees the state of my boots," Lord Fairhurst remarked as he joined them.

"Then let's go inside," Emma suggested.

They pushed forward into the house and promptly became separated from Emma.

"I have never seen so many people in one house." Gwendolyn made a slow pirouette in the foyer. "How will anyone be able to move?"

Lord Fairhurst smiled. "There must be some way to escape." He gestured to the right. "In here?"

"Goodness no." Gwendolyn shook her head. "The musicians have somehow squeezed themselves in the far corner of the room and are about to start playing. We'll become trapped once the crowd starts dancing."

"How about in here?" Lord Fairhurst asked, stopping in front of a half-closed door. "I think it's the library."

Gwendolyn's eyebrow raised. "Mr. Bartwell has a library? How extraordinary. I would hardly consider him a scholarly type."

She moved forward and pressed open the door, leading the way into the chamber. The dark rain clouds cast the room into gloomy, muted tones, but there was enough light to negotiate the room without falling over the furniture.

To Gwendolyn's surprise, the room was indeed a library, boasting floor to ceiling shelves and rows of leather-bound books neatly arranged upon them. There were also several bronze statues and pieces of antique pottery on display, as well as the stuffed head of a large deer. Gwendolyn moved to the far side of the room, hoping to avoid its eerie, glass-eyed stare.

"This is a most impressive collection," the viscount commented as he looked at the book titles. "Greek, Latin, French, Italian. It appears that Mr. Bartwell is a Renaissance man."

Gwendolyn frowned. "That certainly cannot be true. He barely reads English, let alone other languages."

"Ah, then he must be a collector who has made some shrewed investments." Lord Fairhurst removed several books from the shelf and closely examined the contents. "These first editions are rare and worth a great deal."

Gwendolyn ran her fingertips over the book spines, translating the titles in her head, and realized Lord Fairhurst was right. She continued down the line, meeting him in the center of the bookshelf.

As she brushed past him, Gwendolyn felt a tingle of awareness. Instinctively, she stepped back, keeping as much space between them as possible. It made little difference. She was still terribly aware of him. Aware of him as a man, attracted to him with a womanly, sexual feeling that fascinated and terrified her.

Something stirred inside her, something that had laid dormant for many years. Something, sadly, that must remain dormant where he was concerned. He was a married man, a most ill-suited individual about whom to weave romantic fantasies.

For an instant, she was consumed by a physical yearning so strong that it clenched painfully around her heart. Ever practical, she pushed it aside, knowing she was falling in love with an impossibility.

Jason prowled the edges of the library, feeling like a caged tiger, trapped within the constraints of his assumed identity. He knew it was dangerous to be alone with Gwendolyn, even with the door open, yet he found it difficult to do otherwise.

Being near her seemed to emphasize even more his current celibacy and womanless state. Impersonating his brother, a married man, enforced obvious restraints upon him. He was unable to fall into his usual method of an easy flirtation, yet even if he could, he wondered if he would have done so with Gwendolyn.

She had accused him of being too stiff-necked! It was laughable, yet oddly reassuring to know he was succeeding in playing his brother's part. As the rain started and Emma had conveniently left them alone, what he really wanted to do was pull Gwendolyn behind the thick grove of trees and stand there with the rain pouring over them, until they were soaked to the skin and their garments were drenched and plastered to their bodies.

Needing to distract himself from those erotic thoughts, Jason moved away from the tempting Gwendolyn to exam a vase set prominently on the fireplace mantel. The shape and design had an odd familiarity, proclaiming its near eastern origins. Though works of Egyptian origin were currently all the rage, Jason was well acquainted with Asian artifacts, since his father had indulged in their study for many years.

This piece was thickly potted with a creamy, lustrous glaze. The rim was bordered with a classic scrolling chrysanthemum with five large blooms done in blue, while the body had an aquatic scene depicting five shrimp among water-fern, duckweed, delicate wandering eel-grass and other small drifting water plants.

Jason frowned in puzzlement, realizing it was indeed the same patterned vase that his father had collected many years ago. The earl had purchased what he said was the only one in existence and was usually correct in these matters. Still, there could be a logical explanation. Fakes were common in the antiques market and easily passed on to those who were not experts in the field. In this case, however, there was one way to make certain.

Jason lifted the vase and turned it slowly in his hands, searching intently for a particular flaw. "Bloody hell," he muttered beneath his breath as he discovered the small section on the foot that was unglazed and sandy.

As he had painstakingly unpacked his find and showed it to his uninterested sons, his father had explained that this flaw in fact made the vase even more valuable, since an imperfect piece would normally have been destroyed. Instead, it had somehow survived. And somehow ended up in Mr. Bartwell's library, when it should have been on display in the Moorehead Manor drawing room.

"'Tis very pretty." Gwendolyn nodded toward the vase. "Is it from the Ming Dynasty?"

"No. The late Yuan period."

Her eyebrow rose. "I am impressed with your knowledge, my lord, though you could have told me it was from Wedgewood pottery and I would not know the difference."

"My father has a great interest in antiquities. He has made it his life's study, an odd interest for an earl, but something we, his family, have come to accept. Our homes are filled with many treasures he has acquired over the years. In fact, an almost identical vase to this one is in my drawing room at Moorehead Manor."

"How extraordinary. No doubt Mr. Bartwell saw it and when the opportunity presented itself, decided to purchase one for himself." She smiled. "I think you should be pleased at the notion. Is not imitation the sincerest form of flattery?"

Imitation or thievery? Jason was most unsure. But he had every intention of finding out.

Chapter Ten

It was not difficult for Jason to find his way to the city of York, but the distance of more than thirty miles meant he would have to stay overnight once he arrived. After speaking at length with Mr. Bartwell at yesterday's picnic, Jason had in his possession the name and address of the dealer that had sold the antique vase. The *stolen* antique vase, though he had purposely neglected to mention that fact to Mr. Bartwell.

Jason sincerely doubted the man's involvement in anything illegal, but held fast to his determination to keep anything and everything he had discovered a private matter. Jason surmised it would not be an easy task to obtain information on how and where the York antique dealer had come by the vase, but he intended to try.

Jason undertook this journey alone, forgoing the carriage, enjoying the solitude of traveling on horseback. As he passed through the safety of the ancient walls that surrounded the city, the weariness he had been feeling from the long ride vanished. He had spent most of his adult life in London and entering a city again, a place bustling with people and energy and commerce, rejuvenated his spirits.

He found lodging at a respectable inn, ate a hearty meal, slept well and set out with optimism the next morning. On the opposite side of the city, he could clearly see St. Peter's Cathedral towering above all the other buildings, the numerous stained glass windows shimmering in the brilliant sunlight. It was a truly inspirational sight and, while hardly a man to spend a great deal of time inside a church, Jason decided if time allowed he would spare an hour or two to tour the interior.

Following the directions given to him by the innkeeper, Jason made his way cautiously through the narrow cobbled alleyways where the better shops were located. It was a scene from a bygone era, with the half-timbered medieval shops that housed the establishments of the butchers, brewers, bakers, tailors, jewelers, book sellers, wine merchants and antiques dealers lining each side of the street.

A clerk appeared the moment he entered the shop and at Jason's request, obligingly fetched the owner, Mr. Pimm.

"How may I be of service today, sir?"

Jason smiled elegantly. Mr. Pimm was a bit of a surprise. He was a squat, square man with blunt features and sharp dark eyes, dressed conservatively in a finely tailored black coat and matching black trousers. His white cravat was spotless, starched and simply tied, with a small ruby pin twinkling in the center of the fold.

The refined clothing should have looked ridiculous on such a commonly shaped man, but somehow Mr. Pimm managed to look respectable, if not elegant.

"I recently attended a party at the Bartwells and

greatly admired several antiques that grace their home,"
Jason began. "One object in particular caught my eye.
A Chinese vase from the early Yuan period. A rare find,
indeed. Mr. Bartwell told me he purchased the vase from
you. I was hoping you might have others I could view."

"You have an eye for beauty," Mr. Pimm replied with
a smile. "As well as exquisite taste. As you said, pieces of
that era are most rare. I assume you are a collector?"

"It's a passing interest." Jason let his gaze deliberately
drift around the shop. "Tell me, Mr. Pimm, have you
been in this business a long time?"

"More than twenty years, at this very location." The
owner's barrel chest puffed with pride. "'Tis a fascinating way to make a living. These pieces are more than
mere objects, sir. They are memories of history, a
glimpse into the lives of our forebearers. Those who seek
to preserve them are acknowledging the talents of
mankind and the beauty of their marvelous creations."

"A noble ambition, Mr. Pimm, and an impressive philosophy. I would like very much to view more of your
wares."

Mr. Pimm smiled broadly. "This way, please."

He led Jason through a small archway to a larger room
which was crammed with furniture, rugs, statues, paintings and numerous fine porcelain pieces laid out on a
long table. The vases, some encrusted with jewels, glittered in the morning sunlight that poured through the
windows at the back of the shop.

Jason's keen eye carefully surveyed the porcelain,
taking particular time with each one, hoping to find
something that looked familiar. Yet as he feared, there
was nothing. Once again, he wished he had paid more attention to his father's attempts at educating him on the

nuances of various antiquities and the treasures in their family's personal collection.

"I see nothing here of interest," Jason remarked in a regretful tone. "I know you fellows often buy shipments of goods in lots. Perchance, are there any additional pieces available from the lot you sold Mr. Bartwell?"

Mr. Pimm lowered his eyes and said nothing for several seconds. "Objects as rare as a Yuan vase are sold as single items."

"From a particular source?"

Mr. Pimm's chin jerked up. "I receive my stock from numerous sources. Estate sales, other dealers, independent traders."

"And ask few questions, I'll wager, as to how those items came up for sale," Jason said dryly.

"Are you implying that I am selling stolen property, sir?"

"Are you?"

Mr. Pimm started to raise his beefy fist, seemed to think better of it, and instead clasped his hands securely behind his back. "I did not catch your name, sir."

"I did not give it." Jason reached into his pocket and removed a leather purse, fat with coins. "I would be most obliged, Mr. Pimm, if you would check your receipts for more information about the vase. I am especially interested in the name of the individual who sold it to you."

Mr. Pimm's brow was furrowed with caution. His eyes darted from the purse to Jason's face, then back to the purse. "I want no trouble, sir. The success of my business relies heavily on my discretion. If I lose my reputation, I could easily lose my best customers."

"And your best suppliers. I do understand, Mr. Pimm. I have no desire to probe too deeply into your business affairs. Provide me with the information on this one item and I give you my word I shall not trouble you again."

Mr. Pimm's face became taut. "It might take some time for me to locate what you need. Alas, my record keeping is not as detailed it should be."

Judging by Mr. Pimm's tidy appearance, Jason knew the man was lying. "I pride myself on never having paid more for something than I thought it was worth. I am offering you a substantial sum for accurate information. This is my best, and final, offer. You would be wise to take it."

Mr. Pimm seemed torn, sliding several quick, subtle glances at the purse Jason held so tantalizingly close. "If you will return tomorrow afternoon, sir, there is a good chance I will have what you requested."

"An hour."

"Sir—"

"I will return in one hour." Jason turned away, allowing himself a small, triumphant smile. He jammed his hat on head and strode from the shop, calling out loudly over his shoulder. "Pray, do not disappointment me, Mr. Pimm."

Jason returned in forty-five minutes, too jittery to enjoy browsing the many other shops or strolling the busy streets in the fine weather. His arrival sent the clerk scurrying for his boss, who emerged from the back room with a scowling expression.

"'Tis barely an hour," Mr. Pimm protested, letting out a huff of frustration.

"You could not keep such poor records and make a tidy profit," Jason replied. "I therefore decided your accounts were in much better condition than you indicated."

He held out his gloved hand expectantly and Mr. Pimm reluctantly dropped a folded piece of paper into

Jason's waiting palm. The bag of coins Jason offered in exchange quickly disappeared into Mr. Pimm's front pocket.

Too anxious to wait, Jason unfolded the note and read it. His brow furrowed in confusion. The name and address of this particular dealer was located in London.

"You are certain this is correct?"

"Yes." Mr. Pimm flushed. "Rare items often change hands through several dealers before they are bought for a personal or private collection."

Damn! It did make sense that a stolen item would most likely be moved before it was offered for sale. It was probably just bad luck for the thieves that the vase ended up back in York, so close to its original location. Disappointed, Jason turned to leave, but near the exit his eye was drawn to a painting hanging on the far wall.

He moved closer to examine it further, his heart pounding with recognition at each step. Not overly large, the scene depicted a lady in a dark gown trimmed with fur and a gable headdress, surrounded by her six young children, who were also elegantly garbed.

Jason leaned over and consulted the signature in the far left corner, confirming what he already knew. The portrait was done by the great artist Hans Holbein, court painter to Henry VIII.

As an adult, Jason could now appreciate how perfectly balanced the composition of the subjects were, but when he viewed it so often as a child, it had been the two young boys who impishly clutched their mother's skirts that had fascinated him so utterly. They were twins, just like Jason and his brother.

They were also his ancestors. And for as long as he could remember, this portrait had hung in his parents' home. They had given it to his brother several years ago on the occasion of his twenty-first birthday and he had proudly placed it in the portrait gallery at Moorehead Manor.

"That picture, did it come from the same London dealer as the vase?" Jason asked, his tone sharp.

"You said there would be no more questions, sir," Mr. Pimm declared, his voice rising in panic. "You gave your word."

"Is it the same dealer?" Jason repeated, his temper heating.

Mr. Pimm glanced around nervously, refusing to meet his gaze. To Jason's credit, he was able to exercise some restraint on his temper as he repeated the question a third time.

"It was the same London dealer," Mr. Pimm grudgingly admitted.

"Did you get it in the same lot as the vase?"

Mr. Pimm stared at him in stoney silence and Jason allowed the fury he was feeling to blaze from his eyes as he stared back.

"They were different lots," Mr. Pimm said after a long moment. "The painting arrived a few weeks ago."

Jason raised his arm and pointed it around the shop. "Show me everything else from this dealer."

Mr. Pimm hesitated, but the withering glare Jason sent his way loosened his attitude. Silently he led Jason through the shop. There were no additional items Jason recognized, but since he did not keep a running inventory of the contents of his brother's home, it was possible some of them were Jasper's possessions.

"Wrap up the painting," Jason demanded. "I'm taking it with me."

Mr. Pimm sputtered with indignation. "I have two customers who have shown great interest in it. I must give them an opportunity to place a bid before I allow you to purchase it."

With a grunt of annoyance, Jason lifted the portrait in his arms. "I will not give you another farthing, Mr. Pimm. I know that this item was stolen and I intend to return it to its rightful owner. You should consider yourself most fortunate that I am a man of my word and will therefore drop the matter, as I promised."

Cradling the painting in his arms, Jason strode from the shop, his boot-heels clicking loudly on the wooden floor. His earlier plans to enjoy a few of the sights of the city before starting his journey back instantly vanished. He returned to the inn and arranged for the painting to be delivered to the manor house by the next day.

As the sun began to slowly set two nights later, he found himself sitting in the long portrait gallery at Moorehead Manor, a near-empty glass of brandy in his hand, staring intently at one particular painting.

He conceded that whoever painted it had talent. If he had not so recently seen the original, he would never have suspected this was a fake. But as he scrutinized it closely, he saw this copy lacked the maturity and depth of the original. Even with the inclusion of all the intricate details, exactly replicated, the subtle ability to render the inner character of the subjects was missing.

Jason finished the rest of the brandy and sighed. First the vase, then the painting. Not only was someone stealing money from the estate, they were also stealing objects. And replacing them with high-quality fakes. This new revelation brought another troubling dimension to the problem, forcing Jason to rethink his strategy.

It would now be necessary for him to not only catch the culprit, but he must do so in a way that would force him to confess or else there would be no chance of recovering whatever other originals had been taken from the manor house.

The coach bounced along the ruts in the road and turned onto the narrow stretch that would bring them to the Ellingham's home. A bend in the road sent Gwendolyn swaying sideways and Jason felt the softness of her arm briefly press against his shoulder.

"Sorry," she murmured before setting some distance between them again. "I would move to the other side of the carriage next to Dorothea, but riding with my back to the horses always makes me queasy."

"I share the same malaise," he replied.

Her mouth quirked in the barest hint of a grin. "Gracious, who would ever believe that you and I share the same problem, my lord?"

"Who indeed?"

They lapsed again into silence, the moonlight peeking through the thick forest of ash and elm trees. Jason lifted his hand to his jaw and thoughtfully stroked his thumb and forefinger over the stubble that had started to form, despite a close shave in the late afternoon.

Tonight they had attended a musical evening at the Pruit house, where several of the local ladies showcased their vocal talents. Gwendolyn and Dorothea had also participated and Jason thought they made an excellent showing. Dorothea sang an Irish ballad in a clear, pleasant voice while Gwendolyn accompanied her on the harp.

Jason thought Gwendolyn looked like a raven-haired angel as she played, her graceful fingers plucking the correct notes with skill and emotion. The ivory lace over the deep blue gown she wore set off the delicate beauty of her pale, flawless skin. The sparkle of the gold and diamond chain that graced her neck and matching earrings swinging gently from her ears added a touch of elegance and sophistication that he found so irresistibly appealing.

Since their aunt and uncle had left early, Jason had been the girl's carriage escort. Gwendolyn and Dorothea had taken turns engaging him in quiet conversation as the journey to their home started, but their conversation had dwindled and then ended completely. As the miles passed, no one seemed especially eager to introduce a new topic.

Jason could not help but remember the first time he had been alone with the Ellingham sisters—that night in his bedchamber. Dorothea in his bed and Gwendolyn standing beside it, hell-bent on rescuing her sister from certain ruin. Even in that most bizarre moment, something had drawn him to Gwendolyn. Fate?

"The moon shines most brightly tonight," he muttered.

His voice seemed to startle Gwendolyn from her private thoughts. Her head turned swiftly in his direction, then she glanced very briefly out the carriage window. "The moon is nearly full and there is not a cloud in sight."

"Ah, a logical explanation instead of a romantic one. You disappoint me."

She turned her gaze toward him, as he had hoped, but her expression was nearly blank, as if her features were carved from stone. Normally, her eyes would reveal her mood, but they lacked the usual warmth and friendliness. The only thing he was certain about was that she did not look especially happy.

Jason cursed under his breath. This was all his fault. He never should have kissed Gwendolyn. Believing him to be a married man, the gesture had thrown her into confusion and had placed a distance between them he was growing to hate. Her restrained demeanor was like a cold wall of formality between them.

These days, whenever he was with her, he fought a constant battle to reveal his true identity. Yet something unexplainable held him back and Jason forced himself to listen to this inner note of self-preservation, since it had kept him from real harm for all these years.

He knew now those kisses had been a serious error in judgment. Gwendolyn obediently and pleasantly accompanied him on any outing he suggested, but she never ventured anywhere without a chaperone by her side.

And while a part of him applauded her practical nature and diligent quest to maintain her newly discovered reputation, he was frustrated, for he never had a chance to be alone with her. He wanted to talk with her, laugh and tease her, learn more about who she was and what made her happy. But most of all he wanted to do whatever was necessary to stop her from stiffening every time he drew close to her.

Even when he tried so hard to be a gentleman, she tempted the hell out of him. He had never been drawn to the demure, virginal young misses who lined up at every society event searching for a husband. Gwendolyn was a strange mix of innocence and maturity and her straightforward manner of speaking her mind was an odd aphrodisiac.

It made him think of seducing her with slow kisses and soft touches, wooing her with gentle words and truthful flattery. But this was an impossibility as long as he portrayed his married brother. Hell, even if he were still single, the real Viscount Fairhurst would hold tight to the strictest proprieties.

Jason could not help but think again at what a dull and

boring life his brother must have lead before he married. Jason knew that Jasper would have never been bold with a single female, would not even hold her hand, her *gloved* hand, much less steal a kiss or two.

He turned his head and sighed, Gwendolyn's scent teasing at his nostrils. Jason thought again of the evening they had just spent together and conceded he had learned nothing new about the residents of the community or Cyril Ardley. The biggest relief was that he had thankfully not seen any other objects belonging to his brother.

He still firmly believed the estate steward was at the heart of the problem, but at this stage the trail had gone cold. There seemed to be nothing more to learn from the locals, thus making it no longer necessary to attend these society events. The next logical step was to visit the London antique dealer, to learn more about how the dealer came across the vase and the painting.

But if he left Moorehead Manor, he would be leaving Gwendolyn. And that he was not yet prepared to do.

Gwendolyn twitched at her skirts to neaten the folds and Jason shifted his position, closing the distance between their bodies. They were riding in the estate coach this evening, an older model not nearly as elegant or new as the one Jason had brought from London. The interior lamps were not as large, but the dimly lit compartment cast an almost romantic hue over its passengers.

Not that Gwendolyn needed any trick of the light to showcase her looks. He was drawn to her unique combination of boldness and beauty, yet Gwendolyn behaved as if she were unaware of her good looks. The honest lack of artifice intrigued him. Many would call her younger sister's wide-eyed innocence and delicate blond coloring preferable, but Jason disagreed.

In his mind, Gwendolyn was the more breathtaking female, with her sable hair and vivid brown eyes, her flawless skin and full mouth, those luscious lips begging to be kissed. It seemed that whenever he was near, he felt a flash of heat that made him burn to get her in his bed.

Disturbed by these persistent thoughts, Jason cleared his throat. Though he had honestly tried, he had not been able to divest himself of the vividness of his sexual fantasies and the need to make them a reality was becoming almost unbearable.

Yet he admitted that this desire went beyond a sexual satisfaction. Somewhere deep inside lurked the intense desire to know Gwendolyn as well as he knew himself.

"Do I have a smudge of dirt on my face, my lord?"

"Jason," he responded automatically, glancing over at Dorothea, who was dozing and lightly snoring. "Dorothea is nearly asleep, so it is safe. We agreed that when we are alone, you would call me Jason."

"What I call you has no bearing on why you are staring at me," she answered.

"I admire beautiful women."

"Then you should gaze at Dorothea."

"I prefer you."

"Nonsense." Her face went carefully blank. "Everyone knows that Dorothea is the beauty of our family," she said, her voice soft, with but a hint of bittersweet emotion laced in it.

He wanted to argue the point with her. He wanted to enumerate all the reasons he preferred her looks, her personality, to her sister's. But he held his tongue.

Jason looked out the window and noticed they had reached a particularly isolated and empty stretch of road. The stillness of the night was suddenly shattered when something that sounded like a shot rang out, reverberating in the silence. The carriage careened from side to side, lurched, then jerked sharply to the left. It rolled a few more feet, then stopped.

Gwendolyn jerked upright. Her heartbeat faltered, then took off racing. She could hear the coachman shouting, his voice alarmed.

"What's happening?" Dorothea cried, her eyes blinking with sleep and fear.

"I think we have been waylaid," Lord Fairhurst replied calmly. "By a highwayman."

"In Willoughby?" Dorothea squeaked.

"Apparently crime knows no borders." The viscount reached beneath the seat, then cursed softly.

"What? What else is wrong?" Gwendolyn asked.

"I had forgotten this is not my usual coach. I always keep a loaded pistol beneath the seats, just as a precaution."

"My God." Dorothea's voice was breathless with astonishment.

"It might not be my usual coach, but it is my usual coachman driving. He knows what to do." The viscount leaned forward and blew out the lantern, plunging the inside of the carriage into darkness. "I want the two of you to stay in here and remain very, very quiet."

Panic flared in Gwendolyn's chest and for an instant, she could not breathe. The moonlight provided only enough light for her to distinguish the viscount from her sister. She reached out and grabbed his knee. "You cannot go out there unarmed."

"There are plenty of weapons for me on the top of the box," he insisted. "No doubt my two outriders have escaped and ridden for aid, or else they are hiding in the forest, awaiting my orders."

Gwendolyn grimaced. "The outriders could be wounded. Or worse."

"Saints preserve us!" The terror in Dorothea's voice echoed through the carriage.

"I will keep you both safe," Lord Fairhurst promised.

Gwendolyn felt him move and surmised he was reaching to open the door. Blindly, she thrust out her hands, covering his wrist, squeezing her fingers with all her strength. "Wait!"

"Gwendolyn, my dear—"

"Here, take these." She removed her earrings, then fumbled with the clasp on her necklace, her fingers clumsy with fear.

"I cannot take your jewelry."

"Don't be an ass." Frantically, Gwendolyn pressed the earrings and necklace into his hands. "These are worth nothing compared to your life. Maybe they will be appeased at taking our valuables and leave us in peace."

Lord Fairhurst pocketed the jewelry and heaved a sigh. "Stay down," he commanded, and then he slipped out the door and was gone.

Obediently, Gwendolyn fell to the carriage floor. Reaching toward the opposite seat, she grabbed her sister's arm and pulled her down beside her. Above the howl of the wind she heard a man curse, then another shot rang out. Dear God, was Jason safe?

As they huddled on the floor, Gwendolyn's lips began to move in silent prayer. She prayed that Jason and the driver were safe. She prayed that their attackers had been run off. She prayed that no one would get hurt. She prayed that they would all survive.

Gwendolyn heard boots thumping awkwardly on the top of the box and assumed the coachman had climbed down. But beyond that, she heard no other sounds. The quiet was unnerving, the strain was unbearable.

She wished she had a weapon to defend herself, but

then realized it would be useless. She could not fire a pistol and had no chance of fending off a man with a knife. She would have to put her faith in Lord Fairhurst and trust him to keep them all safe.

For at that moment she knew in her heart that she was not as immune to him as she repeatedly told herself.

Chapter Eleven

Jason did not like the odds.

Three men on horseback were off to one side of the coach, their eyes trained to the top of the box where the driver sat, his arms in the air. A fourth man, tall and broad-shouldered, was on foot. He appeared to be the leader and was standing a few feet from the coach. His eyes widened when Jason appeared and the look of surprise registered instantly in Jason's mind.

Clearly the highwayman was expecting someone else to emerge from the carriage. The Ellingham sisters perhaps? Jason's gut twisted at the notion that the men might be out to harm Gwendolyn. Well, they would have to get through him first.

His nerves steadied. Though each man held a pistol, Jason knew above all else he must remain calm and in control of the situation or else they would all be doomed.

"I have but a few coins upon my person, but you are welcome to them if you allow us to proceed in peace," Jason called out.

The man on foot gave him another puzzled look. "Everyone out of the carriage," he demanded.

Jason sucked in air through his teeth. "There are no other gentlemen inside."

"There must be," the man insisted.

"There are not."

"If it's not him, then what do we do?" one of the riders shouted.

Jason glanced at the group of men, taking more careful note of their appearance. They were not masked, as highwaymen usually were, and the poor quality of their horseflesh suggested they must be very new at this line of work. To his knowledge, highwaymen prided themselves on owning the finest horseflesh, bred for the necessary speed in order to escape capture.

This appeared not to be a random robbery, which left Jason at a complete loss. If they were not highwaymen, then why had they stopped the carriage?

"You, get down from there," the leader instructed the coachman.

Slowly the driver obeyed, coming to stand beside his employer. Jason caught his eye and the servant gave him a slight nod. One of the carriage horses whinnied. The brief distraction was exactly the opportunity Jason needed. He swooped down, grabbed the pistol the coachman deliberately dropped and came up with it in his hand.

Several things happened at once. The leader lunged toward him. Jason felled his attacker with a hard blow to the stomach, feeling no sympathy when the man began to retch.

A second man scrambled down from his horse and charged. The coachman's fist connected with his assailant's jaw, knocking him to the ground. Another of the men raised his gun and aimed at the coachman. Reacting with speed and precision, Jason lifted his pistol and blasted the gun out of his hand.

The remaining rider turned his horse and headed in the opposite direction. The disarmed rider followed. And then, as quickly as the confusion arose, it subsided.

"Jason!" Gwendolyn materialized by his side. She rested her forehead on his sleeve. "I was so frightened. Are you all right?"

"Yes. But I told you to stay in the coach."

Horses sounded down the road. The two remaining attackers scrambled to escape. The coachman managed to waylay one of them, but Jason was disappointed to see it wasn't the leader.

Several horses burst into sight—Jason's outriders, along with several servants from the manor. They awaited their orders. The danger seemed past, but Jason certainly did not wish to risk the women's safety by lingering any longer.

"Rodgers, take two other men and see if you can catch our assailants," Jason commanded. "The rest of you will ride with me as I escort the ladies home."

"Is it over?" a timid voice cried from the carriage.

Jason turned. Suddenly, a shot rang out, the horses jumped and Dorothea tumbled out of the open carriage door.

"Take cover!" someone screamed.

The expression of utter fear on Gwendolyn's face twisted him in knots. Jason swallowed hard, and rushed forward, knowing for the rest of his life he would never forget that look on Gwendolyn's face.

He threw her to the ground and protectively covered her body with his own, his senses alert to any sounds, any movements.

"Please, we must see to my sister," Gwendolyn whimpered.

"In a moment. My men must make sure no one else will shoot at us."

Finally, the all-clear was given. Jason grimly rose, then helped Gwendolyn to her feet. They rushed to the fallen Dorothea.

She was slumped on the ground at an awkward angle. Jason gathered her gently in his arms and rolled her carefully on her back. Her forehead was cut, her eyes were closed.

"Is she badly injured?" Gwendolyn knelt beside him.

He leaned over and checked, fearful of what he might discover. "Her breathing is steady and even, her pulse strong."

"Then why won't she open her eyes?"

"She probably needs a few minutes to regain her senses." Jason appreciated how Gwendolyn retained her composure, even though she was unable to completely hide her terror. "She must have hit her head. But there is only a small amount of blood."

"On the outside." Gwendolyn gently brushed the tendrils of hair back from her sister's face. "She could be bleeding in her brain."

Her knowledge startled him. It was exactly what he had feared. "We need to get her to a doctor."

Jason lifted Dorothea in his arms and set her carefully inside the coach. Gwendolyn scrambled in after. Jason saw the pulse beating wildly in her throat, had one quick look at her pale, frightened face before closing the door and climbing up to the driver's box. Gathering the reins, he eased the coach onto the path and drove as fast as he dared.

Gwendolyn sat stiffly in the viscount's drawing room with her feet firmly on the floor, her back primly straight, her hands in her lap and her throat choked with fear. She had refused the tea his servants offered and the wine, and the brandy, knowing she would be unable to swallow anything.

An hour had passed since the incident, though it was mostly a blur to Gwendolyn. After their attackers had fled, the viscount had rushed them to Moorehead Manor, since it was closest, driving the coach himself, while she had cradled Dorothea on her lap. The doctor had been summoned and Gwendolyn waited with growing fear and barely suppressed panic to hear his diagnosis.

Her head jerked suddenly at the sound of footsteps and the murmur of voices in the outer hall. Male voices. The door opened and Lord Fairhurst entered.

"The doctor has just finished his examination. He assures me that Dorothea is fine, resting comfortably. Her ankle is badly swollen, but not broken, and should heal without complications."

Gwendolyn swallowed hard, trying to dislodge the lump in her throat. "The bullet?"

"Never struck her. She must have been startled by the noise of the shot, which caused her fall. I explained how we feared she had bruised her head when she hit the ground, but the doctor believes she must have fainted. He insists she does not have a concussion and the cut on her head was so slight it did not require stitches."

It took a moment for the trembling in Gwendolyn's hands to cease. "When can I see her?" she asked, trying not to sound too anxious.

"Now, if you like. I have sent a servant with a note to your aunt and uncle explaining there was an accident and that you and Dorothea will stay at the manor for the night."

Absently, Gwendolyn nodded her head. She was most

concerned with seeing Dorothea, needing very much to assure herself that her sister was indeed going to recover.

The viscount led her to the second floor. Gwendolyn barely noticed her surroundings as they traversed the corridors. They entered a chamber, well-lit by candles, a soft, comfortable breeze blowing though the partially open window.

Dorothea lay limp and frail on the high four-poster bed, which looked too large for her slender body. Gwendolyn rushed to her side and took Dorothea's hand in hers. There was no response, but her sister seemed calm, almost as if she were in a natural sleep.

"She seems peaceful," Gwendolyn whispered.

"The doctor insists that she is not in any pain," Lord Fairhurst replied, his voice also low. "I have persuaded him to stay the night, just in case there is any change in her condition."

"I am relieved to know he will be here if needed." Gwendolyn released a long sigh. "I will stay at her bedside tonight, so I may attend her if she awakens."

Lord Fairhurst shook his head. "There is no need. I have already arranged for a nurse to sit with Dorothea. The doctor thought it unnecessary, since he has given her a sleep draught that should last until morning, but I knew you would never be able to rest unless Dorothea was given proper care."

"Thank you." Gwendolyn managed a weak smile. "I have been out of my mind with worry over her. It all happened so fast. I saw her fall from the carriage. She did not appear to be badly injured, yet she lay so still, so quiet. For a moment I thought—" Gwendolyn tried to swallow beyond the tightness that had formed in her throat, unable to continue.

Silence filled the air. Gwendolyn struggled with her

emotions, trying to stop the inner trembling and fear. Suddenly, she felt a large, warm hand cover her own. The simple gesture of kindness, the gentle touch that was meant only to comfort and reassure was Gwendolyn's undoing.

For a moment, all she could do was stare at the strong hand that protected hers. It so easily encompassed her own; the long ringless fingers, the pronounced knuckles covered with fine tufts of hair. She turned her hand and laced her fingers with his and he squeezed her hand in apparent sympathy.

Suddenly, the strain of the last few hours tumbled down upon her. Gwendolyn felt her eyes grow moist, and then her lips began to quiver. The ache in her chest turned to a sharp burn and it took every ounce of her inner strength not to burst into sobs.

Goodness, she hated public displays of extreme emotions! Crying should be done in front of sisters, with close female friends, or alone. She knew she should withdraw immediately, to the privacy of an empty room, but she was oddly afraid of being alone.

She stood firm, trying to maintain her composure. But her mind replayed the events of the carriage attack. She heard the gunshot, felt the jolt of the sudden stop, remembered her sister falling to the ground. Gwendolyn gasped out a sob, then another. Her head dropped forward and she covered her face with her free hand, giving in to the emotions that overwhelmed her.

Through her quiet sobs she heard Jason sigh. He took a step toward her, but she backed away, shaking her head. He sighed again and this time did not allow her to protest. He simply tugged the hand he held and pulled her into his arms, holding her tight.

She squirmed for a few seconds, then sagged against

him. Her crying grew louder, the sobs making a deep, bone-shuddering sound.

Thankfully, he made no comments nor did he try to dissuade her from crying. Instead, he gently rubbed between her shoulder blades and rested his cheek against her hair, in a display of comfort and support.

Which made her sob even louder.

After a few minutes she felt him press something into her hand. Opening her eyes, she saw it was his linen handkerchief. She sniffed, dabbed at her eyes, blew her nose and slowly put herself to rights.

As her emotions calmed, she gradually became aware of the warmth of Lord Fairhurst's arms around her waist. He was close; so very close. If she raised her chin and tilted her head back, he could easily reach her lips. Tempting fate, she did just that—and then she waited.

He moved not a muscle. Nor did he make a move to release her. Instead, they stood locked together, savoring the moment. Gwendolyn could feel his chest move with each breath he took and she found herself inexplicably matching him breath for breath. She pressed herself even closer and felt the beating of his heart. For one mad instant she wondered if her own was beating with the same rhythm.

She closed her eyes and let her mind drift, let her fears and anxieties flow out of her body. Another tear leaked from her eyes and she let it fall. Gradually, she realized she was moving. The viscount had shifted his position so they could quit the bedchamber and was taking her away.

Entwined in his arms, Gwendolyn left the room, her mind slightly eased after seeing her sister. They turned down a long hallway that seemed familiar and she realized his bedchamber was located here. They reached his door and she stopped, startling him. His arms slackened.

Wordlessly, Gwendolyn gripped him tighter, not wanting to let go.

"The housekeeper prepared a chamber for you, but I do not mind relinquishing my bedchamber for the night," he said quietly. "Would you prefer to stay in here?"

She nodded. Using his right hand, Jason managed to open the bedchamber door. Still locked in a close embrace, they entered the room. Gwendolyn could not bear the thought of being away from him; she clung to him like a vine of ivy trailing up the garden wall. They stood that way for several long moments as something within her reached out to him, silent and pleading.

Thankfully he heard.

He dipped his mouth down to hers and drew his tongue against her lips in a warm caress. His kiss was everything she remembered and more, tasting all the sweeter since they had cheated death. It was a lover's kiss, filled with sensual hunger and sexual fire. A rush of excitement swept over her senses. Eagerly, Gwendolyn slid her hand over his hip bone and down into the small of his back, drawing his hips into hers.

And then, just as quickly and magically as it had begun, Jason ended the contact. He moved away from her, breaking the comforting touch of his mouth against hers, leaving her feeling lost and alone.

"You should get into bed."

"Not without you."

The words were unplanned. They were spoken from the heart, released tonight through a mixture of fear and shock. She had not meant to say them, had not truly realized she felt them so strongly until that moment. Yet

once they were uttered, she admitted they were true.
And she did not regret it—the words or the sentiment.

A flash of passion crossed his handsome face. "You are
upset and unsettled by this evening's events, Gwendolyn."

"Are you telling me I do not know what I am saying?
What I am asking?" She moved closer until they once
again touched, until the lushness of her thighs was teasing the hardness of his erection.

"I will not take advantage of you when you are in such
a vulnerable state," he declared. "It would be monstrously unfair of me."

A hollow ache bloomed inside her at his tender words.
She knew the wanting and needing she felt whenever
she was near Jason was unwise. The nights spent craving
him, the days spent longing to be in his company were
a fragile emotion she did not truly understand. Un-
doubtedly she would regret this later, but for now she
would choose to be selfish and ask for what she so desperately needed.

They had nearly died tonight. The realization that
she might leave this world without ever knowing him
completely affected her deeply. The need to forget all
the rules she had set for herself overpowered everything
else in her mind. A part of her was very aware that she
was teetering on the edge of reason, toying with all
common sense. But the need inside her, so strong and
deep and compelling that had struggled to be free, was
now released.

This flood of sensation, this honest admission of
desire drove out her sense of propriety. "You may choose
not to take advantage of me, my lord. But alas, I am not
nearly as circumspect." She curled one hand behind his
neck, her fingers gently massaging the cords of tense

muscle. "You may choose to reject my offer. Perversely, I would understand"

"Reject you? What insanity."

Their gazes met, and Gwendolyn clearly saw her own needs and desires mirrored in his eyes. "You see, Jason, I have come to realize that no matter how much I fight it, no matter how many times I tell myself it is wrong, I cannot hide the truth. I want you. Only you."

His arms shot around her, his mouth crushed hers with a fierceness that had her gasping. Gwendolyn's fingers dug into the muscles of his upper arms and she pushed herself tighter against him. She returned his kiss with a sense of urgency, giving herself up to the pure sensual pleasure, desperate with the need to feel *alive*.

His mouth teased and tormented until her skin heated as if it burned, as if her bones were melting like candle wax. His hands never ceased moving, caressing and holding. Shivers ran though her, her breasts tightened, her nipples rigid against the fine material of her undergarments.

She opened herself to him, wanting only to be closer to him, wanting desperately to unleash the magnificent, extraordinary longing that flamed between them. Drawn to his masculine power, she felt her body softening. She burrowed her face in his neck, then set her lips to his throat, her teeth nipping at the strong tendons.

He threaded his hand through her hair, dislodging the pins and scattering them to the carpet as her thick, dark tresses tumbled down her shoulders to the middle of her back. Jason's hands slid to her waist, down to her hips and thighs, then up to her back. She felt the hooks of her gown come loose. With trembling fingers she helped him push the material off her shoulders and over her hips until it fell at her feet.

Then he took her again in his arms and kissed her long and hard, kissed her until it felt as if her bones were melting from the heat and desire, kissed her until his arms were the only thing holding her up.

Her senses were muddled and she was vaguely aware of being lifted in the air. Cradled in Jason's arms, Gwendolyn continued kissing him, her tongue darting in and out of his warm mouth. Softness engulfed her body and then she realized that he had deposited her in the center of his bed.

Startled, she sat up, her breath hitching in delight and excitement as she saw what he was doing. With a wicked smile on his handsome face, Jason untied his cravat and dropped it to the ground. His jacket, waistcoat and shirt soon followed. Gwendolyn's eyes followed the movement of his hands as they rested on the bulge pressing against the front of his black evening breeches. He deftly twisted and released each button, then drew away the flap, leaving himself fully exposed to her.

Gwendolyn swallowed deeply and watched in astonishment as the length of his penis grew. Her gaze returned to his handsome face. He eased the breeches down his hips and thighs and tossed them off. His eyes were smoldering as he approached the bed.

Gwendolyn shivered. She dragged her chemise over her head and pulled it off, then rolled away her silk stockings. Naked, she wantonly reclined on the bed, whispering, "I want you to look at me too."

Cool air floated over her skin. Her breasts peaked and tightened. His eyes ravaged her, his gaze lingering with appreciation over every inch of her exposed flesh.

"You are stunningly beautiful," he whispered into her ear before he took the lobe between his teeth and nibbled.

Gwendolyn squirmed as shivers rippled across her

skin. He moved his lips to kiss her below the ear, then down her throat.

"Open your eyes," he whispered.

The unexpected request caught her unawares. She struggled to lift herself from the languid haze of passion and did as he commanded. Her breath caught. She felt as if she were dreaming. His eyes were staring deeply into hers with a look that told her he found her beautiful and desirable in every way.

But she also thought him beautiful. She slipped her palms upward to feel the defined mounds of muscle on his chest. His skin was smooth, the muscles beneath tight. She dragged her fingers through the crisp mat of hair scattered across his chest and settled them over the steady beating of his heart.

Her fingers quivered as she moved her hand downward. The sound of his harsh breathing filled the room. Gwendolyn watched Jason from under her lashes, using his expression to gauge her direction. She continued her quest until she reached the heated flesh of his erection.

He sucked in a quick breath as her fingers gently curved around the hard length. Curious, Gwendolyn fondled, stroked, then pulled. Jason's eyes were heavy lidded, and he instructed her how to caress him, drawing her hand down his full length, spreading the moisture that seeped out of the tip.

He groaned his approval, making no secret of his enjoyment. His clear pleasure pushed her to boldness. She was aching to give, aching to take all that he offered, trusting him to appease this strange, intense hunger.

He kissed the tip of her nose, then leaned over her chest. She watched in utter fascination as he touched the tip of his tongue to the erect nipple. The sight, as well as the sensation, made her breathless. She laid her hand on his shoulders and let the feel of his wet tongue wash over her.

"Watch," he commanded. "Watch and feel."

He circled the nipple lovingly, then drew it fully into his mouth. A bolt of passion shot through her and Gwendolyn cried out. The sound of his gentle suckling added to the intensity of the moment and Gwendolyn soon found herself arching against him.

He shifted his body and then hers, positioning her across the bed, pressing her thighs wide. Gwendolyn followed his lead, her limbs weakened with desire, her blood pounding with need. He ran his hand up along her inner thigh to the juncture of her legs, then knelt between her legs and kissed his way down to her belly.

She arched wantonly toward him, then lost what little breath she had when he shockingly delivered an open-mouth kiss between her legs.

Gwendolyn bolted upright from the bed. "My goodness, you must not do such a thing!" Her words came out in a breathless pant.

She watched the play of candlelight over his face. His skin was flushed, his devilish eyes dark with passion.

"Trust me, dearest. I know what I'm doing."

Nerves taut with anticipation, Gwendolyn allowed Jason to ease her down on the bed. She tried to do as he bid and relax, but she tensed the moment she felt his breath tease the silky, aching softness between her legs. He ignored her reluctance and continued, slowly coaxing a response.

Gwendolyn felt her muscles go lax. If she shut off her mind, it was easy to find the pleasure. Soon she began to feel tense and strange and almost melting, as if her body had been awakened from a deep sleep. Anticipating that she might again push him away, Jason grasped her wrists and held them at her sides. Ruthlessly, he flicked his tongue up and down along the slick pink folds of her flesh, tasting and teasing until the last vestiges of her reason vanished.

Her body was on fire with the most glorious sensations she had ever known. Gwendolyn started writhing on the mattress, her body begging Jason to release her from this blissful torment. She pushed hard against his tongue, her body jolting with pleasure at each wicked lick.

Oh, Lord, what was he doing to her?

Breathless, she felt herself begin to shudder with an ache so deep she thought she might faint. Her thigh muscles quivered and he threw his arm over her belly to hold her still. Gwendolyn cried out as she felt herself reaching, straining toward that tantalizing something just beyond her reach.

She buried her fingers into the muscles of his shoulders when the first wave broke. Gripping him until her knuckles turned white, Gwendolyn rode out the storm of passion, her spine arching as the spasms overcame her.

Awareness returned in small degrees. Her breathing gradually slowed. She turned her body, and her eyes met his.

He smiled wickedly. "'Tis called an orgasm. Did you like it?"

"You should bottle it, my lord. 'Twould make you a fortune."

He stretched over her, covering her with the hard heat of his body. Gwendolyn sighed and wrapped her arms around him, loving the feel of his weight. It felt beautiful and pure to be with him, which was absurd given their circumstances.

"Open your legs for me."

His voice was deep and gravelly, making her shiver. She lifted her chin and met his sparkling emerald eyes, feeling a stab of illicit pleasure. Boldly obeying his command, Gwendolyn shifted her body, moving her legs, making it clear that she wanted it all. Trapped in the raw hunger of his gaze, her throat constricted, her heart leapt.

Jason's hand slipped beneath her buttocks and gripped it as he positioned himself in between her thighs. Gwendolyn tried to keep her wits focused, but her emotions were too jumbled. Excitement, fear, intense need and desire all warred for dominance in her mind.

She turned her head to kiss his muscular arm and he began to ease himself slowly inside her. A feeling of fullness along with a sharp tension coiled within her. He continued to thrust forward, a fraction at a time and then pull back in a slow deliberate manner, each time keeping his movements shallow.

Gwendolyn's eyes drifted shut. It was amazingly intimate. Every inch of her lower body felt alive as he stretched and heated her flesh. But it was the deeper sense of longing, the awakening of emotions and feelings long suppressed that brought her the greatest gratification.

Suddenly, he stopped moving to press his lips to her ear. "Are you truly certain?"

Gwendolyn opened her eyes to stare up at him. "An odd time to ask that question."

"Not really. Technically you are still a virgin. I have reached the barrier of your maidenhead, but not yet broken it."

"If I told you to stop, what would you do?"

He dropped his forehead to lightly touch hers. "Persuade you to change your mind?"

"You do not need to persuade me," she whispered. She felt caught in a force that demanded the surrender of her entire being and was glad of it, because she knew in her heart she would not be complete until their bodies were joined.

"Thank God." He smiled rakishly, then brushed the tip of his tongue along her lower lip.

She arched in his arms and the tempo of his movements began again. The heat also began again; the yearning, the wanting. Her body throbbed around his, the tantalizing brush of skin against skin made her feel restless, edgy.

Jason felt himself spiraling. He was like a man possessed, worshipping Gwendolyn with his body in a way he had never done with any other female. A fierce need filled him, pounded through his veins. He was enthralled by her naked, unbridled passion and honesty. The sweet scent of her desire filled his nostrils, the tangy taste of her flesh teased his tongue, the silky softness of her body drove him almost beyond restraint.

He could hear the pounding of his heart, the roar of his own blood. The thought that he had summoned her passionate nature gave him a primal sense of satisfaction. Breathing hard, Jason began to move his hips slowly back and forth, pressing himself farther and farther with each thrust. She felt like heat and fire in his arms, but he resisted the lure of ecstasy, wanting to make certain she was ready, hoping he could somehow lessen the pain.

But then she tightened her inner muscles and he could not help himself. Jason thrust deeply, then deeper still into her welcoming body and felt the resistance of her maidenhead burst.

She cried out.

"Are you all right?" he asked before moving to kiss her soft, swollen lips.

"I'm not sure. Is it over?"

Her voice sounded wistful, confused. It was difficult to cling to his control when his body screamed to rush itself to release, but somehow Jason managed.

This moment was too important to be rushed. He knew in his heart that ultimately there would be no pleasure for him if Gwendolyn were not satisfied too.

He leaned close and traced the curve of her ear with his tongue. "Lie back and relax, my love, and let me ravish you. I promise it will be pure delight."

He repeated the slow, deliberate movements until he heard her gasp. His hand drifted down to where they were joined and he began stroking her until she tightened her hold on him and moved faster, drawing him deeper inside her slick warmth.

"Better?"

"Hmm."

His restraint and gentleness slipped as he pleasured them both. She ran her fingers down his back to his buttocks and squeezed tightly. "Don't stop. Oh, please, don't stop."

Her hands felt warm against his skin. He had wondered if she would be shy about exposing herself and was delighted to find that she was honestly uninhibited. She panted softly beneath him, all modesty abandoned.

Jason wrapped his arms around Gwendolyn, drawing her close so their bodies pressed together everywhere. He felt her need, because it so perfectly matched his own. With a whimper, Gwendolyn strained toward him and Jason thrust himself into her harder, striving to complete his conquest, needing her to never regret that she had chosen to give herself to him.

Jason let his breath out in an audible sigh, feeling a soul-wrenching need to hold back his desire so that it could be a shared experience of exquisite pleasure between them.

He felt his release nearing, and he fought harder to hold it back. And then her body began to convulse and shudder beneath him. Jason took Gwendolyn's right hand in his left, twined his fingers through hers and lifted their joined hands over her head.

Her body strained against his, writhing seductively and she cried out his name. He continued to thrust against her over and over until her shudders started to fade.

"Jason," she whispered in awe.

At the sound of her voice, so full of wonder and contentment, something primal and deep hit him hard. His strokes took on an almost frantic urgency and he finally let himself come, spilling himself inside her.

"Hold me," he gasped, and she wrapped her arms around him, then lifted her legs high on his thighs, hugging him close. She shifted her buttocks, rocking her hips upward, taking him even deeper inside.

The sounds of passion filled the air. Jason groaned and grasped her hips, holding her closer, binding her to him completely. With his body and his heart and his very soul. In this moment. And for the rest of their lives.

Jason was unsure how long it took to come back to his senses. He struggled to regain his breath; it seemed like minutes passed before he could move. He was aware of her fingers relaxing around his hand and he released it, then tenderly brushed the damp hair off her brow. What an amazing, humbling experience! The passion, the sweetness, the total surrender and sharing.

He raised himself up on his elbow and gazed down at Gwendolyn. Her eyes were closed, her face turned to one side. Her dark hair was spread in wild disarray across the pillow and he vowed he would relish spending the rest of his days looking at that sight.

He ran his thumb over her cheek and she turned into him. The unconscious gesture of trust made his heart skip and fill with warmth.

Gwendolyn's previous kisses had let him know she would be a passionate lover, but her uninhibited response had surprised him. Though his experience with virgins was extremely limited—she being the only one—he doubted many were such naturals when it came to the physical aspects of making love.

Gwendolyn had been an eager and equal participant, moving against him with joyful abandon, fondling his body, urging and even begging him to bring them both pleasure.

Knowing she was this tempting as a virgin made the idea of teaching her the finer points of the art of love-making an incredibly delightful idea. She was so relaxed and open with him Jason grinned at the notion and his body began to slowly heat.

Gwendolyn sighed and snuggled closer and Jason felt his heart swell with emotion. He bent and kissed her neck. She moved even closer. His heart fairly ached. Then he nuzzled her cheek and whispered, "I love you, Gwendolyn."

Chapter Twelve

The clock on the fireplace mantel seemed to tick very loudly in the silence. For a moment, all Gwendolyn could do was savor the words. She let them wash over her in a wave of sheer joy. *He loved her—perhaps even more than she loved him.*

Delight filled her being. Her mind raced, unable to settle on a single cohesive thought. Her heart fairly ached; it was beating so hard and so fast the moment took on an unreal quality, almost as if it were a dream.

But it was not a dream. The soreness within her body told her this was real, this had truly happened. Gwendolyn's feelings vacillated wildly. To experience love and bliss and then so cruelly have it taken away by the reality of the situation.

Jason was married—all she could ever hope to be in his life was his mistress. A female to be used at his convenience and then when he grew tired of her, sent along her way.

She paled and the heady excitement his nearness evoked vanished abruptly. "The good Lord save me," Gwendolyn whispered in distress. "What have I done?"

He bent his head farther, his mouth brushing her ear. He flashed her one of his lazy, crooked smiles and she wondered at her own stupidity. Love her? How could he? He was married to another woman.

"You have made me the happiest man on earth," Jason insisted.

There was a slight buzzing in her head. She wanted to try and preserve what joy she could out of the moment by not revealing the depth of her jealousy, but that was impossible.

"I have no right to make you happy," she whispered, angling her head so he could not look into her eyes. "You belong to another."

"Gwendolyn, please, I cannot bear to see you look so stricken." He turned her chin and their eyes met. "I did not intend for this to happen. On my word of honor, you must believe me."

Gwendolyn gulped down a deep breath of emotion. "I know. I never believed I would go so far, I never thought at my core I was so weak, that I would act so foolishly." The reality of what they had done began to slowly sink into her conscience and her throat grew painfully tight. Even now, when she knew she had no claim on him, she felt wildly possessive.

I must leave. I must get away.

She started to move, realized she was naked and a shock of modesty overcame her. Pulling the coverlet to her chin, she stared at him mutely.

He sat up in bed, allowing the covers to fall away from his well-muscled chest. "Do you need something?"

Helplessly, her eyes were drawn to the trail of hair that began on his chest and continued down until it disappeared beneath the bed linen cinched around his waist. Disgusted with herself for still feeling such a strong physical and emotional connection to him, Gwendolyn turned away.

"Jason, please, do not speak of this any longer. What we have done is so very, very wrong."

"Ah love, try not to look so miserable. Far worse sins than this can be forgiven."

"That hardly brings me any comfort." Gwendolyn grimaced, her heart hammered painfully against her chest.

"Would it have been better if you had pushed me away, slapped me hard across the mouth when I tried to kiss you?"

"To my utter shame I did not even try."

"Because you wanted me as much as I wanted you."

She rubbed her hand across her forehead, sighing deeply. "Wanting, and having the right to indulge those passions, are not the same."

He leaned across the bed, coming so close their noses nearly touched. "I want to marry you."

Gwendolyn snorted. His outrageous words dissolved her modesty. She sprang from the bed and began fumbling through her clothes, searching for her undergarments. "How terribly inconvenient that you already have a wife. Makes it a bit difficult for me to hold you to that promise, does it not?"

"I do not have a wife."

The chemise she was holding fluttered to the carpet. "What?"

He took her hand and brought it to his mouth, then kissed her knuckles ever-so-gently. "I know this makes no sense and I regret that I am not at liberty to explain it all, not yet at any rate. But know this, my darling. I will marry you."

Gwendolyn lowered her gaze to stare down at their joined hands. He squeezed hers tightly and she yanked her hand from his hold. "I deeply regret ever telling you that you need to be more fun-loving and frivolous, my lord. When I told you that, this is not what I meant. A joke in poor taste is far worse than a somber disposition."

"I am not joking. I am perfectly serious. I adore you. With all of my heart and soul. Mark my words, I will be your husband one day."

He did not elaborate and a deadly stillness came over her. "You mock me," she whispered.

"No! Never!"

It took several seconds for his denials to sink into her mind. Gwendolyn felt even more uncomfortable. She turned and looked into his eyes, hoping to find some clue to his emotional state. His returning gaze was steady and confident, filled with purpose. She continued to stare into his brilliant green eyes and when his gaze never wavered, it gradually became clear that he was perfectly serious and totally sincere.

Gwendolyn slowly sank to the edge of the bed. She reached for the garment at her feet and clutched her chemise to her breast, holding her back rigid with surprise. "You cannot mean that you are planning to divorce Lady Fairhurst? The scandal would be unbearable."

"That is not what I said. There will be no divorce and no scandal."

"How?" she croaked.

"You must trust me."

Gwendolyn bowed her head and studied her twisting fingers. Marry him when he already had a wife? But no, he claimed he did not have a wife, even though everyone knew he had recently acquired one. The London papers wrote about her, wrote about the parties they had attended, the plays they had seen, the charities she favored with her patronage. Surely Lady Fairhurst was a real woman, a true wife?

Suddenly, Gwendolyn could not catch her breath, could not still the thundering of panic in her heart. No divorce, no scandal? How would Lady Fairhurst vanish into thin air? Through foul play?

"There are only two ways to be rid of a wife. Divorce or death. And since you claim you will not divorce Lady Fairhurst, then you must be plotting something far more dire." Gwendolyn shivered at the notion. She shifted her gaze, feeling her eyes glimmering with tears. "You cannot harm her."

Jason eyed her askance. "Well, if that was what I planned, I would be a fool to tell you."

His tone was mocking and filled with indignation. Gwendolyn paused. "I'm sorry." A sigh broke from her. "You are many things, but I do not believe you capable of doing something so vile as murdering an innocent woman."

"Thank you. I think." His hands closed around her shoulders and he looked directly into her eyes. "I would go to extraordinary lengths to have you, but would surely stop short of murder. Do you not know me any better?"

"Perhaps that is part of the problem. Apparently I do not know you very well at all."

"Then we must work toward changing that sad state of affairs."

Gwendolyn's lips quivered. She could not allow herself to know him any better, to get any closer. She was inexperienced and unsophisticated, but not naive. She understood how cruel, how unfair life could be at times. She wondered if she could be happy in an illicit love affair, if she would be willing to sacrifice her reputation to be with the man she loved.

For in that moment she admitted that she loved him. She loved him with all her heart, loved him with a breathless intensity that frightened her for it made her forget her very name. She loved him, even though she would never be free to speak the words aloud within his hearing. Not while he was tied to another woman.

"I do not know if I can be content with what you offer," she said. "'Tis hard for me to accept a devil's bargain."

"I will give you the world, my dearest," he proclaimed.

"I never aspired to anything that grand, Jason."

"Would you settle for my heart?" He stroked her cheek with the back of his hand. "My heart, and my name?"

She tore her gaze away, blinking back the tears of grief and love. Oh, how she wanted to believe him. Confusion licked at her mind. What he was saying was an impossibility and yet if she did not dare to risk believing him, any chance of sharing a life with Jason would slip firmly from her grasp.

Was she foolish or daring enough to try?

Jason's heart was pounding. This was ridiculous. He should just tell her the truth and be done with it, but a deeper part of him desperately needed to know her feelings were true. That she could love him unconditionally, would trust him completely, even when the evidence before her suggested otherwise.

Jason's past with Elizabeth had left a deep wound and Gwendolyn held the power to heal it. For so long he had vowed he would never again be crushed by the needing and wanting that love brought. He would never again allow a woman to fill his mind so completely, to consume the essence of his soul.

He would not be made weak by all that he felt for a

woman. He would never again subject himself to the powerless vulnerability of being the only one who loved. He had made several mistakes with Elizabeth, among them being too hasty to declare his feelings. Years of experience had apparently taught him little, for he had just proclaimed his love for Gwendolyn. And he had fallen just as deeply in love—more perhaps, for now he was a mature man, not a callow youth.

When he looked at her, his heart turned over. At the beginning, he had been so determined to deny any interest or attraction in Gwendolyn. He made assumptions based on her looks and the rumors of her scandalous past. Now that he knew her, now that he could see below the surface, his love flowed freely. She was proud, and opinionated, intelligent and beautiful.

She was also generous, loyal, open-minded and practical. Gwendolyn had not returned a declaration when he expressed his love, but he suspected it was her morality that held her back. If he revealed the truth of his identity, would she feel free to express her feelings?

The debate continued to rage in Jason's head. The confusion and disbelief on her face when he said he would marry her caused a knot of guilt to twist in his gut. He tried to rationalize his actions by telling himself it would not be for too long, and insisting that if she did indeed love him, she would understand and forgive.

"Please, Gwendolyn, say something. Say anything, for Christ's sake!"

She turned her head away and shook it from side to side. "Damn it! I don't know what to say! Hell, I don't know what to feel or think!" Slowly, she calmed herself. "My head is spinning, Jason."

"And you are swearing."

Her head shot up. "This is not funny!"

"Aye, love, you cannot help but be amusing. And adorable. And incredibly beautiful."

She drew taut. "You must not say things like that to me."

"Why not?"

"You know why."

He quelled the frustration that began to gnaw at him. "You must stop feeling so guilty."

"Is that what you do?" she asked, her voice quivering. "Ignore the guilt?"

He slowly moved closer, until the top of their thighs touched as he sat beside her. "I have made a shambles of things, but I vow to set it all to rights. I know it is not easy, but somehow you must find it in your heart to trust me."

Gwendolyn looked at him, unconvinced. "I cannot listen to my heart, Jason. I must listen to my head."

At that moment, Jason almost blurted out the truth, but there was something in her eyes that made him hesitate, a glimpse of feeling that showed she wanted to believe, wanted to trust him.

"Have you never heard of blind faith?" he asked.

Abruptly, she pulled herself away and a sharp exclamation came from her mouth. "I cannot simply toss my good sense out the window because it is what I desire."

Jason also rose to his feet. Needing an activity to occupy his hands, he began to neaten the bed. When it was freshly made, with the sheets pulled tight and the pillows fluffed, he pulled back the coverlet.

"May I join you?" he asked with a wistful smile.

Gwendolyn's astonished expression faded as she jutted her chin forward. "That would be most unwise."

"What if I promised to behave? If I vow to do myself physical harm when the urge to seduce you overcomes me?"

His attempt at humor failed to win a smile from her

and in that moment Jason knew he had to tell her the truth. But not tonight. She looked pale and weary with her gaze focused blindly on the far side of the room and he realized that she must be exhausted, physically and emotionally.

Jason reached for the chemise she clutched tightly in her hand and pryed it from her fingers. Shaking it out, he carefully pulled it over Gwendolyn's head and began to tie the satin pink ribbons, starting at her breasts and working toward her waist.

She blinked as if startled from a dream, her hand reaching for his, no doubt to push them away. "Don't—"

"Let me help you," he pleaded. "Since you have no night rail, this will have to do as a sleeping garment."

She bowed her head. Relieved she no longer fought, Jason finished dressing her, led her to the bed and tucked her beneath the covers. Then he went to the washstand, returning with a flannel cloth and a basin of water that was pleasantly warm. He gently bathed Gwendolyn's face and throat and arms.

He wanted to wash her properly, knowing there must be some virgin's blood clinging to her upper thighs, but he knew the intimacy would most likely startle and agitate her. So he did the best he could and when he was finished, he set the basin aside, pulled on his evening breeches, then climbed into bed beside her.

Gwendolyn stiffened and the lines about her mouth went taut. "Jason, please, you cannot stay here tonight."

He gathered her into the crook of his arm, her head resting against his naked chest. "Just until you fall asleep, Gwendolyn."

She mumbled something inarticulate, but allowed him to remain. At first she was stiff, awkward, but gradually he felt her body begin to relax, heard her breathing settle into a constant rhythm.

Aroused, but content to watch her sleep, Jason spooned her warm body closer. Gwendolyn's face was revealed in the moonlight and when he glanced down at her, his heart melted. She looked younger with her eyes closed, prettier, almost docile.

A strange peace filled Jason's chest, stretched his heart. For the first time in his adult life he felt the warmth of home while lying with a woman in his arms. Felt a sense of deep purpose in his otherwise aimless life, a certainty about his future.

Tomorrow morning he would speak to Gwendolyn, make a clean breast of things and set everything straight. It would not be easy, but it would go better when she was well-rested and calm, when he had her full attention.

She would be his wife, his devoted companion and they would be very, very happy together. He knew that she belonged in his life, knew they were a well-matched pair, kindred spirts who would never be truly content unless they were together.

All he had to do was now was convince her.

By rights, Gwendolyn knew she should never have been able to sleep at all. The enormity of what she had done last night had kept her mind and body in turmoil, yet somehow she had fallen into a restless and dreamless slumber.

She opened her eyes to a stream of sunlight covering the bed. As promised, Jason was gone, but his presence invaded the chamber. Gwendolyn spied his shaving equipment on the low dresser, his hairbrush next to it.

The sight produced an odd lump of emotion in her throat that she had difficulty swallowing back.

She glanced at the clock on the mantelpiece. Nearly eight. The house appeared quiet, though Gwendolyn assumed the staff had probably been up for hours. And what of her sister? Was Dorothea awake? Had she spent a restful night? Was she improving as the doctor had promised?

Needing the immediate answers to these troublesome questions prodded Gwendolyn to arise from the bed. She took several steps forward and became suddenly aware of the tenderness between her legs. Flushed with the memory of her extraordinary night with Jason, Gwendolyn brushed aside her regrets. Her time with Jason was over. Given the circumstances, there was no other choice.

Determined, she crossed the room and opened the viscount's wardrobe. It felt ridiculously intimate, almost intrusive, to see his garments so neatly hung and arranged inside. Lightly she ran her fingertips over the finely tailored garments, puzzled at how bright and vibrant many of them were—a stark contrast to the conservative and somber colors Lord Fairhurst usually wore.

Having no time to deeply consider the matter, Gwendolyn shrugged off the puzzling thoughts and searched through the many coats, grinning when she at last came across what she sought—his dressing gown. Made of black silk, with collar and cuffs trimmed in gold velvet, it was a luxurious garment and the only thing even remotely suitable for her to wear if she wanted to leave the chamber.

Hastily she put it on, tying the belt tightly at her waist to prevent it from dragging on the ground and rolling back the cuffs several times, exposing her wrists. Modestly covered, except for her bare feet, Gwendolyn left the chamber and hastened down the hallway to check on Dorothea.

The nurse rose from her chair and adjusted the draperies to allow in a bit more sunshine. Her eyebrow rose at Gwendolyn's strange attire, but thankfully she made no comment.

"She's had a quiet night," the nurse reported. Her hand went to Dorothea's forehead and she clucked her tongue approvingly. "No sign of fever and that's very good news. Her ankle will hurt and her head will be sore, but she'll recover. The young ones usually do."

"Thank heavens." Gwendolyn went to the bed and stroked her sister's arm. Relief began to flow through her as she noted how natural Dorothea looked. Her cheeks were rosy, her breathing steady, her expression peaceful.

"Best to let her sleep a few more hours," the nurse suggested. "After she wakes and has eaten a light meal she'll be better able to cope with visitors."

Taking the nurse's advice, Gwendolyn returned to her room. She sat on the edge of the bed, then rested her head against the pillow. Her eyelids started to feel very heavy. She let them close, telling herself she would only rest for a few minutes.

Gwendolyn awoke when a maid arrived, carrying in a tray with hot chocolate and toast.

"I've brought a small repast to break your fast, Miss," the maid said cheerily. "Cook will prepare anything you wish once you have washed and dressed and come down to the dining room."

"Thank you." Somehow Gwendolyn managed a polite smile. Her stomach felt too hot and muddled to eat and the scent of the chocolate made it worse. Ignoring the tray, she scrambled out of the large four-poster bed and searched for her clothing, trying not to panic when she could not find her gown.

"I have your clothes right here, Miss," the maid said. "Some of her ladyship's garments arrived last week. The housekeeper checked her chamber, but there was nothing appropriate for you to borrow. So we cleaned the garments you wore last night."

Borrow clothes from Lady Fairhurst? Gwendolyn nearly bit her tongue trying to hold back her exclamation of horror. It was bad enough she had stolen her husband's affections. It would be beyond imagining to then start wearing her clothing.

The very notion made Gwendolyn queasy again. Heart pounding, she leaned against the bedpost and took several deep breaths of air to calm herself. By the time the maid had poured hot water in the china basin, Gwendolyn felt steady enough to wash.

It took a long time to dress. Gwendolyn felt odd wearing an evening gown at this time of day, but at least the garment was freshly cleaned and pressed. And considering all the bizarre and life-altering events of the past twenty-four hours, wearing an evening dress at noon time was hardly the worst infraction.

Gwendolyn raised her chin and looked in the mirror as the maid quickly buttoned the many small buttons down her back. Thank goodness they were all intact. She had worried that in her haste to disrobe last night, several would have been torn away.

No sooner had she completed her toilette, Gwendolyn heard the steady tread of footsteps and then someone knocked on the door. The maid answered it and exited at the same time the visitor entered.

A tremor ran through Gwendolyn as Jason stepped into the room. Oh my, he was in fine form this morning.

He was dressed in a dark green coat, tan breeches, black waistcoat and tasseled riding boots so shiny they gleamed like a mirror.

She assumed his valet must have entered the chamber earlier, when she had gone to visit Dorothea. How else could he have gotten such fine, clean garments?

He bowed, but Gwendolyn's shaking knees made it too difficult to answer with a curtsy. "Good morning, my lord."

"Good morning, my love." He smiled, the expression lighting his emerald eyes. "And please, do call me Jason."

Gwendolyn's resolve faltered. He looked so handsome, so earnest and loving. My God, how could she refuse him anything?

"I saw Dorothea very briefly earlier this morning, but I should like to go and sit with her now." Gwendolyn deliberately spoke in her most polite, impersonal tone, praying he would adopt the same attitude and make it easier for both of them.

"I've just come from her chamber. She was awake for a short time, but has fallen back to sleep, which both the doctor and nurse assured me is perfectly normal."

Gwendolyn drew in a slow breath. "Nevertheless, I would feel more at ease if I were with her."

"Of course. But first we need to talk. I have something very important to discuss with you."

Shaking, Gwendolyn turned away. Jason's arms enfolded her from behind and the unique aroma of spice and masculinity surrounded her. His nearness sent her heart racing to an irregular rhythm. It was too much. Too much.

She pulled away. "There is nothing at all to be said between us."

He pressed his lips together, as if something pained him. "I know this is not easy for you."

"Not easy?" The calm visage Gwendolyn attempted to present crumbled to a grimace. She moved to the other side of the room, needing to place a physical distance between them. He looked at her in mild exasperation.

"There is no need for such melodramatics, Gwendolyn."

Her nerves tightened. Jason moved closer and she slid her hands restlessly up and down her arms.

Without warning, he pulled her against him and kissed her, hard and swift. He moved so fast that she did not even realize his intentions until his mouth was molded against hers.

Initially shocked, she started to pull away, then somehow, her arms found their way around his neck, and Gwendolyn held him closer. As they continued kissing, the pleasure began to unfold itself inside her and a now-familiar ache started to spread through her body.

A loud knock sounded at the door. "My lord?"

Jason pulled back far enough so he could turn his head, and Gwendolyn saw he was glaring at the door.

"Did you recognize that voice?" she whispered.

"It sounds like Snowden. My butler." Jason sighed, but did not release her from his embrace. Instead, he dipped his head and kissed her again.

Gwendolyn's knees weakened when he thrust his tongue inside her mouth. The yearning began and the sweet ache of love swelled in her heart. The feeling was so complete, so intense that it overshadowed her doubts and regrets.

The pressure of Jason's body against hers as he leaned closer caused a shiver to rage through her. All her senses sprang to life and she felt the now-familiar ripple of longing between her quivering legs.

He reached down and cupped her bottom, parting her thighs as he rubbed suggestively against her.

The knock sounded again. "My lord—"

Jason abruptly pulled his mouth away. "If you knock on that bloody door one more time, Snowden, you will be dismissed! Without a reference."

There was an ominous silence on the opposite side of the closed door. For approximately thirty seconds.

"Please, forgive the interruption, my lord. Mr. and Mrs. Ellingham and Miss Emma have arrived and they are most anxious to see Miss Dorothea," the butler said in a nervous, muffled tone. "They are also asking for Miss Gwendolyn. Is she in there with you?"

"Miss Gwendolyn told me she was going to take a morning walk," Jason called out. "I am certain she will return shortly."

"Her family will be relieved to hear it," the butler drawled.

"Please escort the family to Miss Dorothea's bedchamber. I will join them shortly."

"Very good."

"More lies," Gwendolyn muttered. "Will they never end?"

Jason took a harsh breath. "We will talk, Gwendolyn. And soon." He leaned in and kissed her. She could taste his determination, feel his resolve. "Join us in Dorothea's chamber when you feel ready to cope with your family."

He then quit the room, leaving Gwendolyn burning with confusion, her hand pressed tightly against her tingling lips.

Chapter Thirteen

Gwendolyn stood several feet away from the large bed, with a pleasant expression pasted on her face and her hands held behind her back so no one could see them trembling. It had been far more emotional than she expected seeing her family again. Their appearance vividly reminded her of what she might have lost if things had gone differently on the road last night, if the viscount had failed to save them all.

It also reminded her of how she had disgraced herself, and indirectly them, by succumbing to her passion last night. She knew it was unlikely, yet a part of her feared her sins would be clearly reflected in her face. So she tried to stay in the shadows.

"Dorothea, my pet," Aunt Mildred wailed. "Oh, my heavens, how pale and wan you look, my dear. Quick, Emma, remove my vinaigrette from my reticule. I fear I shall faint at the sight of my darling wounded child."

Emma pushed a chair under her aunt's swaying figure. "Gracious, Aunt Mildred, you will frighten Dorothea into a relapse with such nonsense. She looks splendid, does she not, Gwen?"

"Indeed," Gwendolyn agreed. "She is already much improved and we are all thankful."

Aunt Mildred had always been the sort of woman who cried at the drop of a hat and the moment she had set foot inside Moorehead Manor, the floodgates had opened. Honest emotion and upset could be understood; however, Aunt Mildred's prolonged hysterics were another matter entirely.

"And my poor dear Gwendolyn." Aunt Mildred dabbed at her eyes with her handkerchief and sniffled, then turned toward her. Uncle Fletcher, Emma, Lord Fairhurst and even the nurse imitated the gesture, their curious stares cutting through her.

Gwendolyn paled and straightened her back as her aunt reached out her arm. Obligingly she moved forward and grasped her hand. "Hush now, Aunt. We are all fine," she said in a soothing tone.

The remark set Aunt Mildred into a round of noisy sobs. "So brave in the face of such danger, such horror. You are heroes, the pair of you."

"It was Lord Fairhurst who saved them," Emma pointed out, before casting a gaze of pure adoration toward the viscount. "'Tis he who deserved your praise, Aunt Mildred."

"Yes, yes, we are grateful to the viscount," Aunt Mildred said. "Though if he had left the party earlier, as your uncle and I did, you might not have encountered those ruffians upon the road."

All eyes turned to Lord Fairhurst. "It was a most unfortunate incident," he remarked in a neutral tone.

Aunt Mildred sniffed. "'Twas dreadful, my lord. Absolutely dreadful. I wanted to rush over here the moment your servant brought us the terrifying news last night, but my dear Fletcher insisted we wait until morning."

"You would have only gotten in the way last night," Uncle Fletcher said. "Far better to come after Dorothea has rested and started healing. She is nearly herself already."

Aunt Mildred blustered. "She might appear to be herself, but 'tis obvious she will carry these scars for the rest of her life."

Gwendolyn stole a glance at the viscount. He looked slightly exasperated and she imagined her aunt's blubbering was starting to wear on his nerves. But she looked again and decided there was something else. He seemed bothered, even a bit worried.

About what?

"I am fine, Aunt Mildred," Dorothea exclaimed. "Though I do confess to feeling rather tired."

It was the cue the nurse seemed to be waiting to hear. "All right, that's enough." She moved to the center of the bedchamber and clapped her hands together three times. "The patient needs quiet. Too much excitement will do her no good. I must insist you all take your leave at once."

"Yes, you must leave," Aunt Mildred agreed. She shifted in her chair and settled herself closer to Dorothea.

The nurse straightened the coverlet on the opposite side of the bed with an efficient tug. "You too, madame."

"Me?" Aunt Mildred questioned in an affronted tone. "But I must care for my niece."

"They'll be plenty for you to do once we bring Dorothea home," Gwendolyn said.

She placed her hands on her aunt's shoulders. Lips pursed, Aunt Mildred was reluctantly brought to her feet.

Involuntarily, Gwendolyn's eyes sought the viscount's. The worry on his face cleared and he became the charming, welcoming host.

"Cook has prepared luncheon. I shall instruct it to be served immediately."

"We would not wish to impose," Uncle Fletcher said.

"Nonsense. I told Cook to expect guests. She would feel slighted if you did not at least try some of her dishes."

They obligingly followed the viscount. The dining room was elegant and formal, the food plentiful and tasty, but the meal was an ordeal for Gwendolyn. She could hardly wait for it to end, for the questions about the horrible incident last night to cease, for the speculation about the community becoming overrun with ruffians to finally be over.

"When I think of the dreadful nightmare my dear girls went through my heart nearly explodes with emotion," Aunt Mildred said, looking at Lord Fairhurst.

Then don't think about it! Gwendolyn wanted to shout, but she bit back her snippy retort. This melodramatic mood her aunt was in was starting to wear very thin on Gwendolyn's nerves.

"I shall expect a full investigation from the magistrate," Uncle Fletcher blustered. "To think that decent people cannot travel our roads at night is an abomination."

"The Carlyles have canceled their party for this evening," Aunt Mildred revealed. "I heard that Sophia was having heart palpitations over the possibility that her guests could be harmed."

Uncle Fletcher nodded. "Far better to be cautious, under the circumstances."

"One incident hardly constitutes a rash of criminal activities," Lord Fairhurst said casually.

"I dare say, living in London makes you more accustomed to such dangerous behavior, my lord," Aunt Mildred replied. She shuddered, then took a long gulp of wine before continuing. "But here in Willoughby, occurrences such as these give us nightmares."

"I am certain Lord Fairhurst meant no offense, Aunt Mildred," Emma interjected defensively. "And he is right. This was an isolated incident."

"'Tis far too soon to judge exactly what happened," Uncle Fletcher said.

They continued to discuss the incident, though thankfully Aunt Mildred declared her nerves far too frazzled to hear the specific details. Which prompted the viscount to add it would be the height of poor manners to allow such inappropriate matters to be spoken of during a meal in mixed company.

They floundered for a neutral topic, quickly exhausting the weather. Lengthy silences had always made Aunt Mildred nervous and her subsequent attempts to carry the conversation were met with limited results. Uncle Fletcher occasionally grunted a response, the viscount only answered questions directed to him and Emma was too enraptured with the viscount's company to elaborate on her replies, unless they were directed toward him.

Gwendolyn said nothing. Eventually, she abandoned all pretense of eating and placed her fork to the side of her dish. She could see Jason out of the corner of her eye and despite her determination to ignore him, she was painstakingly aware of his every move.

"I agree it is better not to discuss the incident; however, I want to know what you have discovered about these ruffians who attacked you, Fairhurst," Uncle Fletcher demanded.

"Though there were four men, regretfully, we were

only able to capture one of them," the viscount answered. "He was knocked unconscious during the tussle last night and has not yet come to his senses. The doctor assures me he will eventually awaken."

Uncle Fletcher made a scoffing sound. "He'll have a nasty headache, I'll wager."

"He deserves far more than that," Aunt Mildred insisted.

"Has the magistrate taken him away?" Uncle Fletcher asked.

"No. Given his condition and the lateness of the hour, it seemed risky to move him last night. He is currently locked in my cellar."

Dismayed, Aunt Mildred looked at the viscount. "My goodness, the ruffian is right under our noses," she tittered. "Are we safe?"

Uncle Fletcher glared at his wife. "Fairhurst would never be so foolish as to put his household at risk. I'm sure the man is securely contained."

"He is," the viscount confirmed, after taking a long sip of his wine. "Though I will be eager to turn him over to the authorities later today. After I have had an opportunity to question him."

They fell silent as a footman entered with a dessert tray. Nearly everyone declined, claiming they were too full. Except Aunt Mildred, who took a most generous serving of rich chocolate pudding and clotted cream. Gwendolyn, who was beyond anxious to leave the table, nearly groaned out loud.

Would this meal *ever* end?

"I am so very pleased to see that despite your great upset you have managed to retain your appetite, Aunt Mildred," Gwendolyn remarked.

"Yes, it is a blessing." Aunt Mildred smiled.

This time Gwendolyn did groan. The sarcasm was lost on Aunt Mildred, who allowed herself a second helping of the pudding. Feeling guilty for being so waspish, Gwendolyn vowed to keep her temper under control. Still, it was impossible to stay focused on the conversation. She allowed her mind to drift, to think about the future, which at the moment seemed very dark and dismal.

She had been absolutely right to tell Jason they had nothing to say to each other. She had done it for purely selfish reasons, admitting to herself that it might take more self-control than she possessed to resist him if she remained alone in his company. Her only logical form of defense was to keep her distance.

Being near him was dangerous, being alone with him sheer suicide. If she were to survive, she would have to harden her heart against him. There was a deeply sensual connection between them, as the events in the bedchamber last night had proven, and that had not diminished in the cold reality of day.

She was drawn to Jason like a moth to a flame. He made her feel alive with every fiber of her being. He was pure temptation, an irresistible ache. Her body craved the perfect pleasure he could so easily arouse, her heart begged for his sweet touch. Whenever she was near him, she fought an urgent wanton wish to—

"Gracious, are you even listening to us, Gwendolyn?"

Startled, Gwendolyn nearly jumped from her chair. "My apologies."

"We were discussing our favorite books," Aunt Mildred explained. "I told Lord Fairhurst that all my nieces enjoy good literature—in moderation, of course."

"Of course," Gwendolyn repeated. She laughed

sharply. "No bluestockings will be tolerated in the Ellingham family."

Uncle Fletcher snorted in agreement. "Can't abide a
female who tries to be an intellectual."

"It can be a burden," the viscount agreed in a most
solemn tone.

Gwendolyn stiffened with indignation, but suspecting
Lord Fairhurst might be baiting her, she kept silent.

Emma broke the awkward moment. "I have recently
had the great pleasure of reacquainting myself with one
of my favorite books. Perchance, are you familiar with
Pride and Prejudice, my lord?"

The viscount's lips lifted into a thin smile. "I have
heard of the novel, but alas never had the opportunity
to read it."

"Oh, but you must," Emma cooed. "I do believe that
Elizabeth Bennet is my favorite character of all time.
Such spirit, such loyalty. She is more than a match for
the stiff-necked Mr. Darcy."

"'Tis a most emotionally satisfying story," Aunt Mildred said with a small sigh. "Ahh, Mr. Darcy."

"I never understood what Miss Bennet saw in him,"
Gwendolyn could not resist adding. "He was pompous,
opinionated and far too stuffy."

"He sounds perfectly delightful." The viscount smiled.
"Though I generally prefer a story with a bit more adventure, like *Tom Jones*."

"My goodness." Aunt Mildred blushed. "Mr. Fielding
writes such scandalous, rollicking tales. They are hardly
appropriate for young ladies."

"But we have read it anyway," Gwendolyn drawled.
"Since it is not *intellectual* literature."

The arrival of the doctor neatly ended the discussion.
Aunt Mildred rushed to his side and Uncle Fletcher and

Emma quickly followed. Gwendolyn tried to slip from the room while the good doctor was giving her aunt, uncle and sister an update on Dorothea's condition, but the viscount blocked the exit. Deliberately.

"Meet me in the garden, near the rose arbor in ten minutes," he whispered. "We need to talk."

Gwendolyn turned her head away and pretended she did not hear him. And then she felt his hands on her shoulders. With only the slightest pressure he was able to draw her face close.

"The door provides us a bit of much needed privacy along with the perfect opportunity for a stolen kiss."

Gwendolyn hissed out a breath of annoyance and batted his hands away. "You must not say such things. Especially with my family so near."

"I told you that we need to talk."

"And I insisted there is nothing to be said."

He stepped back and bowed his head. "You have got to be the most obstinate, pig-headed female I have ever known, and given the number of my female acquaintances through the years, that is an extraordinary feat."

"Then you should be pleased to be well rid of me." Gwendolyn tried to smile, but it was a shallow, half smile at best.

His brow knit together in suspicion. "What do you mean?"

"I am returning home with my family this afternoon and since it appears that social events in the area will be curtailed for a while, 'tis doubtful I shall see you anytime soon."

He gazed at her with a worried expression. "We had an agreement."

"We did and I have honored it." Gwendolyn drew in a ragged breath and straightened her shoulders. "I have accompanied you to any and all events that you requested. But clearly there will be no celebrations until this mess with those horrid men who attacked our carriage last night is sorted out."

He dragged a hand through his hair. "I will call on you tomorrow."

"I will not be receiving visitors."

"Damn it, woman, you cannot avoid me forever!" Jason opened his mouth, then closed it. He maneuvered her farther behind the large doorway and snared her hands in his. "I love you, Gwendolyn."

The words melted over her. A brief stab of overwhelming joy, followed by a profound sense of sadness. The turmoil inside her was nearly suffocating, the frustration extreme.

In an act of self-preservation, Gwendolyn deliberately stomped on her own toe. The sudden, sharp pain brought her back to her senses, enabling her to pull away. "It does not matter. It cannot matter."

"It grieves me to see you in distress, Gwendolyn. The day following our night together should be one of joy and excitement." He looked unwaveringly into her face. "I should like to think that you came to me last night for other reasons besides loneliness and fear."

She met his eyes with a level stare. His words struck her deeply, compelling her to answer him honestly. "When I remember last night, I concentrate my mind on the undeniable beauty of what happened between us. 'Tis a memory I will cherish. But that is all it can ever be, Jason, a distant memory."

Gwendolyn took a deep breath, trying to ease the light-headed feeling that had suddenly overtaken her. It was such an odd sensation, as though she were standing outside of herself, listening to someone else speak those words. It would never be a distant memory. Jason Barrington would dominate her waking thoughts and haunt her dreams for the rest of her life. Of that she was very certain. But she would never tell him.

He folded his arms across his chest. "You are unaware of the circumstances. You must allow me to explain. Do not shut me out of your life. Please, Gwendolyn, do not toss away this chance for happiness."

She stared broodingly at him for several moments while her mouth grew dry. It was a foolish remark, yet he sounded so sincere. *Would it really be so awful to listen to what he had to say?* They fell into a short silence that was tense and uncomfortable.

Thankfully, Uncle Fletcher claimed their attention. "The doctor informs us that Dorothea has eaten a light luncheon and is taking a nap. He suggests we wait for her to awaken before she starts her journey home."

"But we can hardly continue to impose on Lord Fairhurst's hospitality," Gwendolyn protested. "Would it not be best to go home now and return later when Dorothea is ready to travel?"

"We have no idea when that will occur," Uncle Fletcher replied. "Far better to wait and leave together."

Gwendolyn gritted her teeth, annoyed with her uncle's logic. But it was impossible to argue, without arousing suspicion as to why she was so eager to be gone from Moorehead Manor.

"Might I suggest a visit to the portrait gallery," Lord Fairhurst said. "'Tis a very pleasant way to pass the time."

Uncle Fletcher declined, expressing an interest in an outdoor stroll. After a moment's hesitation Aunt Mildred placed her fingers on the viscount's proffered arm. "You are too kind, my lord. We have heard much about the quality and variety of the artwork in your gallery. 'Tis perfectly splendid to have a tour with you as our personal guide. Come along, girls."

"Stay by my side, Emma," Gwendolyn requested as she grudgingly followed her aunt and the viscount.

Though it was obvious that Emma would prefer to be with the viscount, she obliged. They entered the gallery, which was long and wide, with a procession of windows running along one side of the room. Gwendolyn was well aware of Jason's eyes watching her closely, so she made a point of keeping Emma engaged in conversation.

Gwendolyn knew Emma was excited at the opportunity to view the works of several famous painters and intended to ask her younger sister many questions in an effort to keep herself distracted. Her sister had always been interested in art and her talent was striking, if raw and untutored.

The paintings were all portraits of the viscount's ancestors, and he explained that his father had generously allowed him to transfer some of his favorites from their ancestral home to the manor.

"'Tis like a journey back through time," Emma remarked, as they slowly strolled down the gallery. "Not only is it a lesson in art history, but a reflection of the times in which these individuals lived."

Gwendolyn tried to lose herself in the beauty of the artwork. She was gradually starting to relax when Emma suddenly stopped short. She grasped Gwendolyn's hand and squeezed her fingers. Hard.

"My goodness, what is wrong?" Gwendolyn asked.

Emma's eyes grew wide and she glanced quickly, and fearfully, over her shoulder. Lord Fairhurst and Aunt Mildred were standing several feet away, out of earshot if they kept their voices lowered.

"The painting." Emma lifted her hand and pointed at the group portrait in front of them. Her hand shook noticeably.

Gwendolyn followed the line of her sister's quivering fingers. A noblewoman, dressed in an elaborate Tudor style gown was surrounded by a group of children. They were a solemn, handsome family and Gwendolyn could not help the smile that came to her lips when she beheld the two youngest children, an adorable pair of twin boys.

"What is wrong with the portrait?" Gwendolyn asked.

"I painted it," Emma whispered.

Gwendolyn laughed. "Very amusing."

Emma took a shuddering breath and slumped forward. "I am not joking. I painted that portrait."

"Oh, gracious, Emma, don't be absurd," Gwendolyn exclaimed in astonishment. "How in the world would one of your paintings end up in Lord Fairhurst's gallery?"

"I do not know." A dark ruddy hue tinted Emma's pale complexion. "I only know that is my work."

"Are you certain?" Bright sunlight streaked through the main section of the gallery. Gwendolyn shaded her eyes with her hand and gazed at the painting. "The glare of the sun is extreme and is no doubt distorting the painting. Perhaps if you view it up close, you will discover you are mistaken."

A thunderous expression descended over Emma's lovely face. "For pity's sake, Gwen, I am not a simpleton! I know my own work and I can state emphatically that I painted that picture."

The frantic tone of Emma's voice caught the viscount's attention. He shifted his gaze toward them. Gwendolyn's body tensed with the effort to appear innocent. He moved in their direction, but at that moment Aunt Mildred called out a question. Lord Fairhurst hesitated, then politely turned to answer.

"What are we going to do?" Emma cried out. "This is horrible."

"Tell me exactly what happened," Gwendolyn said. "How did you get permission to enter the manor and even view the paintings?"

"Uncle Fletcher arranged it for me. Through Mr. Ardley." Emma looked down and her clasped hands. "Last year I once again begged Uncle Fletcher to allow me to have proper drawing lessons. As usual, he was not inclined to grant my request and gave a list of reasons as long as my arm. I suppose in the end he felt sorry for me, or else I must have looked so pathetically upset, he said he would reconsider.

"A few days later he told me that perhaps he could arrange for a proper drawing master from London to teach me for several months in the summer. However, in the meantime, he had asked Mr. Ardley for permission for me to view the paintings at Moorehead Manor. Mr. Ardley agreed and even said if I wished, I would be able to study and copy any that I liked."

"I never knew about any of this," Gwendolyn said. "Why did you never tell me?"

Emma blushed to the roots of her hair. "I am very sensitive about my work, Gwen. I wanted to make the piece as perfect as I could before I let anyone see it. And when I realized it would never be good enough, I stopped trying to fix it."

Gwendolyn swallowed a small tightness in her throat. "Then how did it end up here?"

Emma's lids lowered. "I have no idea. The last time I saw it, the painting was hidden beneath a cloth in the small third floor room back home where I store my painting supplies."

"Who else knew about the painting?"

"No one." Emma's brow knit together in a fierce frown. "Except Uncle Fletcher. And Mr. Ardley, I suppose, though Uncle Fletcher was the only one who viewed it. Even though I knew it was flawed, I hoped the picture would show him I had potential and talent and would help persuade him to hire the drawing master."

"'Tis a most extraordinary tale," Gwendolyn mused. She struggled, yet could barely make any sense of what her sister was saying.

"We must tell Lord Fairhurst," Emma decided.

"No!" Gwendolyn reached out and grabbed her sister's arm, forcibly pulling Emma back.

Emma subjected her to an astonished look. "He must be told! The original was extremely valuable."

"Indeed." Gwendolyn cleared her throat. "But we need to consider first how to approach the matter."

"How to approach it! Gwen, have you quite lost your mind? There is nothing to consider. We must relate the truth to the viscount. At once."

"No! We must keep quiet until we have figured out what precisely happened," Gwendolyn insisted. Though she kept her expression impassive, her heart was racing as though she had just seen a ghost.

For a long moment they just stood there, darting uneasy glances at each other.

"Waiting will only make it worse," Emma insisted.

"For whom? Uncle Fletcher? Did he take your painting? You said he was the only other person who saw it."

"Why would Uncle Fletcher take it?"

"I don't know." Gwendolyn pinched the bridge of her nose between her thumb and forefinger, trying to block out the pain of a sudden headache. "We cannot go to the viscount with so many unanswered questions, Emma. Especially without pondering the biggest question of all. If that is your painting, then where in God's name is the original?"

Even as his hands moved swiftly, Cyril Ardley's eyes were trained on the door, ever alert to any interruption. He rummaged through the drawers of the viscount's desk, searching for the small purse of coins kept there to pay any unexpected household accounts.

It was not in its usual position. Cursing loudly, Cyril impatiently yanked open the other drawers. The viscount and his guests were enjoying an afternoon meal, but that could end at any moment. He had to hurry.

He pulled hard on the bottom left drawer, stunned to find it locked. Heedless of the implication, he grasped the silver letter opener. Using the sharp tip, he was able to jam the lock. The drawer slid open. The leather purse lay neatly inside, bulging with coins.

Cyril lifted the fat purse in his hand. The weight of it was a comfort; there was plenty inside. If he took but half, it would make a substantial payment.

"What the devil are you doing, Ardley?"

Cyril jumped and let out a startled gasped. "Bloody hell, you scared ten years off my life. What are you doing in here? I thought you were having lunch with the viscount."

"The meal ended twenty minutes ago." Fletcher Ellingham walked into the study, his eyes widening when he glimpsed the fat purse the steward held. "What have you got there?"

Cyril's hand started moving behind his back, but then

he stopped and sighed, giving up all pretense. "I'm hoping if I make a payment, the moneylender's thugs will go back to York and leave us alone."

"They have contacted you again?"

Cyril snorted. "They believed they were contacting me last night. Instead, they encountered the viscount and your nieces."

Fletcher's jaw went slack. "Those men were after you? It was not a random attack of highwaymen?"

"Hardly." Cyril bowed his head. "Last night Lord Fairhurst took the estate coach that I normally use, since his carriage had broken a wheel. Those ruffians stopped the coach, believing I was inside. They were sent by their leader, Hunter, to remind me that my monthly payment is overdue."

"How can you be certain?"

"I've spoken with the man the viscount captured. I suspected those men might be after me and the prisoner confirmed it."

Fletcher let out a whistle of astonishment. "The moment Lord Fairhurst learns the truth, it will be over, my friend. For you and me."

Cyril sat down hard on the desk chair and dropped his head into his hands. How had it come so far, so fast, and gotten so completely out of control? He thought back on all of his mistakes, wishing with all his heart he could have made better choices, better decisions.

"What am I to do, Fletcher?"

"Buck up, man. We shall think of something."

Cyril shook his head, knowing he had reached the end. He would be dismissed, disgraced, in all likelihood sent to prison. "I need to tell Lord Fairhurst the truth. At least I can salvage a shred of my dignity by revealing it all myself."

"Surely it hasn't come to that!" Fletcher let out a sharp breath. "There might be another way. Where is the prisoner being held?"

Cyril lifted his head. "In the cellar. It has a sturdy lock and no windows, so there is little chance of escape."

"Is there a guard?"

"No."

"Good. Then this should not be too difficult." Fletcher reached for a sheet of parchment, picked up a quill and moved the inkpot in front of the steward. "You need to write a short note. We will give it to this man, release him from the cellar and instruct him to bring it to the man in charge. What did you call him? Hunter?"

Cyril felt his spirits tumble. For just an instant, he had a glimmer of hope that this mess could somehow all be set to rights. "We cannot allow this man to escape! He is a violent criminal, responsible for harming one of your nieces. Don't you care?"

"Of course I care! That's why we need to get him out of Moorehead Manor as quickly as possible. If we aid this man in his escape, it will show good faith."

A cynical laugh escaped from Cyril's lips. "These are not honorable men. They are not interested in good faith. They only want their money."

"Then they shall have it." Fletcher pressed the quill into Cyril's hand. "Write and tell them you shall pay off the debt in full. It will take me a few days, but I know a way to secure a substantial amount of funds."

Cyril felt a bud of hope burst into his heart. "Enough to set everything to rights?"

"No, not everything." Fletcher sighed with genuine regret. "There is not enough to repay the viscount, but I can procure enough to get the moneylenders off your back."

"Good Lord, Fletcher, if you have had the solution within your grasp all these months, why have you not come forward?"

"The money is Emma's dowry. What's left of it. I had been hoping to keep the majority of it intact, but I see now there is no other way."

Cyril dipped the pen and began to write. It was difficult to compose a letter under such circumstances, but he managed to make his position to his creditor clear, including the date, time and location of where he would make the payment. He sanded the page, then held a thick stick of wax over the candle flame and sealed the note closed.

"'Tis done," Cyril said.

"Good." Fletcher nodded. "Now return that purse of coins where you found it. There is no need to be *borrowing* any more from Lord Fairhurst."

Feeling slightly embarrassed, Cyril placed the purse back in drawer and locked it, using the letter opener. He felt a sense of relief, yet it was tempered with true regret. "I wish there was another way," he admitted.

"So do I," Fletcher agreed. "But we have put ourselves in a serious predicament and inadvertently placed others in danger. 'Tis apparent that we must dig our way out before anyone else gets hurt."

Chapter Fourteen

Jason held on to his patience with surprising restraint as Mildred Ellingham oohed and awed with exaggerated pleasure over a portrait done by a lesser-known artist. His only consolation was that the sweet flattery she was now spewing replaced her previous questions about his ancestors and the artwork, both of which had been nearly impossible for him to answer correctly.

It was his brother Jasper who paid attention to such matters. Thankfully, Mrs. Ellingham had no art knowledge to speak of, allowing Jason to simply fabricate his answers. But even his somewhat vivid imagination was being tested to the limit at this point in the afternoon.

The moment he noticed Mrs. Ellingham engrossed in another portrait, Jason quietly slipped away and joined her nieces. He had expected Gwendolyn would keep her distance from him and she had, effectively using her sister as a shield. But he did not intend to let her leave the manor without having a frank and open discussion with her.

"You are scowling, Miss Ellingham," Jason declared. "Is anything wrong?"

Gwendolyn blinked. "Gracious, no. We were just admiring your lovely paintings, were we not, Emma?"

"Yes."

The nearly breathless squeak of that single word answer startled Jason. The response was most unusual for the bubbly, talkative Emma. Curious at what had agitated the sisters, he angled his head to see the painting. The sight made his blood suddenly run cold.

It was the forgery. He had deliberately left it hanging in the gallery, while keeping the original well-hidden in his bedchamber. "Is there something in this portrait that you find of particular interest, ladies?"

He watched the pair closely for a reaction, for a flicker of awareness, some sign that either of them knew there was something wrong with the portrait. Emma's hands twitched and Gwendolyn's back straightened with the perfect posture that would do a military man proud. They exchanged a heated look, but Jason had no idea what that meant.

Emma raised her hand and politely coughed into her fist, leaving Gwendolyn to answer his question.

"We were fascinated by the twin boys," Gwendolyn replied. "And thought it most interesting that twins seem to occur only in certain families. Apparently the phenomenon goes back many generations in yours."

"That is what has captivated you so completely? The twins?" His tone let them know he did not quite believe them.

"Yes," Gwendolyn insisted. "We thought they were adorable."

"Indeed. Very cute," Emma chimed in.

He glared at the women, but Gwendolyn barely flinched. Emma however, let out a half cough, half choke and turned her head away. He noticed Gwendolyn grabbing for her sister's hand and holding on to it tightly.

Jason felt a tic beginning in his left cheek as an awful suspicion began to take root in his mind. Was it possible that they knew something about the forgery? "I seem to recall that you paint, Miss Emma."

"I dabble," she croaked. "As do many other young ladies."

"Come now, you are being far too modest. Why, your own sister has praised your talents to me on several occasions."

"A sisterly prejudice, I am certain."

"I confess that is true." Gwendolyn's brief laugh was a brittle, false sound. "I have exaggerated Emma's talent, though not her enthusiasm and devotion to her art."

His lips curved. Oh, they were a clever pair, but each word they uttered spun them deeper into a web of deceit. Still, he could not ask too many questions without giving away what he knew. "Tell me, Miss Emma, do you subscribe to the notion that copying the works of the great masters improves your own technique?"

The swoosh of breath Emma exhaled was the dominant sound in that section of the gallery. "I have heard it can be of benefit to an aspiring artist," she finally whispered.

"Then you must avail yourself of my gallery," he offered, forcing a smile. "There are so many styles, so many choices. It should not be difficult to find a painting that appeals to you."

"Oh, heavens, I could never even consider doing such a thing." Emma turned wild eyes on her sister. He noticed Gwendolyn squeeze Emma's hand in comfort.

"'Tis a most kind and generous offer, my lord, but Emma's skill is not yet at this level," Gwendolyn added.

"That's right." Emma's head bobbed up and down at a frantic pace. "I would make a real muddle of it if I tried to copy such refined and complicated work."

"Nonsense. Challenging yourself is the only way to improve and sharpen your skills."

"Not always," Gwendolyn interjected sharply. "Attempting something you know is unrealistic is the surest road to failure. And heartbreak."

"I disagree. Though perhaps it would be best to start with a single portrait. A group painting, such as this, might be too overwhelming." Jason made a deliberate show of trying to decide which portrait would be a good subject. "Do you have a particular favorite, Miss Emma?"

"They are all far beyond my humble talent," she answered, her voice rising with panic.

"Truly," Gwendolyn added.

Jason once again considered the women. Gwendolyn remained stoic. Emma looked like a cornered mouse.

"Yes, Aunt Mildred?" Emma called out loudly. "I'm coming."

After hastily excusing herself, Emma rushed away. Jason decided she must have extraordinary hearing because he had not heard Mrs. Ellingham utter a word to her niece. More than likely Emma's quick wit had devised a clever form of escape.

"Oh, no. I'm not allowing you to run away too." Jason planted himself in front of Gwendolyn as she made a motion to follow after her sister.

"Run away? Don't be absurd. I was merely trying to join my aunt and sister. I do not understand why you would make such a ridiculous observation in light—"

"You're babbling, sweetheart. Something that rarely occurs unless you are very nervous or agitated."

Jason watched as Gwendolyn slowly brought herself

under control. The respite gave him time to consider all that he had just discovered and he concluded that in all likelihood Emma had been the one who had copied the painting. But why? And for whom?

Jason almost allowed his frustration to show. He needed to get Gwendolyn alone! It was impossible to have a frank and open discussion with her relatives so near. For a long moment he did not say anything, but his need to know the truth compelled him to ask. "Is there something you wish to tell me, Gwendolyn?"

He looked at her, just looked at her. And waited. There was a heartbeat of silence, then she shook her head from side to side.

Jason's heart sank.

In that instant, he wanted nothing more than to confront her with his suspicions. To drag her upstairs and produce the original painting and then demand to know what she and Emma knew of this matter. Instead, he took a much-needed moment to steady himself, forcing his mind to consider all the implications.

It would do no good to confront her in the heat of emotion, especially when he was missing several important facts. He had no proof that Emma had copied the painting, just a strong suspicion.

Logically, it made little sense. The women had no connection to the manor, no involvement with Ardley, the person Jason was certain was responsible for the missing funds and missing items from the estate. Yet somehow the sisters had become involved.

Still, it stung that Gwendolyn did not trust him enough to reveal the truth. Jason felt his hands tighten into fists, and purposefully relaxed his fingers. How was it possible that an already complicated situation had just become even more of a quagmire?

He caught her eye and was completely distracted when she suddenly smiled at him, going from pretty to beautiful in mere seconds. It reminded him instantly of how deeply he cared for her, how much she meant to him.

The early afternoon light spilling from the long windows haloed around her, but Jason knew she was far from an angel. Which suited him just fine. He wanted a real woman, a female with flaws and faults, with passion and life. After his disastrous relationship with Elizabeth ended, he had vowed that no woman would ever again have such an intense effect on him. That vow was now broken and a part of him rejoiced.

But there were several obstacles that needed to be overcome before he would be rewarded. And the only way Jason knew that would happen was if he and Gwendolyn were truthful with each other.

He was once again distracted from these thoughts by the arrival of the butler. The normally dignified Snowden scurried in and practically yanked Jason away from Gwendolyn, urgently requesting a private word. Jason fully expected to be told that Miss Dorothea was awake and ready to travel home, which made the servant's words even more shocking.

"'Tis the prisoner, my lord," the butler said in an anxious tone. "He's gone."

"Gone? That's impossible. I locked the door to the cellar myself and checked it first thing this morning."

"I know. I watched you as you performed the task." The butler frowned and shook his head in dismay. "At my instruction, Cook prepared a tray of food for the prisoner. I personally selected Collin and Arthur, two loyal footmen of the household who are blessed with common sense and strength, to deliver the food, believing they would be the best men for the job."

"What happened?" Jason asked with concern. "Were the men overpowered? Are they all right?"

"Collin and Arthur are unharmed. When they unlocked the cellar and called out, there was no response. They summoned me. We entered the room most cautiously, fearing a trick. But the joke was on us. The cellar was empty, the prisoner nowhere in sight."

"Are you certain? There are several large crates and heavy barrels down there, providing ample places to hide."

The butler sighed and hung his head. "We searched most thoroughly. The cellar is empty."

Jason's mind rushed through several possibilities, discarding each notion almost as quickly as it occurred to him. "Was the door forced open, the lock broken?"

"No, my lord. The lock is intact. And the door was secured before the footmen attempted to deliver the meal. I had checked it a mere twenty minutes prior."

Jason cursed under his breath as he stabbed his fingers through his hair. "You know what this means, don't you, Snowden?"

"Aye. The lock was opened with a key. And though it pains me greatly to say it, more than likely by someone in the household."

"Exactly."

The butler scowled, his face lined with distress. "What shall I do?"

"Instruct the men to search the grounds, though I suspect it is too late and our bird has flown far away. I also want Collin and Arthur available to give a full statement to the magistrate. He is due to arrive here shortly."

"Gentlemen, is there a problem?" Mildred Ellingham's voice held a sharp note of interest. She drew near, her expression curious.

At that moment Jason realized that Snowden must be

very distressed indeed, for the normally circumspect butler turned toward the older woman and blurted out, "The prisoner has escaped from the cellar!"

Upon hearing that, Mildred Ellingham let out a strangled cry of alarm, then dropped to the floor in a most ungraceful, undignified faint.

The Ellingham family began their journey home amid low clouds, a light drizzle and a rolling fog. Aunt Mildred had expressed deep concern at traveling in such bleak weather conditions, not to mention the danger of an escaped prisoner on the loose, but Uncle Fletcher had quickly dismissed his wife's objections. For once Gwendolyn was glad that her uncle rarely considered the opinions and feelings of the females in the family. Every minute she spent at Moorehead Manor was becoming torturous.

The viscount did insist that his outriders escort their carriage and, after initially presenting a mild protest, Uncle Fletcher agreed, if only to calm his wife's near hysteria. Aunt Mildred was convinced they would all be attacked and brutally slain—or worse.

Personally, Gwendolyn though the idea that a lone man fleeing for his life would attack a large carriage in broad day a perfectly ludicrous notion. But she had no intention of voicing any sort of opinion, fearing any mention of the escaped criminal would set her aunt's emotions over the edge.

Gwendolyn's greater worry was Dorothea, who looked pale and tired even before the journey began. She had limped to the carriage under her own power, but seemed exhausted from the effort. Though Gwendolyn was loath to overwhelm her sister, she found herself joining in with her aunt's fussing, placing a large pillow behind her sister's head and a light blanket upon her lap, even as Dorothea insisted she was far too warm already.

Preoccupied with her efforts to see to her sister's comfort, Gwendolyn was unaware of Lord Fairhurst's approach until Emma leaned over and hissed a warning into her ear. Gwendolyn glanced up, gazed out the carriage window and felt her entire body begin to shiver.

Lord Fairhurst was coming from the stables, looking handsome and surly as he walked in purposeful strides. He had removed his jacket and cravat. His collar was open at the throat, exposing a small part of his tanned chest and a few golden curls. Gwendolyn sucked in her breath sharply. The depth of her yearning shocked her.

"My cook has prepared a basket of treats for Miss Dorothea to enjoy once she is feeling better," the viscount announced, holding it aloft.

"How kind." Dorothea wanly smiled her thanks.

"Gwendolyn dear, fetch the basket from Lord Fairhurst, please," Aunt Mildred requested, as she too smiled at the viscount.

Gwendolyn turned to Emma in mute appeal, but her sister was seated on the far side of the coach, away from the door. Reluctantly Gwendolyn descended from the coach, not understanding why he couldn't just hand the damn basket up to them.

Not bothering to hide her annoyance, Gwendolyn reached for the hamper. "Farewell," she said, backing away the moment it was in her possession, but Jason put a hand on her arm.

"Farewell for now, my dearest. But we both know you cannot hide yourself behind this wall of resolution forever," he replied, his voice low, his deep green eyes darkened. "This is far from settled."

Gwendolyn felt her spine stiffen. Apparently Lord Fairhurst had a streak in him that went far beyond stubborn. No matter how many times she had told him to drop the matter, he refused. And she was hardly in a position to refute his statement without making a total spectacle of herself.

Instead, she leveled a positively frosty stare at him. "Good-bye, Lord Fairhurst."

But before she could make good her escape, he lifted her unencumbered, un-gloved hand to his lips. The heat flashed up her arm, making her breasts tingle as her entire body tightened with response. Gwendolyn swallowed hard, desperately trying to gather herself before anyone noticed.

"Stop," she said thickly, straining away from him. Gwendolyn tugged her arm, trying to pull free. He released her hand slowly, his touch lingering, sending shivers coursing through her body. Gwendolyn wanted to scream. Stamp on his foot, slap his face, anything to remove herself from his hypnotic spell.

The moment she broke free, Gwendolyn bolted inside the carriage, hardly caring how undignified she looked. She thrust the basket at her aunt and maneuvered herself as far away from the window as possible. Still, she had a clear view of Lord Fairhurst and could not help but notice how he stared at her so oddly, as if she were a puzzle he was trying to solve.

The man was most definitely a menace to her peace of mind. Yet try as she might, Gwendolyn could not help from turning for a final look as the carriage pulled away. He was standing where she had left him, one hand on his hip, his eyes on her, his expression part knowing, part inquisitive.

The carriage turned and the viscount faded from view.

Gwendolyn sighed, then closed her eyes, burning the sight of him into her brain.

It was not a long distance home, but the ride seemed interminable. Aunt Mildred babbled, Dorothea dozed, Emma stared out the window pensively and Gwendolyn brooded. She envied her uncle's freedom, riding on his horse beside the coach despite the light rain. Fresh air and brisk exercise were precisely what she needed to occupy her mind, but that was an impossibility, especially since she was dressed in her evening gown from last night.

Eventually, they arrived home safely, in spite of Aunt Mildred's dire predictions. The moment they descended from the carriage, Aunt Mildred began fawning over Dorothea, leaving Gwendolyn and Emma the chance for a private word.

"When shall we confront Uncle Fletcher about the painting?" Emma asked in an anxious whisper. "He is usually in a more congenial state of mind after a good meal. Perhaps it would be best to wait until after supper?"

"*I* will speak with him shortly," Gwendolyn declared.

"But Gwen—"

"No, Emma, I'll not involve you."

"Oh, Gwen, I am already involved," Emma said mournfully.

"Let me handle this, Emma." Gwendolyn drew back her shoulders and raised her chin. "Uncle Fletcher, might I have a word with you, please?"

The older gentleman paused as he handed the reins of his mount to the waiting stable boy and gave her a sour look. "I am rather busy right now. Can it wait until later? Or better still, until tomorrow?"

Gwendolyn shook her head. "No. I must speak with you as soon as possible."

"I don't have time."

"I'm afraid that I really must insist." Gwendolyn pushed her hands behind her back and moved froward, standing toe to toe with her uncle. "I won't keep you long."

Gwendolyn could see the annoyance building in him, from his posture to his tone of voice. "Well, then, girl, speak! I already told you I haven't got all day."

"Not here. Somewhere private. Your study?"

Uncle Fletcher's grimace turned to outright annoyance, but he did not argue. He stomped into the house, down the hall toward his study. Gwendolyn followed close behind.

He moved to sit in the large leather chair behind his desk, indicating she should take the seat on the opposite side. Gwendolyn quickly did as he suggested, surprised to find her knees were knocking together. Schooling herself carefully to hide her nervous agitation, she racked her brain trying to decide the best way to begin.

"Emma and I made a most distressing discovery today in the portrait gallery at Moorehead Manor," she said. "A piece that Emma painted hangs there, in place of the original work."

"What a preposterous notion. Emma's painting, indeed. Naturally you are mistaken." Uncle Fletcher's face creased into a frown. "I certainly hope you did not mention this to the viscount. He would no doubt think you both mad."

"We said nothing to Lord Fairhurst, mainly because we were at a loss to explain how this had happened. That is why I needed to speak with you."

"What could I possibly know about Lord Fairhurst's paintings?"

"A great deal, I believe." Narrowing her eyes, Gwendolyn fixed them on his. "'Tis said that confession is good for the soul, Uncle."

"I have nothing to confess," he insisted with a smug grin. Gwendolyn continued staring at him, saying nothing. Eventually he seemed to realize she was not going to drop the matter until she answered her question. Slowly his smile faded. "It appears you have already drawn your conclusions and they put me in a most unflattering light."

"I apologize," Gwendolyn replied with an uncertain sigh. "I should not speculate. But you must agree 'tis past time that we were truthful with each other."

"Honestly, Gwendolyn, this does not concern you and there is no need for you to worry about it. I have everything well in hand."

"Normally I might be persuaded to walk away, but in this instance I find that I cannot. Not with Emma so directly involved." Gwendolyn folded her hands primly in her lap. "Emma told me that you arranged for her to copy the painting. She also said that you were the only one who viewed it when she was finished. Therefore, I must conclude that you know how it got from the third floor storage room here to the portrait gallery at Moorehead Manor."

Uncle Fletcher picked up the letter opener in front of him and began tapping the tip of it noisily on the desktop. "I was near speechless when I saw it. Such a beautiful painting, a most extraordinary effort. I had never before realized Emma had such talent. Pity she is but a girl. If she were a man, she would already be established as a master artist."

The distraction of her uncle's genuine praise for Emma's talent lasted but a moment. "How did Emma's painting come to hang in the manor's gallery?" Gwendolyn asked.

"I put it there."

Gwendolyn looked at her uncle levelly. "What happened to the original? Was it damaged?"

"No. It was sold."

"By whom?"

Uncle Fletcher's jaw was rigid. "Cyril Ardley handled the actual transaction, but I took an equal share of the money, so I must accept an equal share of the responsibility."

"You stole the original painting?" Gwendolyn asked, trying to keep her wits about her. Suspecting her uncle's involvement and learning the truth were two entirely different matters. Her face pale, Gwendolyn pressed her hand to her forehead.

"We did not steal it. We borrowed it. We always intended to return it, but then time passed and there were other more pressing accounts to settle. The painting had to wait."

Gwendolyn looked at her uncle, dumbfounded, her eyes going so wide she feared she must look like a demented bullfrog. "Oh, Uncle Fletcher, how could you? 'Tis bad enough that you put yourself in such a perilous predicament, but to involve Emma was disgraceful."

Uncle Fletcher walked over to the sideboard and poured himself a drink. "Damn it, girl, I never meant for it to turn out this way. The idea to switch the paintings only came to me after I saw how well Emma was able to copy the original.

"Ardley located a dealer interested in the piece. I wanted to sell him the copy, but Ardley feared an expert would detect it was a fraud. Instead, he struck a deal that would allow us to buy back the original. We both thought the copy would hang in the gallery for a few weeks, a month at most. By then we would have enough funds to reclaim the original and put it back where it belonged. No one would be the wiser."

"But why would you do such a thing?"

"For money!" The serious set of her uncle's face shifted to a grimace. "Our funds were perilously low, so we sold the portrait to a dealer in London who guaranteed us the opportunity to buy it back within six months."

"But you never did." Gwendolyn found herself blinking like the village idiot. "Why do you so desperately need money?"

"I have creditors and bills that must be paid. I tell you, 'tis no small task to keep you and your sisters."

Gwendolyn bristled at the idea that she and her sisters were such an extreme expense. They lived a modest life, genteel and comfortable, but far from extravagant.

"In addition to our dowries, I know my father left an allowance to be paid per annum for our upkeep," Gwendolyn said. "Surely that covers our obligations and places no significant financial burden on you and Aunt Mildred?"

Uncle Fletcher made a face. "Your quarterly allowance is a paltry sum that barely keeps you girls in bonnets and gloves."

Worry shivered down her spine. Were they really such a burden? But why had Uncle Fletcher never mentioned this before? And why had he not asked them to economize more? Gwendolyn opened and closed her mouth several times, trying to think of a way to phrase her next remark without causing too much offense.

"No matter how pressing your debts, you still did not have the right to steal from Lord Fairhurst," Gwendolyn finally muttered.

"I've already explained about that," he replied defensively. With an exaggerated sigh, Uncle Fletcher finished his drink, then poured a second.

"Yes, well, that plan seems to haven fallen short. I think it is paramount that you buy back the painting and return it as soon as possible. Surely there are other funds you can tap? At least temporarily." Gwendolyn gazed out the window as she racked her brain for a solution. "My dowry, perhaps?"

Uncle Fletcher could not hold back a short, closed-mouth cough and Gwendolyn knew she had come painfully close to uncovering another truth.

"It won't help," he said morosely.

"Is it all gone?" she asked quietly. Her uncle nodded and Gwendolyn slowly let out the breath she had been holding.

"After the scandal broke, I knew you would never marry. Initially, I thought the funds could be added to Dorothea's and Emma's portions, but my need became pressing so I used some of the money. Within the year, it was gone."

The assumption that she would never marry, while truthful, still stung. "Yes, Uncle Fletcher, we all know that I am destined to end my days alone, with no family of my own. If I am lucky, I might become a favored aunt to Dorothea or Emma's children. Or else I shall have to be content living alone and raising a large quantity of cats."

Uncle Fletcher's face scrunched in puzzlement. "You don't like cats."

Gwendolyn rolled her eyes. "Then I suppose I must learn to tolerate them."

She jumped up from her chair, crossed the room and joined her uncle by the sideboard. Boldly she poured herself a splash from the crystal decanter, then downed the contents in one long swallow.

"What are you doing? Young women don't drink strong spirits. Especially at this hour of the day."

"And guardians don't spend their charges' dowries to pay off their debts. And by the way, I do not believe it is only household expenses that has gotten you into this mess. I know how much you like to gamble." Gwendolyn glared up at him, almost daring him to deny it.

He was silent for a long moment. The he turned with a jerky movement, picked up the decanter and poured her a second drink. "You've got me there, girl."

Gwendolyn's shoulder's slumped. "What of Dorothea? And Emma? Is there any of their dowries left?"

"Dorothea's is gone. Along with most of Emma's." Uncle Fletcher rubbed his fingers together. "But I have prospects that should offset the losses. There won't be as much as your father left them, but I'll do the best I can. Fortunately there are no prospective suitors for either of the girls, which should give me time to replenish part of what I borrowed."

Borrowed! Stolen was a more apt description. Gwendolyn's head could not seem to stop spinning. It was difficult to dredge up any pity, despite how repentant her uncle looked. She had just discovered that he had spent most of their dowries on gambling debts and had even resorted to stealing from the viscount to pay off additional monies he owed. The truth hurt, cut deep, but Gwendolyn knew lashing out at her uncle would not ease the pain. Nor would it solve the problem.

"What is to be done, Uncle Fletcher?"

"I will make amends, Gwendolyn. I swear it."

Gwendolyn looked down at the whiskey in her glass. The first swig had tasted terrible, burning her throat all the way down to her stomach. But in the ensuing minutes, she had noticed a slight numbing in her fingers and at the edges of her mind. She scrunched her nose tightly and took another sip, shuddering until the liquid hit her nearly empty stomach.

Oh, how she wished with all of her heart that her uncle was telling her the truth. She had to believe that there was a way out of this mess and she knew she had little choice but to wait, hope and pray her uncle could resolve the matter.

"We must stand together or fall alone," Gwendolyn declared solemnly. "I will keep your secret, Uncle Fletcher. And trust that you do right by all of us."

The terrible tension between them broke. "Leave it to me. I will do you proud, my girl. I swear."

Gwendolyn smiled wanly and nodded. The emotions of the day, along with the whiskey she had so rashly consumed, were starting to catch up with her. After her uncle departed, she sat alone in the study, trying to regain her equilibrium.

Emma found her that way, twenty minutes later.

"My goodness, I've been looking everywhere for you. I'm nearly bursting with suspense. What happened?" Emma asked, as she came into the room.

Gwendolyn's eyes found Emma's and she tried to smile with encouragement. "It was Uncle Fletcher, Emma, just as you suspected." Quickly Gwendolyn related the conversation she just had with their uncle. Emma's concerned face turned to sheer panic as she digested the news, so clearly distressed she did not even acknowledge their uncle's praise of her artistic talent.

"Oh, this is horrible! We must tell Lord Fairhurst the truth," Emma insisted.

"I know." Gwendolyn reached up and sharply pinched the bridge of her nose between her thumb and forefinger, trying to ease the ache in her head. "But I promised to give Uncle Fletcher some time to fix this mess on his own. I cannot go back on my word."

Emma bit her lip, her brows lowering. "I do not have a good feeling about this, Gwen."

"Neither do I." Shaking her head, Gwendolyn muttered a stringent oath. "But for now, we must wait and put our fate, and our faith, in our uncle's hands."

Chapter Fifteen

Three days later Jason sat in his bedchamber for more than an hour, with a decanter of his brother's finest brandy as his only companion. Sunshine streamed into the room, making everything glow with nauseating cheerfulness. It was almost more than Jason could bear. Stumbling from his chair, he yanked the heavy window curtains closed, yet was unsuccessful in keeping out all traces of the light. Still, the gloomy dimness was a vast improvement.

Returning to his seat, he lifted the crystal decanter resting on the small table beside him, splashed a liberal amount of the amber liquid into his glass and tossed it back. Then he slowly poured another.

"Hell and damnation!" A male voice swore loudly as the individual stumbled over a low stool, almost toppling to the ground.

Feeling mildly curious at the interruption, Jason glanced over at his valet and grimaced. "Go away, Pierce."

The servant regained his balance and tugged his jacket into place. "I have long suspected that you had the potential to make brooding an art form. I see now my theory is proven correct."

Ignoring his employer's orders to leave, the valet went directly to the window and pulled open the curtains. Sunlight once again filled the room.

"Leave them closed," Jason ordered in a sullen tone.

"And break my neck in this gloom? I think not, sir. I am an aging man with failing eyesight. I do not relish the notion of spending my days limping because a badly broken limb did not heal completely. You may return the chamber to a state of mourning once I have finished with my chores."

Jason grumbled, sipping at his drink. "Has the post arrived? Were there any letters for me? Any correspondence at all?"

"There was nothing."

Damn and blast! Three days. It had been three days since he had last seen Gwendolyn. She had refused to receive him when he called upon her, and she had not responded to the urgent letters he wrote and hand delivered to her home. The one thing she had done, with unfailing determination, was keep her promise to avoid him.

Jason lifted his glass, realized it was nearly empty, then reached for the decanter. He ignored his valet's loud sniff of disapproval and poured himself a generous portion.

"If I may be so bold as to inquire, is there a particular reason why you are swilling such fine brandy like gin?"

"'Tis not the smooth taste or fine quality that I am savoring," Jason responded. "I seek the numbing effect."

"Ah, yes. I saw the sheets the other morning."

Jason paused, the glass at his lips. "The sheets?"

"On your bed. The bed where Miss Ellingham spent the night."

Straightening in the chair, Jason gave his servant a warning glance. "What was wrong with the sheets?"

"The linens were bloodstained. A virgin's blood, if I am not mistaken." The valet removed a coat from the wardrobe, inspected it, then began vigorously brushing one sleeve. "I am also well aware that you did not sleep in the guest chamber that night, even though you asked the housekeeper to air the room and made a point of thanking her the next morning for doing such a fine job."

The liquor burned a path down Jason's throat and hit his stomach sickeningly fast. "Does the entire household know about me and Miss Ellingham?"

"No. I rumpled the bed in the guest chamber and mussed the coverlet so the maids would be none the wiser."

"Thank you."

Pierce scowled. "I did it not only to protect Miss Ellingham, but to preserve your brother's good name. He would not be pleased to be labeled an adulterer. Many individuals do not seem to care one whit about their employee's opinions, but I have been told that the viscount enjoys his staff's greatest respect. Besides, 'tis highly unlikely Lord Fairhurst would become involved with another woman. I understand that he is most devoted to his lovely wife."

"Nauseatingly so," Jason replied, but the bite of sarcasm was missing from his tone. Instead, there was a great feeling of envy. Jasper was devoted to his wife, besotted completely, and she with him. It was precisely the type of relationship that Jason had avoided for so long and now he craved almost compulsively.

Had he come so close yet again, only to lose it at the last moment? He shuddered with regret.

"I assume you will require a bath and a shave later this

afternoon?" the valet asked. "Though perhaps it might be better to wait until tomorrow before you pay a call on the Ellingham household. It would hardly make a stellar impression if you arrive three sheets to the wind when you ask Mr. Ellingham for his niece's hand in marriage."

Jason scrubbed his face with his hands, then laughed darkly. "Mr. Ellingham will think me mad if I say I wish to propose to his niece. They are all very aware that Lord Fairhurst is a married man."

Pierce's left eyebrow rose. "Ah, yes, well that should make it an even more interesting visit, revealing your true identity. Might I suggest that you instruct Miss Ellingham to break the news to her uncle before you arrive? That might make it a more civilized encounter."

"She doesn't know." Jason's chin fell forward onto his chest as he stared into the bottom of his nearly empty glass. "She believes that I am Fairhurst. I waited too long to tell her the truth. I tried several times before she left the manor the other morning, but could never get her alone. Now she refuses to see me."

"This is a dilemma." Pierce scratched his head. "You could write her a letter, yet this is hardly the sort of predicament that is easily explained. It would more than likely confuse her further."

"A letter would do little good. She has returned the first two unopened. My third request was a meeting between us and I have yet to hear from her. But I am not hopeful."

"What are going to do?"

Jason lifted his head. "Drink?"

"That never solved anything." To emphasize the point, the valet moved the decanter to the opposite side of the room. Unconcerned, Jason watched, knowing the servant would not dare to remove it from the bedchamber.

"I have offered to marry her," Jason insisted. "It was the proper thing to do after the night we spent together."

"How romantic." The valet moved to the washstand and straightened the towel placed beside the porcelain bowl. "All women adore the notion of being married due to a guilty conscience."

Jason frowned. "It wasn't like that, Pierce. I love her and I told her of my feelings. I realize of course that she had difficulty believing my sincerity."

"Perhaps that was because she thought you were already married?" The valet rolled his eyes. "Even a female lacking Miss Ellingham's intelligence would doubt your intentions."

"Obviously." Jason drained the final drop of liquor from his glass. "Despite my very inadequate offer of marriage, I am determined to have her for my wife."

"Then you have no reason to act so bleak," Pierce replied. "Things will eventually work themselves out. I would think that being in love would bring you some measure of happiness."

"Unfortunately, there are other complications."

The valet drew in a deep breath and released it slowly. "They will vanish once Miss Ellingham learns the truth."

"Not entirely." Jason rose to his feet and stretched out the stiffness in his back. "I fear she is somehow connected to the financial discrepancies at the estate."

"Are you certain?"

The question made him slightly dizzy, for that was the crux of his dilemma. No matter how hard he had tried, Jason could not wrap his mind around Gwendolyn's involvement. He simply could not believe that she could be so devious, so dishonest. But he had seen for himself how jittery and nervous she was in the portrait gallery around the forgery.

She clearly knew something and had elected to hide it from him. But why? Was she protecting her sister, who had possibly painted the forgery? Or someone else? Her uncle, perhaps? He was a good friend of Ardley's.

"I am only certain of my misery and confusion," Jason replied in a somber tone.

"Then best leave this problem to be solved at another time. I fear you have pressing issues to deal with at the moment."

"Something more pressing than my future, Pierce?"

"Indeed. Forgive me for not mentioning it sooner. The darkness when I first entered the room addled my brain and clouded my memory. Your brother, the *real* Lord Fairhurst, has just arrived. He is waiting in the drawing room to see you."

Three days. It had been three days since she had last seen him. Three days also since she had learned the awful truth about her uncle and his dishonorable way of trying to cover his gambling debts.

Gwendolyn had tried to forget Lord Fairhurst, had tried to push from her mind how much she cared about him, how much she still wanted to be a part of his life. She knew it was an impossibility, yet her stubborn heart clung to the hope that some miracle would occur and she would be free to indulge in her feelings.

However, Gwendolyn was a woman who listened to her head. Though she might dream of a miracle, she knew she must face the reality. There would be no magical fairy tale ending for her and the viscount and she was determined to accept the truth of the situation. It would have been far easier if she could simply walk away from the viscount, but the situation with her uncle made it impossible.

It was imperative that she keep some line of communication open between herself and Lord Fairhurst. If Uncle Fletcher was unable to set things to rights, Gwendolyn knew it would be up to her to plead his case, to somehow convince the viscount not to throw her uncle in jail and ruin all their lives.

So, as much as she would have loved to ignore this latest request from Lord Fairhurst to meet with him, Gwendolyn had decided she must acquiesce. The note had been delivered yesterday. The previous two she had returned unopened, but for some reason she had been compelled to open this one. Already she worried that she had delayed too long in responding.

Even as a child, she was not one to gnaw and wiggle at a loose tooth. Instead, to the sheer horror of her sisters, she would tie a piece of thread around the offending culprit and then swiftly pull. A moment of sharp pain and the problem was solved. Of course, the fact that she was now likening Lord Fairhurst to a tooth was merely a further example of how bizarre her life had fallen.

Telling only Emma where she was going, Gwendolyn had set out on horseback directly after luncheon. The stable boy at the Moorehead Manor greeted her politely, promising to look after her mount. As expected, the butler answered Gwendolyn's knock.

"Good afternoon, Snowden. Is his lordship at home?" she asked as she tugged off her riding gloves and jammed them into the deep pockets of her riding skirt.

"Miss Ellingham! Good afternoon."

Uncharacteristically flustered, the butler glanced over his shoulder. "Is Lord Fairhurst expecting you?"

"Not precisely. But he did request that I call upon him. I will wait in the drawing room."

Barely taking notice of the sudden paleness in the butler's face, Gwendolyn sailed past him. She easily found her way, but drew to a halt when she entered the room, discovering it was already occupied. By Jason.

He turned as she entered, lifting a monocle up to his left eye and peering intently through it. "Good afternoon."

His voice was calm, almost bored. After three days of impassioned notes and messages from him, this was hardly the reception she anticipated. Thinking this might be a deliberate move to keep her off balance, Gwendolyn felt her temper begin to rise.

"For pity's sake, put that thing away. We both know your eyesight is perfectly fine. You look like a fool when you flail it around. A pompous fool."

His eyebrow shot up as he slowly lowered the eyepiece. "Apparently you got up on the wrong side of the bed this morning, and your disposition has worsened as the day wore on. Still, there is no need to take out your sour mood on me. Especially in my own drawing room."

"I am here at your command, my lord." She glared daggers at him, emphasizing her displeasure at his attitude. "Reluctantly, I might add."

"I demanded your presence? Impossible!"

A small sound of frustration escaped from her lips. "I give you fair warning, my lord, I have no patience for your tomfoolery today. So stop acting like a ninny."

"A ninny? Saints above, did you just call me a ninny?"

"'Tis more polite than saying you are an ass," Gwendolyn retorted in a sickening sweet tone.

For a heartbeat he glared at her. She could not read the quick expression that passed behind his eyes, but it made her feel very wary.

"Your sharp tongue and rude behavior are intolerable. I demand an apology," he declared, clenching his jaw.

"You can demand whatever you like. 'Tis what you seem to do best—make endless demands on people."

"Now see here, young woman, if you do not cease behaving in this uncivilized manner immediately, I will have you forcibly removed from my home!"

Young woman? Had he just called her a young woman? What game was he playing out now? Gwendolyn opened her mouth, but the angry retort died on her lips. Lord Fairhurst truly was furious. Though his voice remained calm and never rose in volume, the depth of his anger radiated from every fiber of his being.

She paused, leaned forward and stared closely at the man standing before her. His face and body were etched in her memory, yet there was a small, subtle difference she could not easily discern. His features were handsome, his eyes green, his hair the same shade of blond.

He was dressed rather formally for an afternoon at home. The garments, as usual, were of the finest quality, well cut and expertly tailored, yet somber. Though she could not help but notice they lacked the usual flair and boldness she always associated with the viscount. Finally, she noticed a heavy gold signet ring glittering on his left hand. Her brows drew together in a puzzled frown. Jason never wore a ring.

A sinking feeling of dread washed over her entire being.

"Who are you?" she whispered.

"I am Fairhurst." Squinting, he lifted that ridiculous monocle again. "More importantly, who the devil are you?"

His question was preposterous, yet confirmed her suspicions. He was not Jason. Gwendolyn rubbed her temples with the tips of her fingers. "But that's impossible. You cannot be Fairhurst. I am well acquainted with Lord

Fairhurst. And while 'tis true you bear an amazing resemblance to him—"

Gwendolyn suddenly ceased talking, her mind tripping ahead over the facts. He was not the viscount, yet he looked exactly like him. What was so preposterous to imagine suddenly became crystal clear. This gentleman was Jason's brother, Jason's identical *twin* brother. But why had he referred to himself as Fairhurst?

"Ah, I see the light of truth has gone off in your head and struck you speechless." He brushed an imaginary bit of lint off his navy blue coat and gave her a slight grin. "I confess to enjoying the silence."

"You are Jason's brother," Gwendolyn said slowly.

"I am."

"But you claimed to be Lord Fairhurst?"

"I am Fairhurst." There was a shade of scorn in his tone. "'Tis a peculiar situation, I grant you. Circumstances of fate gave me that title and eventually I shall inherit the earldom from our father. I am the elder twin, the oldest son, though in truth I was born a mere seven minutes before my brother."

For a moment, Gwendolyn could not catch her breath. She felt a peculiar tightness at the back of her throat, as the emotions lingered inside her. Jason was not Lord Fairhurst. But why had he deceived her?

"Have you recently arrived at the manor?" she croaked out.

"Just a few moments ago, actually." He moved toward her, then pulled up short, as if suddenly realizing the extent of her distress. "It appears that you were under the misconception that my brother was the viscount. I assure you there is a logical explanation."

Gwendolyn's eyes glistened as she peered up at him.

Jason had lied to her, had lied to them all. But why? "Logical perhaps, but acceptable? I think not, my lord."

There was a commotion at the door and they both turned to see the intruder. Jason strode into the room, then stopped suddenly. His eyes rounded with shock and a stinging curse fell from his lips.

The nearly mind-numbing confusion gripping Gwendolyn rapidly developed into an overwhelming sense of betrayal. She looked from Jason to his brother, noting once again the subtle differences between the two. Lord Fairhurst was stiffer, more formal, more distant. Jason was more polished, more stylish, in a casual, yet sophisticated way.

Her lips quivered. From anger, from vexation, from pure emotion. Jason took hold of her elbow and she nearly jumped at his touch.

"I can see that you are distressed," he said.

"Because you have lied to me? Lied to us all, *Lord Fairhurst*?" She swallowed deeply. "I have never met a pair of twins before. The resemblance is quite extraordinary."

"It has diminished slightly as we have aged," he insisted.

"Hardly." She bit her lips fiercely to repress her tears, to distract the pain. "Since I now know you are not who you claimed, may I be so bold as to ask your real name?"

"I am Jason Barrington."

"And your brother?"

"He is Jasper Barrington, Viscount Fairhurst."

"Ah! You chose to reveal your true first name to me, Jason. How extraordinary. I suppose I should be deeply flattered at the honor." She curled her hands into fists and faced the viscount. "I must inform you, my lord, that your brother took to being addressed as Lord Fairhurst like a duck to water. I suspect he secretly covets your title."

Jason stepped forward and reached for her hand. "Gwendolyn, please, you must allow me to explain."

"Why? So you can make an even greater fool of me?"

She twisted away, eyeing the door, but Jason blocked her exit. Worried she would lose the very tentative hold she had on her emotions if he touched her again, she turned to his brother.

"I wish I could say it has been a pleasure to finally meet you, my lord." Lifting her chin, she swallowed valiantly to dislodge the lump of emotion in her throat. "But I, unlike other members of your family, prefer not to indulge in lies."

Having distracted Jason's attention to his brother, Gwendolyn seized her slight advantage and ran for the doors. Ignoring Jason's pleas for her to stop, she stepped past him and hurried out the door. Heedless of the fact that the exertion was making the fierce red color she felt blossoming on her cheeks even more prominent, Gwendolyn broke into a run.

The quiet she left behind was complete. Jason's eyes met his brother's, and the two stared at each other for several seconds in stunned silence. Pushing past his brother, Jason tried to follow Gwendolyn, but a strong grip on his arm held him back.

"I take it you refused to follow my advice and have assumed my identity while living here?" Jasper asked.

"My God, Jasper, you have not lost your talent for stating the obvious." Jason leaned his head forward and closed his eyes, desperately trying to sober his mind. The half-decanter of brandy he had recently consumed was still swirling in his head, along with the picture of hurt and horror on Gwendolyn's face. "Could you not have gone along with the charade for a few hours or at least waited to talk with me before revealing your identity?"

"No," Jasper said as he released his grip. "I warned you the idea was ludicrous. No good ever comes of deception, brother."

Jason slowly opened his eyes. "Spare me the two-penny philosophy. What am I going to do? How am I going to fix this mess?"

"Why would it be necessary? I assume she is one of the local girls? From her ensemble, I deduced she was respectable, yet clearly a woman of modest means. Her opinion is unimportant."

"I had forgotten what a pompous ass you can be at times."

Jasper straightened the line of his coat, then glanced at his brother with interest. "She insulted me. More than once."

"Well, she is highly intelligent."

"Spirited, too. And very attractive, if one appreciates such dark, striking hair and eyes." Jasper reached out his hand again, this time patting his brother on the shoulder. "Still, no need to look so glum. I vow you will forget her as soon as you return to London."

"You don't understand. I love her, Jasper."

"Of course you do," Jasper said with a knowing grin. "Just as you love all women. That's hardly a surprising revelation."

"I want to marry her."

Jasper did not even bother to hide his astonishment. "Does she know?"

"Yes, she knows." Jason paced about the room, his eye on the whiskey decanter. But he knew the last thing he needed right now was another drink. "I've already asked her, but she refused, believing I was you and therefore already married." Jason threw himself into a chair and sighed loudly. "God, what a colossal mess I have made of everything."

"No more than usual," his brother said cheerfully.

Jason lifted his head and glared at his twin. "Stuff it! I am in no condition to tolerate your jibes. If you push me, I will probably take a swing at you, and that will do no one any good."

The mood in the room suddenly shifted. "You really are serious about this woman?" Jasper asked.

Jason felt a bit of his heart crumble. "I am."

"Then you had best get your sorry ass out of that chair and hurry after your dear Gwendolyn. If you manage to catch her before she leaves the estate, you can try to explain, apologize profusely and then beg her forgiveness. Trust me, brother, you would be a fool indeed to let a woman like that slip from your grasp."

Jason did not have to be told twice. He raced out of the drawing room, ran down the back hall and out of the house through the French door that led to the terrace. Assuming from her riding costume that Gwendolyn had come on horseback, he rounded the side of the terrace and charged toward the stables.

He caught her just as the stable boy was leading her horse to the mounting block. "I'll take care of that, George," he said.

Gwendolyn's eyes flashed fire at him, but she waited until the servant obediently left before speaking. "Save your breath, sir. I have no interest in hearing anything that you have to say. I only wish to be gone from here as quickly as possible."

"Gwendolyn, please. I beg that you give me a chance to redeem myself. Life is far too short to waste your time being angry over a misunderstanding."

"Oh, so you did not intentionally deceive me? Lie to

me? Lie to all of us? Did I merely misunderstand when you claimed to be Lord Fairhurst?"

He felt his jaw go taut. "I was wrong to continue the deception after we became so close, but you must know that was never my intention. I came here on business for my brother and decided it would be better accomplished if I assumed his identity."

Her eyes flickered, their dark depths turbulent with emotion. "The real Lord Fairhurst seemed surprised at your little masquerade. Did you also neglect to inform him of your plan?"

Jason ran his fingers through his hair, then clasped the back of his neck. "Jasper and I were in disagreement about the best way to handle the situation."

"Why does it not surprise me that you refused to listen to anyone's opinion?"

"All right! I was wrong. I admit it. But I ask you, why do you think I have been so anxious to speak with you these past three days? After the night we spent together, I realized that I should have told you the whole truth. I tried to get you alone, to tell you everything, but you purposely eluded me. And you have continued to rebuff all my attempts to see you."

"I will concede that you have tried to make amends, but 'tis a clear instance of too little, too late," Gwendolyn replied, her voice laden with skepticism. "There were opportunities too numerous to count before that morning when you could have told me the truth, yet you elected to continue with your deception."

"Do not walk away from me, Gwendolyn," he pleaded, his voice sounding hollow, even to his own ears.

She stopped and turned her head. Her face had gone pale. "You leave me no choice."

Her expression was cold and unyielding. But there was

also something unbearably poignant and lonely about her that tugged relentlessly at his heart. He hesitated, trying to find the right words, the right gesture that would somehow make this nightmare end.

"Please, Gwendolyn, think hard before you make this decision. Love is too fragile and fleeting to discard in such haste." He blinked the emotion from his eyes only to find the pain in hers. "Marry me."

She crossed her arms over her chest. "Even now, you dare to insult me."

"Insult you? I have offered you a sincere and forthright proposal of marriage."

Her head dropped, hiding her face from view. "I could never trust you. Therefore, there can be no marriage between us."

"Stop acting like a fool," he said with a harshness he regretted. Her strong mistrust worried him. He continued in a softer tone, without recriminations. "Can you not see that I love you, Gwendolyn?"

She jolted, her head coming up. "I see only that you lied to me, sir. I see only that I cannot trust you or believe you."

"These past weeks have been a joy to me and I would have that joy continue forever. Marry me."

She remained silent for a long time. Anger clouded her eyes, then they cleared as she brought herself under control. Jason's palms began to sweat.

"'Tis too late for us, Jason." Her voice was thick with emotion but he could not distinguish the source. It could have easily been anger or grief. "I beg you, do not speak of it again."

"You cannot simply—"

"I said do not speak of it!"

Jason fell silent. Blood beat at his temples as he tried

to find the words that would somehow stop this nightmare, would prevent his whole world from shattering around him.

Gwendolyn's foot slipped as she started to mount her horse. Jason stepped forward automatically to offer her assistance. At first she tried to push him away and do it herself, but it was impossible. He felt her stiffen when his hand touched her boot, but she said nothing as he hoisted her into the saddle.

She adjusted her seat and gave him a final cold glare, inclining her head gracefully. Then she turned the horse north. He hesitated, on the verge of grabbing for the reins, all the while knowing that physically preventing her from leaving would not change things at this point.

"Gwendolyn—"

"Good-bye, sir," she said, abruptly dismissing him, shutting him out.

His emotions in turmoil, Jason stood in the empty courtyard and watched her ride away, without once looking back.

Chapter Sixteen

Slowly Jason returned to the house, going into the drawing room just as his brother was coming out. The brothers saw each other at the same moment and there was an awkward pause.

"I was going to look for you, to see if I could help in some way," Jasper said.

Jason shook his head. "Too late. She's gone."

"No need to ask how it went. Your expression tells all."

Jason shoved a dangling lock of hair out of his eyes, more shaken than he cared to admit. "I need a drink."

He proceeded into the drawing room, headed straight for the whiskey decanter and poured himself a full glass. But after one sip, he put it down in disgust.

"Doesn't help much, does it?"

He turned and watched as his twin settled into the armchair beside the unlit fireplace, an expression of sympathy shining from his eyes.

"Why are women such stubborn, emotional creatures?" Jason asked, crossing to the fireplace, leaving his glass behind.

Jasper shrugged. "'Tis part of their nature, part of their charm and allure."

"I do not find it in the least bit charming," Jason grumbled.

"Does that mean you intend to give up on her?"

"Hell, no!" Jason felt the already heated blood in his veins rise. "When have you ever known me to let a female get the better of me?"

Jasper considered the question, his gaze thoughtfully focused on his brother's face. "For the most part your affairs have gone as you anticipated, yet there have been a few times I suspect the results were unplanned. I can recall one delicate ballet dancer who walked away from your relationship with an emerald and diamond necklace *and* the tiara to match what must have cost your entire quarterly allowance. And there was that Rubenesque, opera singer—"

"I was speaking metaphorically." Jason grimaced at his brother, taking the chair opposite him.

"What about Elizabeth?"

Jason paused, stretching out his long legs toward the empty fire grate. "I was twenty-two, Jasper. A boy flush with his first love: brash, confident, arrogant. I was too absorbed in my own feelings, my own wants and needs to realize that Elizabeth did not return my deep regard. I fully admit that I handled her rejection badly and in the subsequent years used that hurt to justify my reckless, scandalous behavior."

"And now?"

Jason stared at his brother, but his gaze turned inward. "I made the decision to change the direction of my life before I came here, before I met Gwendolyn. I'm not sure why—perhaps it was seeing you and Claire so happy together that gave me the push I needed to reform, to mature, to finally start acting responsibly.

"'Tis odd, but previously my solitude had never disturbed me and then suddenly I knew that I wanted more from my life. Yet I was not exactly sure what *more* I truly wanted until I met Gwendolyn. With her, it became very clear."

He did want more from his life. He was a gentleman by birth, but had hardly acted that way for several years. He had loved Elizabeth, been hurt by her rejection and had refused to love again. He had refused to be vulnerable or dependant or trusting. He had adopted the attitude of protecting himself, doing what he pleased, and when he pleased, and damn the consequences.

Jasper narrowed his eyes thoughtfully. "Does Gwendolyn return your affection?"

Jason's mouth took on a grim line. "Stop looking so damn worried. I have learned a thing or two about women since Elizabeth. Gwendolyn has very strong feelings towards me."

A wry grin curved Jasper's lips. "Yes, I saw for myself precisely how she feels about you."

"She was upset at learning the truth," Jason insisted defensively. "I know she cares deeply for me. She is a wonderful woman, kind, generous, loving and above all moral. She must love me or else she would not have—"

Jason stopped suddenly, realizing he was revealing far too much. There was a short and very pointed silence. He hoped the moment had passed safely, yet one look at his brother's stormy face and he knew Jasper had caught his meaning.

"Do not tell me that you have bedded this woman? Not while masquerading as me, the recently married Lord Fairhurst?"

"I refuse to answer that vulgar question," Jason retorted, the guilt rising within him as he stood up. "A lady's reputation is at stake."

"If my wife ever suffers one moment of humiliation due to your actions, I will strangle you," Jasper declared in a menacing tone.

"This will never involve Claire." Jason sat back down with a sigh. "I understand your need to protect your wife, but the rest is all meaningless. You have always cared far too much about your all-too-proper reputation and what others think of you, Jasper. 'Tis damn annoying."

"And you care too little," Jasper shot back, his eyes bright, his mouth turned down at the corners with deep disapproval.

They each brooded for a moment, then slowly the tension in the room simmered down a degree. "Whoever said that twins think and act alike was a complete moron," Jason said, attempting a nonchalant tone.

Jasper peered at him. "Indeed."

Jason fidgeted restlessly. He felt irritable and defensive and none too proud of his actions. "I love Gwendolyn. And I will have her, no matter what it takes."

"She looked none too happy when she stormed out of here. You could be in for a long siege."

"I know." Try as he might, Jason could not keep the edge of disappointment from his voice.

Suddenly, a broad grin skimmed Jasper's lips. "I confess, it brings me great pleasure to see you act this way."

"What way? Oh, you mean like a besotted fool?"

"No, like a man with a purpose, a man with a goal he will push himself to achieve, despite the odds."

Jason allowed himself a shallow smile. "You are supposed to boost my confidence, brother. Not force me to see the grim reality."

Jasper looked wry. "If I were a betting man, my coin would be on you."

"Thank you." Jason inclined his head, glad that they were back to a civilized tone. He always hated being at odds with his brother, an unfortunate state that was too often the case in the past.

"Let's move to another subject for the moment," Jasper suggested. "Tell me what has been going on here. Besides impersonating me and ruining my reputation with the community and my good standing among my servants."

"Aside from the one incident, which I will not discuss, everything has gone well. Though I have not yet achieved the results we wanted regarding the missing funds."

Jasper's lips twitched. "Your impersonation was far from successful. Snowden knew who I was the moment he opened the door."

"Of course he knew who you were," Jason said with a snicker. "We are identical twins."

Jasper was shaking his head. "He clearly knew that I was not the same man who had been in residence these past few weeks. He knew that I was the real viscount, and that you, the man who had claimed to be me, were not."

"I don't believe you. He has treated me with the utmost respect and deference since my arrival. He believed I was Lord Fairhurst."

Jasper looked offended at the very idea. "Granted, Snowden was not aware that he had been duped until he saw me. Without the comparison he was fooled. But no longer."

Jason gave a disbelieving snort. "I still do not believe that Snowden knew the truth. Hell, there are times that Mother still gets us confused."

"Mother lacks the keen observation skills of a properly

trained butler." Jasper's face set. "The next time you see Snowden, I fully expect you to apologize to him and explain that I was unaware of your little stunt and upon learning about it, fully disapprove."

Jason waved a dismissive hand. "He's a butler."

"Precisely. And as such should be afforded the respect he is due." Jasper met his eyes very directly. "I stole him away from Lord Devonshire, at a considerable cost, and the man has more than proven his worth."

As if on cue, the butler entered the room, pushing a tea cart laden with savory indulgences. He never hesitated for an instant, coming to place the cart in front of Jasper. The true lord of the manor.

"He most likely remembered what you were wearing," Jason grumbled beneath his breath, still finding it difficult to accept that the butler had been able to unmask the deception.

"Snowden, my brother has something to say to you," Jasper announced.

Feeling ridiculous, yet knowing on some level that he was wrong, Jason stood on his feet. "As you obviously are aware, for personal reasons, I assumed my brother's identity when I arrived at the manor. Lord Fairhurst was unaware of my deception and has just informed me that he is scandalized by my behavior. I therefore feel compelled to offer my apologies to you."

"That is most gracious of you, sir." The butler's face suffused with color. "Since you have brought it up, I will say that there were several occasions these past few weeks when I did puzzle over your behavior, for it was most out of the viscount's character. But you remained a gentleman throughout and the staff held you in the highest esteem and regard."

"So I didn't muck it up too badly?" Jason asked.

"Not at all." The butler's lips twitched into the faintest of smiles. Jason decided this was a sign of approval. "I am certain that I am the only member of the staff to uncover the truth."

"I would be most obliged if you kept it that way," Jasper cut in.

The butler bowed graciously. "You can always count on my discretion, my lord."

"I know. Thank you."

Jason resumed his seat while the butler departed. The tea remained untouched, though Jasper munched on a small sandwich. As the viscount ate, Jason told him what he had uncovered about the estate finance and the missing items.

"Did you find out anything from the London antique dealer?" Jason asked as he concluded his tale. "Did he possess any other items that belonged to you?"

"I don't believe so." Jasper finished his sandwich and reached for another. "I made the mistake of bringing Father with me and compounded it by not telling him the reason I wanted to visit the shop. I feared he would create a scene."

"He does get rather passionate about his antiquities."

"Too passionate." Jasper's eyes narrowed. "It all started fine; Father enjoyed browsing among the various items, but then he spotted two vases he swore were fakes and demanded to see the owner."

"Oh, no."

"A rather heated argument ensued, several harsh words were exchanged, followed by insults, and then we were asked to leave the premises."

"The proprietor was unaware you were peers of the realm?" Jason asked, finding it hard to believe a shrewd businessman would toss an earl and a viscount from his establishment.

"Father saved that bit of information to lend weight to his parting remarks. By then, the damage had been done and we had lost the opportunity to uncover any possible information."

"'Tis unlikely you would have learned anything substantial," Jason replied.

Jasper shrugged. "We will never know."

"How do you wish to proceed?" Jason asked.

"I appreciate all you have done here, but 'tis obvious that you have hit a wall in your investigation. You know how important it was to me to keep this inquiry a private, family matter and I thank you for your efforts."

"My failing efforts."

Jasper's expression hardened. "Hardly. You have determined that Ardley is the logical suspect and I agree. He had the access and the means to accomplish the theft of my funds and my property."

Jason leaned forward in his chair, warmed by his brother's sincere words of praise. Yet he still felt disappointed that he had not been able to neatly solve the problem. "There are inconsistences in the estate ledgers that Ardley has already explained. As for the items taken and replaced with fakes, I have no solid proof that he was involved."

"We don't need it," Jasper said, without rancor. "I am his employer. He is answerable to me for his actions and activities concerning my estate. I will confront him; he will answer."

"What if he lies? Denies all knowledge? We might never recover the items that were stolen."

"That is a risk I am willing to take. They are only things, Jason, objects. They can be replaced."

Jason jerked a little straighter in his chair. "Don't ever let Father hear you say that about his vases."

Jasper smiled and nodded his head. "I will concede that some of these antiques are considered irreplaceable, but no matter. What if a maid accidentally knocked one over while dusting? Or a rambunctious child pulled it to the floor? It would be gone just as completely."

"Are you telling me you place no value on them?"

"Of course they have a value, but I will not put that above the human element," Jasper said, rubbing at his chin. "Ardley has been an excellent steward these past years. I'm sure you don't remember, but his predecessor truly was stealing us blind. The tenant farms were in disrepair, the manor house practically falling down around my ears."

"That was Father's fault. The property had not yet passed to you."

Jasper nodded. "Father was an absentee landlord for decades and therefore must assume part of the responsibility for the sad state of the manor and lands. It was the main reason he was eager to give me the property when I came of age. He admitted he had done a dismal job and hoped that I could do better."

"But it was the influx of your money that has made all the difference, that made the estate profitable. I would think you would take it as a personal insult to discover that someone has been stealing from you."

"I did take offense. That's why I asked you to come and investigate."

"If Ardley is the culprit, he must be punished," Jason said gently.

"Naturally." Jasper shifted uncomfortable in his seat. "But his fate shall be my concern and mine alone. Ardley is a good man. He has worked hard for me for many years. Under his direction, we have nearly tripled the output of these lands. The last thing I want to believe is that he is false and treacherous. That was one of the reasons I needed you to address this matter for me. I knew I would have difficulty being objective."

"Has that changed?"

"I'm unsure. As you say, there is no direct proof." Jasper looked beyond his brother's shoulder for a moment before returning his gaze. "If Ardley is involved, as we suspect, I believe there is an underlying reason. And I fully intend to give the man the benefit of the doubt and the opportunity to explain it to me in person."

"That is your right," Jason concurred.

Jasper nodded. "Shall we summon Ardley now or wait until this evening?"

Jason sighed. "It will have to wait until tomorrow morning. Ardley is gone from the estate; he told me earlier he was traveling to the next county to inspect a bull he was considering for purchase. He will not return until tomorrow morning. If I had known you were coming, I would have requested that he wait and attend to this livestock business next week."

Jasper impatiently drummed his fingertips on the arm of his chair. "We must meet with him the moment he returns. I had not planned to stay at the manor for more than one night and am loath to alter my schedule. I'm most anxious to return to my wife."

Jason smiled at his brother's agitation. "How is my dear sister-in-law these days?"

"Blossoming," Jasper replied with a smug grin.

Jasper continued to smile. Jason, puzzled at the sly expression, tried to figure out what his brother was saying.

"Oh, for Christ sake, she is pregnant," Jasper muttered.

Jason came to attention. "Already?"

"We have been married a few months." Jasper lifted his chin and puffed out his chest a fraction. "Though I will confess we are feeling ridiculously proud of ourselves."

"Aren't you the clever pair? Mother and Father must be over the moon at the prospect of having another grandchild to love and spoil." Jason gave his brother a sidelong glance. "Perhaps you can show up Meredith and Dardington and produce the first grandson."

"It is hardly my goal to outshine our sister and her husband. Though having a son to raise seems far more reasonable to me," Jasper admitted. "But more important is that Claire be safely delivered of a child who is hale and hearty."

"Claire is young and strong. She will do splendidly. Probably better than you."

Jasper bowed his head in slight embarrassment. "I have been fussing quite a lot. That's another reason I decided to journey here. Claire insisted she needed a small respite from my overprotective presence, if only for a fortnight."

Even though he knew Claire loved her husband dearly, Jason could understand his independent sister-in-law's feelings. "She is probably missing you already and will certainly welcome you back with open arms."

"That is my fondest hope." Jasper reached for the final sandwich on the tray. "Is there anything else I need to know before we meet with Ardley tomorrow?"

Jason hesitated. The magistrate had determined the incident on the road was due to highwaymen, prompting a more vigilant attitude toward travel from the locals. As for the estate business, more and more Jason had come to believe his suspicion that the forgery in the gallery was painted by Emma. But the very last thing his tenuous relationship with Gwendolyn needed was more complications.

"I think you are well prepared for the confrontation with Ardley," Jason finally replied, pushing aside the momentary sting of guilt he felt. "If we come up short, I have a few ideas on where to go next for some answers."

It was long after midnight when the two riders neared their destination. The hedgerow along the roadside faded from view as they slowed their horses and turned toward a small copse of evergreens. All was quiet, peaceful. Too peaceful.

"Tell me again why we are meeting in such an isolated area at this time of night?" Fletcher asked, pulling his mount beside his companion, his legs cramping from the long ride.

"It's the only way to preserve our secret," Ardley replied. "We can hardly invite men like these to dinner."

Fletcher gazed skyward, catching glimpses of moonlight and stars through the green canopy of branches. Despite the pleasant warmth of the night, he shivered. He felt chilled to the bone, his confidence in their plan wanning with each mile they rode.

"Why not meet at an inn or an alehouse?" Fletcher asked. "I, for one, would feel safer if there were witnesses about."

"These men would never agree to being seen in such a public place. Anonymity is the key to their success."

Fletcher's brows drew together in a sharp frown. "I don't like it."

"Neither do I." Ardley's face was tight as his eyes anxiously searched the horizon. "But we are hardly in a position to dictate any terms."

"Our circumstances will change once they see what we have brought them." Fletcher patted his coat pocket, which bulged with a heavy purse of coins. "Once we have these money-lending leeches off our backs, we can settle our debt with the manor accounts."

"All in good time." Ardley removed a spyglass from his breast coat pocket and held it to his eye, gazing at the horizon. "Paying off this debt will leave us with little reserve funds. It could take a long time to restore the remaining funds to the estate."

"But this is a most important first step."

"Aye. Let us hope we succeed in solving this problem."

Once again, Fletcher tilted his head back to stare at the night sky. He studied the tree branches that swayed and clattered overhead, trying to keep away the worry niggling at his mind.

Soon, they heard the sound of hoof beats, followed by an abrupt curse, then silence. Fletcher held his breath, sure his rapidly beating heart could be overheard by Ardley. Suddenly, the riders came crashing through the trees, taking the two waiting men by surprise.

Fretfully, Fletcher turned toward Ardley, taking note of the steward's pale face and eyes, which blinked uncertainly.

There were three mounted men facing them. They were all unfamiliar and Fletcher was relieved not to recognize any of these fellows as the man he had released from the manor's cellar, the one who had been involved in the carriage incident.

"Right on time," the man in the center said as he nudged his horse forward. "That bodes well."

"Let's get down to business, then," Ardley said. "We have brought your money, Hunter. Just as you instructed."

"Hand it over," Hunter replied. "I haven't got all night."

With nervous fingers, Fletcher fumbled in his pocket

and withdrew the leather pouch. Hunter held out his hand expectantly, but Fletcher worried about keeping his skittish horse under control if he moved too close to the other man's mount, so he tossed the purse with a high arc directly at the moneylender.

Hunter caught it with his left hand. The hint of a smile that was visible in the dark vanished as he bounced it through the air, weighing it carefully in his palm. "It feels too light."

"It's all there, down to the last coin!" Ardley exclaimed. "We would never be so foolish as to try and cheat you."

"I said, it feels too light," Hunter insisted.

"Well, then count it," Fletcher replied, trying to add an edge of command to his voice. "As we said, 'tis all there, everything that you are owed."

Hunter shoved the pouch into his pocket, then coolly pulled open his coat. A pistol protruded from the waistband of his breeches, the silver handle glittering in the moonlight. "I don't need to count it. I know it's light and I know there isn't enough coin."

Fletcher's vision clouded. Shaking his head, he firmly reminded himself to stay clam. Any display of fear or panic would give Hunter even more of an advantage. "There are over five hundred guineas in that pouch. Enough to clear our debt."

"What about the interest?"

"That includes the interest," Ardley sputtered.

"Says who?" Hunter challenged.

Fletcher stiffened his back. "Really, sir, you are being most unreasonable. If you would—"

"Shut up. I'm not talking to you."

Fletcher swallowed his remaining rant, then dipped his chin and stared down at the reins clutched limply in his riding gloves. He immediately regretted his outburst, for it had drawn Hunter's attention to him.

"We have paid you the agreed upon sum, including interest," Ardley insisted. "Our business is concluded."

Hunter's expression sharpened, his slate-gray eyes narrowing. "Not the way I see it. There is a penalty for late penalties, and the added inconvenience of having one of my men injured and another imprisoned in the manor cellar."

"We released your man," Ardley defended.

"And the injury can hardly be blamed upon us," Fletcher added. "Your men attacked the wrong carriage."

Hunter let out a grunt, then dismounted his horse slowly. Fletcher expelled the breath he had been holding on a sigh of relief. The moneylender was not a tall man. He was fair, willowy, of indeterminate appearance and dress. Hardly a serious foe.

"You have both cost me far more than you are worth," Hunter stated calmly. "And I become a most difficult man when I am angered."

There was a distinct undertone of menace in his voice. Fletcher gulped, knowing with a sickening dread that he and Ardley had seriously underestimated their foe.

"Name your price, Hunter," Ardley said, the panic clearly heard by everyone. "We will pay whatever you demand to end this once and for all."

There was silence. Fletcher could see Ardley twitching nervously. Yet nothing happened. Hunter remained silent and still, as though he had not heard the offer. Fletcher could feel himself beginning to quake in his boots.

"You will never collect any more money if we are dead," Ardley finally said.

"There are two of you. I only need one breathing man to settle the debt. That makes one of you very expendable." Hunter's eyes narrowed into lethal slits and he balanced forward on the balls of his feet, in a clearly threatening gesture. "In my experience, this type of persuasion is most effective. Miraculously, the survivor always produces the necessary funds very quickly."

For a moment it seemed as if Ardley's face might crumble, but his composure held. "Let my friend go. I was the one who contracted the loan with you."

"Then you should be the one to settle the debt." Casually, Hunter bent forward to withdraw a knife from its sheath in his boot cuff.

"But I shared in the use of the money," Fletcher blurted out, helplessly trying to protect his friend. "We carry the burden of debt equally."

Hunter paused to stare at their stricken faces, then threw back his head and laughed. "Maybe I will keep you both alive. For the moment. But this cannot go unpunished. You need to be taught a lesson. One that you will remember, one that others who do business with me will hear about and consider." His voice lowered to a whisper. "No one dares to cross me."

"We did not try to cross you," Fletcher said, desperately trying to hold on to some measure of calm, when he felt such a strong need to yell and scream and vent his growing frustration.

Hunter motioned to his men. They obediently dismounted and advanced. The one moving toward Fletcher was built far differently from his boss. He was a large brute of a fellow, with a misshapen nose that had been broken several times, thick, muscled arms, and large meaty hands.

Fletcher tried to force the bile that filled his mouth back down his throat. Like so much of his life these past few years, this meeting had been a bad idea, a foolish

plan, not well thought out and certainly not well executed. Now they would suffer the consequences.

The brute's boots made a sharp noise as he drew
closer and the gnawing anxiety in Fletcher's belly shifted
to outright panic. With one strong motion the man
reached up and yanked him off his horse. Fletcher stumbled, trying valiantly to stay on his feet. He noted that
Ardley had also been roughly taken off his mount,
though he appeared to have no difficulty in standing.

The ruffian raised his arm, pulling it back. Realizing
what was coming, Fletcher ducked, but not in time. The
blow landed square on his jaw, knocking him to the
ground. The pain exploded behind his eyes, white hot
and fierce. A second blow followed and as the blackness
engulfed him, Fletcher felt a twinge of genuine regret for
all the mistakes he had made, all the wrongs he had done.

But foremost of his regrets, was the realization that he
had been unable to fulfill the sincere promise he had
made to Gwendolyn.

Everything was very far from being set to rights.

Chapter Seventeen

Gwendolyn crossed to the opposite side of her bed-chamber, trying to decide if she could manage the buttons down the back of her gown on her own. It was past time for bed, but she had dismissed Lucy hours ago and did not wish to call for the maid, thinking she had probably already gone to sleep.

Besides, Gwendolyn preferred her solitude. The tumultuous events of the afternoon still resounded in her head. She crossed the room, and stood near her small writing desk. The note from Jason lay partially hidden beneath an inkpot. She reached for it, intending to rip it to shreds and toss it in the unlit fireplace, but the sight of his bold, strong handwriting stirred something in her heart.

Had she made a grave misjudgment turning away from him today? Was she being too harsh and unforgiving? Was she risking her greatest chance for happiness because of her stubborn pride? Or was Jason truly a dishonest, deceptive man?

Dimly she heard the hall clock mournfully sound the hour. It was late; hopefully the rest of the household was asleep. But Gwendolyn doubted she would get any rest tonight.

Occupied with her thoughts on the opposite side of the room, she did not hear the bedchamber door open. But she had a sudden awareness that she was no longer alone.

"Good evening, Gwendolyn."

The sound of his voice gave her gooseflesh. With a sharp sigh, she turned slowly to face him, her heart thumping painfully. "How did you get in here?"

"Emma took pity on me. She snuck me in through the kitchen and made sure the hall was clear before leading me to your room."

Realizing her palms were damp, Gwendolyn dried them on the skirt of her gown. She was not ready for this, not ready to face her feelings, not ready to face him. "Leave at once, or I shall scream. Very loudly."

A disarming smile lit his handsome features. "Nothing would please me more. Your screams will bring your family and the servants running and when I am found in your bedchamber, you shall be well and truly compromised.

"The fact that I am not Lord Fairhurst will be viewed with great relief when it is revealed, for I shall naturally offer to do the right thing. Your aunt will be overjoyed, your uncle will agree to my proposal and you will be forced to marry me."

A rushing noise roared between her ears. "So that is your plan?"

He shrugged. "I am a desperate man, Gwendolyn.

"You are disgraceful!"

He ran his finger slowly over the coverlet on her bed. The movement was slow and sensual. "True, I have no shame, no pride when it comes to you. I will accept you as my wife by whatever means I can. I realize this is not the optimum way to begin a life of wedded bliss. I much prefer it to be your choice."

A hot flush spread over Gwendolyn's cheeks. *Deep breaths,* she admonished herself. She continued until she was composed enough to confront him. "I have already made my position quite clear on the matter. I will not marry you."

"I understand your need to punish me, but dearest, by doing so you are also punishing yourself." He took several steps closer. "Won't you reconsider?"

Gwendolyn's ears warmed with embarrassment. Perhaps the need to strike back at him was a part of her refusal, but it went far deeper. "What you did was no small matter, sir."

"True. Yet I had my reasons, as I tried to explain earlier. And I did attempt to tell you the truth, but you refused to listen."

"I know that, but as I told you before it makes no difference. There were numerous chances to reveal the truth. Good heavens, we spent an entire night and a fair portion of the morning together. Alone. You could have told me who you really were then."

He shot her a chiding look. "With you in my arms, in my bed, I had far more important matters clouding my mind."

She stared back at him, feeling deeply the hurt that was shining from her eyes. "Ever since that night I have been desperately fighting my emotions, trying to understand them so I could cast them away. And that morning! My God, I thought you were deranged, to be speaking of marriage when you already had a wife."

"Gwendolyn." His hand came up to cup her cheek. "I never meant to make it so difficult. To hurt you. If I could change just one thing that I have done in my life, right just one of the many wrongs I have committed, it would be not telling you the truth that night."

His sincerity touched her bruised heart as astonishment took all the words from her mind. "I don't know what to say, what to do," she finally whispered.

Jason languidly moved closer. "I need to know that you have forgiven me, Gwendolyn. That we can get beyond this and move forward with our lives."

Jason's gaze never left hers. Gwendolyn's mind protested vehemently, but her heart, oh, how her heart begged her to reconsider. It seemed that even against her wishes her heart wanted him, needed him.

Everything hung on this moment. If she could well and truly forgive him then they had a real chance for a future life together. But if she could not . . .

"How can I ever trust you?" she muttered.

"It will take time, but I can prove to you that I deserve your trust. And your love." His voice went soft. "Please, for both our sakes, let me try."

For a long moment she thought hard on his words. He made it sound so simple, so easy. Was that all it truly would take? All she need do was open her heart and forgive him?

Gwendolyn leaned toward him, closing the remaining space between them, feeling all the thoughts and warnings and doubts warring within her mind. Rising to the tips of her toes, she kissed him on the cheek.

Jason had his arms around her before she could move away from him. "I need much more than a maidenly kiss from you, Gwendolyn," he said, and then he brought his mouth down hard on hers.

It is amazing how a body's desire can betray you, Gwendolyn thought as she melted against him, her arms twining around his neck. Desire surged through her, hot and hard and completely overwhelming. She found herself remembering the feel of him inside her body, the intense emotions and connection she had experienced when they had made love.

And now, something within him was reaching out to her. She could feel it as substantially as the sun on her face, or the wind in her hair. Jason could be hers. If she dared to truly risk her heart.

Confused, conflicted, Gwendolyn began to move away, breaking the searing touch of her mouth against his. Almost instantly, a hollow ache bloomed inside of her, sharp and painful. Jason tightened his hold on her waist, refusing to allow her to retreat farther. And then he waited.

Gwendolyn stood still, her nerves taut with anticipation, her entire body flushed with restless desire. No matter what the circumstances, she knew that this man was the person who completed her, who made her whole. With all his charm and faults, his sensuality and reckless behavior, she could not deny that he was her one true love.

Gwendolyn looked at Jason. His eyes held a spark of hope for their future and her heart clenched hard enough to tighten her throat. After all she had suffered, all she had lost, was it truly possible to finally find her happiness? Would she be able figure out a way to get beyond her feelings of betrayal and give him a second chance?

It took a long moment to find the courage to say what she was thinking. She raised her chin. "And if I asked you to leave?"

"I would leave." He let out a hard laugh. "But I would return. Again and again and again."

His words shifted through her mind, his intent very clear. He would not give her up. She laid a hand over her heart. "Then perhaps it would be best if we began anew. A fresh start, with no lies between us."

A smile of pure delight crossed his face, but the look in his eye was of hunger, a yearning for her that made Gwendolyn shiver. She felt the heat radiating from his body and drew toward it. She wanted to lose herself in it, to be enfolded in his embrace, in his love, until they were once again joined together.

Her body craved the perfect pleasure that Jason could arouse, but it was her heart, yearning for fulfillment, that pushed her forward. She caught his face in her hands, angled her mouth over his and kissed him and suddenly nothing mattered but the feel and taste and smell of her lover.

Jason insinuated his thighs between her legs, pressing against her sex as their tongues mated. Gwendolyn in turn devoured him with her mouth with a fierce possessiveness. There would be no half-measures in this relationship.

Slowly, his kiss changed. His lips softened, his tongue teased, his hands slid into her hair. Her blood thickened, the dangerous heat began low in her belly. Gwendolyn knew in that instant she had made the right choice. She would never want anyone else in her bed, or in her life. She would never feel this intense connection, this sense of belonging with any other man. Only with Jason.

Gwendolyn could feel the tension growing inside her. She couldn't seem to catch her breath, couldn't halt the rush of sensations assaulting her. She struggled briefly against the fog engulfing her, then gave herself over to it completely, trusting Jason to keep her safe, to bring her joy.

Just as the cravings grew even more intense, he tore his mouth away from hers. His warmth left her and she stumbled forward, her knees weak, her senses muddled. She saw him stride toward the door, securing it tightly before turning the key in the lock. Unbuttoning his shirt, he stormed back across the room. Moments later Gwendolyn was lying on her back on the bed, writhing uncontrollably as Jason worked feverishly to remove her clothing.

The layers of garments melted away as he kissed each part of her before tossing her clothes aside. She watched him through half-closed eyes as her body was unveiled, shivering in anticipation. There was nothing gentle or calm in his movements. Their need was too great, their passion too strong.

When her chest was bared, he bowed his head and drew his tongue over the tipped peak of her nipple. At her urging, he then closed his mouth over it and suckled. She gasped, her hips surging upward and he sucked harder. Gwendolyn closed her eyes and threaded her fingers through the golden waves of his thick, gorgeous hair, wantonly holding him at her breast.

Gwendolyn had never felt so many sensations at the same time. The pleasure was intense, but she knew there was more, much more, to come. And she wanted it all.

As if sensing she was ready, Jason released her nipple, biting and nipping his way up her chest and throat.

"Do you like that, my love?" he whispered in her ear.

She sighed deeply and rubbed against the length of his body. Then she felt his warm hands on her thighs as he slipped her undergarments down past her knees.

He turned slightly, yanked off his coat, ripped away his waistcoat, then pulled his shirt over his head. A wave of passion broke over her at the sight of his naked chest, sculpted with muscle and dusted with golden hair. The moonlight cast a beautiful warmth to his skin and her fingers itched to touch him.

He untied his breeches with one hand and turned back to her. Gwendolyn set her hands on his wide, hard chest and leaned forward for another kiss. His eyes shimmering with heat, Jason obliged her. As they kissed, his hands roamed, molding her hips, sliding down her stomach.

Gwendolyn's bed creaked loudly as he pushed her onto her back and partially covered her with his naked form. The moments of staggering loneliness she had experienced for the past four years faded from her being. Gently, Jason nestled his face in the valley between her breasts, showering kisses on her naked flesh.

Once again he suckled at her breast, his beard softly abrading the tender, delicate mounds. The muscles of his arms and legs held her down, making her feel secure and cherished. His tongue laved and circled her nipple, sending streams of white-hot desire shuddering through her body.

Restless, impatient with excitement, she cried out and pushed him away. He lifted his head, smiled, then kissed his way lower, until his lips were moving along the flat of her naval and then the smooth skin of her upper thigh. The roughness of his jaw grazed lightly against her skin, creating another dimension of tingling sensation.

Gwendolyn's legs shifted restlessly as she felt his warmth breath teasing the aching triangle between her

legs. He kissed her there, sweetly, gently, his hands caressing as he moved a little lower.

"You shouldn't," she whispered, her eyes opening
wide. "'Tis so amazingly wicked."

"You are mine," he insisted. "And I promise to do all
manner of wicked things to you tonight. There are no
more secrets between us, Gwendolyn. We will do anything, everything, to bring us both pleasure."

He grasped her wrists and held them at her sides.
Then he dipped his head and resumed his caresses, his
laving tongue touching her in a sweet, searching circle.
She whimpered as her breathing grew shallow. He
plunged his tongue deep into her most sensitive place,
lapping along the slick pink folds, teasing her until she
sighed and sank deeper into the mattress.

The pleasure began pulsing through Gwendolyn.
Then the tension increased. She shifted and turned beneath Jason's sensual assault, as the restlessness of her
yet-to-be reached climax filled her. Her body strained
against his mouth, her hands gripped the quilt, her heels
dug into the mattress as the sensual torment continued.

Shameless, she opened her thighs wider, reveling in
their wanton, wicked passion. Jason growled his approval
and sucked harder, coaxing her desire. She nearly
screamed with delight when he slipped a finger inside
her and began to thrust. Her response was instinctual.
She pressed herself toward him, gasping at the sensation, wanting more. More of him.

He held her there, a prisoner to his relentless tongue.
All embarrassment fled, even though she was now fully
exposed to him. The sensation was so intense it was
almost unbearable. Every muscle tensed as she arched
and stretched and rocked her hips forward. And then at

last, she started to come apart, shuddering and trembling with the blissful reward of pleasure.

Jason continued kissing her damp curls, her inner thighs, her soft belly until the shivers ended, until her senses returned. Rising up, Gwendolyn leaned forward and threw herself into his embrace. Her eyes welled with emotion, but she blinked back the tears.

"My God, Gwendolyn," he rasped. "How I need you."

She shifted so she could see his face. Heaven help her, he was so handsome. She ran her hands lovingly over his chest, then pressed her lips to his body, flicking her tongue over his nipple. His skin was damp with perspiration, the taste of him wet and erotic. She imitated his earlier actions and swirled her tongue around his flat, hard nipples, tasting the saltiness of his skin, inhaling the masculine scent of his body.

Jason moaned with approval and moved closer. The tip of his enlarged penis brushed against the soft skin of her stomach. She jumped, then pushed herself against the hardness. He reached down, grabbed her hand and led it to his erection. "Touch me."

Gwendolyn's fingers curled lovingly around him. She drew her fingers down his length, amazed at the heat and hardness. It felt as if his penis was encased in warm satin. She stroked him to the base, then reversed directions, allowing her thumb to flick over the moist end of him. Jason made an incoherent sound of need.

He had said they would be wicked tonight, wanton, unrestrained. Did she dare? Filled with passion and daring, Gwendolyn stroked one hand up Jason's chest and then bowed her head to take his penis in her mouth.

He cried out in a choked, astonished voice. Gwendolyn smiled, delighted at the response. She held his throbbing penis in one hand and drew her tongue slowly along the length, paying particular attention to the sensitive tip. Jason growled, started shaking, then began pumping his hips against her mouth.

"You are a wicked woman," he panted, throwing his head back, the muscles in his neck stretched tight.

Feeling awkward, yet aroused, Gwendolyn circled the crest with the tip of her mouth, then closed her lips around him and suckled. He fell back on his elbows and moaned. Feeling confident that she was bringing him pleasure, she dug her fingers into his thighs and held him in place, teasing him with the same rhythm he had used on her.

With another groan, Jason caught her head in his hands, thrust forward a few more times, then slowly eased her head back until his penis slipped free of her mouth. She gazed up at him, her brows drawn together in a frown. "Am I doing it wrong?"

His laugh was a hollow, almost tortured sound. "You are doing it amazingly right, my love."

"Then why must I stop?"

"Because I am starting to lose control."

She smiled. "Good." Moving to a sitting position, she leaned forward, taking one of his small, hard nipples into her mouth. Puckering her lips, she sucked hard. Jason groaned. She continued teasing him with her mouth, while her hands kept busy below, touching him with gentle, then firm, strokes, until his body drew tense and heavy.

"Enough." Jason grabbed her wrist, his body shuddering. "I need to be inside you."

He moved so suddenly that she didn't even realize it was happening until she was flat on her back, pinned beneath him. With a wicked smile, Jason pulled her knees apart and rose over her. A ragged breath escaped her lips as he positioned himself and drove his hard length deep inside her.

Braced on his arms, Jason stilled and gazed lovingly down at her. "Is it all right?"

Gwendolyn felt the tears pool in her eyes. "Yes," she whispered. She brushed her fingers over his cheek and stared up at Jason's beloved face as she lifted her hips against him.

"My God, you are a wonder."

Gwendolyn smiled. She exhaled her breath and closed her eyes, glorying in the moment. They were joined together. In their hearts as well as their bodies.

She opened her eyes and moved her hips again. He groaned. She arched her back, rubbing her breasts against his bare chest. He uttered a low moan and began to move inside her, thrusting and withdrawing, increasing the rhythm slowly, steadily until they were bucking and twisting against each other.

And all the while he gazed deeply into her eyes, never once looking away, never once breaking their complete connection.

"You really do love me," she whispered, her heart aching with joy.

"I do. And I always will."

His words had an instant effect. Gwendolyn felt her body begin to convulse. She cried out sharply and Jason answered her sob by rocking his hips forward, moving them closer, driving into her harder and deeper, until her shaking ceased.

His hands moved from her hips to her buttocks. The strong rhythm of his deep thrust turned to a nearly frantic pace until suddenly he froze and cried out. Gwendolyn held him tightly against her heart as the warm heat of his seed pumped deep into her body. She caressed him in long soothing strokes down his back, whispering words of nonsense and love as his erection pulsed inside, then finally went still.

After a long moment of silence, he lifted himself off her. His handsome face was serene, content, when he bent to kiss her softly on the lips. Smiling, Gwendolyn rolled onto her side and tucked herself against his hard strength.

This time there was no guilt. No shameful regrets that she had betrayed herself by making love with a man who was committed to another. He was hers, utterly and completely, for as long as she wanted.

And oh, how she wanted.

She snuggled into his side, kissing the warm skin of his chest. She felt drowsy and languorous, but fought against falling asleep. "Are you sure about marrying me?" she asked.

Jason shifted his position and glared down at her. "Yes, I want to marry you. Have I not asked you at least a dozen times?"

"You have. But I do not want you to feel that you are obligated to offer for my hand because we have been physically intimate," she replied, playing idly with the curling hair on his chest.

"We have not been physically intimate. We have made love. Several times, and each has been better than the last."

She propped herself up on one elbow and smiled at him. "It has been rather marvelous."

"It has." He leaned forward and nipped the end of her nose. "And I can assure you, dearest, being with you is vastly different from anything that I have ever experienced. I know it is far more than sex. After all, I have not pledged myself to every women with whom I had sexual relations."

"I imagine that would make you a criminal bigamist," she said dryly.

He shrugged. "The number is too high to count."

Gwendolyn snorted. "Now that's a sentiment to warm a woman's heart and inspire confidence in her future."

"You wanted honesty," he replied with a shame-faced grin.

"'Tis one thing to be honest with each other, Jason. 'Tis quite another to be hit over the head with it."

"I cannot change my past," he said solemnly.

"I am not asking for that, Jason. I know I am hardly the first woman in your bed. But I fully expect to be the last."

"You shall be, because I love you. Only you." Jason sobered and frowned. "What an amazingly indecent, indelicate, insensitive subject to be discussing with a woman. With *my* woman. You are unique, my dearest. However, there is something that you need to understand, need to accept, Gwendolyn. My brother Jasper is the *good* son, the proper, responsible, respectable member of our family. I am the reckless, irresponsible, scandalous one.

"When we were young men we were both hellions, mired in scandal, reveling in our inappropriate behavior. But somehow, Jasper was able to contain his wilder nature, to harness this streak of abandon. He became absurdly proper and respectable, a man to be admired and emulated. While I . . . well, I remained the same."

She tilted her head and gazed up at him, then realized he was not teasing her but rather being honest. Perhaps he had not been a model of decorum for most of his adult life, but Gwendolyn knew there was goodness, decency, even nobility in him, for she had seen it.

She pressed a finger to his lips. "Do not say such things."

"They are true."

"Not entirely." Jason's assessment of his own character revealed a vulnerability that went straight to Gwendolyn's heart. Of course he had made mistakes, done things he wished he had not, regretted choices made that were not the best. Didn't everyone? Including her? In Gwendolyn's mind it was far more important to be a man of strong character, with a noble and true heart, rather than an individual who espoused perfect behavior.

"You are a fine, good, remarkable man, Jason Barrington," she said in an authoritative voice. "And I shall challenge anyone who begs to differ. Including you."

For a moment he looked confused. "'Tis an odd experience for me to have so fierce a champion."

She stroked his hair. "Best get used to it."

The bleakness was out of his eyes, replaced with a light of hope. "I fully intend to change, Gwendolyn. To mend my ways, to change my attitudes and behavior. 'Tis said that reformed rakes make the best husbands."

She crinkled her nose and laughed. "What a ridiculous idea! Good men with true hearts and honest intentions make the best husbands."

"Indeed. But men with purpose in their lives have stability."

"And what, pray tell, is your purpose, Jason?"

His smile came straight from his heart. "To make sure you remain the happiest, most fulfilled, most pampered, most cherished female on earth."

He was grinning down at her, with all the handsome, sexy, boyish charm that so completely captured her heart. "I hold no individual responsible for the state of my life. I expect marriage to be a partnership of mutual love and respect," she said. "Yet I cannot help but applaud your lofty goals, my love."

He laughed, a dark, soft sound deep in his throat. "Does this mean you will marry me?"

Gwendolyn smiled, then turned into his arms, enjoying the gentle stroke of his hand against her hip. "Oh, yes, Jason. I will most certainly marry you."

Chapter Eighteen

Gwendolyn's mood was reflective as she made her way to Moorehead Manor the following morning. Though she had taken a long, leisurely bath earlier, she could still smell Jason's scent on her body, could feel the soreness, the tightness in her muscles as a result of their vigorous lovemaking.

They had slept briefly last night, wrapped within each other's arms. Nudging Jason awake, Gwendolyn had whispered that he needed to leave before the dawn broke. Jason had smiled, declaring he would slip out her window and climb down the trellis, in an effort to avoid detection.

She had helped him find his clothing and he donned but a few items: his shirt, breeches and boots. As they said good-bye, Gwendolyn placed a hand on Jason's chest and stretched up, intending to kiss his cheek, but he turned his head and his lips met hers. His arms slid around her and the kiss changed from a simple farewell to the heated sensuality they could not seem to control.

They sank to the floor and Jason rolled her face down on the carpet, then scooped her lower half onto her knees. He pressed her shoulders down, then his hands grasped her hips, holding her firmly while he entered her, then rocked back and forth inside her.

She shivered as the heat raced through her veins, as the pleasure continued to build. Jason bent forward over her back, brushing aside her hair, kissing, biting, sucking at her neck. She could hear his heavy breathing, could see their reflection in the mirror.

They drove themselves to a shattering completion, then slumped together as they waited for their hearts to slow, for their breathing to steady, for the blissful, peaceful aftermath to fade. Jason finally left when the dark horizon began to soften with the promise of the upcoming dawn, vowing to miss her dreadfully until they were once again together.

They had made no specific plan for today, but as she soaked in her bath this morning remembering all the wicked details of their erotic episodes, Gwendolyn realized it illustrated not only the depth of her feelings for Jason, but her complete trust in him. And if she trusted him with her body, with her heart, she could certainly trust him with the truth about her uncle.

"Lord Fairhurst is not receiving visitors this morning, Miss Ellingham," the butler explained when he answered her knock.

"I believe he shall make an exception in my case, Snowden," Gwendolyn replied with a confident smile.

"His orders were most specific." The butler cleared his throat. "However, his lordship's brother, Mr. Barrington, also left instructions to inform him immediately if you happened to call."

Gwendolyn struggled to hold back her surprise, wondering precisely how much the butler knew about Lord Fairhurst and his twin brother. She was sorely tempted to ask, but did not, knowing Snowden was too proper a servant to ever fully reveal his emotions or opinions.

Declining the butler's offer of refreshments, Gwendolyn paced the room impatiently as she waited for Jason.

"I need to talk with you," Gwendolyn announced the moment he entered the room.

He smiled into her eyes. "I'm listening."

"This is serious."

To her relief, he nodded. Crossing to one of the cushioned chairs near the window, he sat and waved to the matching chair facing him. "Best to sit there. I doubt I can control myself if you sit beside me on the settee."

She did as he bid, eager to start, and finish, this conversation, but as she looked into his handsome, curious face, her nerve failed. For a long moment Gwendolyn stared across at him, considering how much to tell him, but then she caught the gleam of love shining from his eyes and her hesitation evaporated. Sinking her shoulders back against the cushions, she began to talk without reservation, telling all she knew about her uncle's financial circumstances.

Jason listened carefully, occasionally asking a question, once offering an observation.

"Ah, so it *was* Emma who painted the portrait that hangs in the long gallery," Jason said, when she was done.

"You knew?"

"I suspected, though to be honest I felt it too good to have been done by someone who lacked years of formal training." He cocked his head to one side. "And I found it difficult to believe she would be a party to such a fraud."

Gwendolyn felt her mouth curve into a grim smile. "Emma was an innocent in the plot and is quite devastated at the outcome. Though it will bolster her spirits to hear your assessment of her talent. I shall tell her—"

"My lord!" The drawing room door burst open, and one of the gardeners, wild-eyed and panicked, entered the room. "You need to come quickly. 'Tis Mr. Ardley. He's hurt bad."

Neither Jason nor Gwendolyn bothered to inform the servant he was not addressing Lord Fairhurst. Instead, they both leapt to their feet and hurried outside.

There was a circle of servants standing in front of the stables, a low buzz of conversation swarming around them. As Gwendolyn and Jason approached, the group parted to make room and Gwendolyn gasped loudly when she saw what they were huddled around.

Prone on the ground was a man, his coat torn, his breeches ripped at the knee. His face was swollen almost beyond recognition, his eyes shut tight, the eyelids puffy and discolored. Dried blood surrounded his lips and stained the front of his shirt. The bruises on his puffy cheek and jaw were already starting to turn a deep shade of purple.

With a sickening lurch of her stomach, Gwendolyn realized she would not have known it was Mr. Ardley if the gardener had not just told them.

"My God, what has happened?" Jason asked as he hunkered down and checked the steward's pulse.

"We have no idea," the gardener replied. "Ned was mucking out the stalls when he heard the horse's hooves clopping on the stone outside the stable. He stuck his head outside just in time to see Mr. Ardley slide off the horse. Ned called for help and we all came running."

Jason turned to the young stable boy. "Did you see anyone else?"

"No. Just Mr. Ardley. He was slouched forward, his

arms around the horse's neck. Don't know how he managed to stay upright for so long."

"How indeed." Jason shuddered. "His pulse is steady, but weak. His leg looks broken in at least two places. His arm too."

"The shoulder?" Gwendolyn inquired, disturbed at the odd angle it presented.

"Dislocated," Jason diagnosed. "And at this point, the very least of his problems."

Lord Fairhurst joined them. "What is happening? Snowden informed me there has been some sort of accident."

"This is hardly accidental," Jason responded grimly.

Gwendolyn observed Lord Fairhurst flinching as he got his first look at Ardley. "Good Lord, who is it? Do we know him?"

"'Tis Ardley." Jason leaned forward and whispered in his brother's ear.

The curious group of onlookers, Gwendolyn among them, moved back a respectful distance, but remained in the yard. It was a testament to the horror and severity of the incident that no one seemed to take particular notice that there were now *two* Lord Fairhursts.

Gwendolyn dropped back farther, standing beside the steward's horse. One of the stable lads held the exhausted animal's reins. Gwendolyn could see the streaks of blood on the horse's flanks. With a sickening jolt she realized they had come from Mr. Ardley.

"We need to put splints on his legs before we try to move him into the house," Jasper decided. He turned and addressed the nearest servant. "Find me four long boards to use as splints along with clean bandages. Then send someone to fetch the doctor. Tell him he is needed here immediately."

"Yes, my lord." The man bowed low and hurried off.

Gwendolyn shook her head in amazement. There might be two men who looked like Lord Fairhurst, but it was very apparent who was the *real* viscount.

The requested supplies quickly arrived, along with a pale-faced Snowden. He tried to disperse the crowd of staff, but succeeded only in getting them to move slightly farther away. Several pretended to attend to their duties, but all were within sight, and earshot.

Gwendolyn noted it was Jason who now directed his brother, instructing him where to grip and hold the splints in place while he quickly tied them with the long strips of linen that had been provided. They worked together in an assured, controlled manner with an economy of movement that bespoke a silent communication.

As she watched Jason's hands move methodically over Ardley's limbs, Gwendolyn wondered where he had obtained such expertise, for he seemed very certain of his actions.

"Do you know what you are doing?" she asked him, moving closer.

"Young hellions with an inclination to neck-breaking carriage races often crash," he replied, never lifting his eyes from his tasks. "It can take hours to find a doctor when you are on a deserted country road. Consequently, I've seen, and set, far too many broken bones in my day."

Jason continued with his attentions to Ardley. He checked the splints on the broken limbs, turned him gently to one side, then with a quick, expert jerk he reset the dislocated shoulder. Ardley did not move or make a sound at what Gwendolyn perceived was a most painful procedure. Her worry increased.

"Did he say anything?" Jasper asked. "Give any information or reason as to what or why this occurred?"

"No," Jason replied. "He has remained unconscious since he was found. Lord only knows how long he was on his horse. If this keeps up too long, I worry that he might never again wake up."

Jasper frowned. "Poor man, he's been beaten within an inch of his life."

"I reckon it was the highwaymen again," one of the stable lads whispered in fear. "The same ones that attacked your carriage, my lord."

Jasper's expression held a flash of surprise, and Gwendolyn realized that he was unaware of the carriage attack. "'Tis to soon to tell," the viscount replied. "But we will not let such a brutal attack go unpunished. I intend to personally lead the investigation into this matter."

"It would be helpful to talk with anyone who saw Ardley before he left last yesterday," Jason suggested. "He told me he was going to the Haslet farm in the next county to inspect some livestock. Perhaps he deviated from his route on the way there or the way back."

"I'll start questioning the servants myself," Jasper declared. "And we need to send someone out to that farm to determine if Ardley ever arrived."

The words swirled around in Gwendolyn's head; the implication hit and her breath caught in her throat.

"I need to return home at once," she cried, turning on her heel, rushing toward the stable to get her mount.

"Wait! Gwendolyn, what's wrong?" Jason asked as he followed after her.

She stopped, turned, hesitated for a heartbeat. "It's my uncle. I believe he accompanied Mr. Ardley on his journey. And when I left the house earlier, he had not yet returned."

* * *

Jason refused to allow Gwendolyn to leave without him. She chafed at the notion of having to wait, but he insisted. After a brief word with his brother and a quick stop in his room to retrieve his pistol, the pair set off.

Nothing appeared amiss as they entered the courtyard of the Ellingham residence. There were a few servants outside, going about their daily chores in the usual manner. Inside the house, Jason and Gwendolyn found her female relations relaxing in the morning room; Aunt Mildred with her embroidery, Emma with her sketch pad and Dorothea reading a magazine.

"No, your uncle has not yet returned from his journey," Aunt Mildred said, in answer to Gwendolyn's tense question. "I do wish he would hurry back. There are things we need to attend to today." She turned her attention to her male guest with a hostess's smile. "May I offer you some refreshment, Lord Fairhurst?"

Jason used his charming, noncommittal smile and looked to Gwendolyn, intending to follow her lead. Now was hardly the time to divulge his true identity, yet he doubted she had the strength to continue with the masquerade.

"This is not Lord Fairhurst, Aunt Mildred," Gwendolyn replied in a distracted tone.

The older woman glanced away and blinked. "Honestly, Gwendolyn, what sort of jest are you trying to play? I might be concerned about your uncle, but my slight distress has not addled my wits nor affected my eyesight. I know Lord Fairhurst when I see him."

Gwendolyn's lips thinned. "This is Mr. Barrington, Lord Fairhurst's twin brother. He arrived in Willoughby yesterday."

Aunt Mildred shifted in her chair, fixing her gaze on him. "Are you certain this is not Lord Fairhurst?"

Gwendolyn huffed and rolled her eyes.

"It is a great honor to make your acquaintance, Mrs. Ellingham." Intent on rescuing Gwendolyn from further explanations, Jason stepped forward, bowing low. "'Tis said the resemblance between myself and the viscount is extraordinary, but I like to think that I am the more handsome of the pair. Do you concur, madame?"

Aunt Mildred giggled, then blushed. Head tilting, she considered him closely. "If pressed, I believe I would have to give you a slight advantage, sir."

"Intelligence as well as beauty." Jason lifted his left eyebrow. "Now I understand how Gwendolyn possess both in abundance. 'Tis clearly a family trait."

Aunt Mildred's chin wobbled as she nodded, her mouth curved in a silly smile. "May I be so bold as to ask if there is a Mrs. Barrington, sir?"

"Alas, not as yet." Jason grinned wickedly. "But I do have aspirations to soon achieve wedded bliss." He turned and stared pointedly at Gwendolyn, who was anxiously gazing out the window toward the front drive, oblivious to the conversation.

"What rubbish!" Emma exclaimed, her nose crinkling in astonishment. "You have only just met my sister."

"It's true, Miss Emma," Jason agreed pleasantly. "One look was all that I needed to know my heart."

Emma's head whirled in his direction. Her pause lasted for no more than a breath. "How can you possibly know my name? I have only met Lord Fairhurst, not his twin brother."

Caught! Jason's smile widened. Though she might be a female, Emma was neither slow-witted nor silly. "Gwendolyn has told me so much about you all, I feel I already know you."

"Odd she never mentioned you," Dorothea said dryly, shooting him a saber-sharp glare.

"There wasn't time," Gwendolyn said wearily. "I met Mr. Barrington yesterday, while visiting Moorehead Manor."

She moved away from the window and came to stand beside him. Jason's heart tightened at her worried expression, but there was nothing to do at this point except wait for her uncle to return. Hopefully, unharmed.

"It was a whirlwind romance," Jason explained.

"Aren't they the very best kind?" Aunt Mildred giggled nervously, her eyes bright with speculation. "Tell me, Gwendolyn, by any happy chance do you share Mr. Barrington's feelings?"

A clearly distracted Gwendolyn turned toward her aunt. "What?"

Jason wrapped his arm around her shoulder and pulled her close. "You aunt wishes to know if you hold me in deep regard."

"Oh, yes, of course. We are madly in love."

"Oh, gracious!" Aunt Mildred squealed with delight, too intent upon her pleasure at this most unexpected news to notice that her niece was hardly acting like a woman smitten. In fact, she had spoken with almost no emotion or interest in her voice. Jason admitted he might have felt slighted if he did not know of the grave worry on Gwendolyn's mind.

Dorothea continued eyeing him with great suspicion; Emma looked equally doubtful. He noticed the three sisters share a number of meaningful looks and prayed this unspoken communication would have a favorable result. Quickly it became clear he need not have worried. Dorothea and Emma loyally took their cues from Gwendolyn.

If she said they had recently met and fallen instantly in love, her sisters would support it. For the time being.

"Oh, I do wish your uncle were home," Aunt Mildred chattered. "I know he would be most pleased to meet Mr. Barrington. Perhaps even have a private meeting together . . ."

Her voice trailed off and she beamed with delight.

"When is Uncle Fletcher due to return?" Gwendolyn asked.

"Four hours ago," Emma answered. "He is very late." Emma sidled up to them and Jason heard her whisper to Gwendolyn. "What in the blue blazes is going on?"

Gwendolyn shook her head. Jason shrugged his shoulders, placing his features under strict control. He would wait for his brother to arrive and learn what he had discovered before questioning the Ellingham sisters.

They spent the next twenty minutes trying to make small talk, deflecting all the avid, curious questions that Emma and Dorothea tossed their way. Then his brother was announced.

Jason was instantly glad they had already revealed he was his brother's twin, for even armed with the knowledge, all three of the Ellingham women were near to speechless as they viewed the brothers side by side.

Jason took advantage of the momentary diversion to question Gwendolyn's aunt. "What can you tell us of Mr. Ellingham's journey, madame?"

Though surprised, Aunt Mildred answered readily enough. "Not much. He left on business late yesterday afternoon, due to return early this morning." She looked from Jasper to Jason. "The resemblance truly is remarkable. If it were not for the different color coats you are wearing, I would never be able to tell you apart."

"A common occurrence," Jasper responded with a tolerant grin. "I suppose my brother has already claimed to be the better-looking twin?"

Aunt Mildred laughed. "He has indeed, my lord. You best be careful with him around."

Emma boldly stepped forward. She had been staring at them both very closely, appraising, assessing, and Jason could tell she was not as easily convinced as her aunt as to which Lord Fairhurst she had known these past few weeks. "I wonder, my lord, if there was a reason other than purely social, for your call this morning?"

"I fear I bring distressing news," Jasper gravely replied. "My steward has been badly injured."

Aunt Mildred frowned. "Fletcher was traveling with Mr. Ardley. Pray, do not tell me that my husband was also hurt?"

"We are uncertain," Jason answered. "Ardley returned to the manor alone and as far as we can tell, Mr. Ellingham is still missing."

"Missing?" Aunt Mildred's lashes fluttered and she began making whimpering noises of distress in the back of her throat. "Oh my, oh my. I just knew something had gone wrong. I had a premonition of disaster all morning, but forced myself to ignore it."

The older woman slumped back against the cushion of her chair, wringing her hands. Dorothea knelt beside her aunt, clasping her fingers comfortingly around Aunt Mildred's fretful ones.

"Have you discovered anything useful about Ardley's attack?" Jason whispered to his brother.

"He has not yet regained consciousness and, given the extent of his injuries, the doctor thought it best to prescribe a strong sedative for the pain. I doubt he will awaken until morning."

"That might be too late for Ellingham." Jason frowned thoughtfully, voicing the theory he had been mulling over in his mind. "I think Ardley and Ellingham might have been attempting to strike a deal with the moneylenders who have been supporting their gambling habit and somehow things went wrong."

"Ardley and Ellingham were in this together?"

Jason nodded. "The funds and objects taken from your estate were used to cover gambling debts and to try and keep the moneylenders at bay. Gwendolyn discovered the truth but a few days ago. She explained it all to me this afternoon, just before Ardley returned to the manor. His condition suggests the moneylenders were not inclined to negotiate."

Jasper let out a low whistle. "If that is true, then they were playing a very dangerous game. Did they not realize what manner of people they were dealing with? Trying to negotiate with a moneylender is tantamount to sticking your hand through a lion's cage."

"They are paying the price for it now," Gwendolyn whispered.

She had barely finished her sentence when the door burst open. They all looked. A maid stood on the threshold, her face contorted in puzzlement. "Cook went outside to gather some herbs for her stew. When she returned, she found this note on the kitchen table."

Aunt Mildred turned to stare at the maid. For an instant, she seemed struck speechless. Then she stiffened. Shock showed briefly on her face as she reached for the note, but the servant shook her head. "It's addressed to Miss Gwendolyn."

Gwendolyn took the note. She broke the plain red seal

and read it. Her jaw fell, then it snapped shut. "They have taken Uncle Fletcher. If we want him released, we must pay them with either coin or jewels. The money is to be left at the Hartfield crossing precisely at six this evening."

Jason snatched the paper out of her hand, not caring if he was being rude. He read it, then passed it to his brother.

"That is preposterous!" Dorothea exclaimed, looking bewildered. "Why would anyone capture Uncle Fletcher with the intent of extorting money from us? We are hardly a wealthy family."

"My dearest Fletcher has no enemies," Aunt Mildred chimed in, rousing herself. "It must be a hoax."

"It does not sound like a hoax." Gwendolyn's lips twisted wryly. "If we do not pay, he will be returned to us in far worse condition than Ardley."

"At least we know now it is the same men," Jason remarked, then, turning to the maid, added, "Did anyone see who left this message?"

The servant shook her head in distress. "I don't know, sir."

"We should question all the servants," Jasper suggested. Jason agreed, though he feared they would be able to tell them very little.

It took several minutes for the small staff to be summoned. As suspected, no one had noticed anyone in the immediate area. Jason began to pace with restless energy once they had been dismissed, his mind formulating and then discarding a variety of wild plans. Finally, he ceased walking and asked his brother, "What should we do?"

Jasper's eyes narrowed. "Giving these scoundrels more coin will only encourage further extortion, yet after seeing what they did to Ardley we cannot risk inciting their ire."

"Perhaps I can bring them a small amount of funds, promising the rest only after Ellingham is safely returned?" Jason suggested.

"The note was addressed to me!" Gwendolyn insisted forcefully, even though she seemed a bit dazed. "It also says that I am the one to bring the money and if I do not follow the instructions to the letter there will be dire consequences."

Jason held up a staying hand. "If you imagine that I will sanction your involvement in dropping off the ransom, then I strongly advise you to think again."

Gwendolyn sighed. "Believe me, I am hardly eager to go. But the instructions are most specific. He expects me, a woman, to leave the money. I cannot jeopardize Uncle Fletcher's safety by doing otherwise."

The thought of Gwendolyn in such danger made Jason catch his breath, made him remember that love could also be very painful at times. "I cannot put you at such risk. I will wear a dress and make the delivery myself before I allow you to come within twenty feet of these bastards."

Gwendolyn caught his hand and held it tightly. "I have no desire to be a martyr, Jason. But they have left us little choice."

"We could make this work," Jasper insisted. "As long as we put the odds in our favor, not theirs." Steepling his fingers, Jasper rested his chin on the tips. "I suppose we could have Jason pretend to be you and disguise himself as a woman, but frankly I think the most advantageous position for him is in the field, monitoring the money drop."

Jason vehemently shook his head. "Jasper—"

"You are the best shot I have ever seen, Jason. I understand your concerns, and I share them, but we both know you can be far more effective guarding Gwendolyn's back."

"See, even Lord Fairhurst agrees," Gwendolyn said.

Jason swore beneath his breath. The color had returned to Gwendolyn's cheeks and sparks lit her velvety brown eyes. "I do not know if I possess the courage to put you in such danger," he whispered honestly.

Jasper swallowed a snort. "Then I will be the decoy and don a gown and cloak."

"No!" Jason and Gwendolyn answered simultaneously.

"If they discover you are a man, both your life and Uncle Fletcher's would be in grave danger," Gwendolyn said.

"As much as it pains me to admit it, Gwendolyn is right," Jason agreed reluctantly. "This area was selected for a specific reason. I suspect there will be a limited amount of trees, and a scant few places for concealment, which works both for and against us. We will quickly know how many of the enemy there are, yet it will be difficult for us to surround them with a large number of men. We can only take a few, those who are the best shots, with the steadiest of heads."

Gwendolyn looked from Jason to his brother. "Then I will make the drop alone?"

Jason moved closer, holding Gwendolyn's stark, questioning gaze. Her courage in the face of her obvious fear humbled him, reinforcing his opinion of her inner strength and character. "Jasper and I and a few other men of our choosing will be there, hidden from view, yet ever alert to any danger. I will keep you safe."

He laid a reassuring hand over Gwendolyn's. With a crooked smile, she said, "I will not be so afraid, knowing you are near."

They spent the next thirty minutes immersed in engineering a solid plan, their voices low as to not be overheard. The note demanded the money by six that evening and perversely Jason was glad they did not have to wait for days to force the resolution of this dilemma. Best to finish it all quickly.

Solemn and serious, Jasper departed, but Jason elected to stay a few more hours with the Ellingham women. A tea tray had been brought to the room, but no one bothered to serve anything. Aunt Mildred remained prostrated against the settee, her three nieces surrounding her.

He noticed some color had returned to her pale cheeks, though she pressed the heel of her hand to her forehead, as if her head ached. When she spied him drawing near, her arm slowly lowered.

"This is a terrible, dreadful occurrence, Mr. Barrington," Aunt Mildred muttered in a trembling voice.

"'Tis awful," he replied.

"What is to be done?"

"You are not to worry, madame. We have devised a solid plan and tonight we shall rescue your husband," he answered, with a confidence he did not entirely feel.

Chapter Nineteen

Jason took a deep breath and forced his mind to concentrate, to examine his surroundings and get his bearings. He could feel his body quivering with agitation, but maintained a cool demeanor, determined that none of his inner turmoil would show. When faced with adversity, men took their cues from their leaders and above all Jason wanted the men he was now leading to feel confident about this mission, to feel sure of its success.

He had known it would not be easy to allow Gwendolyn to play such a major role in the attempted rescue, but he had not expected it to be this hard. Feeling heavily the sense of responsibility for her welfare, Jason focused all of his energies on his task. He did not notice that the wind had quieted, that the sun was starting to dip low on the horizon. He did not feel the coolness of the evening, nor smell the promise of rain which hung in the air.

Instead, he could think only of Gwendolyn. They had less than an hour to stake out positions where they could observe the money drop without being seen and be alert to anyone slinking about in the clusters of trees and bushes that ringed the rendezvous spot.

When he was ready, Jason motioned to Jasper and the small group of men gathered beside his twin. Upon his signal, the group split apart, scattering in various directions. They had left their horses almost a mile away and were covering the remaining ground on foot. Faces intent, the men moved with stealth and precision, running from one cover to the next, trying to find the best position of surveillance before Gwendolyn arrived.

After much deliberation, Jason settled himself behind a boulder that sat at the edge of a slight hill. Within minutes, Jasper joined him, the spot barely sufficient to hide the two of them.

"The other men are scattered around the perimeter," Jasper said. "It will be impossible for these villains to ride out of here without one of us seeing them. If they have brought Gwendolyn's uncle with them, we should be able to rescue him once she has left the money and departed."

Jason gave a tight nod. His concern for Fletcher Ellingham was secondary. All he could think of was Gwendolyn and the urgent need to keep her safe. With effort, Jason straightened his shoulders, feeling as if the weight of the world was pressing them down.

The wait seemed interminable. Silence, cold and tense, filled the air. Jason's legs began to cramp from crouching so long in an awkward position. Shifting, he settled his shoulder against the center of the boulder and continued to scan the open field below. Minute by minute the tension within him escalated, climbing steadily notch by notch.

A movement at the far end of the horizon caught his attention. Jason watched Gwendolyn ride across the field at a strong pace, her progress steady, the jaunty feather on her bonnet bobbing in the breeze. Senses on knife-edge, he strained to see the area in front of her, fearful she might be riding into a trap.

"Are any men positioned closer?" he asked his brother.

"No. The risk of detection was too great." Jasper briefly touched his shoulder, the gesture reassuring and supportive.

Jason kept his eyes trained on Gwendolyn. Though he saw nothing of immediate danger, the tension inside him squeezed tighter as an air of worry and concern enveloped him. Gwendolyn seemed so alone, so vulnerable.

Dear Lord, was this all a mistake? Jason cursed graphically, angry at himself for agreeing to the plan, fearful that Gwendolyn was too easy a prey for these unscrupulous men. A strange hollowness filled his chest, stretched his heart. The prospect of living without Gwendolyn left him desolate. If anything happened to her . . . his breath caught, the thought too horrifying to complete.

His brother looked at him a moment, his lids lowered, his expression intent. "I understand how precious she is to you. We will do all that is necessary to ensure she comes to no harm."

The faintest hint of thickness touched Jasper's voice, easing a bit of the pressure inside Jason's chest. His brother was not a man given to violence, yet Jason knew he could count on him to watch his back. Though Jason modestly conceded his own skill with a pistol, he also knew that no one had a way with a sword like Jasper. Between them they made a formidable pair.

Jason squinted, his eyes glued to Gwendolyn's horse, his attention captivated by her every move. He had planned and prepared the best he was able in the limited time they had been given, had done all he could to ensure her safety. He and the men would have the element of surprise, but he reasoned the moneylenders might suspect Gwendolyn would have some form of assistance, which could put her in even greater jeopardy.

The planes of his face hardened. He could only hope that his adversaries were overconfident, that their greed would cause them to be careless. Anything to tip the odds in his favor.

Either way, it would all be over shortly. One way or another.

Gwendolyn approached the rendezvous spot cautiously, her breath burning in her lungs. The fear that had been steadily building for the past mile had now elevated to a form of mild panic, but she forced it from her mind. A cool head and a steady hand were required and she willed herself to retain both. One mistake on her part could cost Uncle Fletcher his life. And put her own at grave risk.

Though she knew the terrain well, it seemed darkly forboding and dangerous. No singing birds to welcome her, no bright, cheery sunlight to lighten her mood. The closer she drew to the spot where she had been instructed to leave the money, the less certain she was of her ability to remain calm.

What if one or two of the men suddenly appeared and demanded more money? What if she paid them and they still refused to release Uncle Fletcher? What if they threatened her?

And then she remembered Jason. He was here, somewhere, hiding among the trees or bushes or boulders, waiting, watching. A ribbon of relief coursed through her veins. Jason would protect her, would make certain that no harm befell her.

But could he do the same for Uncle Fletcher?

She allowed her horse to pick his way up the small ridge, knowing she was getting close. In the distance Gwendolyn could hear the faint rumbling of thunder, then suddenly a streak of lightning flashed across the sky. She pulled up on the reins, carefully controlling her skittish mare, hoping she would have time to deliver the money and depart well before the summer storm hit.

She resisted the temptation to scan the horizon, fearful the men who were waiting for the money were also watching her, loath to give them any indication that she had disobeyed the instructions and had not come alone.

At last she reached her destination. Bringing her mount to a halt, Gwendolyn took a few moments to collect herself, then nudged her horse toward a small cluster of bushes. She dismounted, tethering the reins on a lower branch.

With careful, deliberate movements, she removed the small leather purse from the saddlebag, taking her time to buckle it closed. Then, ignoring the prickling sensations at the base of her neck, Gwendolyn walked to the large oak tree a few feet away.

The note had said to leave the money at the base of the tree, out in full view. Crouching down, she set the brown leather purse against the trunk, relieved the dark color did not blend into the bark of the tree. Straightening, she gave a final look to ensure the purse was easily seen.

Taking a deep breath, she glanced about nervously, wondering if there was a chance she would see her uncle, hoping that he was near, that he could be easily rescued. A minute passed. And then another. Realizing her uncle would not be immediately released, Gwendolyn did the sensible thing, turned around and marched toward her horse. And safety.

She did not dare look back, though she longed to once again reassure herself she had followed the instructions precisely as they were given. Her heart was pounding so loudly in her ears she did not hear the rustle of the bushes, did not notice the unnatural movement until the stranger was upon her. He leapt out of his hiding place and snatched her, his hand over her mouth before she had a chance to utter a scream.

Lips curled in an angry snarl, he trapped her back against his chest and started to drag her toward the small cluster of dense bushes just beyond where her horse was tethered. Gwendolyn struggled frantically, kicking and wiggling, twisting her body from side to side, but could not break free.

"I told you to come alone," he snarled in her ear.

"I am alone," she mumbled through the fingers pressed against her mouth, a pang of fear momentarily overriding her ability to struggle.

"Not bloody likely," the man insisted. "I've counted at least four men hiding around the perimeter of the field."

"You must be mistaken."

"Damn liar. We've captured two of them, but they are in no condition to talk."

He jerked her forward and she moaned, a combination of pain and fear. Realizing her struggling only succeeded in making her tired, Gwendolyn suddenly sagged in his hold, pretending to faint, hoping to throw him off balance.

But he had anticipated her ploy and was ready to counter the move. Bracing his legs, he lifted her higher, the strong arm around her middle tightening. His other hand pressed harder around her mouth, sealing off any air.

The scream she was trying to lose lodged in her throat. Panting, fighting for breath, Gwendolyn felt all the blood drain from her face. He tightened his grip on her until she was light-headed from lack of air. She clawed at his forearm and willed herself not to truly faint, not to easily succumb.

Roughly he dragged her along the grass. Fearing if he reached the bushes she might never escape, Gwendolyn redoubled her efforts to break away, trying to dig her heels into the soft grass, hoping to slow his forward movement.

But his strength was no match for hers. Tears of frustration filled her eyes and she tried to move her jaw so she could bite the hand across her mouth, but even that effort failed.

Then suddenly, a large shape surged out of the bushes and tackled her assailant. The man yelped in surprise. With a cry of alarm, Gwendolyn too fell to the ground, the breath knocked from her lungs. They tumbled together for a moment, a disjointed array of limbs. It took but a few seconds for Gwendolyn to realize her attacker's grip had been broken in the fall and she was free. Seizing at this chance, she rolled out of his reach.

"Jason!"

Her savior turned. His hair was mussed, his coat torn, his shirt and breeches filthy with dirt.

"Are you hurt?"

Before she could answer, Jason grabbed her arm and hauled her upright. Her captor cursed loudly and Jason thrust her behind his back, standing tall between her and danger.

Gwendolyn stumbled, struggling to remain on her feet. She could clearly see her attacker. He was a slender man, with a strong, wiry frame. His face was wild with anger, his eyes black with rage, his mouth drawn into a thin, cruel line.

For an instant, no one moved.

"He has a knife!" Gwendolyn screamed.

The merest flicker of alarm lit Jason's face, quickly replaced by a look of tough resolve. His face taut with menace, the attacker lunged toward Jason, the long, sharp blade glistening with deadly intent as he drove it toward Jason's throat.

Jason caught the man's wrist and they grappled for the knife. Though Jason was larger, the men appeared equal in strength. Frantically, Gwendolyn searched for something to use as a weapon. Falling to her knees, she rooted through the soft ground, digging furiously with her bare hands until she triumphantly uncovered a sizable rock.

Weapon in hand, she shoved herself unsteadily to her feet, poised to strike the moment it became necessary. The men grunted and staggered, then Jason released his grip on the man's wrist and drove his fist into his attacker's stomach.

There was a loud yelp of anger as the breath whooshed out of him, but instead of slowing his opponent, the blow appeared to energize him. Growling, he slashed the knife intently toward Jason's ribs. Gwendolyn heard herself scream in horror, then a flash of motion caught her eyes and she saw the fading light glint off the polished wood of the pistol that suddenly appeared in Jason's right hand.

The attacker continued to charge, and then suddenly a reverberating crack of thunder echoed through the quiet. Gwendolyn watched in amazement as Jason's attacker slowly slid to the ground, an expression of surprise etched on his face.

The initial small spot of blood spread across his shirt

front, turning his chest quickly from white to red. Slowly she lifted her eyes from the grisly sight to stare at Jason.

"He had a knife," Gwendolyn repeated in a dazed tone.

"Thankfully, my love, *I* had a pistol."

"Oh, Jason!"

Her relief was so great she swayed, but she soon found herself surrounded by Jason's powerful arms. His solid strength calmed her racing heart, soothed her frazzled nerves.

Yet strangely she became aware of a slight tremor from him as the dam of his emotions seemed to burst. "God help me, I have never been so bloody scared in all my life," he whispered hoarsely, burying his face in her hair. "When I saw him touch you, the breath in my body seized. It seemed to take hours as I ran to reach you and I feared I would be too late. I could not have gone on if I lost you, Gwendolyn."

"Nor I you," she whispered. She pushed away a little, looking up into his eyes. Her chest squeezed until it was hard to breathe as she struggled to keep the emotions bubbling inside her carefully suppressed.

A rustling noise startled them both and men seemed to appear of out nowhere. Jason whirled, his position defensive, his empty pistol raised. They both looked up and saw Jasper, sword drawn, leading a small band of men.

"We have captured the others," Jasper said. "With a bit of persuasion, they have told us where Mr. Ellingham is being held."

"We must go to him at once," Gwendolyn cried.

"I have already sent a few of our men," Jasper replied. "If we were told the truth, they should return shortly." The viscount glanced around, wrinkling his nose at the smell of gunpowder wafting through the air. "I see you have things well in hand here, Jason."

Silence fell as they all looked over at the man who had attacked first Gwendolyn and then Jason. The body was eerily still, his eyes glassy as they stared sightlessly toward the horizon.

"Is he dead?" Gwendolyn asked fearfully.

Jasper knelt beside the prone man. "He lives. His pulse is steady and strong. It was a clean shot through the muscles of the shoulder. I believe the bullet passed though to the other side." His lifted his eyes from the body and smiled. "I told you, Miss Ellingham, that my brother has excellent aim."

"I could hardly miss at this distance," Jason drawled modestly. "Though I'll confess it was hard to restrain myself from putting the bullet though his black heart."

"Are you certain you are all right?" Lord Fairhurst asked. "Both of you?"

Gwendolyn nodded. Safe within the circle of Jason's arms, she felt her worries drop away. She lightly stroked his broad back, reveling in the solid feel of him.

"Good God, those hooligans must have struck my head harder than I thought, for I swear I am seeing double."

"Uncle Fletcher!"

Gwendolyn's bottom lip trembled as she hurried to her uncle's side. He hobbled towards her, sporting a black eye and a few other visible bruises, but his embrace was warm and heartfelt.

"How is Ardley?" Uncle Fletcher asked.

"Gravely injured, but there is hope he will recover," Jason answered, stepping forward.

"Fairhurst?"

"No, Jason Barrington, the viscount's twin brother," he replied. "And soon to be your in-law."

The men shook hands. Uncle Fletcher looked shocked.

Gwendolyn was uncertain if it was due to his ordeal or the declaration Jason had just made.

"I owe you and your brother more thanks than I can say." Concern and worry were carved into Uncle Fletcher's features. "Though perhaps once you learn the truth about this wretched business, you will regret coming to my aid."

"They already know," Gwendolyn explained.

The older man regarded them sheepishly. "We will pay back every penny we owe your family. I promise."

"Then I shall take you at your word." Jason heaved a deep sigh. "I would like to escort you and your niece home, Mr. Ellingham," Jason said. "My brother will handle matters here."

Two horses were brought. After assuring them repeatedly that he was able to ride, Uncle Fletcher was assisted into the saddle. Gwendolyn waited patiently beside her mount for Jason's horse to be brought. But he surprised her by first swinging himself up on the animal's back and next hoisting her in the same saddle, in front of him.

"You are riding with me," he declared forcefully, as if he expected a protest.

Gwendolyn adjusted her seat and leaned back against his solid strength. She smiled as his arms snaked around her waist and drew her more closely against him in a possessive, thrilling gesture. Her fear gone, her heart free, her happiness complete, Gwendolyn gave a silent prayer of thanks for the many blessings in her life.

It was a most peaceful, triumphant journey home.

Everyone agreed it was the perfect day for a wedding. In August, the weather could be damp, muggy or on occasion, beastly hot. But today the cloudless blue sky was vibrant with sparkling color, dotted with a few ornamental white clouds and the sun shone with brilliant, pleasant warmth.

The assembled crowd at St. George's in Hanover Square shifted restlessly in their pews as they waited with eager anticipation for their first glimpse of the bride, who was already fifteen minutes late. Many had heard of her, but few had actually seen this mysterious country girl from Yorkshire who had somehow captured the heart of one of the *ton*'s most scandalous bachelors.

Rumors were rampant as to the means she must have employed to land her most elusive prey, for Jason Barrington was not a man who came to mind when one mentioned marriage. Had she blackmailed him, enticed him, used a potent love spell? Did she have a fortune? Or a beautiful face and figure? Or all three?

All these, and as well as other, even more outlandish possibilities had been discussed and analyzed intently ever since the banns had been posted. However, the betting book at White's was giving the best odds that the future groom had put a babe in her belly in record time and was now compelled to do the right thing.

Rake and rogue he might be, but it was a well-known fact that Jason Barrington was nothing if not a gentleman.

Fortunately, Gwendolyn was aware of none of this gossip and speculation as she stepped from the elegant carriage that had brought her to the church. Her future in-laws had been very involved in the planning of this event and their wealth and taste was in evidence.

The specifics of the wedding had not been of paramount interest to either the bride or groom and they were more than happy to let the groom's mother take charge. The countess had been humbly grateful for the chance to finally plan a society wedding, since her daughter had impulsively eloped and her other son had started his married life in a most unconventional manner that was never publicly revealed.

Gwendolyn was content to leave the details of the day to Jason's mother, for the biggest relief had been the genuine regard her new family had bestowed upon her. The scandal in her past that had so worried her was never mentioned and her acceptance into the inner circle of the family—an event Jason had repeatedly assured her was a foregone conclusion—had indeed come to pass.

At Jason's request, they had come to London to be married. It was a far different environment than she had been raised, but she found it intriguing and for the most part pleasant. Though in truth, Gwendolyn knew she would have been happy just about anywhere, as long as Jason was by her side.

In these past few weeks she had come to appreciate the unconventional, yet loyal, devotion the Barringtons had to each other, though it had been a bit hard to understand the occasionally volatile relationship Jason shared with his twin brother.

Jason's sister Meredith had been a wealth of information and support, and his mother a forceful and tactful instructor when it came to the rules of society. Meeting Jasper's wife, Lady Fairhurst, had sent Gwendolyn's nerves into a frenzy and she was relieved to find Claire an unpretentious, modest woman who loved her husband with a fierceness that Gwendolyn admired.

And now it was her turn to become a wife. She could hear the strains of organ music and the low murmur of hushed conversations as she moved into the church vestibule. Dorothea handed her a bouquet of fresh flowers. They were exquisite white roses, bound with a white silk ribbon.

"A gift from your bridegroom," Dorothea exclaimed.

Gwendolyn smiled and held them close to her heart. Then Uncle Fletcher took her arm. She turned and smiled at him, her nerves settling.

They waited at the end of the aisle for the cue to begin. Gwendolyn strained for a glimpse of her groom and her smile widened when she saw him standing beside his brother. Breathtakingly handsome, powerful and utterly splendid in his elegant wedding attire, she was aware only of him.

Her eyes locked with his, her heart swelled with emotion. Depending on Uncle Fletcher to keep pace with the music and lead her up the aisle, Gwendolyn's gaze never wavered from her groom's. There was no shielding of emotions for either of them. Jason's beaming smile was wholly for her, the sincerity and intensity of his feelings shining from his eyes.

When she finally reached him, he lifted her hand into his own, then pressed his lips to the delicate, sensitive spot at the inside of her wrist. The sighs of several women echoed throughout the church at the romantic, courtly gesture.

The service started with a prayer and Gwendolyn strained to concentrate on every word the minister spoke. She wanted to remember, with great clarity, every moment of this day. As she recited her vows, the meaning behind each word surrounded her and she gladly swore to love, honor and yes, even to obey.

"You may kiss your bride."

Jason leaned forward to claim her, but the chaste, brief kiss usually reserved for such a moment quickly turned into a passionate declaration of love and devotion. Gwendolyn sighed as Jason wrapped his arms around her waist, lifted her onto her toes and kissed her with all the skill of a rake and the passion of a lover.

The world melted away. Gwendolyn felt as if she had been waiting for this moment all her life. Delighted, she lost herself in their shared joy, knowing for the rest of her life that only she would have the privilege of sharing kisses with this amazing man.

The minister coughed. Twice.

Finally, the newly wed couple separated. Beaming, Jason turned Gwendolyn to face the crowd. Several gentlemen rose to their feet and started clapping enthusiastically. Such a noisy, boisterous display was most inappropriate on such a solemn occasion, but the blushes of the lovely bride and the satisfied smile of the triumphant groom softened even the sharpest of criticism.

It was later said that the assembled crowd who had made the journey to London at such an unfashionable time of year expected no less from the blacksheep son of the Earl of Stafford.

The luncheon that followed was a lively, happy affair. Still, the crush of more than one hundred family members and close friends was far more than Jason would have preferred. As he watched his wife mingle with the guests, graciously accepting their congratulations and best wishes, all he could think about was breaking away from the party.

Married three hours and already desperately longing to be alone with his new wife. He was a besotted fool and damn happy to admit it! As if sensing his gaze on her, Gwendolyn looked up and smiled. His heart flipped over in his chest and he returned the smile.

His mother strolled up beside him, her face beaming with delight. "I am most pleased with the job the servants have done today. Are you enjoying yourself, Jason?"

"Very much, Mother."

"I hope the food is to your liking. I tried to include many of your favorite dishes, but of course it was also necessary to select a few more elegant choices."

"Everything is excellent," he replied, knowing he could have been eating sand and not noticed. Food was the very last thing he would remember about this day.

His mother was called away and Jason seized the opportunity to corner his bride. Catching her hand, he pressed a kiss on the sensitive pulse at her wrist. "Happy, darling?"

"Oh, yes." Her arms crept around his waist and squeezed. "Is this not the most perfect wedding day?"

He brushed a curl off her forehead. A passing footman offered them champagne and Jason thrust a glass into Gwendolyn's hand. He smiled and drank deeply from his champagne. "'Tis a perfectly lovely wedding. And perfectly chilled champagne. When can we leave?"

"Jason! We haven't had the toasts or the speeches or cut the cake or started any of the dancing."

"Hmm, that sounds like it will take a very long time." He pulled her into his arms. "I suppose you are going to tell me it would be rude if we snuck out now?"

Her eyes twinkled as she pressed herself against him. "Your mother would be hurt if we left so soon."

"I will ask my father to ply her with champagne." Jason nipped her earlobe, then feathered a series of sensual kisses along the column of her throat. "After three glasses, Mother will never even realize we have gone."

"Jason!" She slapped her hand playfully against his solid chest. "How do you even think of such things?"

He shrugged. She smiled, but he could tell by the stubborn set of her jaw she wouldn't be easy to convince.

"I promise we can leave in a few hours."

"Hours!" he growled, but before he could voice any additional complaints, Gwendolyn stood up on her toes and kissed him. It was a long, thorough kiss that whet his appetite with the promise of passion to come.

He returned the kiss with equal ardor, then drew back, his eyes smoldering. "Are you sure we cannot leave?"

She shook her head. "Not yet. We have to cut the cake."

Pulling her close, he let her feel his growing desire, let her know the physical ache he endured, the cravings that were boarding on obsession. "I have the woman of my dreams as my wife and am finally feel free to express the love within my heart. I can assure you, madame, the very last thing on my mind right now is wedding cake."

"We will eat the cake and we will smile appreciatively at the speeches and toasts to our good health and happiness and we will share our joy with all these dear people who have joined us today," Gwendolyn declared primly. "Then we will escape to our honeymoon cottage and lock ourselves in the bedchamber. For at least a week!"

"Will we stay in bed the entire time?"

"Yes."

"Without any clothing?"

"Naked as the day we were born."

He tightened his arms about her and murmured against her hair, "You are sheer perfection, my love. I am not sure I deserve you."

"You are indeed most fortunate." Drawing back, she smiled at him. "As am I. A love like ours is rare and precious, Jason. And I fully intend to remind us both, not only today, but each and every day in all the years ahead."

Epilogue

Three Months Later

The drive from London had taken less than an hour. Gwendolyn sat beside her husband while he drove the sleek phaeton with skill, and a bit more speed than she appreciated, enjoying the fresh autumn air and the chance to be truly alone. As much as she liked living in the city, it was always a delight to escape the noise and dirt, the constant stream of callers, the endless social and family obligations.

The comforting sway of the carriage caused her eyes to feel heavy, but then her attention was suddenly distracted. Jason had drawn the phaeton to a halt, and motioned to Gwendolyn to gaze ahead.

A wide meadow stretched on the right, a few sections of the still-green grass dotted with white sheep grazing contentedly upon what remained of it. To the left was a track of woodlands, dense with oaks and elms, their colors of orange, red and brown a brilliant hue. She smiled, thinking how much Emma would love to paint this pastoral picture.

Directly in the center of all this natural beauty, perched elegantly on the slight ridge, was a house. Four stories high and built of gray stone, it was not particularly majestic, but there was a solid feel to the property along with a sense of intimacy that Gwendolyn found rather comforting.

She especially liked the balcony, which stretched the entire length of the house, boasting long French windows leading out to it and she found it charming that the bottom section of the house was covered with ivy.

"What do you think?" Jason asked.

"'Tis very pretty. Do you know the owner?"

"I do." Jason flicked the reins and drove the carriage between two stone gateposts and covered the relatively short distance across the gravel courtyard to the front door.

"Goodness, Jason, you might have warned me that we would be paying a call," Gwendolyn admonished. She hastily checked her hair, tucking a few stray stands beneath her stylish bonnet. "I must look a fright. I would never have ridden in an open carriage if I knew we were going visiting."

Jason said nothing. He secured the carriage horse to a wrought iron hitching post, then assisted Gwendolyn down the carriage steps, swinging her the last few inches with an arm looped around her waist. Slightly breathless, Gwendolyn accepted the arm he extended and they walked to the front door.

Jason's knock was answered by an older man dressed in work clothes, who seemed to be expecting him. From his outfit, Gwendolyn assumed he was the caretaker. He bowed politely, then left them standing in the foyer. Gwendolyn turned a puzzled, suspicious eye to her husband.

"My parents have very generously insisted that we continue to reside with them in their London townhouse, and have also offered us the use of the family's ancestral home in Kent. But I thought it would be wonderful if I could whisk you away from London whenever I please." Jason removed his hat. "I've made a bid on this property in order to prevent anyone else from buying it, but will not finalize the deal unless you approve."

She smiled and tipped her head sideways, touching her cheek to his gloved hand. "'Tis far from a hardship living with your parents. Their house is quite large; I often go days without seeing either of them."

"Still, it would be nice to have a place of our own."

"It would."

"'Tis not as grand as Moorehead Manor, nor as elegant as any of the properties my parents own," Jason said, as they began a leisurely tour of the first floor.

"Your father is an earl. I hardly expect you to compete with his wealth."

"My allowance is generous, but needs to be supplemented. I admit I do not have the same talent with money as my brother. Or my sister. Which is why I have asked for their advice with my investments, and I am pleased to have achieved some early success."

She turned her head slowly, taking in all the elegant, refined details of the house's interior. "You have been very successful, indeed, if we can afford to buy this place."

"I have done well. And plan to do even better." He smiled, tiny lines fanning in the corners of his eyes. "Many of the furnishing are also for sale. I thought it might be easier if we purchase some items already here and fill in the rest as we need."

Gwendolyn agreed. If they decided to buy the house,

she would want to keep the large mirrors strategically placed throughout the rooms, enhancing the sense of light and space. The downstairs drawing room, which was decorated in tasteful shades of cream and pale gold, with delicate furnishings, also contained items that should be seriously considered.

Gwendolyn stared down at the patterned Aubusson carpet which covered the polished oak floor, the colors reminding her of the carpet in her chambers at the townhouse. In fact, not only the colors, but the pattern was nearly the same.

Her breath quickened with the sensual memory created last night when her overly eager husband had been too aroused to make it to the bed. Instead, they had ended up on the floor, sprawled half-naked on top of each other, Jason's clever hands and sensual mouth creating another earthshaking sexual experience for them both.

"I should like to keep the carpet," she decided.

"The carpet?"

She gave him a clever smile, waiting for him to catch her meaning, to understand why among all these lovely antiques she had singled out this particular item.

"It reminds me of the carpet in my chambers at the townhouse," she prompted.

He glanced down, puzzled, then his lips curved in a sensual smile as he made the connection. "I will pay whatever price they want."

"Thank you."

"Anything to please my lovely wife."

They climbed the stairs to the third floor and began inspecting the bedchambers. Their footsteps echoed loudly as they walked the hardwood floors, as these rooms were unfurnished.

"It all seems to be in very good condition. How many rooms?" Gwendolyn asked as they entered a corner suite, which she decided would be perfect for their bedchamber.

"I didn't ask. Thirty, I think."

"How many bedchambers?"

"Eight? No, maybe ten? I don't recall. We can count them now if you'd like." He stepped into the hallway, glancing left, then right. "One thing I specifically remember is a large nursery on the top floor."

Gwendolyn bowed her head. Her menses had come early last week and she had been sorely disappointed. With as much time as they spent making love she thought for sure she would be pregnant. More than anything she wanted to have Jason's child. "Regretfully, we have no need of a nursery just yet."

"My God, I am an insensitive ass." Jason rushed forward to take her in his arms. "There is nothing that would bring me greater joy than to see you bear my child. But I do not mind waiting a little while. I'm still learning how to be a husband."

"You will be a wonderful father."

"But first, I must make you a mother. A task I find more than delightful."

She relaxed into his warmth, breathing in the familiar scent of his skin, reveling in how good it felt to be held and comforted by the man she loved. "I really do want your child. Our child."

She sighed and kissed the edge of his jaw, then walked to the window and gazed out at the now dormant gardens below. With effort, she closed her mind to her doubts and fears and allowed herself to dream. With Jason's love, anything, everything was possible.

"Shall we work on it now? Making you a mother?"

Gwendolyn turned her head and he gave her a dark grin that sent chills all over her body. It was a look she understood very well.

"There is no bed," she whispered, moving out of reach.

"No bed," he repeated, following after her.

"The floor looks none too clean, either," she said, licking her dry lips. "And rather hard."

"Very hard," he agreed, his voice deep and gravelly.

"The windows," she gulped. "They have no curtains."

"I like the sunlight flooding the chamber. All the better to see your lovely body."

"There are servants about. Anyone could see us!"

"Only the caretaker and his wife. The area is fairly isolated, but honestly, Gwendolyn, I don't care. You are my wife. I love you. I adore you. I burn for you." His eyes glittered with temptation.

"Jason, please."

He threw off his coat and jacket, then loosened his cravat. "You knew I was a rogue when I married you. Remember, I warned you?"

"Yes, everyone warned me what a sinful man I was marrying."

He stopped suddenly. "Everyone?"

"Yes. Even your mother."

"Smart woman."

"Indeed." An irrepressible giggle bubbled in Gwendolyn's throat, but it vanished when she caught the hot look of unabashed lust in Jason's eyes. She felt as if he could devour her in one bite. He kept advancing and she kept retreating, stopping only when her back hit the wall. "Really, Jason—"

"Are we going to buy the house?"

Confused, she shook her head, her mind unable to

focus on anything except the passion and love in his beautiful green eyes. "What?"

"The house, my love? Shall I buy it for you?" His sultry gaze captured hers, enticing her with the promise of sinful pleasure.

"Yes, please."

"Splendid. Then we must make it our own. Right now."

Jason covered the remaining ground between them in a split second, his deep kiss capturing the final protest she tried to utter. Heated sensations began to burn through her body like molten rock, hot, then cold, as she waited anxiously for his touch.

Her hand gripped his shoulders and she shifted to cup his nape, to let him know she approved. He broke the kiss and she exhaled, her breath tight and shaky. He rested his jaw upon the top of her head as she pressed soft, arousing kisses through the fine linen of his shirt upon his shoulder, then his chest.

"Easy," he breathed against her ear, as he slowly ground his hips against her belly so that his stiff arousal rubbed the tender mound of her womanhood. "I'm ready to explode."

"Jason." Gwendolyn moistened her lips, struggling for breath. She leaned forward and pressed her lips to his throat, to a patch of skin left bare by his loosened cravat.

He reached down, slid his hand beneath her skirts, tracing delicate circles on her stomach, then moving lower still, slipping under her drawers, between her thighs to touch her intimately.

"You are already wet," he whispered, his voice thick with desire.

"That happened the moment you smiled so wickedly at me," she answered, rotating her hips in rhythm with his caresses.

His eyes danced wickedly while his fingers continued to tease. Then he sank to his knees before her and lifted her gown, caressing her legs and upper thighs. "You are so damn beautiful," he murmured.

Gwendolyn's throat tightened. Her fingers closed over the edge of her gown and she lifted it higher, past her thighs and hips, holding it with damp palms at her waist.

Jason needed no further encouragement. She could feel the silk tearing as he ripped away her undergarments. The cool breeze on her now-naked limbs made her shiver with excitement. He parted her swollen flesh gently with his fingers and then his mouth, warm and moist, closed over her essence.

She cried out, her knees weakening, but he held her in place, his tongue moving faster, delving deeper. "You are a wicked man, Jason Barrington," she panted.

He answered her with a firm stroke of his tongue, moving it in tight circles around the hooded bud that lay hidden under her nest of curls. A wave of passion broke across her and she gasped, thrusting her hips forward.

Jason stood, fumbled with the button on his breeches, ripping at them with obvious urgency, his eyes never leaving hers. Anticipation shivered down Gwendolyn's spine. Then the rigid length of his erection sprang free. His arm locked around her waist and crushed her to his chest and heavily muscled thighs. She arched in response and he pressed her against the wall, lifting her off her feet.

Her lungs seized and a sharp gasp strangled the back of her throat as he hoisted her higher, spread her thighs wide and stepped between them. Clutching at his shoulders, Gwendolyn clasped her legs about him and drew him forward.

He bent his head to bite a most sensitive spot on her

neck the exact moment his erect penis slid inside her. She moaned, her body feeling heavy and full.

"You are mine," he murmured against her ear.

"Always," she answered.

Slow and controlled, he withdrew, then filled her again inch by inch. He repeated this sensual torture again and again until she was filled with the raw need and love and explosive passion that only Jason could invoke.

Her stomach muscles shivered, contracting as she felt him deep, so deep inside. Taking her wrists, he pinned her arms wide against the wall, holding her solidly captive while he thrust into her.

Her body eagerly welcomed him, as the sensations continued to build, the tantalizing ripples of desire overwhelming her. She was aware of nothing but Jason, of his scent, his strength, his love and desire. Gwendolyn lifted her hips higher as she felt her release nearing the surface, letting out a strangled cry as she climaxed.

Jason answered her by increasing the tempo of his thrusts and she wallowed in the sensation of feeling his seed flooding her womb, rejoicing in the deep, soul-searing contentment that always followed this extraordinary intimacy.

Trembling and clinging, they remained joined together for several moments, each too exhausted to move. Jason leaned on his elbows against the door, his head bent forward, touching Gwendolyn's cheek. His harsh breathing rang in her ears; his heart thudded hard against her fingertips.

Slowly, Gwendolyn moved her legs to the ground, attempting to stand. Her knees weakened and she collapsed, but Jason caught and held her tight against his chest, laughing quietly.

"Isn't this a fantastic house?" he asked. "I think we should make this room our bedchamber. I believe it will bring us good luck. And many babies."

He sank to the floor and settled Gwendolyn on his lap, pulling her skirts into place, while leaving his breeches indecently opened.

"Dear Lord," Gwendolyn squeaked. "We are scandalous. Not only did we lose control in the middle of the day, against a wall, in a strange house, but you were wearing your boots and I was wearing my bonnet."

"It was bloody marvelous." He pressed his lips to her damp brow. "Next time, we shall make love with me in my boots and you wearing *only* your bonnet."

She laughed, scandalized anew. Life with Jason would always be a whirlwind, but given a choice, she would not have it any other way. Her heart filled with joy, contentment and love, Gwendolyn turned once more into the warmth of his solid embrace.

About the Author

Adrienne Basso lives with her family in New Jersey. She is the author of eight Zebra historical romances and is currently working on her next. Adrienne loves to hear from readers and you may write to her c/o Zebra Books. Please include a self-addressed stamped envelope if you wish a response.